KT-154-670

Born in Paris in 1947, Christian Jacq first visited Egypt when he was seventeen, went on to study Egyptology and archaeology at the Sorbonne, and is now one of the world's leading Egyptologists. He is the author of the internationally bestselling RAMSES series, THE QUEEN OF FREEDOM trilogy and several other novels on Ancient Egypt. Christian Jacq lives in Switzerland.

Also by Christian Jacq:

The Ramses Series
Volume 1: The Son of the Light
Volume 2: The Temple of a Million Years
Volume 3: The Battle of Kadesh
Volume 4: The Lady of Abu Simbel
Volume 5: Under the Western Acacia

The Stone of Light Series
Volume 1: Nefer the Silent
Volume 2: The Wise Woman
Volume 3: Paneb the Ardent
Volume 4: The Place of Truth

The Queen of Freedom Trilogy
Volume 1: The Empire of Darkness
Volume 2: The War of the Crowns
Volume 3: The Flaming Sword

The Judge of Egypt Trilogy
Volume 1: Beneath the Pyramid
Volume 2: Secrets of the Desert
Volume 3: Shadow of the Sphinx

The Black Pharaoh
The Tutankhamun Affair
For the Love of Philae
Champollion the Egyptian
Master Hiram & King Solomon
The Living Wisdom of Ancient Egypt

About the translator

Sue Dyson is a prolific author of both fiction
and non-fiction, including over thirty novels, both
contemporary and historical. She has also translated
a wide variety of French fiction.

The Judge of Egypt Trilogy

Shadow of the Sphinx

Christian Jacq

Translated by Sue Dyson

POCKET BOOKS

LONDON • SYDNEY • NEW YORK • TORONTO

First published in France by Plon under the title
La Justice du Vizir, 1994
First published in Great Britain by Simon & Schuster UK
Ltd, 2004
This edition first published by Pocket Books, 2005
A Viacom company

Copyright © Librairie Plon, 1994
English translation copyright © Sue Dyson, 2004

This book is copyright under the Berne Convention.
No reproduction without permission.
All rights reserved.

The right of Christian Jacq to be identified as author
of this work has been asserted by him in accordance
with sections 77 and 78 of the Copyright,
Designs and Patents Act, 1988.

1 3 5 7 9 10 8 6 4 2

Simon & Schuster UK Ltd
Africa House
64–78 Kingsway
London WC2B 6AH

www.simonsays.co.uk

Simon & Schuster Australia
Sydney

A CIP catalogue record for this book is available
from the British Library

ISBN 0-671-01800-0

Typeset in Times by SX Composing DTP, Rayleigh, Essex
Printed and bound in Great Britain by
Cox & Wyman Ltd, Reading, Berkshire

Let the whole rejoice!
Justice has been restored to its rightful place;
All ye righteous ones, come and gaze upon it.
Justice has triumphed over evil,
The wicked have fallen on their faces,
The greedy have been condemned.

Sallier Papyrus I
British Museum 1018, recto VIII.7.

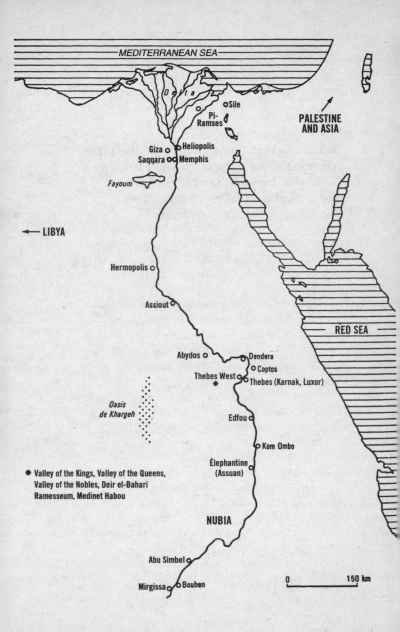

MEDITERRANEAN SEA

Delta

o Sile

Pi-
Ramses

PALESTINE
AND ASIA

Giza o Heliopolis
Saqqara o o Memphis

Fayoum

← LIBYA

Hermopolis o

Assiout o

RED SEA

Abydos o   o Dendera
                 o Coptos
Thebes West o
    ✱   o Thebes (Karnak, Luxor)

*Oasis
de Khargeh*

Edfou o

Kom Ombo o

Éléphantine o
(Assuan)

✱ Valley of the Kings, Valley of the Queens,
Valley of the Nobles, Deir el-Bahari
Ramesseum, Medinet Habou

NUBIA

Abu Simbel o

Mirgissa o o Bouhen

0   150 km

1

Treason was showing a healthy profit: Iarrot had grown red-faced, chubby-cheeked and flabby. He gulped down a third cup of white wine, congratulating himself on his choice. When he had been clerk to Judge Pazair, who was now Ramses II's tjaty, he had worked too hard and earned little. Since he had entered the service of Bel-Tran, the tjaty's worst enemy, his life had improved vastly; he was paid for each piece of information on Pazair's habits. With Bel-Tran's support and the false testimony of one of his henchmen, Iarrot was hoping to obtain a divorce from his wife and custody of his daughter, a future dancer.

The former clerk had risen before dawn with a pounding headache, while darkness still reigned over Memphis, Egypt's economic capital, which stood at the junction of the Delta and the Nile Valley.

From the narrow street outside, which was usually quiet and calm, he heard the sound of whispering.

Iarrot put down his cup. Since he had begun betraying Pazair, he had been drinking more and more, not out of remorse but because he could at last afford the finest wines and beers. His throat constantly burnt with an unquenchable thirst.

He pushed open the shutter and glanced outside. There was no one in sight.

Muttering to himself, he thought of the splendid day in prospect. Thanks to Bel-Tran, he was leaving the city outskirts to live in one of the best districts, close to the centre. This very evening, he was going to move into a house with five rooms and a little garden; the next day, he would take up a post as inspector of taxes, reporting to the ministry that Bel-Tran headed.

Only one thing annoyed him: despite the quality of the information he had given to Bel-Tran, Pazair had not yet been eliminated – it was as if the gods were protecting him. Still, luck would eventually turn against him.

Outside, someone was sniggering.

Perturbed, Iarrot put his ear to the door that led to the street. Suddenly, he realized what it was: that band of urchins again, who enjoyed scrawling on the fronts of the houses with an ochre stone.

Furious, he wrenched the door open.

And was confronted with the open mouth of a hyena. An enormous female with saliva on its lips, and eyes which glowed red. It let out a cry like laughter from beyond the grave, and leapt at his throat.

Ordinarily, hyenas cleansed the desert by eating carrion and they avoided areas of human settlement. Very unusually, ten of them had ventured into the outskirts of Memphis and had killed a former clerk, Iarrot, a drunkard whose neighbours detested him. Armed with sticks, the inhabitants of the district had put the hyenas to flight, but everyone interpreted the drama as a bad omen for the future of Pharaoh Ramses, whose authority had never been contested up to now. At the port of Memphis, in the weapons stores, on the quays, in the barracks, in the districts called Sycamore, Crocodile Wall and College of Medicine, in the markets, and in the craftsmen's shops, the same words were on everybody's lips: 'the year of the hyenas'.

The country would grow weak. The Nile's annual flood would be meagre and the earth barren, the orchards would wither, there would be a shortage of fruit, vegetables, clothes and ointments. Sand-travellers would attack the farms in the Delta. Pharaoh's throne would grow shaky. The year of the hyenas: the shattering of harmony, the breach into which the forces of evil would pour.

It was whispered that Ramses had been unable to prevent this disaster. True, in nine months' time the festival of regeneration would take place, giving the king back the power necessary to confront adversity and overcome it. But would the celebration be in time? Pazair, the new tjaty, was young and inexperienced. Entering office during the year of the hyenas meant he was bound to fail.

If the king did not protect his people, he and they alike would perish in darkness's voracious maw.

It was the middle of winter, and an icy wind swept through the burial-ground at Saqqara, which was dominated by Pharaoh Djoser's stepped pyramid, a gigantic staircase to the heavens. No one would have recognized the couple who, warmly clad in thick, long-sleeved tunics made of strips of fabric sewn together, were meditating before the shrine at the tomb of the sage Branir. Pazair and Neferet silently read the hieroglyphs engraved on a beautiful piece of limestone: '*You who live upon the earth and pass by this tomb, you who love life and hate death, speak my name that I may live, pronounce the offertory words for my sake.*'

Branir had been Pazair and Neferet's spiritual master, and due to become High Priest of Karnak, but he had been murdered, stabbed in the neck with a mother-of-pearl needle, and Pazair had been accused of his murder. Although the investigation to find the real murderer had become bogged down, the couple had sworn to uncover the truth, whatever risks they might run.

A thin man with thick, black eyebrows which joined above the nose, thin lips, very long hands and thin legs, approached the shrine. Djui the embalmer spent most of his time preparing corpses to transform them into Osiris.

'Do you wish to see the location of your tomb?' he asked Pazair.

'Yes, show me.'

Tjaty Pazair had been entrusted by Ramses with the mission of saving Egypt from an evil conspiracy which threatened the throne. When still a minor provincial judge just transferred to Memphis, the young Pazair – whose name meant 'the Seer', 'He Who Sees Far into the Distance' – had refused to sanction an administrative irregularity, and that small deed had led to the uncovering of an appalling series of events, whose key had been given to him by the king himself.

Conspirators had killed the honour-guard of the Great Sphinx at Giza, in order to gain access to a passageway that began between the gigantic statue's paws and ended inside the Great Pyramid of Pharaoh Kufu, the spiritual and energy centre of the country. They had violated Khufu's sarcophagus and stolen the Testament of the Gods, which legitimized each pharaoh's power. If Ramses could not show it to the priests, the court and the people at the festival of regeneration, which was to take place in the summer, on the first day of the new year, Ramses would be forced to abdicate and hand over the ship of state to a creature of the darkness.

Because the young judge had shown that he would never betray justice, even if his career and his life were at stake, Ramses had put his trust in Pazair, and appointed him tjaty: supreme magistrate, keeper of the king's seal, guardian of secrets, director of Pharaoh's works, first minister of Egypt. Pazair must try everything to save the country from disaster.

As they walked along between the tombs, he gazed at his wife, Neferet, whose beauty enchanted him more every day.

With her summer-blue eyes, fair hair and exquisite face with its gentle features, to him she embodied happiness and the joy of living. Without her, he would long since have succumbed to the blows fate had dealt him.

Neferet had become the kingdom's principal doctor after a long series of ordeals. She loved to heal. From Branir, a doctor and dowser, she had inherited the gift of identifying the nature of illnesses and rooting them out. At her throat, she wore a turquoise her master had given her, in order to ward off misfortune.

Neither Pazair nor Neferet had wanted to occupy such important offices. Their dearest wish was to retire to a village in the Theban region and to live out their days in happiness under the sun of Upper Egypt; but the gods had decided otherwise. The couple were the only people who knew Pharaoh's secret, and they would never retreat from the fight, even if the power at their disposal seemed illusory.

'Here's where it will be,' said Djui, indicating a place near the tomb of a former tjaty. 'The stone-cutters will begin work first thing tomorrow.'

Pazair nodded. In accordance with his rank, his first duty was to have his house of eternity built. There he would dwell in company with his wife.

The embalmer went away, his walk slow and weary.

'We may never lie here in this burial-ground,' said Pazair in a sombre voice. 'Ramses' enemies have clearly proclaimed their will to abandon the traditional rites. It is a whole world they want to destroy, not one man.'

The couple headed towards the great open-air courtyard in front of the Step Pyramid. There, at the height of the festival of regeneration, Ramses must hold aloft the Testament of the Gods – which he no longer possessed.

Pazair was sure that Branir's murder was linked to the conspiracy; identifying the murderer would put him on the trail of the thieves and might enable him to spring open the jaws of the trap. Unfortunately, he had been deprived of the irreplaceable help of his friend and spiritual brother Suti, who had been found guilty of infidelity to his wife and sentenced to a year's service in a Nubian fortress. Pazair had thought of many ways to free him, but the tjaty, master of justice, could not show favouritism to someone close to him, on pain of being dismissed from his office.

The great courtyard of Saqqara epitomized the unequalled grandeur of the age of the pyramids. Here the pharaohs' spiritual adventure had taken flesh, here north and south had been united, forming a radiant, powerful kingdom whose inheritance Ramses had taken on. Tenderly, Pazair put his arm round Neferet's waist; awed, they marvelled at the austere structure, which was visible from everywhere in the burial-ground.

Behind them came the sound of footsteps. They turned round.

The man approaching them was of medium height, with a round face and heavy bones; his hair was black, his hands and feet plump. He was walking quickly and seemed nervous.

Incredulously, Pazair and Neferet looked at each other. It was indeed Bel-Tran, their sworn enemy, the heart of the conspiracy.

Bel-Tran had begun at the bottom of the social ladder, as a mere papyrus-maker. But by working hard and by using his prodigious skill in calculations, he had risen to become first principal overseer of all the country's grain-stores, and then head of the Double White House, the minister for Egypt's trade and finances. At first he had pretended to support Pazair, the better to control his actions, but when Pazair had unexpectedly become tjaty Bel-Tran shed his mask of friendship. Pazair could still see his grimacing face and hear his threats: 'Your morality is that of a backward child. Gods, temples, houses of eternity, rituals – all that stupid, outworn stuff. You have no understanding at all of the new world we're entering. Your universe is worm-eaten – I've eaten away the posts that supported it.'

Pazair had not thought it wise to arrest Bel-Tran. First he must destroy the web the traitor had woven, dismantle his networks of spies, and recover the Testament of the Gods. Had Bel-Tran been boasting or had he really corrupted the whole country?

When he reached them Bel-Tran said in a sugary voice, 'We misunderstood each other, and I regret my strong words. Forgive my hot-headedness, my dear Pazair. I deeply respect and admire you. On reflection, I am convinced that we understand each other on the really vital matters. Egypt needs a good tjaty, and that is what you are.'

'What is behind this flattery?' asked Pazair.

'Why should we tear each other to pieces, when an alliance would prevent many . . . inconveniences? Ramses and his regime are doomed – you know that. Let us move in the direction of progress, you and I.'

A peregrine falcon drew circles in the azure blue of the winter sky, above the great courtyard of Saqqara.

'Your regrets are nothing but hypocrisy,' cut in Neferet. 'Do not hope for an alliance with us – ever.'

Anger filled Bel-Tran's eyes. 'This is your last chance, Pazair. Either you submit, or I shall destroy you.'

'Leave this place immediately. Its light cannot agree with you.'

In fury, Bel-Tran turned on his heel and marched away.

Hand in hand, Pazair and Neferet gazed up at the falcon as it flew south.

2

All the dignitaries of the kingdom of Egypt were present in the tjaty's hall of justice, a vast pillared chamber with unpainted walls. At the back was a dais on which Pazair would take his place; on the steps were forty staves of command covered in leather, symbolizing the application of the law. With their right hands on their left shoulders, ten scribes in short wigs and kilts stood guard over the precious staves.

In the front row, seated on a gilded wooden throne, was sixty-year-old Tuya, the Mother of Pharaoh, a thin, haughty woman with piercing eyes. She wore a long linen robe, fringed with gold, and a magnificent wig of human hair whose long tresses fell midway down her back. At her side was Neferet, clad in the official dress of principal doctor: a panther-skin over a linen gown, a striped wig, a cornelian collar, and lapis-lazuli bracelets at her wrists and ankles. In her right hand, she held her seal; in her left, a writing-box. The two women greatly respected each other; Neferet had cured Tuya of serious eye complaints, and the Mother of Pharaoh had fought successfully against Neferet's enemies and facilitated her accession to the highest medical post in the land.

Behind Neferet was one of Pazair's greatest allies, Kem, a Nubian. As a young man, Kem had been wrongly convicted of theft and had had his nose cut off; he now wore a false one made of painted wood. While serving as a security guard in Memphis, he had got to know and like the young, inexperienced judge, who was in love with a justice in which Kem no longer believed. After many adventures, and at Pazair's request, the Nubian had been given command of the forces who maintained order in Memphis. So it was not without pride that he grasped the emblem of his office, an ivory hand of justice decorated with a wide-open eye, to detect evil, and the head of a lion, evoking vigilance. At his side, held on a leash, was his huge, immensely strong guard-baboon, Killer. Killer had just been promoted in recognition of his remarkable service in the guards. His main role was to watch over Pazair, whose life had been threatened several times.

A good distance away from the baboon was Pazair's predecessor as tjaty, Bagey, whose stooping back showed the weight of the years he bore. Bagey was tall, pale and stern-looking, his long face dominated by a prominent nose. As tjaty he had been both feared and celebrated for his inflexible character. Now he was enjoying a peaceful retirement in a small house in Memphis, while continuing to advise his successor.

Half hidden behind a pillar Silkis, Bel-Tran's wife, stood smiling at her neighbours. A child-woman, she had resorted to the doctor's knife so that she would continue to be attractive to her husband. Her greed, especially for rich cakes and pastries, had made her fat, and she was obsessed with her weight. She often suffered from severe headaches, but no longer dared consult Neferet since Bel-Tran had declared war on the tjaty. Discreetly, she dabbed on her temples a lotion made from juniper, pine-sap and laurel-leaves; ostentatiously, she adjusted her blue porcelain necklace and played with her delicate bracelets made from pieces of red fabric joined by little cords in the form of lotus-flowers in full bloom.

Her husband was with her. Although Bel-Tran obtained his clothes from the best kilt-maker in Memphis, they never seemed to fit properly: either they looked too small for him or else he was swamped by them. At this moment of worrying gravity, he forgot his pretensions to elegance and anxiously awaited the tjaty's arrival. No one knew the reason for the solemn judgment that Pazair had decided to proclaim.

When the tjaty appeared, all talk ceased. Only his shoulders were visible above a stiff gown made from thick fabric, which enveloped the rest of his body; the garment was weighted down, as if it strove to emphasize the difficulties of the office. Accentuating still further the austerity and simplicity of his costume, Pazair had contented himself with a short wig in the old style.

He hooked a figurine of the goddess Ma'at* on to a small gold chain which hung round his neck, signifying that the court was in session.

'May we distinguish truth from falsehood and protect the weak to save them from the powerful,' declared the tjaty, using the ritual words on which each judge, from the lowliest to the most high, must base his rule of life.

Ordinarily, forty scribes formed a line on either side of the central aisle along which the accused, the plaintiffs and witnesses passed as they were ushered in by guards. This time, the tjaty simply sat down on a low-backed chair and gazed for a long time at the forty staves of command laid out before him.

'Egypt is in great danger,' revealed Pazair. 'Dark forces are trying to unleash themselves upon the country. That is why I must hand down justice, in order to punish the guilty parties who have been identified.'

---

*Ma'at was the goddess of justice, whose name meant 'She Who Is Straight', 'She Who Gives the Right Direction'. Embodying the universal rule, which will live on after the human race is gone, she was symbolized by a seated woman holding an ostrich feather.

10

Silkis clutched her husband's arm. Would the tjaty dare to attack powerful Bel-Tran head on, despite having no proof against him?

'Five former soldiers who formed the honour-guard of the Great Sphinx at Giza were murdered,' Pazair went on. 'This horrible deed resulted from a conspiracy to which Qadash the tooth-doctor, Sheshi the inventor and Denes the ship-owner belonged. By reason of their various crimes, which have been well established through official inquiries, they must receive capital punishment.'

A scribe asked for and received permission to speak. 'But, Tjaty, they are all dead.'

'Indeed, but they have not been judged. The fact that destiny has struck them down does not remove the duty of this court. Death does not enable a criminal to escape from justice.'

Although those present were astonished, they had to agree that the tjaty was respecting the law. The charges were read out, detailing the crimes of Bel-Tran's three accomplices; his name, though, was not mentioned.

No one contested the facts, no voice was raised to defend the accused.

'The three guilty parties will be devoured by the fire of the royal cobra in the afterlife,' declared the tjaty. 'They will not lie in the burial-ground, will receive no offerings or libations, and will be offered up to the knives of the slaughterers who stand at the gates of the underworld. There they will die a second time, of hunger and thirst.'

Silkis shivered. Bel-Tran remained imperturbable. Cracks appeared in Kem's scepticism; the baboon's eyes widened, as if it was satisfied with this posthumous condemnation. Neferet, overwhelmed, had the feeling that the spoken words had taken on the power of reality.

'Any king, any head of state, who offers an amnesty to the condemned,' concluded the tjaty, repeating ancient words, 'will lose both crown and power.'

3

The sun had been up for almost an hour when Pazair arrived at the gate of the royal palace. Pharaoh's guards bowed before the tjaty, and admitted him.

He walked down a corridor whose walls were decorated with delicate paintings depicting lotus-flowers, papyrus and poppies, crossed a pillared hall containing a pool full of playful fish, and reached the sovereign's office.

Ramses' personal scribe greeted Pazair. 'His Majesty is expecting you.'

This morning, as every morning, the tjaty must give an account of his actions to the Lord of the Two Lands, Upper and Lower Egypt. The place was idyllic: a vast, light-filled room, with windows opening on to the Nile and the palace gardens, porcelain floor-tiles decorated with blue lotus-flowers, bowls of flowers on gilded pedestals. On a low table lay unrolled papyri and writing-materials.

The king was gazing eastwards, deep in contemplation. He wore a simple white kilt, and his only items of jewellery were some gold and lapis-lazuli bracelets, whose upper part was shaped like the heads of two wild ducks. A strongly built man of medium height, with reddish hair, a broad forehead and a hooked nose, he gave the impression of power. As a young boy he had been linked to the throne by his father, the remarkable Seti I, who had built Karnak and Abydos. Since succeeding to the throne, Ramses had led his people to peace with the Hittites and to a prosperity which many other countries envied.

'Pazair, at last! How did the trial proceed?'

'The guilty men were condemned, Majesty.'

'How did Bel-Tran react?'

'He was tense and nervous, but he stood firm. Majesty, I wish that I could say to you the customary words: "All is in order, the kingdom's affairs are proceeding well," but I cannot lie.'

Ramses seemed troubled. 'What are your conclusions?' he asked.

'As regards Branir's murder, I am certain of very little, but with Kem's help I am planning to explore several leads.'

'Will you be investigating the lady Silkis?'

'She heads the list of suspects.'

'One of the conspirators was a woman.'

'I have not forgotten that, Majesty. Three of them are dead; it remains for us to identify their accomplices.'

'Bel-Tran and Silkis, it would appear.'

'That is probable, Majesty, but I have no proof.'

'But did Bel-Tran not unmask himself to you?'

'Indeed, but he has many important supporters.'

'What have you discovered?'

'I am working night and day with those in charge of the various government departments. Dozens of officials have sent me written reports, I have listened to senior scribes, departmental heads and junior employees. The situation is more serious than I thought.'

'Explain that.'

'Bel-Tran has bought a good many consciences. Blackmail, threats, promises, lies – there are no depths he will not stoop to. He and his friends know precisely what they want to do: take over the country's trade and finances, and fight and destroy our ancestral values.'

'How?'

'I do not yet know, Majesty. But arresting Bel-Tran would be a mistake, because I could not be certain of cutting off all the monster's heads and identifying the many snares he has laid for us.'

'On the first day of the new year,' said Ramses, 'when Sopdet appears in the crablike group of stars, signifying the beginning of the Nile's annual flood, I must show the people the Testament of the Gods. If I cannot, I shall have to abdicate and offer the throne to Bel-Tran. Will you have time, in the few months until then, to render him powerless?'

'Only the gods can answer that question, Majesty.'

'It was the gods who created royalty, Pazair, in order to build monuments to their glory, to make men happy and to drive away the envious. The gods gave us the most precious of riches, this light whose guardian I am and which I must spread around me. Humans are not equals; that is why pharaohs offer support to the weak. For as long as Egypt builds temples where the energy of light is preserved, her lands will flourish, her ways will be secure, the child will sleep peacefully in its mother's arms, the widow will be protected, the canals will be maintained, and justice will be done. Our lives do not matter at all; it is this harmony which must be preserved.'

'My life belongs to you, Majesty.'

Ramses smiled and laid his hands on Pazair's shoulders. 'I have the feeling that I have chosen my tjaty well, even if his task is a most arduous one. You have become my only friend. Do you know these words one of my predecessors wrote? *"Trust no one; you shall have neither brother nor sister. It is the one to whom you have given much who will betray you, the poor man you have made wealthy who will strike you in the back, he to whom you have stretched out your hand who will foment unrest. Be wary of your subordinates and those close to you. Rely only upon* *yourself. No one will help you, on the day of misfortune.'"* *

'But, Majesty, does the text not add that the pharaoh who is wise in his choice of those around him shall preserve his own greatness and that of Egypt, too?'

'You know the words of the sages well. I have not made you wealthy, Tjaty. I have weighed you down with a burden which a reasonable man would have refused. Never forget that Bel-Tran is more dangerous than a sand viper. He was able to outwit the vigilance of those close to me, allay their mistrust, infiltrate himself into the government like a worm into fruit. He pretended to be your friend so that he might destroy you more easily. Now his hatred will grow constantly, and he will never again leave you in peace. He will attack where you least expect, will cloak himself in shadows, will wield the weapons of traitors and liars. Are you still willing to face all that?'

'Once one's word is given, it cannot be taken back.'

'If we fail, you and Neferet must submit to the law of Bel-Tran.'

'Only cowards submit. We shall resist to the end.'

Ramses sat down on a gilded wooden chair, facing the rising sun. 'What is your plan?'

'To wait.'

The king could not hide his astonishment. 'Time is not our ally!'

'Bel-Tran will think I am desperate and will move forward across conquered territory; he will remove other masks, and I shall respond in an appropriate manner. In order to persuade him that I have lost my way, I shall direct my efforts into a secondary area.'

'Those are risky tactics.'

'They would be less risky, Majesty, if I had an additional ally at my side.'

*The quotation is from *The Teachings of Merykara.*

'Whom do you mean?'

'My friend Suti.'

'Why is he not with you? Did he prove disloyal?'

'He was sentenced to a year in a Nubian fortress for marital infidelity. The judgement was in accordance with the law.'

'So neither you nor I can overturn it.'

'But if he were to escape, should our soldiers not devote themselves to guarding the border, rather than to pursuing a fugitive?'

Ramses smiled. 'It is possible that they will receive an order telling them not to venture outside the fortress because an attack by some of the Nubian tribes is expected.'

'Human nature is changeable, Majesty, particularly that of nomads. Perhaps, in your wisdom, you knew intuitively that a rebellion was imminent.'

'But it will not take place . . .'

'The Nubians will give up the idea when they see that our garrison is on its guard.'

'Draw up that order, Tjaty Pazair; but in no way facilitate your friend's escape.'

Pazair bowed. 'Destiny will provide for that.'

4

Panther was hiding in a shepherd's hut in the middle of a field. The man had been following her for two hours. He was tall, pot-bellied and dirty, a papyrus-gatherer who spent most of his time in the mud cutting the precious stems. He had been spying on her while she bathed, naked, and had crawled towards her.

Always on the alert, the beautiful young Libyan had spotted him and run away, though she had been forced to abandon her shawl, which she would need against the cold of the night. Panther had been expelled from Egypt because of her open liaison with a married man, Suti, but she refused to accept her fate. She was determined not to abandon her lover, because she feared he might be unfaithful to her – after all, during their affair he had married the lady Tapeni. Panther had resolved to travel to Nubia in order to free him from his prison and live with him again. Never again would she be deprived of his strength and his passionate caresses, never again would she let him wallow in another woman's bed.

The vast distance to Nubia did not daunt her. Making full use of her charms, she had travelled on cargo-boats from port to port, until she reached Elephantine and the First Cataract. Once past the mass of rocks that prevented vessels from passing through, she had allowed herself a moment's relaxation in a water-course which snaked away into a farming area. It was then that the papyrus-gatherer had seen her.

She would not be able to shake him off. He knew every cubit of the terrain, and would soon find her hiding-place. The thought of being taken by force did not frighten Panther; before meeting Suti, she had belonged to a band of looters and had fought Egyptian soldiers. She adored love-making, its violence and its ecstasy. But this man was disgusting – and she had no time to lose.

When the papyrus-gatherer slipped into the hut, he saw Panther lying on the ground, naked and asleep. Her fair hair, which was spread across her shoulders, her generous breasts, her golden womanhood with its luxuriant curls, made him throw caution to the winds and pounce on his prey. His feet were instantly caught in a noose laid out on the floor, and he fell heavily. In the blink of an eye, Panther leapt on to his back and strangled him. As soon as his eyes rolled up in their sockets, she stopped squeezing, undressed him so as to have something warm to wear at night, and continued her journey towards the Great South.

The commander of the fortress of Tjaru, deep in Nubia, pushed away the revolting broth his cook had served him.

'A month in the cells for that incompetent fool,' he decreed.

A cup of palm wine consoled him for his disappointment. So far from Egypt, it was difficult to eat well; but occupying a post like this would bring him promotion and a better retirement. Here, in this desolate, arid land, where the desert constantly threatened the few fields and where the Nile sometimes raged violently, he played host to men who had been sentenced to periods of exile varying from one to three years. Usually, he was rather lenient with them and assigned them domestic tasks which were far from exhausting. Most of the poor fellows had committed only minor crimes, and would take advantage of their enforced stay to reflect on their past.

With the prisoner called Suti, however, the situation had gone rapidly downhill. That fellow would not accept authority and refused to submit. So the commander, whose main duty was to keep watch on the Nubian tribes so as to foresee and forestall any rebellion, had placed his recalcitrant charge well out in the front line, unarmed. Suti would act as bait, and experience a few salutary minutes of fear. Of course, the garrison would rush to his aid if there was an attack; the commander liked to free his guests in good condition and keep his record clean.

A junior officer brought him a sealed papyrus. 'Special message from Memphis, sir.'

'It's the tjaty's seal!' Intrigued, the commander cut the strings and broke the seal.

The officer awaited orders.

'The Information secretariats fear there may be trouble brewing in Nubia. We must be doubly alert and check our defences thoroughly.'

'Yes, sir. Should we close the gates of the fortress and see that no one leaves?'

'Pass the order immediately.'

'What about prisoner Suti?'

The commander hesitated. 'What do you think?'

'The whole garrison loathes that fellow – he's been nothing but trouble. At least he's useful where he is now.'

'Yes, but if something were to happen . . .'

'We would report, sir, that there had been an unfortunate accident.'

Suti was a strong, fine-looking man, with a long face, a frank, direct gaze, and long black hair; he moved with great suppleness and elegance. After escaping from the great scribes' school in Memphis, where his studies had bored him deeply, he had lived the adventurous life he had always dreamt of. He had known beautiful women, and had become

19

a hero of Egypt by identifying a corrupt general and helping his friend and blood-brother, Pazair. Despite his youth, Suti had had many brushes with death: without Neferet's skill, he would have died in Asia, of wounds inflicted by a bear which had struck him down in single combat.*

Seated on a rock in the middle of the Nile, and attached to it by a heavy chain, he could do nothing but gaze into the distance, at the mysterious, disturbing South, whence hordes of formidably brave Nubian warriors emerged from time to time. He, as the advance sentry, would have to sound the alert by shouting at the top of his voice. The air was so clear that the lookouts at the fortress could not fail to hear him.

But Suti would not shout; he would not give the commander and his underlings that satisfaction. Although he had not the slightest wish to die, he would not humiliate himself. He thought of the marvellous moment when he had killed that traitor and criminal General Asher, who had tried to escape from justice, taking with him his stolen gold.

Suti and Panther had found the gold, taken it back with them and hidden it with great care. It was worth a fortune, and would have enabled them to revel in every pleasure they could think of. But he was chained to this rock, and she had been banished to her native Libya, forbidden ever to set foot on Egyptian soil again. She had probably already forgotten him, and was enjoying herself in someone else's arms.

As for Pazair, his position as tjaty tied his hands; intervention in Suti's favour would be punished, and in any case would not lead to his friend's being freed. Suti thought his exile doubly unjust, because the only reason he had married the pretty and spirited Tapeni was to further the judge's investigations. He had thought it would be easy to get a divorce once Tapeni had given him the information he wanted, but he had underestimated her possessiveness. The

*See *Beneath the Pyramid*.

hussy had accused him of adultery with Panther, taken her case to court, and had him sentenced to a year in the fortress. And when he returned to Egypt he would still have to work for her, to provide her with money for when she was old.

In fury, Suti punched the rock and wrenched at his chain. He had done so a thousand times, in the hope that it would eventually break, but this prison without walls or bars had proved unyielding.

Women, his happiness and his misfortune . . . But he had no regrets. Perhaps a tall Nubian girl with high-set breasts, firm and round, would lead the rebels, perhaps she would be taken with him, perhaps she would free him instead of cutting his throat. To die like this, after so many adventures, conquests and victories, was too stupid.

The sun was past its zenith, and beginning its descent towards the horizon. A soldier ought to have brought him something to eat and drink long ago. Lying down, he scooped up some river water in his hands and slaked his thirst; with skill and a little luck, he could catch a fish and so would not die of hunger. But why this sudden change of routine?

When the next day dawned and still no one had come, he was obliged to conclude that he had been abandoned to his fate. If the garrison were staying huddled inside the fortress, it must be because they expected a raid by the Nubians. Sometimes, after a drunken festival, a troop of warriors with a longing for a fight had the mad idea of invading Egypt and set off in quest of a massacre.

Unfortunately, he was directly in their path.

He must break this chain, get away from here before the attack; but he did not even have a hard stone. His mind empty, rage in his heart, he let out a roar.

When evening fell, turning the Nile to blood, Suti's practised eye detected an unexpected movement behind the bushes that lined the bank.

Someone was spying on him.

21

5

Bel-Tran applied pomade made from acacia-flowers and egg-white to the area of red, scaly skin, bordered by spots, that had spread across his left leg. Then he drank a few drops of aloe juice, without much hope of a spectacular cure. He refused to admit that his kidneys were not functioning properly and that his liver was congested; anyway, the head of the Double White House had no time to look after himself.

His best remedy was constant activity. Perpetually charged with irresistible energy, sure of himself, talkative to the point of wearing out those who heard him, he was like an unstoppable torrent. He was only a few months away from the goal that the conspirators had set themselves, supreme power, and a few petty ailments were not going to interrupt his triumphal march.

Right from the beginning of the conspiracy, Bel-Tran had followed the plan laid down, and he had made not even the smallest mistake. Everyone thought he was a faithful servant of Pharaoh, that his dynamism was being deployed to the benefit of Ramses' Egypt, that his powerful capacity for work was worthy to be compared to that of the great sages who worked for the temple and not for themselves.

True, three of his allies were dead; but he still had plenty of others. The dead men had been second-rate and often stupid – he would have had to get rid of them anyway, sooner or later. Even the death of the corrupt clerk Iarrot hardly troubled him, for his source of information had threatened to dry up. The hyenas had solved a problem for him.

Bel-Tran smiled as he mused that he had succeeded in deceiving the whole government and in spinning his strong web without any members of Pharaoh's entourage noticing. Pazair might be trying to fight him, but it was too late.

He constantly travelled around the large towns and provincial capitals to reassure his accomplices that a revolution was going to occur soon and that, thanks to him, they would become rich and powerful, beyond anything they had imagined in their wildest dreams. The appeal to human greed, upheld by cogent arguments, never failed to strike a chord.

The minister for trade and resources massaged his podgy ankles with a paste of crushed acacia-leaves, mixed with beef-fat; it eased tiredness and pain. He chewed two pastilles designed to sweeten the breath; olibanum, scented grasses, terebinth resin and Phoenician reeds mixed with honey produced an extremely smooth mixture. While he chewed, he gazed out of the window with satisfaction.

A huge house, at the centre of a garden enclosed by walls; a stone gateway, its lintel decorated with palm-fronds; a façade regularly punctuated by tall, thin pillars imitating papyrus stems, of which he was the principal producer; an entrance hall and reception rooms whose splendour deeply impressed his visitors, ten bedchambers, dressing-chambers with dozens of linen chests, two kitchens, a bakery, stone privies, a well, grain-stores, stables, a large garden with a pool fringed by palm-trees, sycamores, jujube-trees, perseas, pomegranates and tamarisks. Only a rich man could own such a dwelling, especially in Memphis.

He was proud of what he had achieved, he, once an insignificant employee, an upstart whom senior officials had disdained – before they came to fear him and submit to his law. Wealth and material possessions: no other lasting

23

happiness or success existed. Temples, gods and rites were nothing but illusions and daydreams. That was why Bel-Tran and his allies had decided to wrest Egypt out of an outdated past and make her set forth on the path to progress, in which all that would count was the truth of money. In that realm, no one could equal him; Ramses and Pazair could only endure the blows and then die.

Bel-Tran picked up a jar set into a hole in a raised plank and sealed with a stopper made from silt; covered in clay, it preserved beer marvellously well. Taking out the stopper, he inserted a pipe linked to a filter, which removed any impurities, and savoured a drink that was cool and aided digestion.

Suddenly, he felt a desire to see his wife. He had succeeded in transforming a rather awkward, plain little provincial girl into a great lady of Memphis, decked in finery of such magnificence that it drove her rivals wild with jealousy. The doctors had charged high prices for the operations, but Silkis's pretty new face and the disappearance of her rolls of fat were worth it. In many ways she was still a child-woman: her moods were changeable, and she sometimes suffered from attacks of hysteria, which only the dream-interpreter could soothe; but she obeyed him without question. At today's receptions, and tomorrow's official meetings, she would appear at his side as a suiitable consort, her duties to keep silent and look ravishingly beautiful.

He found her in her bedchamber, rubbing her skin with oil of fenugreek and powdered alabaster. When that was done, she applied a preparation composed of honey, red natron and northern salt, then painted her lips with red ochre, and lined her eyes with green kohl.

Bel-Tran smiled. 'You look delectable, my darling.'

'Would you hand me my best wig?'

Bel-Tran turned the mother-of-pearl button on an old chest made of cedarwood from Phoenicia, and took out a wig made with human hair. Silkis opened a jewellery box and selected a pearl bracelet and an acacia-wood comb.

'How are you feeling this morning?' he asked as he set the wig on her head.

'Still very fragile; I'm taking carob beer mixed with oil and honey.'

'If that doesn't help, consult a doctor.'

'Neferet would cure me.'

'You are not to mention Neferet's name!'

'But she's such a good doctor.'

'She is our enemy, like Pazair, and she'll be destroyed with him.'

'Couldn't you save her . . . for my sake?'

'We shall see. But enough of that. I've brought you something.'

'A surprise!'

'Some juniper oil for your delicate skin.'

She leapt up and threw her arms round his neck. 'Are you staying at home today?'

'Unfortunately, no.'

'Our son and daughter would like to talk to you.'

'Let them obey their teacher; that is more important. Soon, they will be among the most important people in the kingdom.'

'Aren't you afraid that—'

'No, Silkis, I'm not afraid of anything, because I'm untouchable. And no one knows what a powerful weapon I have.'

A servant interrupted them. 'A man is asking to see the master.'

'What is his name?'

'Mentmose, my lord.'

Mentmose, the former head of Memphis's security guards, who had been replaced by Kem. Mentmose, who had tried to get rid of Pazair by accusing him of murder and sending him to a prison camp. Although he did not belong to the circle of conspirators, he had served his future masters well. Bel-Tran thought he had disappeared for ever, exiled to Byblos in Phoenicia, and reduced to the rank of a workman in a boatyard where warships were built.

'Show him into the lotus room, next to the garden,' said Bel-Tran, 'and serve him some beer. I shall be there directly.'

Silkis was anxious. 'What can he want? I don't like him.'

'Don't worry.'

'Will you be travelling again tomorrow?'

'I have to.'

'And what am I to do?'

'Go on being pretty, and don't speak to anyone without my permission.'

'I'd like a third child with you.'

'You shall have one.'

Now aged over fifty, Mentmose had got fat. He had a bald red scalp, a pointed nose and a nasal voice which became shrill and piercing when he was angry. He was a cunning man who had built a brilliant career by using other people's failings. Never could he have imagined falling into an abyss like this, for he had taken a thousand precautions. But Judge Pazair had wrecked his system and brought his incompetence to light. Now that his enemy had become tjaty, Mentmose had no chance of regaining his lost splendour. Bel-Tran was his last hope.

Bel-Tran's opening words were not promising. 'Aren't you forbidden to set foot in Egypt?'

'I am here illegally, it's true.'

'Why have you taken such a risk?'

'I still have a few relations in high positions – all Pazair has is friends.'

'What do you expect from me?'

'I have come to offer you my services.'

Bel-Tran seemed doubtful.

'When Pazair was arrested,' Mentmose reminded him, 'he denied having murdered Branir. I did not believe for a second that he was guilty and I was aware I was being used, but that situation suited me. Someone sent me a warning message, so that I could catch Pazair red-handed when he was bending over his master's corpse. I've had time to reflect on that episode. Who was it that warned me, if not you yourself or one of your allies? Qadash, Denes and Sheshi are dead; you are not.'

'How do you know they were my allies?'

'A few tongues are wagging, and and they say you're the future master of Egypt. I hate Pazair as much as you do, and I have some information which may prove embarrassing.'

'What is it?'

'The judge said he ran to Branir's house because he'd had a written message saying, "Branir is in danger. Come quickly." Suppose that, contrary to what I said at the time, I didn't destroy that document, and that the writing could be identified? And suppose I kept the murder weapon, the mother-of-pearl needle, and it belonged to someone dear to you?'

Bel-Tran thought for a moment. 'What do you want?'

'Rent me a house in the city, let me work against Pazair, and give me a post in your future government.'

'Nothing else?'

'I am convinced that you are the future.'

'Your requests seem reasonable to me.'

Mentmose bowed before Bel-Tran. All that remained was for him to take his revenge on Pazair.

6

As Neferet had been called urgently to the main hospital in Memphis for a difficult operation, Pazair was feeding Mischief, his wife's little green monkey. Although the wretched creature spent her time annoying the servants and stealing from the kitchens, Pazair had a great weakness for her. When he had met Neferet for the first time, it was only because Mischief had splashed water over Brave, his dog, that he had dared speak to his future wife.

Brave put his forepaw on the tjaty's wrist. Long-legged with a long tail and drooping ears that pricked up at meal times, the sand-coloured dog wore a pink and white leather collar bearing the legend 'Brave, companion of Pazair'. While Mischief peeled and ate palm-nuts, the dog feasted on mashed vegetables. Fortunately, peace had been established between the two animals. Brave had agreed to have his tail pulled ten times a day, and in return Mischief left him alone when he curled up to sleep on Pazair's old mat, which had been the young judge's only valuable possession when he arrived in Memphis. It was indeed a fine item, which could serve as bed, table, floor-covering and, if the need arose, coffin. Pazair had sworn to keep it for ever, no matter how rich he became, and since Brave had adopted it, disdaining cushions and soft chairs, he knew his mat would be well guarded.

A gentle winter sun awoke the dozens of trees and flowerbeds that made the tjaty's great dwelling look like one of the eternal paradises where the righteous dwelt. Pazair walked a little way along a garden path, enjoying the subtle scents that arose from the dew-moistened earth. A friendly muzzle touched his elbow: his faithful donkey, Way-Finder, was greeting him in his usual way. A fine animal, with gentle eyes and an acute intelligence, he had an astonishing sense of direction – which the tjaty himself lacked utterly. Pazair was delighted to be able to offer Way-Finder a life in which he no longer had to carry heavy loads.

The donkey lifted his head. He had detected an unexpected presence at the main gateway, and set off rapidly towards it. Pazair followed.

Kem and Killer were waiting for the tjaty. Kem was impervious to both cold and heat, and despised luxury: he was wearing only a short kilt, like any ordinary man of modest standing. At his belt was a wooden case containing a dagger, a gift from the tjaty, with a bronze blade, and a hilt made from a mixture of gold and silver, with marquetry rosettes in lapis-lazuli and green feldspar. The big Nubian preferred this splendid weapon to the ivory hand he was obliged to carry at official ceremonies. He loathed the atmosphere of offices, and continued, as in the past, to patrol the streets of Memphis and work on the ground.

Killer had a massive head, a band of rough hairs running from the top of his back to his tail, and a red cape on his shoulders. He was calm now, but when he was enraged and unleashed his full strength he was capable of felling a lion. The only creature that had ever dared fight him in that state was another baboon of the same size and strength, sent by an unknown assassin who wanted to kill him so as to be able to attack Pazair. Killer had defeated and killed his attacker, but had been gravely wounded. Neferet had treated him, and soon put him back on his feet, and he felt undying gratitude to her.

When Pazair and Kem had exchanged greetings, Kem said, 'There's no visible sign of danger, and no one's been watching you these last few days.'

'I owe you my life.'

'And I owe you mine. However, since it seems our destinies are linked, let's not waste our breath thanking each other. Our quarry is in the nest – I've checked.'

As if he had divined the tjaty's intentions, Way-Finder immediately set off in the right direction. He trotted composedly through the streets of Memphis, a few paces in front of the baboon and the two men. Killer liked to walk upright and gaze all around him; as he passed, everything instantly went quiet.

There was a cheerful bustle in front of the main weaving-workshop in Memphis; weaving-women were chattering, and men were delivering bales of linen thread, which a female overseer checked minutely before accepting them. The donkey halted before a heap of forage, and Pazair, Kem and Killer entered the workshop where the looms were set up.

They headed for the office of the weavers' overseer, the lady Tapeni. Her appearance was deceptive: she might be a small, lively, seductive thirty-year-old with black hair and green eyes, but they knew she ran the workshop with an iron hand and thought of nothing but her career.

The trio's appearance seemed to disconcert her. 'You . . . you want to see me?'

'I believe you can help us,' said Pazair in a firm voice.

Already, rumours were flying round the workshop. The tjaty of Egypt himself and the head of Memphis's security guards were in Tapeni's office! Was she about to be suddenly promoted, or had she committed a serious crime? Kem's presence rather implied the latter.

'I must remind you,' Pazair continued, 'that Branir was murdered with a mother-of-pearl needle. Using what you had told me, I formed several hypotheses, but unfortunately none of them bore fruit. Now, you claimed to have conclusive information. It is time you revealed it.'

'I was boasting.'

'Among the conspirators who murdered the Sphinx's guards, there was a woman – and she was as cruel and determined as her accomplices.'

Killer's red eyes fixed on the pretty brunette, who was increasingly nervous.

'Suppose,' Pazair went on, 'that this woman was also an excellent needlewoman and that she was ordered to kill Branir so as to stop his investigation in its tracks.'

'All this is nothing to do with me.'

'I should like to gain your confidence.'

'No!' she shouted, on the verge of hysteria. 'You want revenge because I had your friend Suti sentenced, but he was in the wrong and I was in the right. Don't threaten me any more or I'll lodge a complaint against you. Get out of here!'

'You should speak more respectfully,' warned Kem. 'You are addressing the tjaty of Egypt.'

Trembling, Tapeni lowered her voice. 'You have no evidence against me.'

'We shall obtain some eventually. I wish you good health, Lady Tapeni.'

The two men bowed and left.

When they were outside, Kem asked, 'Well, are you satisfied?'

'Indeed I am.'

'We may have stirred up a hornets' nest.'

'That young woman is very nervous. She attaches great importance to her social success, and our visit doesn't bode well for her reputation.'

'So she's likely to react.'

Pazair nodded. 'Straight away.'

'Do you think she's guilty?'

'Of iniquity and meanness, certainly, but . . .'

31

'Then who do you think is? Surely you can't mean Silkis?'

'A childish woman can, like a child, become a criminal on a mere whim. Besides, she's an excellent needlewoman.'

'But she's said to be very timid,' Kem objected.

'She bends to her husband's slightest wish. If he told her to act as bait, she'd obey him. And if the head of the Sphinx's guard saw her suddenly appear in the middle of the night, he wouldn't have been able to think clearly.'

'Committing a crime . . .'

'I shan't make a formal accusation until I have proof.'

'But what if you never get it?'

'Let us trust in the work.'

Kem looked closely at his friend. 'You're keeping something important from me, aren't you?'

'I must – I have no choice. But you should know that we're fighting for Egypt's very survival.'

'Working with you isn't exactly restful.'

'All I want is to live quietly in the country, with Neferet, my dog and my donkey.'

'Then you'll have to be patient, Tjaty Pazair.'

Tapeni could not sit still. She knew how stubborn Pazair was, how determined he was to uncover the truth, and how unshakeable was his friendship with Suti. Perhaps she had dealt too harshly with her husband, but he had married her and she would not tolerate his being unfaithful to her. He would pay for his affair with that Libyan bitch.

But now, in the light of what the tjaty had said, she knew she must find a protector at once. If recent rumours were to be believed, there could be no doubt to whom she must apply.

Tapeni hurried to the offices of the Treasury secretariat, and asked the guards if she might wait. After only half an hour an empty travelling-chair arrived in front of the offices. It had a high back, a footstool and broad armrests, and woven palm-fronds shaded the user from the sun's rays. Twenty bearers, under the command of a leader with a powerful voice, ensured that it travelled quickly. They hired out their services at a high price, and would not take on journeys that were too long.

A few minutes later, Bel-Tran came out of the secretariat's main door and hurried towards his chair.

Tapeni barred his way. 'I must speak with you.'

'Lady Tapeni! Are there problems at your workshop?'

'The tjaty is bothering me.'

'He sees himself as a righter of wrongs.'

'But he's accusing me of having committed a crime.'

'You?'

'He suspects me of having murdered Branir.'

'What evidence has he got?'

'None, but he's threatening me.'

'An innocent woman has nothing to fear,' said Bel-Tran smoothly.

'It wasn't just Pazair. Kem and his baboon were there, too, and I'm afraid. I need your help.'

'I can't see how I—'

'You're rich and powerful, and people say that you'll rise to still greater power. I'd like to become your ally.'

'In what way?'

'I control the trade in fabrics, and noble ladies like yours have a passion for them. I know how to contrive the best conditions for buying and selling – believe me, the benefit to you wouldn't be negligible.'

'Is there a great deal of such trade?'

'Yes, and with your qualities you'll easily be able to make it grow still further. As a bonus, I promise to do harm to the tjaty – may he be accursed.'

Bel-Tran's eyes narrowed. 'Have you a specific plan in mind?'

'Not yet, but you can rely on me.'

'Very well, Tapeni, you may consider yourself under my protection.'

7

The shadow-eater* was a perfectionist. So far his attempts to destroy Pazair had come to nothing, but he was determined to succeed in the end. After following his trail for a long time, Kem had resigned himself to failure. Working alone, without help, the murderer would never be identified. Thanks to all the gold he had been paid for crimes committed in the conspirators' service, he would soon be the owner of a house in the country, where he would enjoy a peaceful retirement.

The shadow-eater no longer had any contact with his employers; three were dead, and Bel-Tran and Silkis had made themselves inaccessible. However, Silkis had not been exactly shy at their last encounter, when she had passed on the order for him to disable Pazair. She had neither screamed nor called for help when she submitted to his lust. Soon Bel-Tran and Silkis would mount the throne of Egypt, so the shadow-eater felt obliged to present them with the head of the tjaty, their worst enemy.

He had learnt from his previous failures, and would no longer attack head-on; Kem and Killer had proved too effective for that. The baboon always sensed danger, and the Nubian constantly watched over Pazair. The shadow-eater would act indirectly, by setting traps.

*A literal translation of the Egyptian expression used for an assassin.

34

In the middle of the night, he climbed the wall of the main hospital in Memphis, crawled on to the roof, and slipped inside the building by means of a ladder. Setting off along a corridor full of the smells of healing ointments and pomades, he made for the rooms where dangerous substances were kept. In several workshops the saliva, excrement and urine of toads and bats were stored, along with the venom of snakes, scorpions and wasps, and other toxic substances derived from plants, from which the remedy-makers prepared very effective medicines.

The presence of a watchman did not hamper the shadow-eater in the least. He struck the man unconscious with a blow to the base of the neck, then seized a phial of poison and a black viper imprisoned in a basket.

Aghast, Neferet enquired after the watchman's condition before she even inspected the workshops, and was relieved to hear he was not seriously injured.

'Has anything been stolen?' she asked the hospital's head doctor.

'Almost nothing. Only a black viper in a basket.'

'No poisons?'

'It's difficult to say. We received a new batch yesterday evening, and I was going to enter them in the records this morning. But the thief didn't break anything.'

'From tonight, the guard is to be doubled. I shall inform Commander Kem of the break-in myself.'

Anxiously, the young woman thought of the attempts to murder her husband. Might this odd incident be the prelude to a new threat?

Having crossed the security barriers that prevented unauthorized persons from entering the Treasury district, the tjaty arrived at the door of the Treasury, together with Kem and Killer. For the first time since his investiture, Pazair was

35

inspecting Egypt's reserves of precious metals. He felt as though his mind were still half asleep. He and Neferet had been woken before dawn by a messenger from the hospital, and had not even had time to exchange a few thoughts before Neferet dashed off to the scene of the break-in. Unable to get back to sleep, Pazair had risen very early, taken a burning-hot shower, and then set off for the centre of Memphis.

The tjaty placed his seal on the register handed to him by the guardian of the Treasury, an elderly, slow and meticulous scribe. Although he knew Pazair's face, he checked that the imprint matched the one that had been sent to him by the palace when the new tjaty was appointed.

'What do you wish to see?' the scribe asked.

'All the reserves.'

'That will take a long time.'

'It is part of my duties.'

'I am at your disposal, Tjaty.'

Pazair began with the immense building in which were stored ingots of gold and silver from the Nubian mines and the eastern desert. Each ingot had been given an order number, and their arrangement was impeccable. A consignment was due to leave soon for the temple at Karnak, where the goldsmiths would work the precious metal into ornamentation for two great gates.

Once he recovered from his initial bedazzlement, Pazair saw that the strong-rooms were half empty.

'Our reserves are the lowest they've ever been,' said the scribe.

'Why is that?'

'Orders from above.'

'Where exactly?'

'The Double White House.'

'Show me the documents.'

The scribe was not mistaken: for several months, gold and silver ingots, as well as large quantities of other rare minerals,

had been regularly leaving the reserves on Bel-Tran's orders.
Waiting was no longer an option.

Walking fast, Pazair, Kem and Killer soon reached the
Double White House, a collection of two-storey buildings
housing offices separated by small gardens. As usual, it was
as busy as an anthill. Since Bel-Tran had been placed at the
head of the great body of state, he had stamped out laxity, and
he ruled like a tyrant over an army of busy scribes.

In a large enclosure were fat oxen destined for the temple;
specialists were examining the animals, which had been
received as payment of taxes. In a shed surrounded by a brick
wall and protected by soldiers, accounting-scribes were
weighing gold ingots before placing them in chests. The
internal message system was in operation from dawn till
dusk; young men with strong legs ran from one place to
another, carrying instructions which had to be carried out
immediately. Stewards took charge of tools, the making of
bread and beer, receiving and distributing ointments,
materials for the great construction sites, amulets and
religious items. One whole department was devoted to
scribes' palettes, reed pens, papyri, and clay and wooden
tablets.

While Kem and Killer waited in the entrance-hall, Pazair
made his way though pillared halls where dozens of officials
were writing notes and reports. As he went, the tjaty began to
realize the full extent of the system Bel-Tran had come to
control. Little by little the man had learnt about its various
components, and he had not pushed himself to the forefront
until he had mastered them all.

The leaders of the teams of scribes bowed before the tjaty,
while their employees continued to work; they seemed to fear
their master far more than the first minister of Egypt. A
steward led Pazair to the threshold of a vast hall where Bel-
Tran was pacing up and down, dictating his instructions to

three scribes, who were obliged to write with remarkable speed and dexterity.

The tjaty observed his sworn enemy. Ambition and lust for power impregnated every fibre of his being, every word he spoke; the man had no doubts about his own qualities, or about his ultimate triumph.

When he spotted Pazair, he stopped, tersely dismissed the scribes and ordered them to close the wooden door behind them. 'Tjaty, your visit is an honour,' he said.

'Don't waste your breath on hypocritical words.'

'Did you take the time to admire my administration? Hard work is its abiding law. You could dismiss me and appoint another minister, but the system would take hold and you would be its first victim. You would need more than a year to take back the rudder of this heavy vessel, and you have only a few months before the appointment of the new pharaoh. Give up, Pazair, and submit.'

'Why have you emptied our reserves of precious metals?'

Bel-Tran gave a smug smile. 'Have you inspected them, by any chance?'

'That is my duty.'

'And I'm sure you were very thorough.'

'I demand an explanation.'

'The higher interest of Egypt! We had to keep our friends and vassals happy – the Libyans, Phoenicians, Syrians, Hittites, Canaanites and many others – in order to maintain good relations and preserve the peace. Their governments like presents, especially gold from our deserts.'

'You have hugely exceeded the usual quantities.'

'In certain circumstances, one has to show generosity.'

'Not one speck more of precious metal is to leave the Treasury without my authorization.'

Bel-Tran smiled again. 'As you wish. But everything was done legally and correctly. I can see what you're wondering: did I use a legal procedure in order to misappropriate wealth for my own benefit? A shrewd idea, I admit. Allow me to leave you in doubt, with just one certainty: you cannot prove anything.'

8

From his rock in the middle of the Nile, Suti peered through the darkness at the bushes on the bank where the Nubian spy was hiding, watching him. Wisely, the spy kept absolutely still, probably suspicious of a trap: Suti was too easy a target.

The bushes rustled again; the spy must have decided to attack. No doubt an excellent swimmer, like all his race, he would swim underwater and try to take Suti by surprise.

With the rage of despair, Suti wrenched at his chain; it groaned and grated, but did not break. He was going to die here, stupidly, without even a chance to defend himself. Turning round, he tried to work out where the attack would come from; the night was dark, the waters of the river impenetrable.

A slender shape darted up out of the water, very close to him. He charged, head down, stretching the chain to its maximum. The figure dodged out of the way, slipped on the wet rock, fell into the water and came up again.

'Keep quiet, you fool!' it hissed.

That voice . . . He would have recognized it in the kingdom of the underworld! 'Panther? Is it really you?'

'Who else would come to your aid?'

Naked, her fair hair tumbling over her shoulders, she came towards him, bathed in a ray of moonlight. Her beauty and her sensuality entranced him yet again.

She pressed herself against him, put her arms round him and kissed him passionately. 'I've missed you a lot,' she whispered.

'I'm chained up.'

'At least you haven't been unfaithful to me.'

Panther grew hot with passion, and Suti did not resist this unexpected assault. Under the Nubian sky, lulled by the song of the river, they gave themselves to each other lustily.

When passion was spent, she stretched out beside him, overwhelmed with pleasure, and he gently stroked her hair.

'Fortunately,' she said, 'your strength hasn't been sapped. If it had been, I'd have abandoned you.'

'How did you get here?'

'Boats, chariots, carts, on foot, donkeys . . . I knew I'd find you in the end.'

'Did you have any problems?'

'Rapists and thieves here and there, but nothing really dangerous. Egypt's a peaceful country.'

'Let's get out of this place – fast.'

'I like it here.'

'If the Nubians attack, you'll soon change your mind.'

Panther got up, dived into the river, and surfaced with two sharp-edged stones. With strength and accuracy, she attacked one of the links in the chain, while Suti smashed the metal ring encircling his wrist.

At last, their efforts were crowned with success. Mad with joy at being free again, Suti seized Panther and hoisted her up; the Libyan wound her legs round her lover's back and his manhood reawoke. He slipped on the wet rock and, joined together, they fell into the river, overcome with laughter. Their bodies were still united as they rolled on to the bank. Intoxicated with each other, they found a new energy in their embrace.

At last the cold of dawn calmed them down. 'We must go,' said Suti, suddenly serious.

'Go where?'

'South.'

'But that's unknown territory, and there'll be wild animals and the Nubians . . .'

'We must get away from the fortress and its soldiers. When they realize I've escaped, they'll send out patrols and alert their spies. We must hide until their vigilance dies down.'

'What about our gold?'

'We'll get it back, never fear.'

Panther frowned. 'It won't be easy.'

'Together, we'll succeed.'

'If you ever deceive me again with that woman Tapeni, I'll kill you.'

'Kill her first – it would be a relief.'

'You're the one responsible for that marriage. You obeyed your friend Pazair, and then he abandoned you, and look where we are now!'

'I shall settle all my accounts,' said Suti grimly.

'If we escape from the desert.'

'It doesn't frighten me. Have you got any water?'

'Two full skins. I hung them on a branch of a tamarisk.'

They hurried down a narrow track, between sun-scorched rocks and hostile cliffs. Then Panther led the way along a dry riverbed, where they found and ate a few tufts of grass. By mid-morning the sand burnt their feet, and white-necked vultures circled overhead.

For two days, they did not meet a living soul. At noon on the third day they heard horses galloping, and hastily took shelter behind an outcrop of granite rocks eroded by the wind. Two Nubian horsemen appeared, dragging behind them a naked boy. He was clinging to a rope attached to one horse's tail, and was breathless from running. The riders stopped, and ochre-coloured dust rose up into the azure sky. One cut the prisoner's throat, the other sliced off his testicles. Laughing merrily, they abandoned the corpse, and headed back towards their camp.

Panther had watched unflinchingly. 'You see what awaits us, my sweet one,' she said. 'Nubian bandits know no pity.'

'Then we'd better make sure we don't fall into their hands.'

'This place is hardly suitable for a happy retirement. Let's go on.'

As they went, they fed on palm-shoots which they found growing wild in the lonely black rocks. A lugubrious moaning accompanied them: a strong wind had begun to blow, and clouds of sand soon hid the horizon. They staggered and fell, holding each other tightly, and waited for the storm to end.

A slight shiver ran over Suti's skin. He awoke, and shook the sand out of his nose and ears.

Panther lay motionless.

'Get up,' he said. 'The storm's over.'

She did not move.

'Panther!' In panic, Suti lifted her up. She lay limp in his arms. 'Wake up, I beg you!'

'Do you love me, just a little bit?' she asked in a sultry voice.

'You were play-acting!'

'When you're in danger of becoming enslaved to a faithless lover, you have to put him to the test.'

Suti set her on her feet. 'We've no water left,' he said. 'We must go on.'

Panther walked ahead, scanning the sand for traces of moisture. When night fell, she managed to kill a rodent. She stuck two pieces of palm-leaf rib into the ground and held them firmly with her knees, then between them she rubbed a length of very dry wood, holding it in both hands; vigorous repetition produced sawdust, which caught fire. The cooked meat, little though there was, gave them back some strength.

As soon as the sun rose, the modest meal and the relative

43

cool of the night were forgotten; they must find a well, and soon, or they would die. But how could they do that? There was not a single oasis in sight, not even a few tufts of grass or thickets of thorn bushes, which sometimes revealed the presence of water.

'Only one sign can save us,' said Panther. 'Let's sit down and watch for it. There's no use walking any further.'

Suti acquiesced. He did not fear the desert or the sun; dying free, at the heart of this ocean of fire, held no terrors for him. The light danced on the rocks, time dissolved in the heat, eternity imposed itself, burning and indomitable. In Panther's company, he felt a form of happiness which was as precious as the gold of the mountains.

'Over there,' she suddenly whispered in his ear, 'on your right.'

Suti turned his head slowly. On the summit of a sand-dune, he saw an oryx stag: at once proud and wary, it was sniffing the air. It weighed at least much as two men, and its long horns could run a lion through. He knew that these animals could tolerate unbearable heat, wandering in the desert even when the sun beat down vertically.

'We must follow it,' decreed Panther.

A slight breeze lifted the black hairs on the tail of the oryx, whose breathing grew faster as the heat intensified. The animal of the god Set, lord of storms and incarnation of nature's extremes, the oryx knew how to capture the smallest breath of air in order to refresh the circulation of its blood. The stag made a mark in the sand with its hoof, and then set off southwards along the dunes, surefootedly avoiding the areas of soft sand.

The couple waited a few minutes before going to examine the mark. It was like an X, the hieroglyph signifying 'to pass'. Was the oryx showing them a way of getting out of this great barren waste? They followed it, staying a safe distance behind.

Suti marvelled at Panther. She never complained, never balked at even the most strenuous effort; she fought for survival with the same determination as a wild animal.

Just before sunset, the oryx began to walk faster and disappeared behind an enormous dune. Suti helped Panther to climb the slope, which gave way beneath their feet. She fell, he lifted her up, and fell in his turn. Lungs aflame, legs aching, they crawled to the summit.

The desert was tinged with ochre. The heat came not from the sky but from the sand and the stones. The mild warmth of the wind could not cool their burning lips and throats.

The oryx had disappeared.

'It's tireless,' said Panther. 'We have no hope of catching up with it. If it scents greenery, it'll carry on without stopping, for days on end, if need be.'

Suti was staring at something in the far distance. 'I think I can see . . . No, it's a mirage.'

Panther looked, too, but her sight was clouded.

'Come on,' said Suti, 'keep going forward.'

They forced their legs to move again, despite the pain. If Suti was wrong, they would have to drink their own urine before dying of thirst.

'Look!' panted Suti. 'The oryx's tracks.'

After a succession of leaps, the antelope had settled back into a slow walk towards the mirage that had cast a spell on Suti. In her turn, Panther began to hope: could she make out a minuscule patch of green?

They forgot their exhaustion, and followed in the animal's tracks. And the green dot grew and grew, until it became a grove of acacia-trees.

Under the tree with the broadest canopy, the oryx was resting. It watched the new arrivals carefully. They admired its long horns, its fawn pelt, its black and white face. Suti knew it would not flinch in the face of danger; sure of its own power, it would gore them if it believed itself under threat.

'The hairs of its beard,' croaked Panther. 'They're wet!'

The oryx had finished drinking. It was eating acacia-pods, a good part of which would pass, undigested, into its droppings and would result in the growth of new trees wherever it went.

'The earth is soft,' Suti observed.

They walked very slowly past the animal and entered the heart of the grove, which was bigger than it seemed. Between two date-palms lay the mouth of a well, surrounded by flat stones.

Suti and Panther embraced, before running to the well and slaking their thirst.

'This is a real paradise,' declared Suti.

9

Anxiety reigned in the narrow street where Bagey, Pazair's predecessor as tjaty, lived in retirement: the old man was gravely ill.

In his time as tjaty, Bagey had been known as a cold, intransigent, austere man, who was impervious to flattery and who hated sloppiness; he had ruled his subordinates with an iron fist. Eventually, worn out by his burdens of office, he had asked Ramses to release him from his duties so that he might end his days in peace in his little house in Memphis.

Pharaoh, who had closely watched Pazair's career and his clashes with certain eminent persons, had put his faith in the young judge's sincere desire for truth and determination to unravel the conspiracy menacing Egypt. Bagey had approved of that decision. Pazair had proved honest in the pursuit of his investigation and had unfailingly fulfilled his duties as a judge, so Bagey told Ramses that, though he himself was no longer strong enough to fight, the younger man had his full support.

Bagey's wife, a plain, brown-haired woman, had alerted their neighbours as soon as her husband's illness worsened. Usually he rose early, went for a walk in the great city, and came back a little before the midday meal. But this morning he had complained of a terrible pain in his back. Despite his wife's insistence, Bagey refused to call a doctor, convinced that the pain would soon ease. But it had not, and in the end he had been compelled to see reason.

The neighbours had gathered in the street, advocating a thousand and one remedies, accusing all kinds of demons of having caused Bagey's illness. Silence fell with the arrival of Neferet, the kingdom's principal doctor, accompanied by Way-Finder, whose job was to carry her medical equipment. He walked straight through the crowd and headed for Bagey's house, where he halted before the door. The housewives in the crowd called out greetings and congratulations to Neferet, who was very popular, but she was in a hurry and answered only with smiles.

Bagey's wife was put out. She had been expecting a proper doctor, not this radiantly beautiful, alluring creature in a long linen gown. 'You should not have troubled,' she said.

'Your husband helped mine at a difficult time. I shall always be grateful to him for that.'

The two women went into the little white, two-storey house. crossed a drab entrance-hall devoid of ornament, and climbed the narrow staircase to the upper floor.

Bagey was lying down in a somewhat airless room, which had not been repainted in a long time.

'You!' he exclaimed when he saw Neferet. 'Your time is too valuable to—'

'Didn't I cure you once before?'

'You even saved my life. Without your treatment, my portal vein would have killed me.'*

'Don't you trust me any more?'

'Of course I do.'

Bagey sat up, his back propped up against the wall, and looked at his wife. 'Leave us.'

'Don't you need anything?'

*See *Beneath the Pyramid*.

'The doctor's going to examine me.'

His wife withdrew, with a heavy, hostile tread.

Neferet took her patient's pulse in various places, and consulted the portable clock she carried on her wrist, in order to calculate the reaction times of the organs and their proper rhythm. She listened to the voice of the heart, and checked that the hot and cold currents were circulating correctly.

Bagey remained calm, almost indifferent. 'What is your diagnosis?'

'One moment.'

Neferet took a thin, strong cord at the end of which swung a fragment of granite, and passed her pendulum over the different parts of the patient's body. Twice, the granite described wide circles.

'Tell me the truth,' commanded Bagey.

'This is a sickness I know and can treat. Are your feet always so swollen?'

'Quite often. I soak them in tepid salted water.'

'Does that bring relief?'

'Yes, but these days it doesn't last long.'

'Your liver is congested again: the blood is thick. Too much fatty cooking, I expect.'

'My wife has her ways; it's too late to change them.'

'Take more chicory, and drink a potion made of bryony, fig-juice, grape-juice, and the fruits of the persea and sycamore. You must urinate more.'

'I'd forgotten that remedy. But there's something else wrong, I'm sure.'

'Try to stand up.'

With difficulty, Bagey did so. Neferet brought forward a wooden seat with transverse supports and a concave frame on which lay a cover of cords plaited like fish scales. The old man sat down stiffly, and the seat creaked under his weight.

Neferet used her pendulum again.

When she had finished, she said, 'You're suffering from the early stages of kidney disease. Four times a day you must drink a mixture of water, beer leaven and the juice of fresh dates. Keep it in an ordinary terracotta jar, which must be closed with a stopper of dried earth covered with cloth. It's a simple but effective remedy; if it doesn't work quickly, and if you have difficulty passing water, tell me at once.'

'I shall owe my recovery to you again.'

'You certainly won't if you hide part of the truth from me.'

'Why do you say that?'

'I can sense that you're deeply worried, and I must identify the cause.'

'You're a remarkable doctor,' said Bagey.

'Will you tell me?'

Bagey hesitated, then said, 'As you know, I have two children. My son has given me cause for worry from time to time, but he seems to like his work checking baked bricks. But my daughter. . .' He looked down at his feet. 'She spent only a short time in the temple – the rituals bored her. She has become an accounting-scribe on a farm, and the owner seems pleased with her work.'

'Are you angry with her for doing that?'

'Indeed not – my children's happiness comes before all else, and I respect their choices. She wants to start a family, and I am encouraging her to do so.'

'Then what is it that's worrying you?'

'It is stupid, deplorable! My daughter has been given bad advice, and has started proceedings against me in order to obtain her inheritance before the appropriate time. But I have nothing to give her except this house.'

Neferet smiled. 'I cannot cure an ill like that, but I know someone who has proven skill.'

Brave begged for a pastry, and Pazair gave in.

Bagey was seated on a comfortable chair, which he had

told the servants to put in the shade: he disliked the sun's fierce rays.

'This garden is much too big, Pazair,' he said. 'Even devoted gardeners would have trouble keeping it up. I prefer my little house in the town.'

'The dog and the donkey enjoy the space.'

'How have your first days as tjaty been?'

'It all seems almost impossibly difficult.'

'The words of the investiture rite should have put you on your guard: it is a task "more bitter than bile". You are young, so don't try to go too far too fast; you have time to learn.'

Pazair longed to confide in the old man and tell him he was much mistaken. Instead, he said, 'The less I master the situation, the more the country's balance will be compromised.'

'Why are you so gloomy?'

'More than half of our reserves of precious metals have been squandered,' said Pazair.

Bagey sat bolt upright. 'What? More than half? That's impossible! My last checks did not reveal anything of the kind.'

'Bel-Tran used – perfectly legally – all the administrative resources at his disposal, and transferred a good part of the Treasury abroad.'

'What justification did he offer?'

'To ensure peace with our neighbours and our vassals.'

'The argument is not without weight. I should have been more wary of that upstart.'

'He has deceived the whole government. He has always worked hard and shown the will to succeed, an obsessive desire to serve his country. Why should anyone have doubted his sincerity?'

'He's taught us a harsh lesson.' Bagey was downcast.

'At least we are now aware of the danger.'

'You are right,' agreed Bagey. 'Of course, no one can replace Branir, but I may perhaps be able to help you.'

51

'My vanity made me assume I would get the measure of my office quite quickly, but Bel-Tran has locked many doors. I fear that my power may be an illusion.'

'If your subordinates think that, your position will rapidly become untenable. You are the tjaty: you must lead.'

'Bel-Tran's henchmen will block my decisions.'

'Go round the obstacle.'

'How?'

'In each government secretariat,' said Bagey, 'there is always one especially important, experienced man – not necessarily the one in the highest position. Find him and cultivate his acquaintance: you'll soon understand the subtleties of how the different components of that secretariat work.' He gave Pazair names and details. 'Be absolutely scrupulous,' he warned, 'when you attest your actions before Pharaoh. Ramses is highly perceptive, and if you try to deceive him you will fail.'

'In case of difficulty, may I consult you?'

'You will always be welcome, even if my hospitality is not as lavish as yours.'

'The heart matters more than appearances. But now tell me, are you in better health now?'

'Your wife is an excellent doctor, but I am sometimes an undisciplined patient.'

'You must take care of yourself.'

Bagey smiled. 'I am a little tired. Will you allow me to retire?'

'Before you are escorted home, I have something to confess: I met your daughter.'

'Then you know . . .'

'Neferet asked me to see her, and there was nothing wrong in my doing so.'

Bagey frowned angrily.

'It was not a misuse of privilege,' insisted Pazair. 'A

former tjaty deserves due consideration. It was my duty to resolve this disagreement.'

'What did my daughter say?'

'There will be no court case. You will keep your house, and she will build her own, using a loan which I have guaranteed. Now that her dearest wish is being met, harmony will reign in your family again. Oh, and you can expect to be a grandfather soon.'

Bagey's stern demeanour crumbled; he could not hide his emotion. 'You have given me many joys at once, Tjaty Pazair.'

'It is a small thing compared with the help you have given me.'

10

The great market in Memphis was a daily festival, in which as many words were exchanged as goods. The traders, who included women with an inexhaustible gift for talking, had their own allocated places. Barter was practised, along with the necessary haggling and gesticulations. The tone became heated from time to time, but transactions always ended in good humour.

Kem, always accompanied by Killer, liked walking through the main square. Killer's mere presence prevented thefts, while his master listened to snatches of conversation reflecting the people's state of mind, and, using a secret code, discreetly questioned his informants.

The big Nubian paused in front of a stall selling preserved food; he was hoping to find a trussed goose which was ready for roasting, having been dried, salted and put in a jar. The stallholder was sitting on a mat, his head hanging low.

'What's the matter?' asked Kem. 'Are you ill?'

'It's much worse than that.'

'Have you been robbed?'

'Look at my goods, then you'll understand.'

The jars used for preserving food were very efficient. They were also attractive, being made of clay from Middle Egypt, decorated with garlands of flowers and glazed with luminous blue. Kem examined the inscriptions of those on the stall: water, wine, but no meat at all.

'I didn't receive my deliveries,' lamented the trader. 'It's a disaster.'

'Have you been given any explanation?'

'None at all. The ship sailed empty – I've never known such misfortune!'

'Has it happened to anyone else?'

'To everyone. Some traders have stocks in reserve, but no one has received fresh supplies.'

'Perhaps it's simply that they've been delayed.'

'If we don't get our deliveries tomorrow, there'll be a riot, I promise you.'

Kem did not take the matter lightly; no one, rich or poor, would accept such disruption. Well-off people demanded meat for their banquets, more humble people needed dried fish.

So he went to the warehouse where jars of meat were stored centrally. When he arrived, he found the scribe in charge standing outside gazing at the Nile, hands folded behind his back.

'What's going on?' demanded Kem. 'Why aren't you working?'

'Nothing's arrived for a week.'

'And you didn't tell anyone?'

'Of course I did.'

'Whom?'

'The scribe I'm responsible to: the man in charge of salting.'

'Where can I find him?'

'In his workshop, near the Temple of Ptah's butcheries.'

The butchers were talking and drinking sweet beer. At this time of day, they would normally have been busy plucking geese and ducks hung on a long pole, gutting them, salting them, and putting them into large, clearly labelled preserving-jars.

'Why aren't you working?' asked Kem for the second time.

'We've got the birds and the jars,' replied one of them, 'but no salt. That's all we know. You'd better go and see the scribe in charge of salting.'

The scribe was a small man, entirely round and almost bald; he was playing dice with his assistant. The appearance of Kem and Killer instantly banished his desire for amusement.

'It's not my fault,' he declared in a shaky voice.

'Did I accuse you of anything?'

'If you're here—'

'Why haven't you given the butchers the salt they need?'

'Because I haven't got any.'

'Why is that?'

'I have two sources of supply, the Nile Valley and the oases. After the great heat of summer, the foam of the god Set solidifies on the surface of the soil near to the river, so that the earth is covered with a white sheet. This salt contains fire which is a danger to the temple stones, so it's collected at once and stored. At Memphis we also use salt gathered from the oases, because we preserve a great many different kinds of food. But as of today we have none left.'

'Why not?'

'The salt warehouses on the Nile have been placed under lock and key and the caravans are no longer arriving from the oases.'

With Killer at his heels, Kem hurried to the tjaty's office, which, he found, had been invaded by ten angry senior scribes. Each was trying to speak louder than the others, with the result that a deplorable cacophony had taken the place of a discussion. Eventually, after a firm instruction from Pazair, they spoke in turn.

'The same price is paid for an untreated skin and a treated skin. The craftsmen are threatening to stop work unless you take action to re-establish the difference.'

'Not only are the hoes delivered to the farm-workers on the estate of the goddess Hathor of poor quality, but their price has doubled: four *deben** instead of two.'

'The humblest pair of sandals costs three *deben*, which is three times their normal price – and I'm not talking about luxury items.'

'A ewe costs ten *deben* instead of five; a fat ox two hundred instead of one hundred. If this madness goes on, we shan't be able to feed ourselves any more.'

'Haunch of bull will soon be unaffordable, even for the rich.'

'And I'm not talking about dishes or vases made of bronze or copper. One will soon have to barter an entire wardrobe for a single dish.'

Pazair got to his feet. 'Please, calm yourselves.'

'Tjaty, this explosion of prices is intolerable.'

'I agree, but who is behind it?'

The scribes looked at each other.

The one who had been angriest spoke up. 'But . . . you did.'

'Did the directives to that effect bear my seal?'

'No, but they bore the seal of the Double White House. And no one has ever heard of a tjaty being at odds with his minister for finance and trade.'

Pazair could see their point. Bel-Tran's plan, he reflected, was a cunning one: artificial price-rises, discontent among the population, and the tjaty accused of being responsible.

'I made a mistake, and I shall rectify it. Prepare a scale of prices conforming to the normal one, and I shall ratify it. Excessive increases will be punished.'

*One *deben* was the equivalent of 91 grams of copper; it was a reference value used to calculate the value of products.

'Shouldn't the value of the *deben* be altered?'

'That will not be necessary.'

'The traders won't like it. Your mistake was making them a lot of money.'

'Their prosperity does not seem compromised to me. Pray make haste. First thing tomorrow, my messengers will go into the towns and villages to proclaim my decisions.'

The scribes bowed and withdrew.

Kem looked around the large office, which was filled with shelves groaning under the weight of papyri and tablets.

'If I understand rightly,' he said, 'we've had a narrow escape.'

'I found out only yesterday evening what was going on,' said Pazair, 'and I worked all night to stem this devastating tide. Bel-Tran is trying to make everyone discontented, to show that I'm carrying out a disastrous policy and that Pharaoh no longer runs the country. We've escaped disaster this time, but he'll try again, concentrating on particular trades. His goal is to divide the country, setting the rich against the poor, spreading hatred, and turning those destructive forces to his own advantage. We shall have to be constantly on the alert.' Pazair sighed. 'I hope you've brought me some good news?'

'I'm afraid not.'

'Has something else happened?'

'Salt is no longer being delivered.'

Pazair turned pale. There was a danger that people would run out of staple food like dried meat and fish. 'How can that be?' he asked. 'Ample supplies were gathered.'

'Seals have been placed on the doors of the warehouses.'

'Let us go and remove them.'

The seals were in the name of the Double White House; in the presence of Kem and two scribes, the tjaty broke them. A deed was immediately drawn up, signed and dated.

The scribe in charge of salt opened the doors himself.

'But the salt's all damp!' he cried in dismay.

'It was wrongly collected and stored,' said Kem. 'It was moistened with stagnant water.'

'It must be washed in clean water and filtered,' ordered Pazair.

'Hardly anything will be saved.'

In fury, Pazair turned on the scribe. 'Who spoilt this salt?'

'I don't know. When Bel-Tran examined it, he judged it unsuitable for consumption and for preserving food. Legal documents were drawn up, in good and due form.'

The scribe trembled under Killer's piercing gaze, but stood his ground; he truly knew nothing else.

The secretariat in charge of trade with the oases was an annexe of the Foreign Affairs secretariat. Although the oases had belonged to Egypt since the time of the earliest pharaohs, these far-off lands remained mysterious in the eyes of those who lived in the Nile Valley. But they produced natron, which was vital for cleanliness and mummification, and salt of excellent quality. Caravans of donkeys travelled the routes ceaselessly, bearing heavy and precious loads.

A former hunter of sand-travellers who looted caravans – his face was still brown and lined from the desert sun – had been placed in charge of the oases secretariat. He had a square head and powerful chest, and it was immediately clear that he knew the value of hard work and danger. All the same, Killer made him uneasy.

'Put that baboon on a leash,' he said. 'Baboons are dangerous when they're angry.'

'Killer has taken an oath,' replied Kem. 'He has sworn to attack only people who are doing wrong.'

The former hunter turned purple. 'No one has ever doubted my honesty.'

'Haven't you forgotten to greet the tjaty of Egypt properly?' said Kem.

The man did so, his back stiff.

'How much salt is there in your storehouses?' asked Pazair.

'Very little. The donkeys from the oases have delivered nothing for several weeks, neither to us nor to Thebes.'

'Weren't you surprised by that?'

'No. I'm the one who gave the order to halt all trade.'

'Were you acting on your own initiative?'

'I had received instructions.'

'From Bel-Tran?'

'Yes, that's right.'

'What reasons did he give?'

'To bring down prices. The people of the oases refused point blank to obey, because they were sure the Double White House would back down. But now the whole situation has become a morass. My demands for more supplies of salt go unanswered – fortunately, we have the salt from the Valley.'

'Fortunately,' repeated Pazair, aghast.

Clean-shaven, wearing a wig which covered half his forehead, and dressed in a long tunic, the shadow-eater was unrecognizable. Leading two donkeys by a long rope, he arrived at the gate of Pazair's estate that gave access to the kitchens.

He presented the steward with a basket of soft cheeses, creamy fermented milk in a jar, and curds with alum. When the steward bent over the basket, the shadow-eater knocked him unconscious and dragged his body inside the gate.

At last he could get down to work.

11

The shadow-eater had a map of the tjaty's villa and grounds. Leaving nothing to chance, he had established that at this time of day the servants were busy in the kitchen, where the gardeners were eating their midday meal. The absence of Kem and Killer, who were with Pazair in the town, meant that he could act with the minimum of risk.

Although usually impervious to the beauties of nature, the murderer was amazed by the garden's luxuriance. A hundred cubits long and two hundred wide,* it had terraced fields, squares interlaced with water-channels, and a kitchen garden. In addition, it contained a well, an ornamental lake, where blue lotuses were in flower, a hut providing shelter from the wind, a line of shrubs shaped into cones along the edge of the Nile, a double row of palm-trees, a shady path, an arbour, clumps of flowers dominated by cornflowers and mandragora, a vine, fig-trees, sycamores, tamarisks, date-palms, perseas and rare species imported from Asia to charm the eye and the nose. But the man of darkness did not linger in this enchanting place. Carefully carrying the black viper in its basket, he walked along one side of the lake until he reached the house, then stopped and crouched down, on the alert for the faintest sound.

*About 5,400 square metres.

Neither the dog nor the donkey had detected his presence, for they were eating their midday meal, too, on the other side of the estate. According to the map, he was outside the bedchambers used for guests. He climbed through a low window into a rectangular room furnished with a bed and storage chests. He kept tight hold of the handle of the basket; the black viper was thrashing about.

Emerging from the room, he discovered, as he had expected, a fine hall with four painted pillars. The painter had depicted, in vivid colours, ten species of birds frolicking in a garden. The shadow-eater decided he would have this sort of decoration in his future home.

Suddenly, he stopped in his tracks.

He heard snatches of conversation coming from his right, from a bathing-room where a serving-girl was pouring warm, scented water over Neferet's naked body. The mistress of the house was listening to her servant's worries about her family problems, and trying to suggest solutions. The shadow-eater would have liked to gaze at the young woman, whose beauty fascinated him, but pleasure would have to wait until his mission was accomplished. He retraced his steps, and opened another door. It was that of a large bedroom. Vases filled with hollyhocks, cornflowers and lilies stood on pedestal tables, and the two beds had gilded wooden headrests; this was where Pazair and Neferet slept.

His first task accomplished, the shadow-eater recrossed the four-pillared hall, passed the bathing-room, and entered an oblong room full of different-sized phials made of wood, ivory, many-coloured glass and alabaster, and taking such varied shapes as a pomegranate, a lotus, a papyrus stem and a duck. This was Neferet's private workshop. Each remedy was identified by its name, with the corresponding instructions for treatment. He had no difficulty in finding the one he was looking for.

Once again he heard the sound of female voices, and the

song of cascading water; the sounds were coming from the next room. At the top left-hand corner of the wall, he noticed a hole which the plasterer had not yet blocked. Unable to bear it any longer, he climbed on to a stool and stretched up.

He saw her.

Neferet was standing up, receiving the delicious water poured by her servant, stood on a raised brick bench. Her ablutions done, Neferet lay down on a stone bench. Still complaining about her husband and children, the serving-girl gently smoothed lotion into her mistress's back. The shadow-eater drooled at the sight. The last woman he had taken, Silkis, with her opulent curves, was an ugly bitch beside Neferet. For a moment, he thought about rushing into the bathroom, strangling the servant and raping the tjaty's beautiful wife; but time was getting on.

From a box shaped like a swimming girl pushing a duck before her, the servant scooped up a little pomade and spread it over Neferet's lower back to soothe tiredness and ease muscle spasms. The shadow-eater contained his desire and left the house.

When the tjaty crossed the threshold of his house, a little before sunset, his steward rushed up to him.

'Master, I was attacked this morning! It was the time when the travelling sellers come by . . . The man said he was a cheesemonger. I was wary, because I didn't know him, but his cheeses seemed of very good quality. He knocked me unconscious.'

'Did you tell Neferet?'

'I thought it better not to alarm her. Instead, I carried out my own investigation.'

'What did you find out?'

'Nothing worrying. No one saw the man anywhere on the estate – he must have left straight after knocking me out. He probably planned to steal something, but saw that that was impossible.'

'And how do you feel now?' asked Pazair.

'Still a bit shaken.'

'Go and rest.'

Pazair did not share his steward's optimism. If the attacker was the mysterious assassin who had tried several times to kill him, he had probably got into the house. What had he intended to do?

Tired after a long, hard day, during which he'd hardly had time to draw breath, the tjaty put the problem aside for the moment, intent on joining Neferet. He walked quickly down the main garden path, beneath the branches of the sycamores and the palm-trees, admiring the way the leaves undulated in the wind. He liked the taste of the water from his well, and of his dates and his figs. The rustling of the sycamores reminded him of the sweetness of honey; the fruit of the persea looked like a heart. The gods had granted him the privilege of enjoying these marvels and, moreover, of sharing them with the woman he had loved with all his heart since the first moment he set eyes on her.

Seated under a pomegranate tree, Neferet was playing a portable seven-stringed harp. Like her, the tree kept its beauty all year long, for as soon as one flower fell another opened. In her pure, high voice full of gentle emotion, she was singing an ancient song telling of the happiness of lovers who were faithful for ever. He went to her and kissed her neck, in the place where the touch of his lips always made her shiver.

'I love you, Pazair.'

'I love you more.'

'You don't – that's impossible.'

They kissed with the fervour of youth.

'You don't look well,' she observed.

'My cold and cough are coming back.'

'That's because you work too hard and worry too much.'

'These last few days have been exhausting. We came close to two major disasters.'

'Because of Bel-Tran?' asked Neferet.

'There's no doubt about it. He organized a rise in prices in order to sow discontent among the population, and cut off the trade in salt.'

'So that's why our steward couldn't find any preserved geese. And what about dried fish?'

'Stocks in Memphis are exhausted.'

'You'll be held responsible, won't you?' said Neferet worriedly.

'That is the rule.'

'What are you going to do?'

'Get things back to normal straight away.'

'As regards the prices, a decree will be enough. But what about the salt?'

'Not all the stores were spoilt by damp, and the caravans will soon start leaving the oases again. Besides, I've opened up Pharaoh's reserves, in the Delta, at Memphis, and at Thebes. We shan't be without preserved food for long, and in order to reassure people the royal granaries will distribute free food for several days, as in periods of famine.'

'What about the merchants?'

'They will receive fabrics as compensation.'

'So harmony has been restored.'

'Only until Bel-Tran's next attack – he'll never stop harassing me.'

'But can you not bring a case against him? Surely what he did was illegal?'

'He can claim to have acted in the interests of the Double White House, and therefore in Pharaoh's. Raising food prices and making the salt vendors lower theirs would have enriched the Treasury.'

'And made the people poor,' said Neferet angrily.

'Bel-Tran doesn't care about them. He's only interested

making allies of the rich, whose support will be vital if he takes power. To my mind, these were only skirmishes, intended to test my reactions. He has far greater control of the country's trade and finances than I have, so his next attack may well be decisive.'

'Don't be so gloomy. It's tiredness making you feel like that – and a good doctor will cure you of it.'

'Do you know a remedy?'

'The massage room.'

Pazair let himself be led, as though this was the first time he had been there. After washing his feet and his hands, he took off his official robe and his kilt, then lay down on a stone bench. Neferet massaged him gently, smoothing away the ache from his back and the stiffness from his neck. When he turned on to his side, Pazair gazed at Neferet. Her gossamer-fine linen dress scarcely concealed her curves, and her body was perfumed.

He drew her towards him. 'I have no right to lie to you, even by omission. Our steward was attacked this morning, by a man pretending to be a cheese-seller. He couldn't identify his attacker, and nobody saw the man afterwards.'

'Do you think he was the man who's tried to kill you, the one Kem hasn't yet tracked down?'

'Probably.'

'We shall eat different dishes from the ones planned for this evening,' decided Neferet. 'He tried to kill you with poisonous fish, once, remember?'

Pazair admired his wife's composure; and his rising desire made him forget the worries and the dangers.

'Have you changed the flowers in our bedchamber?' he asked.

'Yes. Would you like to see them?'

'I'd like nothing better.'

They walked down the passage between the massage room and the bedchamber, and went into their room.

Pazair undressed Neferet very slowly, covering her with fevered kisses. Each time they made love, he gazed at her soft lips, her slender neck, her firm, round breasts, her shapely hips, her slim legs, and thanked heaven for granting him such insane happiness. Neferet responded to his ardour, and together they experienced the secret joy that the goddess Hathor, queen of love, granted to her faithful worshippers.

The huge house was silent. Pazair and Neferet lay side by side, hand in hand.

A strange noise caught Pazair's attention. 'Can you hear something that sounds like a stick tapping?'

Neferet listened for a moment. The sound was repeated, then silence fell again. She concentrated; distant memories were slowly surfacing.

'It's coming from over there, on my right,' said Pazair.

Neferet lit an oil-lamp. A chest containing Pazair's linen kilts stood where he was pointing. He got out of bed and went over to it.

He was about to lift the lid when a horrible scene rushed back into Neferet's memory. She caught him by the arm and pulled him back.

'Call a servant,' she said, 'and tell him to bring a stick and a knife. I know what the false cheesemonger came to do.'

She was reliving each moment of the ordeal during which she had had to catch a snake and extract its venom to prepare a remedy. When its tail tapped against the sides of the basket in which it was contained, it made a sound exactly like the one she and Pazair had just heard.

Pazair put on his kilt and went to fetch the steward and a gardener. When he returned with them, the steward carried a long stick, and the gardener a very sharp knife.

'Take great care,' advised Neferet. 'There's an angry snake in this chest.'

The steward opened the lid with the end of his stick – and with a hiss the black viper's head instantly appeared. The gardener, used to dealing with this sort of undesirable visitor, chopped the snake in two.

Pazair sneezed several times and was overcome by a fit of coughing.

'I shall go and fetch your medicine,' said Neferet.

Neither of them had touched the delicious grilled lamb their cook had prepared; Brave, on the other hand, had done ample justice to it. Replete, his chin resting on his crossed paws, he was enjoying a well-deserved rest at his master's feet.

From her workshop, Neferet fetched a phial of bryony-based potion, which would clear Pazair's breathing-passages.

'First thing tomorrow,' he said, 'I shall tell Kem that from now on our house must be guarded by some of his most reliable men. This kind of thing won't happen again.'

Neferet put ten drops of potion in a cup, and added water. 'Drink this,' she said, 'and you are to take the same quantity again in an hour's time.'

Thoughtfully, Pazair took the cup. 'The killer must be in Bel-Tran's pay. Was he one of the conspirators who violated the Great Pyramid? No, I don't think so. He's an element outside the conspiracy proper. Which leads me to suppose there are others—'

Brave growled and bared his teeth.

This astounded the couple: he had never behaved to them like that.

'Be quiet,' ordered Pazair.

Brave stood up on his hind legs, and growled more loudly.

'Whatever has got into him?' said Pazair.

The mongrel leapt up and bit Pazair's wrist.

Stunned, he dropped the cup and shook his fist.

White-faced, Neferet blocked his way. 'Don't hit him! I think I understand.'

His eyes filled with love, Brave licked his master's hand.

Her voice shaking, Neferet said, 'That isn't the smell of bryony tincture. The assassin replaced your usual medicine with a poison he stole from the hospital. In treating you, I was meant to kill you.'

12

Panther set a hare to roast, while Suti put the finishing touches to a bow he had made from acacia-wood. It looked much like his favourite bow, which was capable of shooting arrows sixty paces in a straight line, and more than a hundred and fifty in a curved trajectory. Since adolescence, Suti had shown an exceptional gift for hitting the very centre of small targets, even from a long way away.

King of this small oasis, which was rich in pure water, succulent dates and game that came there to drink, Suti was happy. He and Panther lived naked, sheltering from the sun at the hottest times of day and enjoying the shade of the date-palms and the greenery. When desire took hold of them, their bodies united with an ever-renewing passion.

Suti loved the desert, its power, its all-consuming fire which led a man's thoughts towards infinity. For long hours, he gazed at the sunrise and sunset, the imperceptible movements of the dunes, the dance of the sand, its rhythm set by the wind. Immersing himself in silence, he communed with the burning immensity over which the sun reigned unchallenged. Suti had the feeling that he was touching the absolute, beyond the gods. Was it really necessary to leave this unknown patch of earth, forgotten by men?

'When are we leaving?' asked Panther, snuggling up against him.

'Perhaps never.'

'Are you planning to put down roots here?'

'Why not?'

'It's a hellish place, Suti!'

'What do we need that we haven't got?'

'What about our gold?'

'Aren't you happy?'

'This sort of happiness isn't enough for me,' said Panther. 'I want to be rich and command an army of servants, on a vast estate. You will pour me out the finest wines, and rub my legs with perfumed oil, and I shall sing you songs of love.'

'There's no vaster estate than the desert.'

'Where are the gardeners, the ornamental lakes, the musicians, the banqueting-halls, the—'

'All things we don't need.'

'Speak for yourself!' retorted Panther. 'I loathe living like a pauper. I didn't get you out of your Nubian prison just to rot away in this one.'

'We've never been freer. Look around you: no one to bother us, no parasites, only the world in all its beauty and its truth. Why should we leave such splendour?'

'Your imprisonment has weakened your brain, my poor darling.'

'Don't pour scorn on what I said. I've fallen in love with the desert.'

'And what about me? Don't I matter any more?'

'You're not only a fugitive from justice but a Libyan, Egypt's hereditary enemy.'

'Monster! Tyrant!' She rained blows on him with her fists.

Suti seized her arms and threw her down on to her back. Panther struggled, but he was the stronger.

'Either you become my slave of the sands, or I'll throw you out.'

'You have no rights over me – I'd rather die than obey you. You still think about your slut of a wife, Tapeni, don't you?'

'Well, yes, I admit I do occasionally.'

'You're unfaithful to me in your thoughts.'

'Don't you believe it. If I had the lady Tapeni to hand, I'd deliver her to the demons of the desert.'

Panther frowned, suddenly anxious. 'Have you seen them?'

'At night, while you're asleep, I watch the summit of the great dune – that's where they appear. One has the body of a lion and the head of a snake, another has the body of a winged lion and the head of a falcon, and there's a third with a pointed nose, long ears and a forked tail.* No arrow can reach them, no rope can capture them, no dog can pursue them.'

'You're making fun of me.'

'Those demons protect us, because you and I belong to their race – we're as unyielding and ferocious as they are.'

'You were dreaming,' scoffed Panther. 'Those creatures don't exist.'

'You do.'

'Get off me. You're too heavy.'

'Are you sure about that?' He started caressing her.

'No!' she shouted, shoving him hard to one side.

A hatchet-blade sliced into the ground a hair's breadth from where they had been a second before; it was so close that it brushed Suti's forehead. Out of the corner of his eye, he glimpsed the attacker, a tall Nubian who retrieved his weapon and, with a dancer's leap, placed himself in front of his prey.

Their eyes met, each filled with the other's death; talk was futile.

The Nubian swung his hatchet in circles. He was smiling, sure of his strength and his skill, obliging his opponent to back away.

---

*The fantastic animals believed to people the desert are depicted, notably, in the tombs of the nobles in the burial-ground at Beni-Hassan, in Middle Egypt.

Suti's back met the trunk of an acacia-tree. The Nubian raised his weapon, but Panther seized him round the neck. Underestimating her strength, he tried to push her away by elbowing her in the chest. Indifferent to pain, she put out one of his eyes with a stick. Roaring in agony, he brought down the hatchet, but Panther had let go, dropped to the ground and rolled clear.

Head first, Suti butted the man in the belly and knocked him flat on his back.

Panther instantly straddled his chest and forced her stick down across his throat. The Nubian's arms flailed, but he could not free himself. Suti allowed his mistress to finish her victory alone. Their enemy suffocated to death, his larynx crushed.

'Do you think he was on his own?' she asked anxiously.

Suti shook his head. 'Nubians usually hunt in groups.'

'I fear your beloved oasis may be about to become a battlefield.'

'You really are a demon – you're the one who's shattered my peace by attracting them here.'

'Shouldn't we leave as quickly as possible?'

'But supposing he was alone?'

'You said just the opposite a minute ago. Give up your illusions and let's go.'

'Go where?'

'North.'

'The Egyptian soldiers would arrest us – they must be deployed all over the region.'

'If you follow me, we'll avoid them and we'll get our our gold back, too.' In her exzcitement, Panther flung her arms round her lover. 'They'll have forgotten you. They'll think you're lost, or perhaps dead. We'll cross their lines, avoid the fortresses and get rich!'

The danger had excited the Libyan girl; only Suti's arms would calm her. He would gladly have answered her expectations, if he hadn't seen an unexpected movement at the summit of the great dune.

'Here are the others,' he whispered.

'How many?'

'I don't know; they're crawling forward.'

'Let's take the oryx's path.'

Panther was brought down to earth when she saw several Nubians crouching behind the rocks on the rounded summit. 'Then we'll head south.'

But that direction was blocked, too: the enemy had encircled the oasis.

'I've made only twenty arrows,' Suti reminded her, 'and that won't be enough.'

Panther's expression grew hard. 'I don't want to die.'

He held her close. 'I'll kill as many as I can, by climbing to the top of the tallest acacia-tree and shooting from there. I'll let one enter the oasis, then you kill him with the hatchet, take his quiver and bring it to me.'

'We haven't a chance of winning.'

'I trust you.' Suti kissed her, then quickly climbed his chosen tree.

From his perch up there, he could see the Nubians clearly. There were about fifty of them, some armed with clubs, others with bows and arrows. Escaping from them would be impossible. He would fight to the end and kill Panther before she could be raped and tortured. His last arrow would be for her.

Far behind the Nubians, on the crest of a dune, he spotted the oryx that had guided them. It was struggling against an increasingly fierce wind; tongues of sand were detaching themselves from the little mountain and flying up into the sky. Suddenly, the animal disappeared.

Three black warriors ran forward, roaring. Suti drew his bow, aimed instinctively and fired three times. The men fell, face forward, hit in the chest.

Three others followed them.

Suti hit two; the third, mad with rage, entered the oasis. He fired an arrow at Suti, but missed his target by a long way. Panther hurled herself on him, and the two entangled bodies tumbled out of Suti's field of vision. Not a single cry was uttered.

The trunk moved; someone was climbing up. Suti readied his bow.

A hand emerged from the leaves, holding a quiver full of arrows.

'I've got it!' cried Panther.

Suti hauled her up beside him, and found that she was shaking. 'Are you hurt?' he asked.

'I was faster than he was.'

They had no time to congratulate each other; another attack was being launched. Despite his rudimentary bow, Suti shot with great accuracy. But to Panther's surprise it took him two shots to hit an archer who was aiming at him.

'The wind's deflecting my arrows,' he explained.

The branches began to toss in the growing storm. The sky became copper-coloured, the air filled with dust. An ibis, caught by the wind, was almost flattened to the ground.

'Climb down,' ordered Suti.

The trees groaned and made sinister cracking noises; uprooted palms were being sucked up into a yellow whirlpool of sand.

When Suti reached the ground, a Nubian charged at him, axe raised.

The desert's breath was so powerful that it held back the attacker's arm, but even so the blade sank into the left shoulder of the Egyptian who, with his clenched fists, broke his enemy's nose. The raging wind tore them apart, and the Nubian disappeared.

Suti seized Panther's hand; if they escaped the Nubians, the desert's terrifying anger would not spare them.

In waves of unheard-of violence, the sand burnt their eyes and rooted them to the spot. Panther dropped her hatchet, Suti his bow; they crouched at the foot of a palm-tree, whose trunk they could scarcely make out. Neither they nor their attackers could move any further.

The wind howled, the ground shifted beneath their feet, the sky had disappeared. Clasped together, already covered with a winding-sheet of golden grains which whipped their skin, Suti and Panther felt as if they were lost in the middle of a furious ocean.

Closing his eyes, Suti thought of Pazair, his blood-brother. Why had he not come to his aid?

13

Kem walked along the quays in the port of Memphis, watching the unloading of merchandise and the loading of cargos of food for Upper Egypt, the Delta or foreign countries. The deliveries of salt had recommenced, and the people's rising anger had been appeased. Nevertheless, the big Nubian was still uneasy: there were strange and persistent rumours about Ramses' failing health and the country's decline.

He was also furious with himself. Why had he failed to identify the man who was trying to kill Pazair? At least the murderer could no longer get inside the tjaty's estate, which from now on would be under strict guard day and night, but Kem had no leads at all, and none of his informants had given him any useful clues. The criminal worked alone, without help, trusting no one. When would he at last make a mistake? When would he leave a significant trace behind him?

Unlike Kem, Killer was calm, though his sharp eyes took in every detail of the scenes unfolding around him. In front of the Pine House, the buildings that housed the scribes in charge of the transport of wood, Killer halted. Sensitive to the baboon's smallest reactions, Kem did not hurry him along.

Killer's red eyes fixed on a tall man dressed in a red woollen cloak who was hurrying aboard a large boat, her cargo protected by sheets of tough cloth. The man was obviously on edge: he was haranguing the sailors, ordering them to hurry up. It was an odd attitude to take at the start of a long voyage. Why was he irritating the dockmen instead of celebrating the rites of departure?

Kem entered the central building of the Pine House, where scribes were registering on wooden tablets all the details of the cargos and the movements of the boats. He made for one of his friends, a man from the Delta who enjoyed the good things in life.

'Where is that big boat over there going?' asked Kem.

'To Phoenicia.'

'What's she carrying?'

'Water-jars and water-skins.'

'Is that the captain, the one who's in such a hurry?'

'Who do you mean?'

'The man in the red cloak.'

'He's the ship-owner.'

'Is he always so nervous?'

'No, he's usually a rather quiet fellow. Your baboon must have frightened him.'

'To whom does he report?'

'The Double White House.'

Kem left the Pine House, and saw that Killer had taken up position at the foot of the gangplank, preventing the owner from leaving the ship. The man tried to escape by jumping on to the quayside, at the risk of breaking his neck, but Killer seized him by the throat and flattened him out on the dock.

'Why are you so afraid?' asked Kem.

'He's going to strangle me!'

'Not if you answer my questions.'

'This boat isn't mine. Let me go.'

'You're responsible for the cargo. Why are you loading jars and water-skins in the Pine House sector?'

'All the other quays are full.'

'No, they aren't.'

Killer twisted the ship-owner's ear.

'Killer hates liars,' said Kem.

'The cargo covers . . . Roll them back.'

While Killer guarded his prisoner, Kem did so. He made a most surprising discovery: trunks of pine and cedar, planks of acacia wood and sycamore.

Kem felt a surge of joy: at last, Bel-Tran had put a foot wrong.

Neferet was resting on the terrace. Little by little she was recovering from the terrible shock she had suffered, though she still had nightmares about it. She had checked and rechecked the contents of her private workshop, terrified that the assassin might have poisoned other phials, too; but he had restricted himself to the one intended for Pazair.

The tjaty, closely shaven by an excellent barber, came out of the house. He kissed his wife tenderly, and asked, 'How do you feel this morning?'

'Much better. I'm going back to the hospital.'

'I've just had a message from Kem. He says he has good news.'

Neferet put her arms round his neck. 'Please, let yourself be guarded while you are travelling from place to place.'

'Don't worry. Kem's sent Killer to protect me.'

When Pazair got to his office, Kem was waiting for him. The big Nubian had lost his legendary calm, and was fingering his wooden nose in unheard-of agitation.

'We are holding Bel-Tran,' he told Pazair. 'I took the liberty of summoning him immediately. Five of my men are bringing him here.'

'Is there a solid case against him?'

'The evidence of my own eyes.'

Pazair was well versed in the laws regulating the trade in wood. Bel-Tran had indeed committed a serious offence, and one which carried a severe penalty.

However, Bel-Tran's quietly ironic manner betrayed no sign of anxiety. 'Why such a show of force?' he asked with astonishment. 'I'm not a bandit, as far as I know.'

'Sit down,' suggested Pazair.

'I can't – there's a mountain of work waiting for me.'

'Kem has just seized a cargo boat destined for Phoenicia. She was chartered by a ship-owner who reports to the Double White House – in other words, to you.'

'A lot of people do.'

'According to custom, cargos for Phoenicia consist of alabaster vases, crockery, pieces of linen, oxhides, rolls of papyrus, ropes, lentils and dried fish. In exchange, the Phoenicians send us the wood we lack.'

'You are not telling me anything new.'

'This boat would have carried cedar- and pine-trunks, and even planks cut from our acacias and sycamores, whose export is forbidden. In other words, you would have sent out again wood we had paid for, and we would have been short of wood for our buildings, for the masts set up before the doorways of our temples, and for our sarcophagi.'

Bel-Tran did not lose his composure. 'You know nothing about this affair. The planks were ordered by the Prince of Byblos for the coffins of his courtiers, because he admires the quality of our acacias and our sycamores. After all, Egyptian material is a guarantee of eternity, isn't it? To refuse him this gift would have been a grave insult and a political error, with many harmful consequences.'

'And what about the cedar- and pine-trunks?'

'Being young, Tjaty, you are probably unfamiliar with the subtleties of our trade exchanges. Phoenicia undertakes to provide us with varieties which are resistant to fungi and insects. These are not, so I ordered the consignment to be sent back. Specialists have confirmed those facts; the documents are at your disposal.'

'Experts from the Double White House, I presume.'

'By common consent, they are the best. May I leave now?'

'I am not a fool, Bel-Tran. You organized an illegal trade with Phoenicia, hoping to make big profits and to benefit from the support of one of our most important trading partners. I am cutting off that branch. From now on, imports of wood will come solely within my remit.'

'As you wish. But if you go on like this you'll soon collapse under the weight of all your responsibilities. Now, call me a travelling-chair, please. I'm in a hurry.'

Kem was devastated. 'I made you look a fool – I'm very sorry indeed.'

'Not all,' said Pazair. 'Thanks to you, we've taken away one of his powers.'

'The monster has so many heads . . . How many must we cut off before we weaken it?'

'As many as necessary. I'm drawing up a decree calling upon the heads of all the provinces to plant dozens of trees so that people can rest in their shade. Moreover, no tree is to be cut down without my authorization.'

'What are you hoping for?

'To restore confidence to the people, who are being deluged by rumours, and to indicate to them that the future is as bright as a tree's foliage.'

'Do you believe that yourself?'

'Do you doubt it?'

'Being tjaty of Egypt, you can't lie. Bel-Tran is eyeing the throne, isn't he?'

Pazair did not answer.

'I understand that your lips are sealed, but you can't stop me heeding my own intuition. You're fighting a battle to the death – and you stand no chance of winning. Right from the beginning this affair has been rotten, and we're bound hand and foot. I don't know why, but I'll go on fighting beside you.'

*

81

On his way home, Bel-Tran congratulated himself on his foresight. He had surrounded himself with strong defences, and had bribed enough officials to ensure that he could not be toppled, no matter who attacked, no matter how. The tjaty had failed, and would fail again. Even if he did manage to uncover some of Bel-Tran's schemes, he would win only paltry victories.

Bel-Tran was followed by three servants bearing gifts for Silkis: a costly ointment for oiling and perfuming the hair of her wigs; another, made from powdered alabaster, honey and red natron, which would make her skin very soft; and a large quantity of the best-quality cumin, a remedy for indigestion and colic.

When he reached home, he was met not by his wife but by her personal maid. The girl looked concerned: it was Silkis who should have welcomed him and massaged his feet.

'Where is my wife?' he asked.

'She is in bed, my lord.'

'What's the matter with her now?'

'She has pains in her belly.'

'What have you given her?'

'What she asked for, my lord: a little pyramid stuffed with dates, and an infusion of coriander. But they don't seem to be working.'

The bedchamber had been ventilated and fumigated. Silkis, who was very pale, was twisting and turning in pain. When she saw her husband, she tried to smile.

He did not smile back. 'Have you been overeating again?'

'No, really – all I had was one tiny pastry. But the pain's getting worse, darling.'

'Tomorrow evening, you must be out of bed and in your best looks. I have invited several provincial leaders here, and you must do me honour.'

'Neferet would make me better.'

'I told you to forget about that woman.'

'But you promised me—'

'I promised you nothing. Pazair won't give up: he's fighting as fiercely as ever – that puppet! Asking his wife for help would be a show of weakness on our part, and I won't do it.'

'Not even to save me?'

'You aren't very ill – it's just a temporary indisposition. I shall send for the doctors at once. In the meantime, concentrate on getting well for tomorrow so that you can use your charms on our guests.'

Neferet was sitting in the garden, talking with a voluble old man with sun-browned, deeply furrowed skin. He presented her with a terracotta jar, and she bent over it with interest.

As he went towards them, Pazair recognised the old bee-keeper who had been unjustly sentenced to prison and who had helped Pazair escape.

The old man stood up and greeted him. 'Tjaty of Egypt! What a pleasure to see you again. Getting in here wasn't easy, I must say. I was asked a thousand questions, my identity was checked, and they even inspected my pots of honey.'

'How are your bees?'

'Extremely well – that's why I am here. Just you taste this.'

The gods, who were often made bitter by humans' behaviour, recovered their gaiety by eating honey, according to storytellers. When Ra's tears fell to earth, they had been transformed into bees, magicians who could transform pollen into edible gold.

The flavour astonished Pazair.

'Never seen a harvest like it,' said the bee-keeper, 'for quantity and quality.'

'The hospitals will all be supplied,' put in Neferet, 'and we'll still have plenty in reserve.'

A gentle substance, honey was used in eye treatments and to treat blood-vessels and the lungs; it was also used for women's problems, and was incorporated into numerous medicines. And was used in most dressings.

'I only hope the kingdom's principal doctor won't be cruelly disappointed,' the old man went on.

'Why do you say that?' asked Pazair.

'News travels fast. Since word of the amazing harvest got round, the area of the desert where I and my assistants work hasn't been as peaceful as it used to be. We're secretly watched while we take the liquid sunshine out of the hives, put it in jars and seal the jars with wax. When all the honey's been collected, I think it's going to be stolen.'

'Aren't there guards watching over you?'

'Yes, but there aren't enough of them. My honey's worth an absolute fortune, and they won't be able to protect it.'

Of course, thought Pazair: Bel-Tran must have been told about the exceptional yield of honey. Depriving the hospitals of such a vital ingredient of medicine would lead to a grave crisis.

'I shall inform Kem – the delivery will take place in complete safety.'

'Do you know what day it is?' asked Neferet.

Pazair said nothing.

'It's the eve of the Garden Festival.'

The tjaty's face lit up. 'Hathor speaks through you. We shall give much happiness.'

On the morning of the Garden Festival, every betrothed girl and young wife planted a sycamore-tree in her garden. In town and village squares, and beside the river, gifts of cakes and bunches of flowers were exchanged, and everyone drank beer. After rubbing themselves with scented lotion, the beautiful girls danced to the sound of flutes, harps and tambourines. Boys and girls talked of love, and the old folk turned a blind eye.

When scribes handed the mayors jars of honey, the names

of the tjaty and the king were hailed: the bee was one of the symbols of Pharaoh. For most families the edible gold was unaffordable, an almost impossible dream, but that dream would be realized and relished on this festival day, which was being celebrated under Ramses' protection.

From their terrace, Neferet and Pazair listened in delight to the echoes of the songs and dances. The armed thieves who had been preparing to attack the honey caravans had been ambushed and captured. The old bee-keeper was feasting with his friends, proclaiming loudly that the country was well governed and that the festival honey would ward off bad luck.

14

The oasis had been utterly destroyed. The palm-trees had been decapitated, the acacias torn apart, their trunks split and their branches ripped off; the well was blocked, the dunes disembowelled, and little mountains of sand covered the paths. All around was desolation.

When Suti forced his eyes open, he recognized nothing of his haven of peace. So much yellow dust was floating in the air that the light could not shine through, and he wondered at first if he had descended to the shadowy realms that the sun never reached.

Pain awoke in his left shoulder, where the hatchet-blade had caught it. He stretched his legs, which were so painful that he thought they were broken – fortunately, they were only scratched. Beside him lay the bodies of two Nubians, who had been crushed by the trunk of a palm tree. One of them, stiff as a board, was still brandishing his dagger.

Panther! Although his thoughts were confused, Suti remembered the Nubians' attack, the beginning of the storm, the ferocity of the wind, the desert's sudden madness. One minute she had been beside him, the next a savage gust of wind had separated them. Where was she? On all fours, gasping for breath, he began digging.

He could not find her. But he refused to give up. He would

not leave this cursed place without the woman to whom he had given back her freedom.

He searched every corner of the oasis, often having to push aside other Nubian corpses. Then, at last, he heaved aside the crown of a big palm-tree, and saw her. Panther looked like a young girl sleeping, dreaming of a handsome suitor. There was no trace of injury on her naked body, but she had a huge lump on the back of her neck. Suti rubbed her eyes and gently brought her back to consciousness.

'Suti,' she said faintly. 'Thanks be to the gods that you're alive.'

'Don't worry, you're not badly hurt, just stunned.'

'My arms, my legs!'

'They hurt, I know, but they aren't broken.'

She threw her arms round him, like a child. 'Let's get away from here, quickly.'

'We can't, not without water.'

For long hours, Suti and Panther toiled to unblock the well, and in the end they had enough silty, bitter-tasting water to fill two water-skins; then they made a new bow and fifty arrows from the wood of the broken trees. After a restorative sleep, wrapped against the night cold in faded finery taken from the corpses, they set off northwards, under the protection of the starry night.

Panther's resilience amazed Suti. Their narrow escape from death had given her a new energy, a determination to win back her gold and become a rich woman, respectable and respected, able to satisfy all her wishes. She believed in no destiny but the one she made for herself, moment after moment, and gleefully tore off the fabric of her existence, proclaiming the nakedness of her soul with perfect shamelessness. She feared nothing except her own fear, which she stifled ruthlesssly.

She permitted only brief stops, kept a close watch on the

water rations, and chose their direction and paths, which led through a jumble of rocks and dunes. Suti let himself be guided, enthralled by the chaotic landscape; it acted on him like an enchantment and filled him with its magic. Resisting it was pointless; wind, sun and heat created a land whose every line and curve he loved.

Panther was constantly on the alert, and as they got closer to the Egyptian lines she redoubled her vigilance. Suti, though, grew uneasy: he was moving further and further away from his true freedom, the immensity where he loved to live with the nobility of the oryx.

As they were filling their water-skins at a well marked by a circle of stones, more than fifty Nubian warriors, armed with clubs, short swords, bows and slings suddenly appeared in a circle round the well. Panther and Suti were horrified: neither had heard them approach.

Panther clenched her fists. She could not bear to fail like this. 'Let's fight,' she murmured.

'It's hopeless.'

'Then what do you suggest?'

Suti look slowly around. If they tried to run for it, they'd stand no chance – he wouldn't even have time to draw his bow.

He said, 'The gods forbid suicide, but if you like I'll strangle you before they smash my head. If they take you alive, they'll all rape you in the vilest way.'

'I'll kill them all.'

The circle round them tightened.

Suti decided to charge at two huge warriors who were advancing side by side; at least he'd die fighting.

Before he could move, an old Nubian addressed him. 'Was it you who wiped out our brothers?'

'I, and the desert.'

'They were brave men.'

'So am I.'

'How did you do it?'

'My bow saved me.'

'You're lying.'

'Try me – I'll soon show you.'

'Who are you?' asked the old Nubian.

'My name is Suti.'

'Are you Egyptian?'

'Yes.'

'What are you doing here in our land?'

'I escaped from the fortress at Tjaru.'

'Escaped?'

'I was a prisoner there.'

'You're lying again.'

'I was chained to a rock in the middle of the Nile, to act as bait for men like you.'

'You're a spy, aren't you?' said the Nubian angrily.

'No, I'm not. I was hiding in the oasis when your men attacked it.'

'If the great storm hadn't come, they'd have defeated you.'

'But they're dead, and I'm still alive.'

'Proud of yourself, aren't you?'

'If I could fight you one by one, I'd prove my pride is justified.'

The Nubian looked around at his fellow countrymen. 'This defiance is contemptible, and you'll pay for it. You killed our leader at the oasis, and I, an old man, have had to take the head of our tribe.'

'Let me fight your best warrior, and give me back my freedom if I win.'

'Fight them all.'

'You're a coward,' sneered Suti.

A stone from a slingshot whizzed through the air and hit Suti on the temple; semi-conscious, he collapsed. The two big Nubians went over to Panther, who glared at them defiantly and did not move a muscle. They tore off her clothes and the strip of fabric concealing her hair.

Stunned, they drew back.

Panther did not try to conceal her breasts, or the golden curls of her sex. Arms hanging loosely at her sides, she walked forward as regally as a queen.

The Nubians bowed.

The rites in honour of the golden-haired goddess lasted all night. The Nubians had recognized the terrifying creature whose power had been spoken of by the ancestors. She came from far-off Libya, and if angered she could spread disease, cataclysms and famine. To appease her, the Nubians offered her date-wine, snake cooked on hot coals, and fresh garlic, which would protect against snakebite and scorpion stings. They danced round Panther, who had been crowned with palm-leaves and anointed with scented oil; prayers passed down from age to age were addressed to her.

Suti was forgotten. Like the others, he was merely the servant of the goddess, which part Panther played to perfection.

When the celebrations were over, she took command of the little band, and immediately gave orders that they should circle round the fortress of Tjaru and follow a track towards the north. As they neared Tjaru she sent out scouts who, with great surprise, reported that the Egyptian soldiers had gone to earth behind their walls and had sent out no patrols for several days.

They halted at the foot of a rocky peak, which offered shelter from the sun and the wind, and Panther stepped down from her travelling-chair, which was carried by four enthusiastic fellows.

Suti went over to her and bowed. 'I daren't raise my eyes to look at you.'

'Just as well – they'd disembowel you.'

'I can't bear this situation.'

'We're on the right road.'

'But not in the right way.'

'Just be patient.'

'That's not in my nature.'

'A taste of slavery will improve your nature a lot.'

'Don't count on it.'

Panther smiled. 'No one can escape the power of the golden-haired goddess.'

Furious, Suti withdrew.

After some thought, he decided to learn the use of the slingshot from his new companions as they travelled. He soon became very skilful, and thus earned their respect. A few sessions of unarmed combat, which he won, confirmed their good opinion, and it was firmly established by a demonstration of his prowess at archery. A friendship between warriors was born.

Most evenings were passed the same way: after their meal, the Nubians talked about the golden goddess, who had come to teach them music, dancing and the joys of love. One evening, though, while the storytellers were embroidering the myth, Suti saw two men go apart from the main group and light a fire. He went over to watch. Over the fire they hung a pot containing glue made from antelope fat. When it was hot enough, the glue became runny. The first man dipped in a brush, and the second handed him an ebony waist-plate, which the first meticulously brushed with glue. Suti yawned. Just as he was walking away, something gleamed in the darkness. Intrigued, he retraced his steps. The man with the brush, who was concentrating hard, was applying something to the buckle.

Suti bent closer. His eyes had not deceived him: it really was gold leaf.

'Where did you get that?' he asked.

'It was a present from our chief.'

'And where did he get it?

'When he came back from the Lost City, he brought back jewels and thin sheets of gold like this.'

'Do you know where the Lost City is?'

'I don't, but our leader does.'

Suti woke the old man, and made him draw a map in the sand. Then he gathered the whole band together round the fire.

'Listen to me, all of you,' he said. 'I was a chariot officer in the Egyptian army. I know how to use the great bow, and I have killed dozens of sand-travellers and meted out justice by killing a treacherous general. But my country showed me no gratitude for any of that, so now all I want is to become rich and powerful. This tribe needs a chief, a man who is battle-hardened and a proven victor. I am that man. If you follow me, the gods will smile on you.'

Suti's impassioned face, his long hair, his height and his bearing impressed the Nubians, but before they could react the old warrior cut in: 'You killed our chief.'

'I was stronger than he. The law of the desert does not spare the weak.'

'It is up to us to choose our next chief.'

'I shall lead you to the Lost City, and we'll kill anyone who tries to stop us. You have no right to keep this secret for yourself. Soon our tribe will be the most respected in the whole of Nubia.'

'Our chief went to the city alone.'

'We shall go together,' countered Suti, 'and you'll all have plenty of gold.'

Suti's supporters and opponents began to debate. The old man's influence was such that Suti thought defeat looked certain. So he seized Panther and, with a brutal gesture, tore off her clothes. The flames lit up her fair hair.

'See?' he shouted. 'She doesn't resist me. I'm the only one who can be her lover. Unless you accept me as chief, she will unleash a new sandstorm, and you'll all die.'

Suti knew the Libyan girl held his fate in her hands. If she rejected him, the Nubians would know he was boasting and would slaughter him. Now that she had been raised to the rank of goddess, had she grown drunk with vanity?

Panther pulled free. The Nubians warriors pointed their arrows and daggers at Suti.

He cursed silently. He'd been wrong to trust a Libyan. Still, at least he would die gazing at a beautiful woman.

With the grace of a wild cat, Panther lay down beside the fire and held out her arms to him.

'Come,' she said, smiling.

15

Pazair awoke with a jolt. He had been dreaming about a monster with a hundred heads and with countless clawed feet which cut into the stones of the Great Pyramid and tried to topple it over. Its belly was a human face: that of Bel-Tran. Covered in sweat despite the chill of the winter night, the tjaty fingered the wooden frame of his bed, with its base made from plaited vegetable ropes, and its feet in the form of lions' heads.

He turned towards Neferet's bed. It was empty.

Pushing back the fine mesh that kept mosquitoes off, he stood up, put on a cloak and opened the window that looked out on to the garden. The gentle sun was awakening trees and flowers, and birds were singing. He saw Neferet, wrapped in a thick blanket, standing barefoot in the dew.

She blended into the dawn, surrounded by its light. Two falcons, soaring up from the ship of Ra, flew around her when she laid an offering of lotus-flowers on the ancestors' altar, in memory of Branir. Making the space fertile, linking Egypt to the celestial ship, the birds of prey flew back to its prow, beyond the sight of men.

When the rite was over, Pazair went out into the garden and put an arm round his wife.

'You are the star of the morning, at the dawn of a happy day. No woman has a radiance like yours, and your eyes are as soft as your lips. Why are you so beautiful? Your hair has captured the brightness of Hathor herself. I love you, Neferet, as no one has ever loved before.'

In the amorous dawn, they made love.

Standing at the prow of the boat as she headed towards Karnak, Pazair looked admiringly out across his country, where the marriage rites of the sun and the water were celebrated with such splendour.

On the banks, the peasants were maintaining the irrigation channels while a body of specialists was cleaning out the canals, Egypt's vital arteries. The crowns of the palm-trees offered generous shade to the men lovingly bending over the black, fertile earth. Seeing the tjaty's boat pass by, the children ran along the banks and towpaths, shouting and waving enthusiastically.

Killer sat on the roof of the central cabin, guarding Pazair. Kem brought the tjaty some fresh onions.

Pazair thanked him and asked, 'Anything new on the shadow-eater?'

'No, nothing.'

'What about Tapeni?'

'She had a meeting with Bel-Tran.'

'So she's found a new ally . . .'

'We should be wary of her,' said Kem. 'She could do you more than a little harm.'

Pazair sighed. 'Yet another enemy.'

'Does that worry you?'

'Thanks to the gods, ignorance serves me as courage.'

'It would be fairer to say that you have no choice.'

Pazair shook his head, and changed the subject. 'I take it all is quiet at the hospital?'

'Yes – your wife can work in peace.'

'She must reform the system of caring for the people's health as quickly as possible. Nebamon cared little about it, and serious inequalities have opened up.' He sighed again. 'Neferet's office and mine are sometimes very burdensome, and we weren't properly prepared for them.'

'Prepared?' said Kem. 'How do you think I feel, becoming commander of the very guards who cut off my nose?'

The wind was blowing hard, and was against the current, so sometimes the sailors used their oars, though they did not take down the mast or the rectangular sail, which was tall and narrow. The captain, who was well used to sailing on the Nile all year round, knew its dangers and how to use the weakest breeze to convey his illustrious travellers swiftly. The vessel's design, with its keel-less hull and raised bow and stern, had been perfected by Pharaoh's shipwrights so that it would glide easily over the waves.

'My friend,' said Kem, 'I can't help wondering when the assassin will strike again.'

'Don't worry about it.'

'But I do. It's become a personal matter – that demon is soiling my honour.'

'Well, have had you any news of Suti?'

'The order to sound the alert definitely reached Tjaru. The soldiers are taking refuge in the fortress until further orders.'

'Was he able to escape?'

'According to the official reports no one's missing, but I have had some rather odd information. A hot-headed prisoner had apparently been chained to a rock in the middle of the Nile, to serve as a lure for Nubian looters.'

'It must have been Suti.'

'In that case, don't be hopeful.'

'He'll find a way out of his situation – he'd escape from the kingdom of darkness itself.'

The tjaty's thoughts flew to his spiritual brother, then communed with the magnificent Theban landscape. The cultivated strip on either side of the river was the widest and the most luxuriant in the Nile Valley. More than seventy villages worked for the immense Temple of Karnak, which employed no fewer than eighty thousand people – priests, craftsmen and peasants. But even those riches were as nothing before the majesty of the area consecrated to Amon, which was surrounded by a brick curtain-wall that undulated like a wave.

When the boat reached Karnak, the High Priest's head steward and other senior household officials greeted the tjaty at the landing-stage. After formal greetings had been exchanged, they offered to escort Pazair to the office of High Priest Kani. However, Pazair said he would rather go alone, and he set off along the central aisle of the vast pillared hall, which only those initiated into the great mysteries might enter. Kem and Killer stayed outside the great double golden doors, which were opened on the occasion of great festivals, when Amon's ship left the shrine to flood the earth with its light.

Pazair meditated for a long time before a sublime depiction of the god Thoth, whose elongated arms provided the basic measurement used by the overseer of works. He read the columns of hieroglyphs and deciphered the message of the god of knowledge: it urged his worshippers to respect the proportions that presided over the birth of all life.

It was this harmony that the tjaty must maintain in daily life, so that Egypt might be the mirror of heaven; it was this harmony that the conspirators wanted to destroy, replacing it with an ice-cold monster ready to torture men the better to gorge itself on material goods. In truth, Bel-Tran and his allies were a new race, more fearsome than the cruellest invaders.

Pazair left the pillared hall, and allowed himself a moment to enjoy the perfect blue of the sky over Karnak. He paused in the little open-air courtyard, at the centre of which a granite offering-table marked the birth of the temple, many years before. Sacred above all others, it was constantly covered with flowers. Why must he tear himself away from this profound, otherworldly peace?

'I am happy to see you again, Tjaty.' Shaven-headed and carrying a golden cane, Kani bowed to Pazair.

'It is I who should bow to you,' protested Pazair.

'No so, Tjaty. I owe you respect, for the tjaty is the eyes and ears of Pharaoh.'

'May they see and hear acutely.'

'You look troubled.'

'I have come to ask for help from the High Priest of Karnak.'

Kani's face fell. 'I was going to beg you for yours.'

'What is happening?'

'Grave problems, I fear. I would like to show you the temple, which has just been restored.'

Kani and Pazair passed through one of the gates into the enclosure of Amon, walked along the curtain-wall, greeted painters and sculptors at work, and went into a modest sandstone shrine to Ma'at. It contained two stone benches where the tjaty sat when judging a senior priest or priestess.

As soon as they were inside, Kani said, 'I am a simple man. I have not forgotten that it was your master, Branir, who should have reigned over Karnak.'

'Branir was murdered, and Pharaoh chose you.'

'He may have made a bad choice.'

Never had Pazair seen the old man so dejected. Before being raised to the dignity of supreme ruler of the biggest city-temple in Egypt, Kani had been a gardener, accustomed to dealing with the caprices of nature and the pitiless realities of the earth. Despite his humble origins, he had nevertheless imposed himself upon his subordinates and the college of priests, and he enjoyed general respect.

Kani went on, 'I am unworthy of my office, but I shall not try to escape from my responsibilities. Before long I shall appear in this very place before your court, and you will have to condemn me.'

'This trial is proceeding far too quickly!' said Pazair. 'Will you allow me to investigate?'

Kani sat down on one of the benches. 'You won't have much difficulty. All you need do is consult the recent archives: in only a few months, I have brought Karnak close to ruin.'

'How?'

'Just examine the returns for cereals, dairy produce, fruit . . . Where food is concerned, my management of our resources has been an appalling failure.'

Pazair was troubled. 'Could someone be deceiving you about it?'

'No, the reports are accurate.'

'What has the weather been like?'

'The annual flood was abundant, and there were no plagues of insects to destroy the crops.'

'Then what has caused this disaster?'

'My incompetence,' said Kani. 'I wanted to tell you straight away, so that you can alert the king.'

'There is no hurry.'

'The truth will come out. As you can see, my help will be no use to you. I shall soon be nothing but an old, despised man.'

The tjaty shut himself away in the archive chamber of the Temple of Karnak and compared Kani's records with those of his predecessors. The difference shattered him.

He soon became certain of one thing: someone was trying to ruin Kani's reputation and force him to resign. His replacement was bound to be someone hostile to Ramses – and without Karnak's support it would be impossible to control Egypt. But who would have dreamt that Bel-Tran and his underlings would dare attack a High Priest whose integrity was so widely known? The consequences would be devasting: Kani would be universally blamed, and Karnak,

Luxor and the temples of the west bank would soon find themselves short of offerings. The rites would be poorly celebrated, and everywhere people would shout the name of the man responsible, Kani the incompetent.

Despair overwhelmed Pazair. He had come to ask a friend for help, but instead would be forced to incriminate him.

He jumped as someone tapped him on the shoulder.

'Stop poring over your papyri,' advised Kem, 'and let's get out into the fields.'

The first villages they inspected, those nearest the great temple, were living their normal, peaceful lives, following the eternal rhythm of the seasons. The two men questioned the village headmen and field scribes, but learnt of nothing abnormal. After three days of fruitless investigations, the tjaty's thoughts returned to the evidence. He must go back to Memphis and explain the situation to the king, before opening the trial of High Priest Kani. Reluctantly, he told Kem of his decision.

But the wind was so strong that it would have been unsafe to sail. Kem suggested that they spend the extra day investigating and the two men, the baboon and their escort went to a village at some distance from the temple, on the far edge of the province of Kebet.

When they arrived, they found that here, as elsewhere, the peasants were getting on with their livelihoods, while their wives took care of the children and prepared the meals. On the banks of the Nile, a washerman was at work; in the shade of a sycamore, a country doctor was seeing his patients. Everything seemed normal.

But Killer became edgy; his nostrils quivered, and he scratched at the ground.

'What has he detected?' asked Pazair.

'Harmful energies,' said Kem. 'We haven't made the journey for nothing.'

16

The village headman was a pot-bellied man of around fifty, the father of five children. He was affable and courteous when he performed the duties of his office, which he had inherited from his father.

He was informed at once of the arrival of a small group of strangers, and regretfully interrupted his afternoon nap. Accompanied by a servant carrying a fan of palm-leaves to protect his bald head from the sun, he went to meet the unexpected visitors.

When his gaze encountered that of an enormous, red-eyed baboon, he stopped in his tracks.

'Greetings, my friends,' he said uncertainly.

'And greetings to you,' said a tall, imposing Nubian.

'Is that monkey tame?'

'He is an official member of Memphis's security guards.'

'Ah . . . and you are?'

'I am Kem, commander of the guards, and this is Pazair, tjaty of Egypt.'

Dumbfounded, the headman pulled in his stomach and bowed as low as he could, hands stretched out before him in a sign of veneration.

'What an honour,' he gabbled, 'what an honour! Such a humble village, welcoming the tjaty . . . What an honour!'

As he straightened up, the headman began a flow of sugary

compliments, which stopped abruptly when Killer growled.

'Commander, are you absolutely sure you can keep that animal under control?'

'Except when he smells an evildoer.'

'Fortunately, there aren't any in my little village.'

The tall, deep-voiced Nubian seemed as fearsome as his baboon. The headman had heard stories about this strange commander: he had little or no interest in administrative work, but was so close to the common people that no criminal ever escaped him for long. Seeing him here, on the headman's own territory, was a decidedly unpleasant surprise. And the tjaty! Too young, too serious – and bound to be too inquisitive. Pazair's natural dignity, his direct, piercing look, the straightness which which he held himself: these things did not bode well.

'Forgive my astonishment,' said the headman, 'but such eminent persons in this insignificant little village . . .'

'Your fields extend as far as the eye can see,' observed Kem, 'and they are extremely well irrigated.'

'Please do not judge by appearances, Commander. In this area the earth is very hard, so it's difficult to work – my poor ploughmen break their backs.'

'Why? Last year's flood was excellent.'

'We were unlucky. It was too strong here, and our irrigation pools were in poor condition.'

'But you had an excellent harvest, from what I hear.'

'Alas, I'm afraid you have been misinformed. It was much smaller than the year before.'

'What about the vines?'

'Oh, such a disappointment! Clouds of insects attacked both the leaves and the grapes.'

'No other villages in this area shared your bad luck,' said Pazair.

The tjaty's voice was heavy with suspicion; the headman had not expected such a tone.

'Perhaps my colleagues were boasting?' he said. 'Perhaps my poor village was the victim of fate?'

'What about livestock?'

'A lot died of sicknesses. An animal-doctor did come, but it was too late. This place is very remote, and—'

'The earthen road is in excellent condition,' objected Kem. 'The officials appointed by Karnak see that it is well maintained.'

The headman hastily changed the subject. 'Although our resources are meagre, it is an immense privilege to invite you to eat your midday meal with us. I am sure you will forgive the frugal fare – it comes with our heartfelt welcome.'

No one could violate the laws of hospitality. Kem accepted in the tjaty's name, and the headman sent his servant to inform the cook.

As the headman escorted them to his house, Pazair noted that the village looked very prosperous: several white housefronts had just been repainted, the cattle and donkeys had shining coats and plump bellies, the children wore new clothes. At the corners of the pleasantly clean streets, there were statuettes of the gods; in the main square, opposite the headman's office, were a fine bread oven and a large mill, which was obviously almost new.

'Congratulations on the way you run things,' said Pazair. 'Your people lack for nothing, and this is the prettiest village I have had the privilege of seeing in a long time.'

'You honour us too much, too much! Please, come in.'

The house's size, number of rooms and decoration would have befitted a Memphis noble. The important visitors were greeted by the headman's wife, who bowed her head and laid her right hand on her chest – she had hastily painted her face and put on an elegant dress – and by all five children.

They sat down on best-quality mats and ate sweet onions, cucumbers, beans, leeks, dried fish, grilled beef ribs, goat's cheese, watermelon and cakes topped with carob paste. Red wine with a delicious aroma accompanied the food. The headman tucked into each dish with gusto.

'That was a delicious meal and a notable welcome,' said Pazair when they had finished eating.

'Oh, my lord,' said the headman, 'it's such an honour to have you here.'

'May we consult the field scribe?'

'I'm sorry, my lord, but he's away. He's visiting his family, to the north of Memphis, and won't be back for a week.'

'His records must be accessible.'

'I'm afraid not. He has locked his office, and of course I cannot—'

'Well I can.'

'You are the tjaty, of course, but would it not be a—' The headman broke off, afraid of saying something highly inappropriate. 'My lord, it's a long way to Thebes, and the sun sets early at this time of year. Consulting those boring scrolls might delay you till after dark.'

Killer, who had been sitting gnawing a rib of beef, broke the bone; the crack made the headman jump.

'Where are they?' insisted Pazair.

'Well . . . I don't know now. The scribe must have taken them with him.'

Killer stood up. On his feet, he looked even bigger and more dangerous, and his red eyes glared at the headman, whose hands began to shake.

'Please, Commander, tie him up,' he quavered.

'The archives,' ordered Kem, 'or I can't answer for his actions.'

The headman's wife fell to her knees in front of her husband. 'Tell them the truth, I beg you!'

'I . . . I have the scrolls here,' he admitted. 'I'll go and get them.'

'Killer and I will accompany you. We can help you carry them.'

The three soon returned and set a heap of papyri on the table in front of Pazair.

The headman unrolled some of them. 'Everything's in order, my lord,' he muttered, 'and the observations were all made on the correct dates – the reports are very dull.'

'Let me read in peace,' demanded Pazair.

Looking feverish, the headman went back to his seat; his wife left the room.

The pernickety field scribe had gone over the numbers of livestock and sacks of cereals several times. He had given not only the names of the owners but also those of the animals, plus their weight and their state of health. The sections concerning fruit and vegetables were just as detailed. General conclusions were written in red: in every area of production the results were excellent, much better than average.

Perplexed, the tjaty did a simple calculation. The area of agricultural land was such that its wealth almost made up for the deficit Kani would be accused of, so why did it not feature in his records?

'I attach great importance to respect for other people,' he declared.

The headman nodded.

'But if those other people persist in concealing the truth, they are no longer worthy of respect. Is that not true of you?'

'I've told you everything, my lord.'

'I dislike using harsh methods, but in certain circumstances, when urgency demands it, a judge must force himself to do so.'

As if he had read the tjaty's thoughts, Killer leapt at the headman, took him by the throat and pulled his head back.

'Stop him! He's breaking my neck!'

'Where are the rest of the scrolls?' asked Kem calmly.

'I haven't got anything else – nothing at all!'

Kem turned to Pazair. 'I suggest we go for a walk while Killer conducts the interrogation as he sees fit.'

'Don't leave me!' gasped the headman.

'The rest of the scrolls,' repeated Kem.

'Tell him to take his hands off me first.'

The baboon relaxed its grip, and the headman rubbed his painful neck.

'You're behaving like savages,' he complained. 'I reject this arbitrary judgment, and I condemn this unspeakable act, this torture inflicted on a village headman.'

'I shall formally charge you with concealing official documents,' said Pazair.

The threat made the headman blanch. 'If I give you the rest, I demand that you recognize my innocence.'

'What crime have you committed?'

'I acted for the common good.'

From a chest used to store plates and dishes, the headman took a sealed papyrus. His expression had changed: it was no longer afraid but fierce and cold. 'Very well, look!'

The scroll indicated that the village's riches had been delivered to the capital of the Kebet province. The field scribe had signed and dated it.

'But this village is part of the Karnak estate,' Pazair reminded him.

'You have been misinformed, Tjaty.'

'It is shown in the list of the High Priest's properties.'

'Old Kani's as ignorant as you are. His list doesn't show the real state of affairs, the land register does. Go to Thebes and look at it, and you'll see that my village comes under the jurisdiction of Kebet, not the Temple of Karnak. The boundaries prove it. I'm going to lay a complaint against you for causing me bodily harm – you'll have to arrange your own trial, Tjaty Pazair.'

17

The guard at the land registry office in Thebes was awoken with a start by an unusual sound. At first he thought he must have been dreaming, but then he heard someone hammering on the door.

'Who is it?' he shouted.

'The commander of the Memphis security guards, accompanied by the tjaty,' said a deep voice.

'I hate practical jokes, especially in the middle of the night. Go away, or you'll regret it.'

'You'd do better to open up at once.'

'Go away, or I'll call my colleagues.'

'By all means do so. They can help us break down the door.'

The guard wondered; he looked out of a window with stone cross-pieces and, by the light of the full moon, made out the shapes of a huge Nubian man and an enormous baboon. It must be Kem and Killer! He had heard all about that fearsome pair: their reputation had spread throughout Egypt. Then the man coming forward to join them must be the tjaty himself!

He slid the bolt open. 'Forgive me, but this is so unexpected . . .'

'Light the lamps,' ordered Kem. 'The tjaty wishes to examine the maps.'

'I think I had better inform the director.'

'Yes, do. Bring him here.'

When he arrived, the director's face was screwed up in anger, but he soon calmed down when he realized that the guard had not been lying. The tjaty, Egypt's first minister, really was there, in his registry, even if it was at an unexpected hour of the night! He suddenly became obsequious and eager to help.

'Which maps do you wish to consult?' he asked.

'Those showing the properties belonging to the Temple of Karnak,' said Pazair.

'My lord, I warn you, they're enormous.'

'Let's start with the most distant villages.''

'To the north or the south?'

'The north.'

'Small or large?'

'The largest.'

The director spread out the maps on long wooden tables. The land registry scribes had shown the boundaries of each piece of land, the canals, and the settlements.

But Pazair looked in vain for the village he had just visited. 'Are these plans up to date?' he asked.

'Of course, my lord,' said the director.

'Have they been altered recently?'

'Yes, at the request of three village headmen.'

'Why?'

'The Nile flood had swept away the boundary stones, so a new survey was needed. An experienced man carried out the work, and my scribes took account of his observations.'

'He has cut off the Karnak estate,' Pazair pointed out.

'That is not for me to judge. I confine myself to registering land.'

'Did you by any chance forget to inform High Priest Kani?'

The director moved away from the lamp, so that his face was hidden in the shadows. 'I was just about to send him a full report.'

'And why has there been such a deplorable delay?'

'My lord, I'm very short of staff, and—'

'What is the name of the scribe who did the survey?'

'Sumenu.'

'Where does he live?'

The director hesitated, then said, 'He isn't from here.'

'Not from Thebes?'

'No, he came here from Memphis.'

'Who sent him?'

'My lord, it was the royal palace, of course.'

On the processional route leading to the Temple of Karnak, pink and white laurels provided walkers with an enchanting sight, whose gentle sweetness lessened the austerity of the monumental wall that encircled the sacred area. High Priest Kani had agreed to leave his retreat to speak with Pazair. The two most powerful men in Egypt after Pharaoh walked slowly between the two lines of protective sphinxes.

'My investigation is progressing,' said Pazair.

'What good will it do?'

'It will show that you are innocent.'

'But I'm not.'

'You were deceived.'

Kani shook his head. 'I deceived myself about my abilities.'

'No, you didn't. The three villages furthest away from the temple delivered their produce to Kebet. That's why it doesn't show in your records.'

'Do they come under Karnak's jurisdiction?'

'The land register was altered after the last flood.'

'Without consulting me?'

'At the instigation of a surveyor from Memphis.'

'That's inconceivable!'

'A messenger has just left for Memphis with orders to bring back the person responsible, a scribe named Sumenu.'

109

'But what can be done, if it was Ramses himself who took the villages away from me?'

Meditating on the banks of the sacred lake, taking part in the dawn, noon and sunset rites, observing the star-watchers at work on the temple roof, reading the old myths and guides to the afterlife, and conversing with great dignitaries who had withdrawn into the enclosure sacred to Amon: these were Pazair's main occupations during his retreat. He felt the radiant eternity engraved in the stone, listened to the voices of the gods and the pharaohs who had adorned the structure over the course of the dynasties, and steeped himself in the immutable life that inhabited the relief carvings and sculptures.

Several times, he meditated before the statue of Branir, who was depicted as an aged scribe kneeling down and was unrolling a papyrus bearing a hymn to creation.

When Kem brought him the information he was awaiting, Pazair went immediately to the land registry. The director was extremely gratified: receiving another visit from the tjaty would confer an unhoped-for importance upon him.

'Remind me of the name of the surveyor from Memphis,' said Pazair.

'Sumenu, my lord.'

'Are you sure about that?'

'Yes – at least, that's the name he gave me.'

'I have checked.'

'There was no need for that, my lord. Everything's in order.'

'Ever since I was a minor provincial judge, I have had a mania for checking everything. It often takes a long time, but it's extremely useful. Sumenu, you said?'

'Well, I might be mistaken. I—'

'Sumenu, the surveyor attached to the royal palace, died two years ago. And you yourself replaced him.'

110

The director's lips parted, but he could not utter a sound.

'Altering the land register is a crime,' said Pazair sternly. 'And you appear to have forgotten that the assignment of villages and lands to any partiular jurisdiction is the responsibility of the tjaty. Whoever bribed you was relying on the High Priest of Karnak's inexperience and on my own. He was wrong.'

'My lord, you are talking nonsense.'

'We shall soon know. I have requested an immediate second opinion from the leader of the guild of the blind in Thebes.'

The guild's leader was an imposing man with a broad forehead and a heavy jaw. After the annual flood, if the river had swept away the boundary stones, thus erasing the marks of ownership, the government called upon him and his colleagues to adjudicate in disputes. He was the earth's memory; from many years of criss-crossing the fields and cultivated areas, his feet knew their exact dimensions.

He was eating dried figs under his vine, when he heard footsteps.

'There are three of you,' he said, 'a very big man, a man of average height, and a baboon. Could it be Commander Kem and his famous baboon, Killer? And might the third be—'

'Tjaty Pazair,' cut in Kem.

'So this must be an affair of state. Which lands has somebody tried to steal? No, don't say anything! My judgement must be completely objective. Which is the area concerned?'

'The rich northern villages bordering the province of Kebet.'

'The farmers complain a lot in that area – they say the worms eat their harvests, the hippos trample on them, and mice, grasshoppers and sparrows eat what's left. They're incorrigible liars. Their lands are excellent, and the year was fruitful.'

'Who is the recorder of those estates?'

'I am – I was born and grew up there. The boundaries have not altered for twenty years.' He smiled. 'I won't offer you figs or beer, for I assume you are in a hurry.'

In his hand the blind man held a cane whose top was shaped like the head of an animal with a pointed snout and long ears.* At his side, a surveyor uncoiled a rope, according to his instructions.

Not once did the blind man hesitate. He accurately identified the four corners of each field, re-established the locations of the boundary stones, the statues of the gods – notably the cobra that protected the harvests – and the stelae, a gift from Pharaoh, that marked the limits of the Karnak estates. Scribes noted everything down, made maps and drew up lists.

Once the process was over, there could be no doubt about it: the land register had been wrongly altered, and rich lands belonging to Karnak had been assigned to Kebet.

'"It is the tjaty's responsibility to draw the borders of each province, to oversee the offerings, and to bring before him anyone who has illegally seized a piece of land": is that indeed the order Pharaoh gave me, as each pharaoh gives it to each tjaty on his enthronement?'

The governor of Kebet province went pale.

'Answer,' ordered Pazair. 'You were present at the ceremony.'

'Yes . . . the king did indeed say those words.'

'Then why did you accept riches that did not belong to you?'

'The land register had altered—'

*This ritual staff was identical to the *was* sceptre, which only the gods, with this almost sole exception, could carry, for its head was that of the animal of the god Set, master of the storm, of thunder and of celestial fire.

'The alteration was a forgery, which did not bear my seal or that of the High Priest of Karnak,' said Pazair coldly. 'You should have alerted me. What were you hoping for? That the months would pass quickly, that Kani would resign, that I would be dismissed, and that the position would be given to one of your accomplices?'

'Tjaty, I cannot permit you to—'

'You gave aid to conspirators and murderers. Bel-Tran will have been shrewd enough to leave no trace of a link between you and the Double White House, so I cannot prove your allegiance to him. But your dishonesty is sufficient: you are unworthy to govern a province. Consider your dismissal final.'

The tjaty convened his court at Thebes, before the great gate of the Temple of Karnak, where a wooden shelter had been built. Despite Kem's advice to be careful, Pazair had refused to hold the trial without an audience, as the accused had requested; a large crowd had gathered.

The tjaty read out the charges, after summarizing the principal stages in his investigation; the witnesses appeared and the court scribes noted down their testimony. The jury, composed of two priests from Karnak, the mayor of Thebes, the wife of a noble, a midwife and a senior army officer, delivered a verdict which Pazair judged was in accordance with both the spirit and the letter of the law.

The erstwhile governor of Kebet was sentenced to serve fifteen years in prison and to pay enormous compensation to the temple. The three guilty headmen were found guilty of falsehood and stealing food, and would henceforth work as agricultural labourers. Their land would be shared out among the humblest folk. The head of the Thebes land registry would spend ten years in a labour camp.

The tjaty did not ask for the penalties to be increased; none of those convicted sought to appeal.

One of Bel-Tran's networks had been wiped out.

18

'Look at the desert sky,' the old Nubian warrior urged Suti. 'That is where precious stones are born. It gives birth to the stars, and from the stars metals are born. If you know how to speak to them, and if you can hear their voices, you will learn the secret of gold and silver.'

'And do you know their language?'

'I reared livestock before I left with the tribe on the road to nowhere. My children and my wife died in a year of great drought, so I left my village and entrusted my footsteps to faceless tomorrows. What do I care about the shore from which no one returns?'

'Isn't the Lost City just a dream?'

'Our former chief went there several times and brought back gold each time: that is the truth.'

'And is this the right road?'

'If you're a real warrior, you ought to know that.'

With his regular, unflagging stride, the old man resumed his place at the head of the tribe; they were in a region so arid and desolate that they had not seen even an antelope for several hours.

Suti moved back to join Panther, who was reclining on a rudimentary travelling-chair carried by six Nubians, all delighted to be bearing the golden goddess.

'Put me down,' she said. 'I wish to walk.'

The warriors obeyed, then roared out a war-song, promising that they would cut their enemies into thin strips and devour their magic power.

Panther was sulking.

'Why are you angry?' asked Suti.

'This adventure is stupid.'

'Don't you want to get rich?'

'We know where our own gold is. Why chase a mirage and probably die of thirst doing so?'

'Nubians don't die of thirst, and I'm not chasing a mirage. Are those promises enough for you?'

'Swear that we'll go and fetch our gold from its hiding-place in the cave.'

'Why are you so stubborn?'

'You almost died for that gold,' Panther reminded him. 'I saved you, and you killed that traitor, General Asher, to get it. You mustn't defy destiny any more.'

Suti smiled. Panther was expressing a very personal vision of those events. Suti had not coveted the traitor's gold, but had applied the law of the desert by killing a liar and murderer who was trying to escape the tjaty's justice. The fact that fortune had smiled upon him proved that his deed had been just.

He said, 'Supposing the Lost City's full of gold and—'

'I don't care about your crazy plans! Promise me we'll go back to the cave.'

'You have my word.'

Satisfied, the golden goddess got back on to her travelling-chair.

The track stopped at the foot of a mountain whose slopes were dotted with blackish rocks. The wind swept across the desert; neither falcon nor vulture circled in the stifling sky.

The old warrior sat down; his companions did likewise.

'We will go no further,' he told Suti.

'What are you afraid of?'

'Our old chief used to talk to the stars, but we can't do that. Beyond this mountain, there is not a single source of water. Everyone who has tried to find the Lost City has disappeared, swallowed up by the sands.'

'Your chief didn't.'

'The stars guided him, but his secret has been lost. We shall not go any further.'

'But you said you're in search of death.'

'Not that death.'

'Didn't the chief give you any clues?'

'A chief doesn't talk, he acts.'

'How long did his journey last?'

'The moon rose three times.'

'The golden goddess will protect me.'

The old man shook his head. 'She will stay with us.'

'Are you defying my authority?'

'If you want to die in the desert, you're free to do so. We shall stay here until the fifth moonrise, then we shall leave for the oasis.'

Suti went across to Panther, who was more beautiful than ever. The wind and sun had turned her skin an amber hue, made her hair golden, and emphasized her wild, indomitable nature.

'I'm leaving,' he told her.

'Your city doesn't exist.'

'Yes, it does, and it's full of gold. I'm not going to my death. I'm going to another life, the life I have been dreaming about ever since I was shut away in the scribes' school in Memphis. Not only does this city exist, but it will belong to us as well.'

'Our gold is enough for me.'

'I see things on a grander scale, much grander! Just suppose the soul of the Nubian chief I killed has passed into me and is guiding me towards a fabulous treasure . . . Who'd be mad enough to reject such an adventure?'

'Who'd be mad enough to try it?' snorted Panther.

'Kiss me, golden goddess. You'll bring me luck.'

Her lips were hot as the southern wind.

'Since you're determined to go, I suppose I must wish you good luck,' she said.

Suti took two skins filled with brackish water, some dried fish, a bow, arrows and a dagger. He had not lied to Panther: the soul of his defeated enemy would show him the way.

From the top of the mountain, he looked out over a landscape of unusual power. A gorge with reddish soil wound between two steep cliffs and then joined another desert, which stretched to the horizon. Suti set off into it, like a swimmer sliding into a wave. He felt the call of an unknown land, whose luminous essence called to him irresistibly.

He crossed the gorge without difficulty. There was not a single bird, animal or reptile: it was as if no life at all existed there. Quenching his thirst with small sips, he rested in the shade of a rock until night fell.

When the stars appeared, he raised his eyes to the sky and tried to decipher their message. They drew strange shapes; in his mind, he linked them with lines. Suddenly, a shooting-star flashed through the heavens, tracing a path which Suti engraved in his memory. That was the direction he would take.

Despite his instinctive collusion with the desert, the heat became almost unbearable, each step painful; but he followed the invisible star, as if he were somehow outside his pain-racked body. Before long, thirst forced him to empty his water-skins.

Eventually, Suti fell to his knees. In the distance was a red mountain, but it was far out of reach and anyway he would not have the strength to explore it in search of water. And yet he was certain he had not been mistaken. He wished he were an oryx, capable of bounding towards the sun and forgetting his exhaustion.

He dragged himself to his feet again, to prove to the desert that its strength was nourishing him. Slowly he advanced, his legs moved by the fire that ran across the sand. When he fell again, his knee broke a fragment of pottery.

Incredulously, he picked up the fragments of a jar. Men had lived here; probably it had been a nomads' encampment. As he staggered forward, the ground gave beneath his feet. Everywhere there were the remains of pots, vases and jars, so many that they formed small hills which barred his way. Although his body was increasingly heavy, he climbed one of the hills.

Down below, he saw the Lost City.

A guard-post built of brick, half-collapsed, gutted houses, a roofless temple whose walls were threatening to fall into ruin . . . And the red mountain was pierced with galleries, tanks to collect the winter rainwater, sloping stone tables for washing gold, stone huts where the miners had stored their tools. Everywhere, reddish sand.

Suti ran towards a water-tank, demanding a final effort from his failing legs; he gripped the stone rim, and let himself drop down inside. The water was lukewarm, divine; every pore of his skin drank it in while he quenched his thirst.

No longer parched, and filled with an unknown intoxication, he explored the city.

He found not a single human or animal bone. The entire population had suddenly abandoned the site, leaving behind an enormous mining operation. In each house there were jewels, cups, vases, amulets made from solid gold and silver; these alone were worth a vast fortune.

Suti wanted to check that the seams of ore could still be mined, so he went into one of the deep galleries that ran into the heart of the mountain. By hand and eye, he identified long veins, easy to work. The quantity of metal exceeded his wildest dreams.

He would teach the Nubians how to extract the incredible

treasure. With a little discipline, they would be excellent miners.

That morning, as the Nubian sun decked the red mountain in magnificent radiance, Suti became master of the world, confidant of the desert, as rich as a king. He explored the narrow streets of the city of gold, of *his* city, until, suddenly, he caught sight of its guardian.

At the entrance to the city sat a lion with a flaming mane, watching the explorer. With one blow from its paw, it could tear open his chest or his belly. The legend said that the lion always kept its eyes open and never slept. If that was true, how could Suti overcome its vigilance?

He drew his bow.

The lion stood up. Slowly and majestically, it entered a ruined building. Suti ought to have passed it at a distance, but his curiosity was too strong.

Ready to let loose an arrow, he followed the lion into the ruins.

It had disappeared. In the half-light, he saw ingots of gold. A forgotten reserve, a treasure offering him the spirit of the place, which had appeared in the form of a wild animal before returning to the realms of the Invisible.

Panther was astounded. So many marvels, such riches – Suti had succeeded! The city of gold belonged to them.

While she examined the city's treasures, her lover directed a team of Nubians who were skilled at extracting metals from rock. They attacked the quartz with hammers and pick-axes, shattered the rock, then washed it before separating out the metal; brilliant yellow, dark yellow, tinged with red, Nubian gold was decked in admirable hues.

In several galleries they found gold-bearing silver which thoroughly deserved its name of 'luminous stone', because it was capable of lighting up the darkness; it was valuable as gold. According to custom, the Nubians would transport it in the form of nuggets or rings.

Suti joined Panther in the old temple whose walls were threatening to collapse. She could not have cared less about the danger, engrossed as she was in trying on collars, earrings and bracelets.

'We shall restore this place,' he declared. 'Can you imagine it with golden gates, a silver floor, and statues decked with precious stones?'

'I'll never live here,' said Panther. 'There's a curse on the place: it drove its inhabitants away.'

'I'm not afraid of the curse.'

'Don't try your luck too far.'

'Then what do you suggest we do?'

'Take with us as much as we can carry, get our gold back, and then settle down somewhere peaceful.'

'You'd soon get bored.'

Panther pouted; Suti knew that he had hit home.

He said, 'You've dreamt of ruling an empire, not a village. Wouldn't you like to be a great lady, reigning over an army of serving-women?'

She turned away.

'Where could you wear collars like those, except in a palace, in front of a sea of admiring, envious noblewomen? But I can make you still more beautiful.'

With a fragment of perfectly polished gold, he rubbed her arm and her neck.

'How gentle that is . . . Go on.'

He moved down to her breasts, then her back, and finally more intimate places.

'Am I going to turn into gold?' she asked.

Panther swayed to Suti's rhythm. At the contact of this precious metal, this flesh of the gods which so few mortals had the chance to touch, perhaps she was indeed becoming the golden goddess the Nubians revered.

Suti forgot not one inch of his mistress's body. The gold acted like smooth balm, and drew delectable shivers from her.

She lay down on the floor of the temple, fragments of gold glittering all around her; he lay down beside her.

'As long as Tapeni lives, you won't belong to me,' she said bitterly.

'Forget her.'

'I shall burn her to ashes.'

'What? A future queen lowering herself to such vulgar work?'

'Are you trying to defend her?'

'She's much too clever for me to argue with.'

'Will you fight Egypt at my side?'

'I could strangle you.'

'The Nubians would slaughter you.'

'I'm their chief, and—'

'And I am their goddess! Egypt has rejected you, and Pazair has betrayed you. Let's take our revenge.'

Suti suddenly cried out in pain, and threw himself to one side. Panther saw the attacker: a black scorpion, hiding under a stone.

The young man bit the sting, which was on his wrist, until he drew blood, sucked out the venom, and spat it out.

'You'll be the richest sham widow in the world,' he said.

19

Pazair held Neferet close. Her tenderness wiped away the tiredness of the journey and gave him back his taste for the fight. He explained to her how he had saved Kani and foiled one of Bel-Tran's plans. But he sensed that, despite her joy, she was weighed down with cares.

'There's been news from Tjaru,' she said.

'Suti!'

'He's been reported missing.'

'What happened?'

'According to the commander's report, he escaped. The garrison had had orders to stay inside the fortress, so no patrols went after him.'

Pazair raised his eyes to the heavens. 'He'll come back, Neferet, and he'll help us. But you look anxious. What is it?'

'It's only tiredness.'

'Tell me, I beg you. Don't carry the burden alone.'

'Bel-Tran has begun a campaign of defamation against you. He eats his midday and evening meals with high dignitaries, senior officials and provincial governors; Silkis smiles and keeps quiet. Your inexperience, your uncontrolled zeal, your insane demands, your incompetence, your ignorance of how the ministries really work, your ignorance of the realities of the present time, your devotion to outdated values . . . those are his favourite themes.'

'Talking too much will only do him harm.'

'But it's you he's harming – day after day after day.'

'Don't trouble yourself with it.'

'I can't bear to hear you slandered like that.'

Pazair smiled. 'Actually, it's rather a good sign. If Bel-Tran is acting like that, it's because he still isn't certain of success. The blows I've just dealt him may have been more painful than I thought. Yes, it really is an interesting reaction, and it encourages me to continue.'

'There's something else,' said Neferet. 'The Overseer of Writings has asked several times to see you.'

'Why?

'He won't tell anyone but you.'

'Have there been any other visitors of note?'

'The Director of Secret Missions and the Overseer of the Fields. They want to see you, too, and they deplored your absence.'

The three men belonged to the Brotherhood of the Nine Friends of Pharaoh, the most influential group in the kingdom, and were therefore accustomed to making and unmaking reputations. This was the first time they had intervened since Pazair's appointment.

'Why don't I invite them to to join us for our midday meal?' he suggested.

The Overseer of Writings, the Overseer of the Fields and the Director of Secret Missions had foregathered. Mature men, profound thinkers, with grave voices and solemn bearing, they had climbed the ladder of the scribes' hierarchy and given the king full satisfaction in their work. Wearing wigs, and linen tunics over shirts with long, pleated sleeves, they arrived together at the gate of the tjaty's estate, where Kem and Killer identified them.

Neferet came to the gate to greet them, and led them through the garden towards the house. They admired the ornamental lake, the vine, and the rare plants imported from Asia, and congratulated her on the flowers. At the house, she took them to the winter dining-chamber, where Pazair was conversing with Bagey; the three visitors were surprised to find the former tjaty there.

Neferet withdrew.

'We would like to see you alone, Tjaty,' said the Overseer of Writings.

'I assume you are here because of concerns about the way I am fulfilling my duties. Why should my predecessor not help me? His advice may be valuable.'

Bagey glared sternly at the newcomers. 'Until recently we worked together; do you now consider me a stranger?'

'Of course not,' replied the Overseer of the Fields.

'In that case,' said Pazair, 'the matter is decided. All five of us shall eat together.'

They took their places on their allotted chairs; before each stood a low table on which the servants placed trays laden with food. The cook had prepared succulent pieces of beef cooked in an earthenware cauldron with a rounded base, and poultry roasted on the spit; peas and courgettes in sauce accompanied the meat. To one side were plates of fresh bread, and of butter made with fenugreek and caraway, without water or salt, and kept in a cool cellar in order to avoid browning.

A cup-bearer poured red wine from the Delta, set the jar down on a wooden stand, and left the room, closing the door behind him.

The Director of Secret Missions said, 'We speak in the name of the highest authorities in the land—'

'With the exception of Pharaoh and myself,' cut in Pazair.

The director looked offended. 'Such objections seem pointless to me.'

'Your tone is extremely unpleasant,' said Bagey. 'Whatever your rank and age, you must respect the tjaty Pharaoh appointed.'

124

'Our conscience forbids us to spare him deserved reprimands and criticism.'

Annoyed, Bagey got to his feet. 'I do not accept such a course of action.'

'It is neither unfitting nor illegal,' the director pointed out.

'I disagree. Your role is to serve the tjaty and to obey him.'

'Not when his actions compromise Egypt's well-being.'

'I will not hear another word,' snapped Bagey. 'You shall eat your lunch without me,' and he stalked out of the room.

Taken aback by the fierceness of the attack and by Bagey's reaction, Pazair felt very alone. The meat and vegetables grew cold, the fine wine was undrunk in the cups.

'We have spoken at length with the head of the Double White House,' said the Overseer of Fields, 'and his worries seem to us to be justified.'

'Why is he not with you?'

'We did not tell him what we were going to do. He is a young and impulsive man, who might get carried away over such a serious matter. Indeed, there is a risk that your own youth will lead you into an impasse, unless reason wins through.'

Pazair had had enough. 'You all occupy important posts in which unnecessary words are inappropriate. My time is as precious as yours, so you will oblige me by coming straight to the point.'

'That is just the sort of attitude we mean. Governing Egypt requires much greater flexibility.'

'Pharaoh governs, I see that Ma'at is respected.'

'Daily life sometimes lags far behind the ideal.'

'If that is how Egypt's most senior scribes think,' said Pazair, 'the country is heading for ruin.'

'You are inexperienced,' said the Overseer of Fields, 'and you blindly follow old ideas which no longer have any real substance.'

'I think differently.'

'Was it in the name of those old ideals that you sentenced the governor of Kebet, heir to a noble and famous family?'

'The law was applied, without taking account of his rank.'

'Are you planning to dismiss many more respected, highly skilled officials like that?'

'If they plot against their country, they will be charged and tried.'

'You are confusing serious offences with the necessities of power.'

'Falsifying the land register is hardly a minor offence, is it?'

'We all recognize your integrity,' said the Overseer of Writings soothingly. 'Ever since the start of your career, you have demonstrated your commitment to justice and your love for the truth – no one is contesting that. The people greatly respect and admire you. But is that enough to avert a disaster?'

'What are you reprimanding me about?'

'Perhaps nothing, if you can reassure us.'

The opening skirmishes were over; now the real battle was beginning.

These three men knew everything about power, the system of government and the mechanisms of society. If Bel-Tran had managed to convince them of the rightness of his views, Pazair would have little chance of overcoming their opposition. Isolated and disowned, he would surely be as easily broken as a child's toy.

'My departments,' said the Overseer of Fields, 'have drawn up a list of landowners and farmers, re-counted the heads of livestock, and assessed the harvests. They have also set the year's taxes, taking account of the peasants' opinions, but all this work will result in wholly inadequate revenue. The taxes on fodder and cattle should be doubled.'

'I refuse.'

'Why?'

'In the event of difficulty, increasing taxes is the worst of all solutions. It seems to me more urgent to eliminate injustice – our food reserves are quite sufficient to see us though several bad harvests.'

'Besides, the arrangements are too favourable to country-dwellers. If a tax demand is unjust, some living in a town has only three days to lodge an appeal, while someone who lives in the provinces has three months.'

'As I know very well – I was myself a victim of that ruling,' Pazair reminded him. 'I shall lengthen the appeal period for town-dwellers.'

'At least increase taxes on the rich!'

'The highest-taxed person in Egypt, the governor of Elephantine, pays the Treasury the equivalent of four gold ingots. The governor of a medium-sized province pays a thousand loaves, as well as calves, oxen, honey and sacks of grain. There is no need to demand more, because they maintain extensive households and look after the well-being of the villages they control.'

'Then do you intend to target the craftsmen?'

'Certainly not. Their houses will remain exempt from taxes, and I shall maintain the ban on seizing their tools.'

'Then will you give way on the wood tax? It should be extended to all the provinces.'

'I have closely studied the wood centres and how they receive brushwood, palm-fibres and small pieces of wood. During the cold season, distribution was carried out correctly. Why alter the work of teams whose rotation is satisfactory?'

'You do not understand the situation,' said the Director of Secret Missions. 'The way our trade and finances are is organized no longer meets the demands of the day. Production must be increased, and profits—'

'Those are words Bel-Tran is fond of.'

'Of course he is – he is the head of the Double White House! If you are at odds with your minister for the economy,

127

how can you carry out a coherent policy? You might as well get rid of him – and get rid of us too!'

'We shall continue to work together, according to Egypt's traditional laws. The country is rich, the Nile provides us with abundant food, and prosperity will endure as long as we struggle each day against injustice.'

'Are you sure your views have not been distorted by your own past? The economy—'

'The day the economy takes precedence over justice, disastrous misfortune will be unleashed upon this earth.'

'Very well. But at least the importance of the temples' role should be reduced,' suggested the Overseer of Writings.

'Why do you say that?' asked Pazair.

'They gather in almost all of the agricultural produce and other items, and then distribute them according to the people's needs. Would a more direct route not be preferable?'

'It would be contrary to the rule of Ma'at and would destroy Egypt in a few years. The temples are our energy-regulators, and the priests, shut away behind their walls, have no concern but harmony. Through the temples, we are linked to the Invisible and to the vital forces of the universe. Their schools and workshops produce people who have been fashioning our country for centuries. Do you wish to cut off its head?'

'You are twisting my words.'

'I fear your thoughts resemble a twisted staff.'

'You insult me!'

'You are turning your back on the values upon which Egypt was founded.'

'You are too single-minded, Pazair – a fanatic.'

'If that is what you think, do not hesitate to ask the king for my head.'

'You benefit from the support of Kani, whose opinion Ramses values. But his favour will not outlast your popularity. Resign, Pazair. That would be the best solution, for you and for Egypt.'

20

The head gardener of the Temple of Iunu was devastated. Sitting at the foot of an olive tree, he was in tears. Pazair, who had been summoned urgently by Kem, shivered: a cold wind was gusting, turning over the silver-backed leaves.

'Tell me what happened,' he said to the gardener.

'I oversaw the harvest myself . . . The oldest olive trees in Egypt! What a tragedy! And why? Why this vandalism?'

The gardener could not say any more. Pazair abandoned him to his sadness, after assuring him that he did not consider him responsible, and followed Kem into the largest storehouse of the Temple of Ra, where the country's best lamp-oil was kept.

The floor was a viscous lake.

Not one jar had been spared: every single stopper had been removed, and the contents emptied out.

'What have you found out?' asked Pazair.

'It was one man acting alone,' replied the Nubian. 'He got in through the storehouse roof.'

'Just as he did at the hospital.'

'It was the man who's trying to kill you, I'm certain of it. But why should he carry out this destruction?'

'The temples stand in Bel-Tran's way. Destroying the lamp-oil will slow the work of the scribes and priests, because they won't be able to work after dark. Send out messages immediately: guards must be set to watch all oil reserves. In the Memphis region, we'll use the palace reserves. Not one lamp shall go unfilled.'

Bel-Tran's reaction to the tjaty's firm stance had not been long in coming.

Every single serving-man was wielding a broom made from long, stiff fibres bundled together, every single serving-maid was armed with a brush of reeds held together by a ring: the tjaty's household was zealously sweeping the floors. A delicious smell of incense and cinnamon floated in the air; the smoke from the burning essences would purify the great house and cleanse it of insects and other undesirable guests.

'Where is my wife?' Pazair asked his head steward.

'In the grain-store, my lord.'

Pazair found Neferet on her knees, pushing cloves of garlic, dried fish* and natron into a corner.

'What's hiding in there?' he asked.

'It may be a snake. If it is, these things will suffocate it.'

'Why all this cleaning?'

'I'm worried that the murderer may have left other traces of his visit.'

'Why? Have you had some unpleasant surprises?'

'Not so far, no, but I'm not going to leave a single suspicious place untouched. But tell me, what did Pharaoh say?'

Pazair helped her to her feet.

'He was surprised at the Friends' attitude, which proved to him that the country is gravely sick. I fear I may not be as effective a doctor as you are.'

'What will his answer to them be?'

'It is up to me to deal with their requests.'

'Did they demand your resignation?'

'It was just a suggestion.'

*To be precise the fish called *bulti* [*Tilapia nilotica*].

'So Bel-Tran is still spreading his lies.'

'He has his weaknesses – it's up to us to find them.' The tjaty sneezed uncontrollably, and began to shiver. 'I need a doctor.'

Pazair's cold pounded in his skull; it felt as though his bones were being shattered and his brain hollowed out. Neferet gave him onion juice, considered very effective against chills, purged his nostrils with palm-juice, made him inhale the steam of a potion containing sulphur of arsenic, which doctors called 'that which makes the heart open', and prescribed mother-tincture of bryony to prevent lung problems. She treated his cough with a decoction of the roots of marshmallow and fresh colocinth. Copper-water would soon finish off the infection for good.

Delighted to have his master at home, Brave slept at the foot of his bed, enjoying a soft blanket and, into the bargain, a spoonful of honey.

Despite his fever, Pazair consulted the papyri brought to him by Kem, the only intermediary between the tjaty and his office. The more time passed, the more the tjaty was mastering his job. This period of withdrawal was in fact an advantage, because he noticed that the large temples, in both the north and the south, were not under Bel-Tran's control. They regulated matters according to the teachings of the ancients, and oversaw the distribution of supplies from their store-houses. Thanks to Kani and to the other High Priests – who were in full agreement with their colleague at Karnak – the tjaty could maintain the stability of the ship of state, at least until the fatal day when Ramses would have to abdicate.

When the tall Nubian fingered his wooden nose, Pazair knew his friend had some important information.

'First,' said Kem, 'a worrying piece of news: Mentmose, my predecessor of sad memory, has left Byblos, where he was living in exile.'

'He's taking an enormous risk. When you catch him, he'll be sent to a prison camp.'

'He knows that, which is why his disappearance doesn't bode well.'

'Is Bel-Tran behind it?'

'Possibly.'

'Or has Mentmose simply run away?'

'I'd like to think so, but he hates you as much as Bel-Tran does. You fascinate both of them, because they don't understand your honesty or your love of justice. So long as you were merely a junior judge, it didn't matter. But you as tjaty? That's intolerable. Mentmose doesn't want to live out his life in peace. He wants revenge.'

'And is there still no progress on Branir's murder?'

'Not directly, but . . .'

'But?'

'I believe that the man's who's been trying to kill you is the one who killed Branir. He came from nowhere, and has disappeared again, faster than a greyhound.'

'Are you telling me he's a ghost?'

'Not a ghost, no . . . But a shadow-eater the like of whom I've never come across before. He's a monster – he's in love with death.'

'Has he at last made the mistake you were hoping for?'

'Yes, when he attacked Killer. That's the only time he's had to use outside help, and therefore to make contact with others. I was afraid this thread might be cut off, but fortunately one of my best informants, a man called Short-Thighs, has a few problems at the moment. A judge has just increased the amount of the food contribution he has to give his former wife, so his memory seems to have been jogged.'

'And does he know who the shadow-eater is?'

'If he does, he'll ask for an enormous reward.'

'It's granted. When are you seeing him?'

'This evening, behind the docks.'

'I'll come with you.'
'Not in your state of health, you won't.'

Neferet had summoned the principal suppliers of rare and expensive ingredients used in the medical workshops. Although stocks were by no means exhausted, she judged it wise to replenish them as quickly as possible, because of the difficulties of harvesting and delivery.

'Let us begin with myrrh,' she said. 'When is it planned to send the next caravan to the land of Punt?'

The man responsible coughed. 'I don't know.'

'Why not?'

'No date has been set.'

'It's up to you to set it, I should have thought.'

'I have no boats or crews at my disposal.'

'And why is that?'

'I am awaiting the goodwill of foreign countries.'

'Have you consulted the tjaty?' asked Neferet.

'No. I applied to the usual secretariats.'

'You should have told me about this problem.'

'There was no hurry . . .'

'But there is now – it's urgent.'

'I'd have to have a written order.'

'You will have it today.'

Neferet turned to another trader. 'Have you ordered green gum resin of galbanum?'*

'Yes, but it won't arrive for some time.'

'Why won't it?'

'It comes from Asia, and we're dependent on the whim of the gatherers and sellers. The government scribes strongly advised me not to bother them. Apparently, our relations with those countries are rather strained, because of certain incidents – the details escape me. But as soon as it's possible . . .'

---

*These gum resins [*galbanum* and *ladanum*], extracted from trees or shrubs, and still used today in perfumery, were considered medicinal.

'And what about the dark ladanum resin?' Neferet asked the third supplier. 'I know it comes from Greece and Minoa, and they're are always ready to trade.'

'Not at the moment, I'm afraid. The harvest was poor, so they've decided not to sell any to other countries.'

Neferet did not even ask the other merchants. It was clear from their embarrassment that they would also answer in the negative.

'Who receives these products when they reach Egyptian soil?' she asked the myrrh-supplier.

'The border trade-control guards and scribes.'

'To which secretariat do they report?'

The man stammered, 'To . . . to the Double White House.'

Neferet's eyes, usually so gentle, filled with anger and revulsion. 'By becoming henchmen of Bel-Tran,' she said coldly, 'you are betraying Egypt. As the kingdom's principal doctor, I shall ask that you be charged with damaging the people's health.'

'That certainly isn't our intention, but the circumstances . . . You must admit that the world is changing and Egypt must change, too. Our way of doing business is altering: Bel-Tran holds the key to our future. However, if you were to increase our profits, and review our margins, deliveries could start again quite quickly.'

'That's blackmail!' said Neferet furiously. 'Blackmail which compromises the health of your fellow countrymen!'

'That's putting it much too strongly. We have open minds, and in well-conducted negotiations—'

'Given that this is a matter of urgency, I shall ask the tjaty for a requisition order and I shall deal with our foreign partners myself.'

'You wouldn't dare!'

'Greed is an incurable disease, which I cannot treat. Ask Bel-Tran for new jobs. You no longer work for the medical services.'

21

Fever did not stop Pazair signing the requisition order enabling Neferet to ensure the acquisition of the ingredients the doctors needed. Armed with the papyrus, Neferet left immediately for the Foreign Affairs secretariat. There, she would personally oversee the drafting of the documents ordering the caravans to set out.

Her favourite patient's condition gave her no cause for concern, but he must stay in his bedchamber for two or three more days, to avoid any risk of a relapse.

The tjaty did not allow himself to rest. Surrounded by papyri and wooden tablets sent by scribes in different ministries and departments, he searched for weak points which Bel-Tran would be sure to exploit. He tried to imagine his enemy's plans, and took measures to counter them, but he did not delude himself: Bel-Tran and his allies would soon find other means of attack.

The head steward came in and told his master someone was requesting an audience. When Pazair heard the visitor's name he could hardly believe his ears. Despite his astonishment, he agreed to see him.

Full of confidence, fashionably dressed in a luxurious linen robe that was too tight at the waist, Bel-Tran greeted the tjaty warmly.

'I have brought you a jar of white wine dating from year

two of the reign of Seti II, father of our illustrious king. It's a virtually unobtainable vintage – I'm sure you'll enjoy it.' Without waiting for an invitation, he took a chair and sat down opposite Pazair. 'I heard you were ill. Nothing serious, I hope?'

'I shall soon be on my feet again.'

'It is true that you benefit from the skills of the best doctor in the kingdom, but, all the same, I think this attack of fatigue is significant. The burden of being tjaty is almost impossible to bear.'

'Except for shoulders as broad as yours.'

'There are a lot of rumours circulating at court. Everyone knows you're having great difficulty performing your duties properly.'

'That's true. I am.'

Bel-Tran smiled.

'In fact, I'm not sure I shall ever succeed,' added Pazair.

'My friend, this illness is doing you a world of good.'

'Enlighten me about something. Since you have the decisive weapon, and since you're certain of gaining supreme power, how can what I do be a hindrance to you?'

'It's like being bitten by a mosquito all the time – unpleasant. However, if you agree to obey me and to follow the way of progress at last, I shall allow you to remain tjaty. You are, after all, popular with the people, and they admire your capacity for work, your upright character, your clear-sightedness . . . You'd be useful in carrying out my policies.'

'High Priest Kani would disapprove of my doing that.'

'It's up to you to deceive him. You foiled my plan to acquire a good part of the temple's lands, so you certainly owe me that much. The temples' power over Egypt's trade and resources is archaic, Pazair. The production of wealth must not be held back and restricted – we must encourage continued growth.'

136

'Will it ensure the happiness of men and the balance between peoples?'

'Oh, that doesn't matter. Money gives power to whoever controls it.'

'Perhaps. But I can't stop thinking about my master, Branir.'

Bel-Tran made an airy gesture. 'He was a man of the past.'

'According to the annals of the past, no crime went unpunished then.'

'Forget that wretched story and turn your thoughts to the future.'

'Kem is still investigating, and he thinks he has identified the murderer.'

Bel-Tran kept his composure, but there was alarm in his eyes.

'However, my hypothesis differs from Kem's. Several times, I've come close to charging your wife with the killing.'

'Silkis? But . . .'

'I believe she is the woman who lured the commander of the honour-guard aside, and distracted him from his duty. Right from the beginning of the conspiracy, she's obeyed you unquestioningly. In addition, she's an excellent weaver, and handles needles better than anyone else. There's no one more dangerous than a child-woman, according to the old sages. I believe she's quite capable of having murdered Branir by stabbing him in the neck with one of her mother-of-pearl needles.'

'I was wrong. Your fever's doing you harm, not good.'

'Silkis needs your wealth, but you're her slave, too – much more than you think. It's only evil that binds you together.'

'That's enough of your miserable thoughts! Will you at last submit?'

'Thinking I might betrays a clear lack of lucidity on your part.'

Bel-Tran stood up. 'Don't try to take action against Silkis,

137

or against me. You and your king have lost: the Testament of the Gods is out of your reach for ever.'

That evening the wind heralded the coming of spring: warm and scented, it bore with it the soul of the far-away desert. People went to bed later, chatted in one another's houses, discussed the day's events.

Kem waited until the last lamps had been extinguished, then he and Killer stole out into the narrow lanes leading to the docks. Killer moved forward slowly, looking up and down, and from right to left, as if he sensed danger. Edgily, he sometimes retraced his steps, then suddenly increased his pace. Kem respected the baboon's instinct; in the darkness, it was a valuable guide.

The docks area was silent; guards were keeping watch outside the storehouses. Kem and Short-Thighs had agreed to meet behind an abandoned building which was due to be rebuilt. Short-Thighs often conducted his illicit dealings there, and Kem turned a blind eye to them in exchange for the sort of information that an office-bound guard would never be able to get.

Short-Thighs had left the path of truth virtually from the moment of his birth. He was a dedicated trafficker, whose only pleasure was his next theft, and the little folk of Memphis could keep no secrets from him. Ever since the start of his inquiry, Kem had thought the thief would probably be the only one likely to give him firm information about the assassin, but he also knew he must not push too hard, or he would come up against a wall of silence.

Killer halted, on the alert. His hearing was much better than a man's, and his time in the guards had developed his faculties. Clouds hid the first quarter of the moon; darkness extended over the abandoned, doorless warehouse. He started moving forward again.

Short-Thighs' goodwill derived from a legal problem.

Acting on shrewd advice, his ex-wife was stripping him of the small fortune he had amassed, so he had resolved to sell his most precious possession: the identity of the shadow-eater. What would he demand in exchange? wondered Kem. Gold, certainly, and Kem's silence on a bigger smuggling deal than usual: a cargo of jars of wine. Kem would soon find out.

Killer gave an ear-splitting howl. Kem thought he was hurt, but a swift examination showed that all was well. Killer agreed to continue and walked round the warehouse.

There was no one at the agreed meeting-place.

Kem sat down beside Killer, who was now calm. Had Short-Thighs changed his mind? The Nubian thought not: the man was in urgent need of money.

The night passed.

A little before dawn, Killer took Kem by the hand and led him inside the warehouse. Abandoned baskets, broken chests, the remains of tools . . . Killer forced a path through this chaos, halted before a pile of grain sacks and howled as he had done a few hours earlier.

Kem quickly pulled away the sacks.

Propped up against a wooden pillar, Short-Thighs had indeed come to the meeting. But, as the shadow-eater had broken his neck, he would not be selling his big secret.

Pazair did his best to reassure Kem. 'Short-Thighs' death is entirely my responsibility,' he said.

'Of course it isn't. It was he who contacted you.'

'I should have had him protected.'

'How?'

'I don't know, I—'

'Stop blaming yourself,' said Kem. 'The shadow-eater must have got wind of Short-Thighs' intention, followed him and killed him.'

'Or else Short-Thighs tried to blackmail him,' suggested Pazair.

'He was greedy enough to do something as mad as that. And now the trail has gone cold again. Of course, I am maintaining the watch over you.'

'Do what's necessary. We're leaving tomorrow for Middle Egypt.' Pazair's voice had darkened.

'Is something wrong?'

'I've had worrying reports from several provincial governors.'

'What about?'

'Water.'

'What's happened?'

'The worst.'

Neferet had carried out a long and delicate operation on a young craftsman who had fallen from the roof of a house, breaking his skull and cracking several neck-bones; one of his temples was stove in. Fortunately, though, he had been brought to the hospital straight away, so she was confident he would live.

Worn out, she had fallen asleep in a rest-chamber.

One of her assistants woke her. 'I'm sorry, but I need you.'

'Ask another doctor; I haven't the strength to operate again.'

'It is a strange case – we really do need you to look at the patient.'

Wearily, Neferet got up and followed her assistant.

The patient was a woman aged about forty. She wore an expensive dress; that and her well-cared-for hands and feet showed that she belonged to a wealthy family. Her eyes were open, but staring blankly.

'She was found lying in an alleyway in the northern district,' explained the assistant, 'but the people living there didn't recognize her. She looks as though she's been numbed for an operation.'

Neferet listened to the voice of the woman's heart in her arteries, then examined her eyes. 'She has been drugged,' she concluded, 'with extract of pink poppy – which should be used only in hospital.* I shall ask that an investigation be begun immediately.'

In the face of his wife's insistence, Pazair had delayed his departure for Middle Egypt and asked Kem to investigate the case of the drugged woman. She had died without regaining consciousness.

Thanks to Killer, tongues were loosening. The unfortunate woman had gone three times to the alleyway, where a man had been waiting for her. He was a Greek, Kem was told, a seller of precious vases, who lived in a beautiful house.

When Kem arrived there, the suspect was not at home. A serving-woman asked him to take a seat in the receiving-chamber and brought him some cool beer. The vase-seller had gone to deal with a business matter at the quayside, she said, and would soon be back.

When he returned, the Greek, a tall, thin man with a beard, took flight the moment he saw his visitor. Kem did not move, confident that Killer would see to things. He was right: the baboon dived at the fugitive's legs and brought him down on his face on the tiled floor.

Kem pulled him up by his tunic.

'I haven't done anything!' protested the Greek.

'You killed a woman.'

'I sell vases, that's all.'

For a moment, Kem wondered if he was holding the shadow-eater; but the man had been much too easy to catch. He said, 'Unless you tell me what I want to know, you'll be sentenced to death.'

The Greek's voice turned into a sob. 'Have pity! I'm only a go-between.'

---

*From the *shepen* or pink poppy, opium and morphine were extracted for use as sedatives and analgesics.

'From whom do you buy the drug?'

'From Greece – from people who grow the plants there.'

'They are beyond my reach. You, however, are not.'

Killer's red eyes signalled his full agreement.

'I'll tell you their names,' said the vase-seller.

'Tell me the names of your customers.'

'No, not that!'

Killer's hairy hand came down on the man's shoulder. He shivered with fear, and began to speak volubly, naming officials, merchants and a few nobles.

Among them was the lady Silkis.

22

On the morning of his departure, while Pazair and Neferet were in the garden, sitting in the shade of a persea, an invitation arrived. It was from Bel-Tran. At the end of winter, it was incumbent upon the head of the Double White House to host a magnificent reception and banquet, attended by all the principal court dignitaries, senior officials and several provincial governors. And it was customary for the tjaty to honour the reception with his presence.

'He is laughing at us,' said Neferet.

'Bel-Tran bows to tradition when it is useful to him.'

'Arc wc rcally obligcd to takc part in this masquerade?'

'I'm afraid so.'

'Charging Silkis would cause a fine scandal.'

'I shall try to be discreet.'

'Has the drugs traffic been halted?'

'Kem has been spendidly efficient. The Greek's accomplices were arrested on the quayside, and so were all their customers – except Silkis.'

'But you can't move against her, can you?'

'Bel-Tran's threats won't stop me.'

'The important thing is to have put an end to this horror. What good would it do to imprison her now, today?'

Pazair put his arm round his wife. 'It would be justice.'

Christian Jacq

'But isn't the moment when a deed is done more important than the deed itself?

'Are you advising me to wait? The days and weeks are passing; Pharaoh's abdication is not far off.'

'We must fight clear-headedly right up to the last second,' insisted Neferet.

'The darkness is so dense! Sometimes, I—'

She hushed him by putting a finger to his lips. 'A tjaty of Egypt never gives up,' she said.

Pazair loved the countryside of Middle Egypt, the white cliffs bordering the Nile, the vast green plains and the bright hills where the nobles built their houses of eternity. The region possessed neither the lofty character of Memphis nor the sun-drenched splendour of Thebes, but it retained the secrets of the country-dwellers' soul, which had withdrawn into middle-sized farms run by families jealous of their traditions.

During the voyage, Killer gave no warning of danger. The spring air was growing more and more gentle, and he seemed to delight in it, though without ever softening the fierce energy in his eyes.

The province of the Oryx was proud of its water management. For centuries, it had ensured its inhabitants' prosperity, driving away the spectre of famine and drawing no distinction between great and small. In years of low annual floods, skilfully built ponds held enough water to irrigate the land. Canals, sluice-gates and earthen retaining-banks were watched constantly by dedicated specialists, especially during the crucial period following the floodwaters' retreat. At that time, many fields remained flooded, absorbing the precious silt that had given rise to Egypt's nickname of 'Black Earth', and the villages, perched on mounds which rose clear of the water, were alive with songs honouring the Nile's fertilizing energy.

Every ten days, the tjaty received a detailed report on the country's water reserves, and he often went, without warning,

144

to check the local scribes' work. Now, as he travelled towards the capital of the Oryx province, Pazair felt less anxious. The retaining-banks were in excellent condition, the pools lining the way were full, and men were at work maintaining the canals – it was all a reassuring sight.

The tjaty's arrival caused a happy tumult. Everyone wanted to see the great man, present a petition to him, ask for justice. There was no hostility; quite the opposite. The people's esteem and trust moved Pazair to the bottom of his heart and filled him with new strength. For these people's sake, he must safeguard the country and prevent the kingdom from falling apart. He called upon the sky, the Nile, and the fertile land; he implored the creative powers to open his spirit so that he might save Pharaoh.

The governor of the province was descended from a long line of officials of the province. A rotund sixty-year-old who enjoyed good living, he was called Iau, meaning 'the Fat Ox'.

He hastily summoned to his fine white-painted house his principal colleagues: the overseers of retaining-banks and canals, the distributor of water reserves, the official land-surveyor and the recruiter of seasonal workers. Pazair was surprised to find that they all looked sombre. They bowed before the tjaty, to whom Iau at once ceded his place and the leadership of the gathering.

'This visit is a great honour for me,' Iau declared, 'and a great honour for my province.'

'Your reports alerted me. Do you stand by them?'

The bluntness of the question surprised Iau, but did not shock him. Tjaties, overburdened with work, seldom had time for polite formalities.

'I initiated them.'

'Several provinces share your anxiety. I have chosen to come to yours because of its exemplary record over several generations.'

'I shall be blunt, too,' said Iau. 'We no longer understand

the orders from central government. Usually I am left free to run the province, and my results have never disappointed Pharaoh. Now, since the end of the last flood, we're being ordered to do things which make no sense.'

'Explain.'

'This year, as every other year, our surveyor calculated the volume of earth to be moved and piled up to make the retaining-walls impermeable. But his figures have been revised downwards. If we accept the correction, the walls won't be strong enough – they'll be destroyed by the tides.'

'Where did this correction come from?'

'From the Surveying secretariat in Memphis. But that isn't all. Our recruiter of seasonal workers knows exactly how many men he needs to carry out the maintenance work, when the retaining-banks are repaired and sealed. But the Employment secretariat will let him have only half that number, and refuses to say why.

'More serious still is the question of the irrigation pools. Nobody knows better than we do how long water takes to pass from a pool upstream to a pool downstream, according to the needs of the kinds of plants to be grown. But the Double White House wants to impose on us dates which are incompatible with the demands of nature. And I haven't even mentioned the increase in taxes that will result from the increase in production. Whatever is going on in the minds of those people in Memphis?'

'Show me these documents,' requested Pazair.

Iau called for the papyri.

Pazair looked at them closely. All the signatories were scribes either from the Double White House itself or from departments which Bel-Tran controlled more or less directly.

He said, 'Give me writing-materials.'

A scribe presented him with a palette, fresh ink and a writing-brush. In his swift, precise hand, Pazair cancelled the orders. Then he affixed his seal to each papyrus.

'These errors have been put right,' he announced. 'Take no notice of these out-of-date orders, and follow your usual procedures.'

Stunned into silence, the provincial administrators exchanged looks.

Eventually, Iau found his voice. 'Are we to understand—'

'From now on, only directives bearing my seal will be valid.'

Delighted by the tjaty's unexpected and rapid intervention, the administrators applauded him and went cheerfully back to their daily tasks.

But Iau still looked careworn.

Pazair said, 'Is there something else worrying you?'

'Doesn't your attitude rather imply an open conflict with Bel-Tran?'

'One of my ministers can make a mistake.'

'In that case, why do you retain him in his position?'

Pazair had been afraid that question would be asked. Up to now, the skirmishes had been fairly discreet, but this matter of the water had brought into the open the serious disagreements between the tjaty and the head of the Double White House.

'Bel-Tran has a great capacity for work,' he said.

'Do you know that he is taking steps to convince the provincial governors that his policies are the right ones? My colleagues and I have been wondering, are you the tjaty or is he?'

'You have just had your answer.'

Iau smiled. 'That's very reassuring – I didn't like his offer.'

'What was it?'

'An important post in Memphis, a tempting increase in pay, fewer responsibilities . . .'

'Why didn't you accept?'

'Because I'm satisfied with what I have – but Bel-Tran

147

can't seem to accept that ambition may be limited. I love this region and I loathe large cities. I'm respected here; in Memphis, I'd be nobody.'

'Have you officially refused the offer?'

'That man frightens me, I admit, so I preferred to play at being hesitant. But other governors have agreed to help him – as if you didn't even exist. It looks as though you have taken a snake into your house.'

'If I have, it is up to me to put things right.'

Iau did not hide his concern. 'From what you say, I think the country is likely to face difficult times. As you have preserved my province's integrity, I pledge you my full support.'

Kem and Killer were sitting on the threshold of Iau's beautiful house. Killer was eating dates, and Kem was watching the street, obsessed by the shadow-eater and convinced that the man of darkness was thinking about him with the same intensity.

As soon as Pazair came out of the house, Kem stood up.

'Is everything all right, Tjaty?' he asked.

'Another disaster narrowly averted. We must inspect several other provinces.'

Iau caught up with them, on the road back to the landing-stage.

'Tjaty,' he said, 'there's something I forgot to ask. Was it really you who sent me a man to check the drinking-water?'

'Absolutely not. Describe him to me.'

'About sixty, medium height, with a bald, red pate he scratches a lot, very irritable, with a nasal voice and a peremptory tone.'

'Mentmose,' murmured Kem.

'What did he do?' asked Pazair.

'He carried out a routine inspection,' said Iau.

'Take me to the drinking-water stores.'

The most beneficial drinking-water was collected a few days after the start of the flood. Rich in mineral salts, it helped digestion and also promoted fertility in women. Being turbid and muddy, it had to be filtered, after which it was stored in large jars which preserved it wonderfully well for four or five years. The Oryx province sometimes exported it to the South, in years of great heat.

A guard drew back the heavy wooden bolts and opened the heavy wooden door of the largest storehouse.

The breath fled from Iau's body when he saw the disaster: the stopper had been removed from every single jar, and all the water had been spilt on the ground.

23

How could a woman be so beautiful? wondered Pazair as he gazed at Neferet, who was decked in her finery for Bel-Tran's banquet. She was wearing the seven-stringed collar of cornelian beads, embellished with Nubian gold, that the Mother of Pharaoh had given her; hidden beneath it was her gift from Branir, a turquoise a designed to ward off evil. Hcr wig's fine plaits and ringlets showed off her beautiful face, with its clear, radiant complexion. Bracelets of small beads encircled her wrists and ankles, and a belt of amethysts, a gift from Pazair, emphasized the slenderness of her waist.

'It is time for you to get dressed,' she remarked.

'Just one last report to read.'

'About the reserves of drinking-water?'

'Mentmose destroyed ten; the others are protected, for the time being. The heralds are proclaiming the criminal's description, so either he'll fall into the hands of the security guards or he'll be forced to go to ground.'

'How many of the governors have sold themselves to Bel-Tran?'

'A third, perhaps. But the work to maintain the retaining-banks will be carried out correctly. I have given orders to that effect, with a ban on reducing the number of workmen involved.'

Neferet sat down on his knee, to stop him working. 'It

really is time for you to put on your best kilt, a traditional wig and a collar worthy of your rank.'

As commander of Memphis's guards, Kem had had an invitation to the banquet. The Nubian was very ill at ease at this sort of affair, and his only jewellery was his dagger with the gold-and-silver alloy hilt, with inlaid rosettes of lapis-lazuli and green feldspar. Standing inconspicuously in a corner of the great pillared hall where Bel-Tran and Silkis received their guests, he watched the tjaty, who was sur-rounded by people. Killer had taken up a position on the roof of the house, from where he kept watch on the area around.

Garlands of flowers decorated the pillars; the guests, the cream of Memphis's nobility were dressed in their most splendid clothes; roast geese and grilled beef were brought in on dishes of silver, and the finest wines were poured into cups imported from Greece. Some guests sat on cushions, others chose chairs. A constant stream of servants frequently changed the guests' alabaster plates.

The tjaty and his wife sat in state behind a well-laden table; servants washed their hands with perfumed water and hung necklaces of cornflowers about their necks. Each female guest received a lotus-flower, which she set in her wig.

Girls playing harps, lutes and tambourines enchanted their listeners. Bel-Tran had hired the best players in the city, demanding new melodies from them, which music-lovers would appreciate for their true worth.

One very old courtier, who could no longer walk, was enjoying the benefit of a comfortable commode, which enabled him to participate in the evening. After use, a servant removed the earthenware jar from under the seat, and replaced it with another, filled with perfumed sand.

Bel-Tran's cook was a genius with fine herbs. For this feast he had united the tastes of rosemary, cumin, sage, anise and cinnamon, which was known as 'truly noble'. Food-lovers were effusive in their congratulations, while everyone extolled the generosity of the head of the Double White House and his wife.

At last, Bel-Tran stood up and called for silence.

'My friends,' he said, 'on this wonderful evening, which your presence makes still more beautiful, I should like to pay homage to a man whose benevolent authority we all respect: Tjaty Pazair. The post of tjaty is a sacred institution, and through it the will of Pharaoh is expressed. Despite his youth, our dear Pazair has given evidence of a remarkable and surprising maturity. He has earned the people's love, he takes decisions quickly, and he works every day to preserve the greatness of our country. In your name, and as a sign of homage, we present him with this modest gift.'

The steward placed before Pazair a glazed blue earthenware cup, the bottom of which was decorated with a four-petalled lotus.

'My thanks to you,' said Pazair, 'and I hope you will permit me to present this beautiful work of art to the Temple of Ptah, the god of craftsmen. We must never forget that the temples have a duty to collect food and other resources, and to redistribute them according to the people's needs. Who would ever dare to lessen their role, thus damaging the country's harmony and destroying the balance created since the days of our earliest pharaohs? If food is nourishing, if the earth is fertile, if our society rests on the duties of the man and not on his rights, it is because Ma'at, the eternal Rule of life, is our guide. Whoever betrays her, whoever attacks her, is a criminal to whom no mercy must be shown. As long as justice is our central value, Egypt will live in peace and have cause for celebration.'

The tjaty's words were greeted with enthusiasm by one half of the audience and frozen horror by the other. When conversation began again, the two halves clashed in muffled voices, either praising the tjaty's words or criticizing them.

Was a banquet an appropriate occasion for such a declaration? While Pazair was speaking, Bel-Tran's face had hardened. The tight smile he wore now deceived no one. After all, was there not talk of a profound divergence of views between the two men? Because of all the contradictory rumours, it was difficult to tell truth from falsehood.

After the meal, the guests took the air in the gardens. Kem doubled his vigilance, assisted by Killer; the tjaty listened to the grievances of a few senior officials who complained, justly, about the slowness of government. Bel-Tran, who was never at a loss for a cheery word, was holding the rapt attention of a group of courtiers.

Near the lake, Silkis came up to Neferet. 'I have been wanting for a long time to talk to you. At last, this evening gives me the chance.'

'Have you decided to get a divorce?' asked Neferet.

'But I love Bel-Tran so much – he's a wonderful husband. Besides, if I intervene on your behalf, perhaps the worst can be averted.'

'What do you mean by that?'

'Bel-Tran feels real esteem for Pazair. Why can't your husband be more reasonable? Together, the two of them could do wonderful work.'

'The tjaty doesn't believe that.'

'He's wrong. Can't you make to change his mind?' Silkis spoke in the naive, sugar-sweet voice of a child-woman.

'Pazair doesn't comfort himself with illusions.'

'There's so little time left – soon it will be too late. Surely the tjaty's obstinacy is a bad counsellor?'

'Compromise would be considerably worse.'

'And what about you? Rising to the position of principal doctor was far from easy. Why wreck your career?'

'Curing the sick is not a career,' said Neferet firmly.

'In that case, you won't refuse to treat me.'

'Yes I shall – I do.'

'A doctor can't choose her patients!'

'In the present circumstances, I can.'

'Why? What have I done wrong?'

'Are you daring to say you aren't a criminal?'

Silkis turned away. 'I don't understand . . . To accuse me, and . . .'

'Unburden your conscience and confess. That's the best remedy in the world.'

'What am I supposed to have done?'

'At the very least, you have taken illegal drugs.'

Silkis closed her eyes and hid her face in her hands. 'Stop saying these horrible things!'

'The tjaty has proof of your guilt.'

Close to an attack of hysteria, Silkis ran to hide in her apartments.

Neferet rejoined Pazair. 'I'm afraid I was clumsy,' she said.

'Judging by Silkis's reaction, I'm sure you weren't.'

Bel-Tran cut in on them. 'What's happened?' he asked irritably. 'You—'

Neferet's gaze choked the words in his throat. It showed no hatred, no violence, but was full of a light which pierced him through and through. Bel-Tran felt himself laid bare, stripped of his lies, his connivings and his plots. His soul burnt, and a spasm clenched his chest. Feeling as though he were going to be sick, he withdrew from the fight and left the great pillared hall.

His part in the reception was at an end.

Followed discreetly by Kem, Pazair and Neferet moved to a quiet place, near the house, where they could talk privately.

'You are surely a sorceress,' said Pazair.

'One can't fight a sickness like that without magic. In fact, Bel-Tran looked inward, upon his true self. What he saw doesn't seem to have made him very happy.'

The gentle warmth of the night delighted them. For a few

moments, as they strolled in the garden, they forgot that the passage of time was against them. They began to dream that Egypt would never change, that the scent of jasmine would always fill the garden, that the Nile flood would for all eternity nourish a people united in the love of their king.

The slight figure of a woman leapt out of a clump of bushes in front of them. She screamed in fear when, with an enormous bound, Killer leapt from the roof and landed between her and the couple, freezing her where she stood. With his mouth open and his nostrils dilated, he was obviously ready to attack.

'Stop him, please!'

'Lady Tapeni!' said Pazair in astonishment, laying a hand on Killer's shoulder. 'What an extraordinary way to approach me. You might have been badly hurt.'

Killer calmed down and went over to Kem, who had also leapt to the couple's defence, but Tapeni went on shaking for some time.

'I must search you, my lady,' said Kem.

'Get back!'

'If you refuse, I'll ask Killer to do it.'

Tapeni gave in. Pazair concluded that the priest who had given her her name, which meant 'the Mouse', had clearly detected her true nature: vivacious, nervous and sly.

Kem had hoped to find a mother-of-pearl pearl needle, proof of her wish to attack the tjaty, and of her guilt of Branir's murder, but she was carrying no weapons or tools.

When Kem had finished, Pazair asked her, 'What do you want to speak to me about?'

'Soon you won't be questioning anyone any more.'

'How do you know that? Are you a seer?'

She bit her lip.

'Once again, Tapeni, you have said both too much and too little.'

'No one in the whole of Egypt supports your rigorous government. The king will have to dismiss you.'

'That is for Pharaoh to decide. Is that all you have to say?'

'I've heard that Suti escaped from the fortress where he was serving his sentence.'

'You're well informed,' said Pazair.

'Don't hope that he'll come back.'

'I shall see him alive again – and so will you.'

'No one survives the harsh Nubian desert. He'll die of thirst there.'

'The law of the desert is in his favour. No only will he survive but he'll settle his accounts.'

'That flies in the face of justice.'

'I'm afraid that's true, but I cannot control him.'

'You must ensure my safety.'

'As I must the safety of all the inhabitants of this country.'

'You must have Suti hunted down and arrested.'

'In the Nubian desert? That's impossible. We shall just have to be patient and wait until he reappears. I wish you good night, Tapeni.'

Hidden behind the enormous trunk of a sycamore, ears straining, the shadow-eater saw the tjaty pass by, with Neferet, Kem and that damned Killer. After his recent failure, the assassin had wanted to try again during the reception. But Kem had been watching inside, and Killer outside. He might, through mere vanity, have wasted several years of success on trying to prove that no one, not even a tjaty, could escape him.

He must keep his nerve. After killing Short-Thighs, the shadow-eater had felt his hands shake for the first time. Killer impressed him no more than before, but not succeeding in killing Pazair exasperated him. Was a strange force protecting the tjaty? No, it was just a Nubian guard and a baboon with a keen intelligence.

The shadow-eater would win the fiercest battle of his career.

24

Suti fingered his lips, his cheeks, his forehead, but did not recognise the contours of his face. It was no more than a puffed-up, painful mass, and his eyelids were so swollen that he couldn't see. Nor could he could move his legs, so he had to be carried on a litter by six sturdy Nubians.

'Are you there, Panther?' he asked.

'Of course,' she replied.

'Then kill me.'

'You'll live. Another few days, and the scorpion's venom will disperse. The fact that you can speak shows that your blood is circulating again. The old warrior can't understand how you've resisted the poison.'

'But my legs . . . they're paralysed.'

'No, just tied to the litter. You were having convulsions – probably because of nightmares – and kept nearly tipping it over. Were you dreaming of Tapeni?'

'Certainly not. I was floating deep in an ocean of light, where no one could bother me.'

'You deserve to be abandoned at the side of the road.'

'How long have I been unconscious?'

'The sun has already risen three times.'

'Have we made any progress?'

'We're still going towards our gold.'

'Have you seen any Egyptian soldiers?'

'We haven't seen anyone, but we're nearing the border now – the Nubians are getting restive.'

'I'm taking back command,' said Suti.

'In your state?'

'Untie me.'

'Do you know how dreadful you are?'

But she told the Nubians to set the litter down, untied him and helped to his feet.

'It's good to feel the earth under my feet again,' he said. 'Quick, give me a staff.'

Leaning on a rough cane, Suti walked to the head of the tribe. Panther was impresssed by his determination.

The band passed to the west of Elephantine and the border post of the first Southern province. A few isolated warriors had joined them during their slow journey northwards. Suti trusted these valuable, experienced fighters: if they encountered desert guards they would not hesitate to take them on.

The Nubians followed the goddess. Laden with gold, they dreamt of conquests and victories, led by Suti, who was stronger than a scorpion. They crossed a barrier of granite by means of narrow paths, walked along the bed of a dried-up river, killed game for food, drank sparingly and made their way without complaint.

Suti's face had recovered its good looks, and the young man his energy. The first to rise, the last to go to bed, he fed greedily on the desert air and became tireless. Panther loved him all the more: he was taking on the stature of a true warrior chief, whose word was law and whose decisions were not open to debate.

The Nubians had made him several bows of varying sizes, which he used to bring down antelopes and a lion. With unerring instinct, as if he had roamed the unexplored tracks all his life, he led his little army to the water-sources.

'A band of desert guards is coming towards us,' one of the warriors warned him.

Suti recognized them at once: the All-Seeing Ones and their ferocious dogs roamed the desert to ensure the safety of caravans and to capture sand-travellers found pillaging. They did not usually venture into these parts.

'Let's attack them,' suggested Panther.

'No,' replied Suti. 'We'll hide, and let them go by.'

The Nubians hid in a massive rocky outcrop while the guards skirted it. The dogs were thirsty and tired, and did not sense their presence. The All-Seeing Ones had nearly finished their patrol, and were heading back to their base in a nearby valley.

'We could easily have killed them,' muttered Panther, lying down beside Suti.

'If they hadn't got back, the post at Elephantine would have raised the alarm.'

'You don't want to kill Egyptians – but I dream of it. You're a pariah, and you're the leader of rebel Nubians whose only trade is war. You'll have to fight soon. It is your nature, Suti, and you can't escape it.'

Panther caressed her lover's chest. Hidden by the granite rocks, oblivious of the danger, they embraced in the midday heat. Covered in gold jewellery from the Lost City, her skin golden and warm, the Libyan girl played her body as if it were a lyre and sang a burning melody whose every note Suti adored.

'This is the place,' said Panther. 'I recognize the country-side.' She gripped Suti's wrist tightly enough to break it. 'Our gold's over there, in that cave. To me it's more precious than any other gold in the world, because you killed an Egyptian general to get it.'

'We don't need it any more.'

'Yes we do! With it, you will be the master of gold.'

Suti could not take his eyes off the cave where he had hidden General Asher's treasure. Panther was right to bring him here. Rejecting that episode in his life and running away from it into oblivion would have been cowardly. Like his friend Pazair, Suti loved justice. If he hadn't struck down the fugitive traitor, no one would ever have done it. The gods had granted him the traitor's gold, which he intended to use to buy a life of peace from the Libyan warlord Adafi.

'Come on,' Panther demanded. 'Come and marvel at our future.'

As she walked forward, blinding flashes of light came from her magnificent collar and her bracelets. The Nubians knelt down, awed by their golden goddess's slow walk towards a shrine which only she knew: she had led them this deep into Egyptian territory in order to increase their magical power and make them invincible. When she and Suti went into the cave, the warriors sang an ancient chant which hailed the return of the far-off betrothed, ready to celebrate her wedding to the soul of her people.

Panther was convinced that taking possession of the gold would seal her destiny by uniting it with Suti's. This moment was the forebear of a thousand brilliant tomorrows.

Suti was reliving his execution of that vile murderer General Asher, who had been intent on escaping the tjaty's court and living to a happy old age in Libya, where he would have stirred up trouble against Egypt. Suti had no regrets about killing him. Engraved on his soul was the righteousness of the desert, where falsehood could not flourish.

The interior of the cave felt cool. Disturbed by their arrival, bats flew in all directions before once again hooking themselves on to the cave roof, their heads hanging down.

'It's gone!' cried Panther. 'It was here, I know it was, but where's the chariot?'

'Let's go further in.'

'There's no point. I remember exactly where we hid it.'

Suti searched every corner, every cranny, of the cave. But

it was empty. 'Who could have known? And who would have dared . . . ?'

Mad with rage, Panther tore off her golden collar and smashed it against a rock. 'We'll rip out the belly of this cave of ill fortune!'

Suti picked up a piece of cloth. 'Look at this.'

She bent over the find. 'Dyed wool,' she said. 'Our thieves aren't demons of the night, they're sand-travellers. When they took the chariot out, one of them tore his robe on a jagged piece of rock.' All at once, her hopes revived. 'We must go after them.'

'It wouldn't be any use,' said Suti.

'I'm not giving up.'

'Neither am I.'

'Then what do you suggest?'

'We stay here and wait – they'll come back.'

'Why are you so certain?'

'In our haste to explore the place, we forgot about Asher's body.'

'He's definitely dead.'

'His bones should still be where I killed him.'

'Perhaps the wind . . .'

'No, his friends have taken him away. They're lying in wait for us, hoping for revenge.'

'Have we fallen into a trap?'

'Lookouts saw us arrive.'

'Supposing we hadn't come back?'

'That was unlikely. They'd have stayed at their posts for a long time – for several years, if need be – as long as they weren't sure we were dead. Wouldn't you have done the same in their place? Identifying us is vital; killing us will be a pleasure.'

'We'll fight them.'

'As long as they give us time to prepare our defence. They've even taken my old bow – they'd be delighted to shoot me with my own arrows.'

161

The two of them left the cave and returned to their companions.

Naked to the waist, her magnificent, firm breasts bare to the sun, Panther addressed the faithful. She explained to them that sand-travellers had looted the golden goddess's shrine and stolen her possessions. A fight looked inevitable, and she was entrusting Suti with the task of leading them to victory.

No one protested, not even the old warrior. He felt rejuvenated at the thought of making the sand drink the sand-travellers' blood: the Nubians would demonstrate their prowess – no one could match them in hand-to-hand fighting.

Although he agreed with that assessment, Suti had the Nubians create a well-entrenched camp, using big stones and rocks behind which their archers would shelter. In the cave, they stored their full water-skins, food and weapons. Some distance from their position, they dug holes, equal distances apart.

Then the days of waiting began.

Because of the heat, according to the custom which Nubians and Egyptians shared outside towns, they lived naked. Panther never tired of admiring her lover's splendid body, and he responded in kind; their bronzed skin took no harm from the sun, which only intensified their desire. Each day, Panther wore different jewellery; gold emphasized the curves of her body, and made her inaccessible to anyone but Suti.

Suti enjoyed the lull. Sitting cross-legged, at one with the rocks and sand, he listened to the desert's secret songs, to its invisible movements and to the wind's words; he hardly noticed the heat. He feared the clash of weapons much less than the noise and bustle of the city; here, even the smallest action must be in harmony with silence, bearer of the nomads' steps.

Although Pazair had abandoned him, he would have liked to have his friend beside him, to share the moment when his wandering would come to an end. Without saying a word, they would have fed upon the same fire, their gaze lost in the ochre-coloured horizon, the devourer of all things ephemeral.

Catlike, Panther came up behind him and put her arms round him. As softly as a spring breeze, she caressed the nape of his neck.

'Supposing you're wrong?' she said.

'There's no chance of that.'

'Perhaps the looters will be satisfied with stealing our gold.'

'We disrupted their smuggling operation. Getting the gold back won't be enough: they must find out who we are.'

'If the Libyans are allied to the sand-travellers, will you fight them?'

'I shall kill the thieves whoever they are.'

Their kiss was worthy of the immense open spaces, their interlaced bodies rolled in the soft sand as it drifted in the northerly breeze.

The old warrior told Suti that the man sent to fetch water had not come back.

'When did he leave?' asked Suti.

'When the sun leapt above the cave. Judging by its position in the sky now, he should have got back long ago.'

'Perhaps the spring had dried up.'

'No, it would have supplied us for several weeks.'

'Do you trust him?'

'He was my cousin.'

'He might have been attacked by a lion.'

The old man shook his head. 'The wild animals drink at night, and in any case he knew how to avoid being attacked.'

'Shall we go and look for him?

'If he isn't back by sunset, it means he's dead.'

The hours went by. The Nubians no longer talked or sang. Motionless, they stared along the track that led to the spring, the direction from which where their comrade ought to have appeared.

The day-star sank low in the sky, entered the Peak of the West and descended into the ship of night. It would sail across the subterranean spaces, where it would confront the enormous dragon that would try to drink the water of the universe and dry up the Nile.

The track remained empty.

'He is dead,' declared the old warrior.

Suti doubled the guard. Perhaps the attackers would approach the cave. If they were sand-travellers, they wouldn't hesitate to break the rules of war and launch a night attack.

Sitting facing the desert, he wondered without grief if he was living his last hours. If so, would they be imbued with the peaceful gravity of the immemorial rocks, or with the fury of a last battle? He lay down and prepared to sleep.

Panther came and lay down beside him. 'Do you feel ready?'

'As ready as you are.'

'Don't try to die without me – we'll step through the gateway of the afterlife together. But before then we shall be rich and live like kings. If you really want it, we'll succeed. Be a true leader, Suti, and don't waste your energy.'

As he did not answer, she respected his silence and joined him in sleep.

The cold air woke Suti. The desert was grey, the morning light dimmed by thick mist.

Panther opened her eyes and shivered. 'Warm me up.'

He held her to him, but suddenly drew away, his eyes fixed on a point in the distance.

'To your posts,' he shouted to the Nubians.

Dozens of armed men and chariots were emerging out of the mist.

25

The sand-travellers stuck close together. With their straggly hair, unkempt beards, turbans, and long robes with coloured stripes, they did not look impressive. Some of them were starving and had jutting collarbones, hollow shoulders and staring ribs; they carried rolled-up mats on their bent backs.

As one, they drew their bows and let fly a first volley of arrows, but hit no one. When there was no response – Suti had given the order not to return fire – the sand-travellers took heart. Shouting loudly, they came nearer.

The Nubian archers showed that they deserved their reputation: not one missed his target. Moreover, their firing rhythm was rapid and sustained, and, although outnumbered ten to one, they quickly redressed the balance.

The surviving sand-travellers retreated to make way for light chariots, whose platforms were made of criss-crossed leather strips and which were covered with hyena-skin; the outside panels were decorated with the aggressive figure of a horse-god. In each chariot, one man drove the horses, while a second brandished a javelin. All the men had goatee beards and coppery skin.

'They're Libyans,' observed Suti.

'That's impossible!' cried Panther, sickened.

'Libyans allied to sand-travellers: remember your promise.'

'I'll talk to them – they won't attack me.'

'Don't deceive yourself.

'At least let me try.'

'It isn't worth the risk.'

The horses were pawing the ground. Each javelin-thrower raised his shield to chest height; once within range of their opponents, they would throw their weapons.

Panther stood up and left her shelter. She picked her way through the rocks, and took a few steps across the flat expanse that separated her from the chariots.

'Lie down!' roared Suti.

A javelin was hurled, powerfully and accurately.

Before the Libyan had even finished his throw, Suti's arrow pierced his throat. Flinging herself aside, Panther avoided the lethal javelin. She crawled back towards the rocks.

The Libyans charged forward, while the Nubians, enraged by the attack on their golden goddess, fired arrow after arrow.

Too late, the charioteers saw the holes the Nubians had dug in the sand, and tried to swerve. A few avoided them, but most did not: some overturned, wheels came apart, chariot-shells broke, and their occupants were thrown to the ground. The Nubians charged at them and gave no quarter; they brought back horses and javelins from the field of battle.

When the attackers withdrew, Suti had lost only three men and had inflicted heavy losses on the enemy. The Nubians acclaimed their golden goddess, and the old warrior composed a song to her glory. Despite the lack of palm-wine, the men were drunk on victory; Suti had to shout himself hoarse to stop them leaving their positions. Every man wanted to wipe out the remainder of the enemy single-handed.

A red-painted chariot emerged from a cloud of dust. An unarmed man got out, his arms hanging loosely at his sides. He was haughty, with a curiously large, square head, out of proportion to his body. His harsh voice carried a long way.

'I want to speak to your leader.'

Suti stood up and showed himself. 'Here I am.'

'What is your name?'

'What is yours?'

'They call me Adafi.'

'And I am Suti, an officer of the Egyptian army.'

'Let us move closer together. Shouting is not conducive to a constructive conversation.'

The two men advanced towards each other.

'So,' said Suti, 'you are Adafi, Egypt's sworn enemy, the conspirator, the troublemaker.'

'And it was you who killed my friend General Asher.'

'I had that honour, though the traitor's death was too easy.'

'An Egyptian officer leading a band of Nubian rebels. Doesn't that make you a traitor, too?'

'You stole my gold.'

'It belonged to me. It was the price agreed with the general for his peaceful retirement in my lands.'

'That treasure is mine.'

'By what right?'

'War booty.'

Adafi smiled grimly. 'You aren't timid, are you, young man?'

'I demand what is due to me.'

'What do you know of my dealings with the miners?'

'Your gang was wiped out and you have no support inside Egypt. You'd better withdraw as quickly as possible and hide in some far corner of your barbarous country. Perhaps Pharaoh's anger won't reach you there.'

'If you want your gold, you'll have to earn it.'

'Is it here?'

'It's in my tent. Since you killed Asher, whose bones I buried, why don't we become friends? To seal the pact, I offer you half the gold.'

'I want all of it.'

'You're too greedy.'

167

'You've already lost a lot of men,' Suti pointed out. 'My warriors are better than yours.'

'That may be true, but I know where your traps are now, and there are more of us.'

'My Nubians will fight to the last man.'

'Who is the woman?'

'Their golden goddess. Because of her, they fear nothing and no one.'

'My sword will soon cut off the head of that superstition.'

'If you live.'

'Unless you join me, I'll kill you.'

'You won't escape, Adafi. You'll be the most notable of my trophies.'

'Pride has turned your head.'

'If you want to spare the lives of your troops, fight me in single combat.'

The Libyan stared at Suti. 'Against me, you don't stand a chance.'

'I'll be the judge of that.'

'You're very young to die.'

'If I win, I shall take back the gold.'

'And if you lose?'

'You can take mine.'

'Yours? What do you mean?'

'My Nubians are carrying a lot of it.'

'You've taken over the general's smuggling ring, have you?'

Suti said nothing.

'You'll die,' prophesied Adafi, his broad forehead furrowed.

'What weapons shall we use?'

'Each unto his own.'

'I demand that a pact is signed, and approved by both camps.'

'The gods will bear witness.'

The ceremony was organized straight away. Three Libyans

and three Nubians, including the old warrior, took part. They called upon the spirits of fire, air, water and earth to destroy either man if he committed perjury, then agreed upon a night's rest before the duel.

Near the cave, the Nubians formed a circle round the golden goddess. They implored her protection and begged her to grant victory to their hero. Using crumbling stones, which left red marks on the skin, they decorated Suti's body with signs of war.

'Don't let us be turned into slaves,' they besought him.

The Egyptian sat down facing the sun, deriving from the desert light the strength of the giants of yore, who could move huge granite blocks to build temples in which the Invisible was embodied. Though he had rejected the way of scribes and priests, Suti still felt the presence of a hidden energy in both sky and ground; he absorbed it as he breathed, channelled it as he concentrated on the goal that must be attained.

Panther knelt beside him. 'This is mad,' she said. 'Adafi has never been beaten in single combat.'

'What's his favourite weapon?'

'The javelin.'

'My arrows will fly faster.'

'I don't want to lose you.'

'As you want to be very rich, I've got to take risks. Believe me, there was no alternative. Seeing those Nubians slaughtered sickened me.'

'Does the thought of my being widowed leave you unmoved?'

Suti smiled. 'You're the golden goddess. You'll protect me.'

'When Adafi has killed you, I shall stab him in the belly with my dagger.'

'Then your countrymen will kill you.'

'The Nubians will defend me – and it'll be the massacre you dread.'

'Unless I win.'

'I shall bury you in the desert and then go and burn Tapeni alive.'

'Will you give me permission to light the pyre?'

'I love you when you dream. I love you because you dream.'

The mist had covered the desert again, smothering the dawn light. Suti walked forward; the sand squeaked under his bare feet. In his right hand he carried a medium-range bow, the best he had, and in his left a single arrow: he would not have time to fire another.

Adafi had the reputation of being an invincible fighter, whom no opponent had even come close to beating. As elusive as the mist, he had evaded a number of military forces sent to catch him. His favoured form of action was arming rebels and looters so as to maintain instability in the western provinces of the Delta. His abiding dream was of reigning over the North of Egypt.

Rays of sunlight pierced the grey mist. Very dignified in his red and green robe, his hair hidden by a black turban, Adafi took up position fifty paces from his opponent.

Suti knew he had lost.

Adafi was wielding not a javelin but Suti's own favourite acacia-wood bow, the one he had hidden in the cave. It was of exceptional quality, and could fire an arrow more than seventy paces in a direct shot. The one Suti was using seemed pathetic by comparison. Its accuracy was unpredictable, and it wouldn't enable him to kill the Libyan, only to wound him at most. If he tried to go any nearer, Adafi would fire first, giving Suti no chance to respond.

The Libyan's face had changed: hard and closed, it no longer showed the slightest trace of humanity. Adafi wanted to kill: his entire being embodied death. His eyes were cold, and he was waiting for his victim to start trembling.

170

Suti suddenly realized why the Libyan always emerged victorious from his duels. Flat on his belly behind a small mound of rocks on the left, a Libyan archer was protecting Adafi. Would the archer shoot before his master? Were they coordinating their efforts?

Suti cursed himself for his stupidity. An open, honest fight, respect for a man's word . . . Adafi hadn't wasted a moment's thought on that. The young Egyptian's first instructor had taught him that sand-travellers and Libyans often stabbed you in the back. Forgetting that warning might well have cost him his life.

Adafi, Suti and the Libyan archer all drew their bows at the same moment. Suti did so progressively, increasing the tension little by little. His behaviour amused Adafi, who had assumed that Suti would first try to kill the man to his left, then fire another arrow at Adafi. But he was armed with only one arrow.

Out of the corner of his eye, Suti saw something which was as quick as it was brutal. Panther snaked out of the rocks behind the archer and cut his throat. Adafi saw, too, and aimed his arrow at Panther, who flattened herself in the sand. Suti took advantage of that mistake, drew the bowstring as far as it would go, put his soul into the arrow and fired.

Aware of having made a mistake, Adafi hurried his shot, and his arrow merely grazed Suti's cheek. The Egyptian's plunged into Adafi's right eye. He dropped to the ground, face down, stone dead.

While the Nubians shouted with joy, Suti cut off the defeated man's right hand and brandished his bow at the heavens.

The sand-travellers and the Libyans laid down their arms and prostrated themselves before the embracing couple of Suti and Panther.

The golden goddess was radiant with happiness. Rich,

happy, an army at her feet, Libyan soldiers forced to obey her: her wildest dreams were coming true.

'You are free to leave or to submit to me,' Suti told the Libyans. 'If you follow me you'll have a lot of gold, but at the first sign of disobedience I'll kill you with my own hands.'

No one moved. The promised reward would have seduced even the most suspicious of men.

Suti examined the chariots and the horses, and was well satisfied with what he found. With a few well-trained charioteers, and Nubian archers who were better than any rival, he had an effective, unified army at his disposal.

'You are the master of gold,' said Panther joyfully.

'You saved my life again.'

'I've told you before: without me, you won't achieve anything great.'

Suti distributed a first payment, which dispelled any lingering hostility towards him. The Libyans offered the Nubians palm-wine, and their fraternization took the form of a drinking-session punctuated by songs and laughter. Their new chief went off on his own, preferring the silence of the desert.

After a while, Panther joined him. 'Have you forgotten me, in your dream?'

'Of course not. You're the one who inspires me.'

'You have done Egypt an enormous service by killing Adafi and eliminating one of her most tenacious enemies.'

'What am I to do with this victory?'

26

Patchily shaven, and dressed in a shabby kilt and worn-out sandals, Pazair walked through the great market at Memphis, mingling with the crowd – there was no better way of finding out what people were thinking. He noted with satisfaction that all the usual produce was on sale. Boats were circulating freely on the Nile, and food was being delivered regularly. A recent check on the ports and on the artificial lakes, where boats were overhauled twice a year, had shown that the trading-fleet was in an excellent condition.

Pazair noted that bartering was proceeding well, and that exchanges were taking place normally. Prices were under control, and did not penalize the poor. Among the traders were many women who held respected and coveted positions. When barter went on a long time, water-bearers offered the participants a drink. 'I'm very happy with that,' exclaimed a peasant, pleased to have acquired a pitcher in exchange for some juicy figs.

People gathered in curiosity around a magnificent piece of linen which two cloth-merchants were unfolding.

'What a beautiful piece of material,' commented a prosperous-looking woman.

'That's why it's expensive,' said the clothmaker.

'Since the new tjaty was appointed, unseasonal price rises are frowned upon.'

'So much the better. People will come to the market more often and buy better quality. If you take this linen, I'll throw in a scarf.'

While the transaction was being concluded, Pazair moved to another stall, that of a man selling sandals, which hung by strings from a wooden bar supported by two small uprights.

'You'd do well to buy a new pair of shoes, my lad,' commented the seller. 'You've walked too far in the ones you're wearing, and the soles will soon give way.'

'I can't afford it.'

'You have an honest face. I'll give you credit.'

'That's against my principles.'

'The man who has no debts gets rich! All right, I'll mend yours very cheaply.'

Feeling hungry, Pazair ate a honey-cake, while listening to a conversation about preparing the next meal. There was no anxiety in people's words, and no one was contesting the tjaty's actions. And yet Pazair was far from reassured: the name of Ramses was almost never uttered.

Pazair went over to a woman selling ointments, and began haggling over a small phial.

'It's rather expensive,' he said.

'Are you from the city?'

'No, the country, but the stories I heard about Memphis made me want to see it. Ramses has made it the most beautiful city in the world. I'd love to see him. When will he come out of his palace?'

'No one knows. People say he is ill and living at Pi-Ramses, in the Delta.'

'What, Ramses? But he's the healthiest man in Egypt.'

'People are whispering that his magical power is exhausted.'

'Then let it be regenerated.'

'If that's still possible,' said the seller.

'If it isn't there'll have to be a new king.'

174

The seller shrugged.

'Who will succeed Ramses?' asked Pazair.

'Who knows?'

Suddenly, shouts rang out. The crowd scattered, opening a way for Killer, who in a few bounds was at Pazair's feet. Thinking she was dealing with a thief and that the baboon was going to arrest him, the seller immediately put a rope round the delinquent's neck to stop him getting away. For once, Killer did not bite his victim in the leg, but merely sat in front of her until Kem arrived.

'I arrested him myself!' boasted the seller. 'Am I entitled to a reward?'

'We'll see,' replied Kem, leading Pazair away.

'You look angry,' said the tjaty.

'Why didn't you warn me you were coming here? You've been extremely rash.'

'No one would have recognized me.'

'Killer found you easily.'

'I needed to listen to people.'

'And did you learn any more?'

'The situation is not heartening: Bel-Tran is preparing people for the fall of Ramses.'

Neferet was late, despite the importance of the meeting of the doctors' council over which she was to preside. A few people grumbled, accusing her of taking her job lightly, but she had in fact been giving emergency treatment to Mischief, who was suffering from indigestion, Brave, who had coughing spasms, and Way-Finder, who had scorched his foot. Taking care of the household's three good spirits seemed to her to be a priority.

The assembled dignitaries all stood up when she entered, and bowed to her. Neferet's beauty instantly dispelled all criticism; when she spoke, her voice acted like a soothing balm, and the old doctors never tired of that remedy.

Neferet was very surprised to find Bel-Tran present.

'The government has asked me to be the economic spokesman,' he explained. 'Today measures are to be adopted concerning the people's health. I must be sure those measures don't unbalance the state's resources, for which I am responsible to the tjaty.'

The Double White House was usually content to send a delegate. The direct intervention of the director signalled a battle for which Neferet was not prepared.

'I am not satisfied with the number of hospitals in the provincial capitals and the small towns. I propose that ten establishments are created, on the model of the one in Memphis.'

'Objection,' cut in Bel-Tran. 'The cost would be enormous.'

'The provincial governors will finance their construction; the Health secretariat will provide them with skilled doctors and ensure their proper running. We shall not require assistance from the Double White House.'

'It will affect taxes.'

'According to Pharaoh's decree, the governors have a choice: either to pay taxes to your ministry, or to improve health provision. They have chosen the second solution, on my advice, and have done so perfectly legally. We shall continue next year, I hope.'

Bel-Tran was obliged to give way. He had not expected Neferet to act so quickly and skilfully. She was quietly creating solid bonds with local officials.

She said, 'According to the *Book of Protection*, which dates from the times of the founding ancestors, Egypt must not neglect any of her children: it is up to us, as doctors, to heal those who suffer. At the start of his reign, Ramses promised a happy life to the young generations, and for everyone health is an essential element of that happiness. I have therefore decided to train more doctors and nurses, so that everyone, irrespective of where they live, may benefit from the best treatment.'

'I should like to see a change in the medical order,' said Bel-Tran. 'We ought to give much more importance to specialists and much less to ordinary doctors. When Egypt is opened up to the outside world, as she soon will be, not only will the specialists soon grow rich, but we'll be able to profit greatly from sending them to work abroad.'

'So long as I am principal doctor,' declared Neferet, 'we shall follow tradition. If the specialists are given too much power, medicine will lose sight of the most important thing of all: the human being as a whole, the harmony of mind and body.'

'Unless you accept my proposal, the Double White House will actively oppose you.'

'Is this a case of blackmail?'

Bel-Tran stood up and addressed the assembly imperiously. 'Egyptian medicine is the best in the world – many foreign doctors spend time with us to learn the elements of it. But we must reform our methods, and make more profits from this resource. Your skill and learning deserve better, believe me! Let us produce many more remedies, and use the drugs and poisons whose secrets we know. Above all, let us concern ourselves with quantity. That is the future.'

'We reject it,' said Neferet.

'You are wrong. I came here to warn you, you and your colleagues, in a friendly manner. Refusing my help would be a disastrous mistake.'

'Accepting it would mean destroying our vocation.'

'A vocation is not something which can make us money.'

'Neither is health.'

'You're wrong, just like the tjaty. Defending the past will lead nowhere.'

'I cannot cure the disease from which you suffer.'

*

Bagey had come to consult Neferet because of unbearable pains in his kidneys and blood in his urine. After examining him for more than an hour, she diagnosed the presence of parasites in his blood, and prescribed a preparation made from pine-kernel seeds, grasses, henbane, honey and Nubian earth,* to be taken each evening before retiring. She reassured her patient that the treatment would be highly effective.

'My body is wearing out,' lamented Bagey.

'You're stronger than you think.'

'My hardiness is failing.'

'It's the infection making you feel weak. I promise you'll soon feel better, and will enjoy many more years of good health.'

'How is your husband?' asked Bagey.

'He'd like to see you again.'

Pazair and Bagey walked in the shade of the tall trees in the garden. Pleased with this unexpected walk, Brave accompanied them, sniffing at the flowerbeds as he passed.

'Bel-Tran is attacking on all fronts,' said Pazair, 'but I'm managing to slow him down.'

'Have you gained the trust of the main government officials?'

'Some of them agree with me and distrust him. Fortunately, his brutality and over-obvious ambition have bothered certain people's consciences. Many scribes are faithful to the ancient wisdom that created this country.'

'I sense that you're calmer, more sure of yourself.'

'I only seem that way. Every day is like a battle, and I cannot predict where the next attack will come from. I wish I had your long experience.'

---

*Two unidentified ingredients, the plant *shames* and the fruit *shasha*, were also added.

'Don't deceive yourself. I no longer had the strength for the fight. Pharaoh was right to choose you. Bel-Tran realizes that now: he wasn't expecting such strong resistance on your part.'

Pazair shook his head. 'How can anyone be treacherous as that?'

'Human nature is capable of the worst things imaginable.'

'Sometimes I lose heart. The small victories I win cannot hold back the passage of time. Spring has begun, and people are already talking of the next flood.'

'What does Ramses say?'

'He urges me to keep working. By yielding not a cubit of ground to Bel-Tran, I get the impression that his deadline is being delayed.'

'You've even conquered part of his territory.'

'That is the only thing that gives me hope. By weakening him, perhaps I shall make him begin to doubt himself. If he tried to seize power without enough support, he'd fail. But is there enough time left for me break down the pillars on which his scheme rests?'

'The people like you, Pazair – they fear you, but they like you. You carry out your duties impeccably, in accordance with the duties the king indicated to you. Coming from me, this is not flattery.'

'Bel-Tran would gladly buy my services! When I think back over his demonstrations of friendship, I wonder if he was sincere for a single moment, or if he was playing a part from the very first second, in the hope of including me in his plot.'

'Why should hypocrisy have limits?'

'You have no illusions, have you?'

'I eschew fervour: it is futile and dangerous.'

'I'd like to show you some documents concerning the land registry and surveys. Would you be kind enough to check whether some of the information has been altered?'

'Gladly, particularly as it falls within my original speciality. What are you worried about?'

'That Bel-Tran and his allies are trying to steal land legally.'

The evening was so beautiful and so mild that Pazair allowed himself a brief rest beside the pool in his garden. Sitting on the edge, her feet in the water, the faintest line of green kohl on her eyelids, Neferet was playing a lute whose strings, tuned in unison, were knotted at the base of the neck. Its gentle, mellow tone delighted him, and the melody harmonized with the quiver of the leaves as the northerly breeze stirred them.

Pazair thought of Suti, who would have loved this music. Where was he wandering, and what dangers was he facing? The tjaty was banking on his heroism to wipe away his faults, but he would come up against the ferocity of the lady Tapeni. According to Kem, she was spending less and less time in the weaving-workshop and was running all over the city. How would she try to harm him?

The voice of the lute soothed his anxieties. Eyes closed, Pazair gave himself up himself to the magic of the music.

The shadow-eater decided to act.

There was only one possible observation post near the tjaty's home, a tall date-palm set in the middle of the court-yard of a small house which belonged to a retired couple. The murderer had got inside, knocked them out, then climbed to the top of the tree, armed with his weapon.

Luck was smiling on him. As he had hoped, this beautiful evening, when the declining sun caressed the skin, the tjaty had come home earlier than usual and was relaxing with his wife, in a clear, unobstructed area.

The shadow-eater gripped a curved throwing-stick of the kind used by bird-hunters. Killer was perched on the roof of the tjaty's house, and so would not have time to take action.

The throwing-stick, a fearsome weapon when handled skilfully, would break Pazair's neck.

The criminal found himself a stable position, holding on to a branch with his left hand; he concentrated, and worked out the trajectory. Although the distance was considerable, he would not miss: with this weapon he had, from a very young age, displayed exceptional ability. Shattering birds' skulls amused him enormously.

Mischief was constantly on the alert, ready to gather any fruit that fell from the tree, or to play with the first blackbird on the date-palm. When the shadow-eater's arm drew back, she gave a cry of alarm.

Killer reacted with lightning speed. In a split second, he understood the monkey's call, saw the throwing-stick cleave the air, identified its target and hurled himself from the roof in a prodigious leap. He caught the weapon in mid-air, and landed a few paces from the tjaty.

Stunned, Neferet dropped her lute. Brave, who had been dozing, awoke with a start and jumped on to his master's lap.

His body spear-straight, one bloodstained paw firmly holding the throwing-stick, Killer gazed proudly at Egypt's first minister, whom he had just, once again, saved from the jaws of death.

The shadow-eater was already running away down an alley, his mind in turmoil. What god inhabited the soul of that baboon? For the first time in his career, the murderer doubted his own abilities. Pazair was not a man like other men; a supernatural force seemed to protect him. Could it be that the goddess Ma'at, the tjaty's justice, was making him invulnerable?

27

Killer allowed himself to be cosseted. Neferet washed his paw with copper-water, cleaned the wound, and bandaged it. Although she had seen it before, Killer's strength astonished her: despite the heaviness of his fall, the wound was not deep and would quickly scar over. Hardened to pain, he would need only one or two days of relative rest, and would not even stop patrolling.

'It's a fine weapon,' said Kem as he examined the throwing-stick, 'and perhaps the start of a new lead. The shadow-eater was kind enough to leave us an interesting clue. It's a pity you didn't see him.'

'I didn't even have time to be afraid,' confessed Pazair. 'If Mischief hadn't cried out . . .'

The monkey dared approach the enormous baboon and touched him on the nose; Killer did not move a muscle. Growing bolder, Mischief laid her tiny paw on his huge thigh. His gaze seemed to soften.

'I've doubled the guard around your estate,' said Kem, 'and I shall question the makers of throwing-sticks myself. At last we have a chance of identifying the murderer.'

A fierce quarrel had set Silkis against Bel-Tran. Although Bel-Tran admired his son, who was his designated heir, he intended to be master in his own home. But Silkis refused to discipline the little boy, and still less to discipline their daughter, whose lies and insults she accepted without a murmur.

When her husband criticized her for this, Silkis flew into a rage. Losing her temper, she ripped up lengths of costly fabric, smashed a valuable chest and trampled on expensive gowns. Before leaving for his office, Bel-Tran uttered the terrifying words: 'You are mad.'

Mad . . . the word frightened her. She was a normal woman, in love with her husband, the devoted slave of a rich man, and an attentive mother. By taking part in the conspiracy, by distracting the Sphinx's guard commander with her nakedness, she had obeyed Bel-Tran, trusting in his destiny. Before long, he and she would reign over Egypt.

But ghosts haunted her. By letting herself be raped by the shadow-eater, she had plunged into dark shadows which had not melted away. The crimes to which she was party troubled her less than that wantonness, that source of disturbing pleasure. And then there was the break with Neferet . . . Was it madness, falsehood or perversion to want to remain her friend?

Nightmare succeeded nightmare, sleepless night followed sleepless night.

Only one man could save her: the dream-interpreter. He charged exorbitant fees, but he would listen to her and guide her.

Silkis told her maid to bring a veil, to hide her face.

The servant began to cry.

'What's the matter?' asked Silkis.

'Oh, my lady, something terrible's happened. It's dead.'

'What is?'

'Come and see.'

The aloe, a superb shrub crowned with orange, yellow and red flowers, was no more than a dried-up stalk. Not only was it a rare specimen, a gift from Bel-Tran, but also it had produced remedies which Silkis used every day. Oil of aloe, applied to the genitals, prevented inflammation and favoured bodily union. In addition, when applied to the red patches on Bel-Tran's leg, it reduced the itching.

Silkis felt bereft, and the sight of it brought on an atrocious headache. Soon she, too, would wither, like the aloe.

The room where the Syrian dream-interpreter saw his clients was painted black and kept dark to soothe his clientele, which consisted solely of rich noble ladies. Instead of becoming a workman or a trader, he had studied grimoires and keys to dreams, determined to calm the anxieties of a few idle women in exchange for a well-deserved reward. The fish were not easy to catch in a happy, free society, but once in his net they never got out again. To be effective, the treatment must be of unlimited duration. Once that principle had been accepted, all he had to do was interpret his patients' fantasies, more or less roughly. They were unbalanced when they arrived, and unbalanced when they left; but at least he settled them in their madness, be it slight or otherwise, and made a lot of money. Up to now, his only problem had been avoiding the close attention of the taxation scribes, so he paid heavy taxes in order to carry on his activities without trouble. But the appointment of Neferet as Egypt's principal doctor worried him: according to reliable people, she could not be bought and showed no lenience to charlatans like him.

When she arrived, Silkis lay down on a mat, closed her eyes, and prepared to answer his questions.

'Have you had any dreams lately?' he asked.

'I had a horrible one. I was holding a dagger and plunging it into the neck of a bull.'

'What happened?'

'My blade broke, and the bull turned on me and trampled me underfoot.'

'Are your relations with your husband . . . satisfactory?'

'His work takes all his energy. At night he's so tired that

he falls asleep straight away. And when he does have time for lovemaking, he's always in a hurry – too much of a hurry.'

'You must tell me everything, Lady Silkis.'

'Yes, yes, I understand.'

'Have you ever in fact wielded a dagger?'

'No.'

'Or anything like that?'

'No, I don't think so.'

'A needle?'

'A needle, yes.'

'A mother-of-pearl needle?'

'Yes, of course. I can weave, and that's my favourite tool.'

'Have you ever used it to attack someone?'

'No, I swear I haven't.'

'A middle-aged man . . . He turns his back on you, you approach soundlessly and plunge the needle into his neck.'

Silkis howled, bit her fingers, and twisted and turned on the mat. Alarmed, the dream-interpreter was on the point of calling for help, but the attack of dementia subsided and Silkis sat up, dripping with sweat.

'I didn't kill anyone,' she declared in a hoarse, hallucinatory voice. 'I didn't have the courage. But if Bel-Tran ever asks me to, I will. To keep him, I'll do it.'

'You are cured, Lady Silkis.'

'What . . . what are you saying?'

'You no longer need my care.'

The donkeys were loaded and ready to leave for the port when Kem approached the dream-interpreter.

'You've finished packing, have you?'

'The boat's waiting for me. I'm going to Greece, where I won't be given any trouble.'

'A wise decision.'

'I have your promise: the trade-control officers won't stop me?'

'That will depend on your goodwill.'

'I questioned the lady Silkis, as you asked me to.'

'Did you ask her the right questions?'

'I didn't understand, but I obeyed you.'

'And what was the result?'

'She didn't kill anyone.'

'Are you absolutely certain of that?'

'Absolutely. I may be a charlatan, but I know that type of woman. If you'd seen her in her delirium, you'd know she wasn't play-acting.'

'Forget all about her – and about Egypt.'

Tapeni was on the verge of tears. Opposite her, in front of a low table covered with unrolled papyri, sat an angry Bel-Tran.

'I've asked everyone in Memphis, I promise you,' she said.

'That makes your failure all the more bitter, dear friend.'

'Pazair is faithful to his wife, he doesn't gamble, has no debts, and isn't involved in anything illegal. It's insane, but the man is irreproachable.'

'I warned you: he is the tjaty.'

'Tjaty or not, I thought that . . .'

'Your greed distorts your thinking, Tapeni. Egypt remains a land apart, whose judges, particularly the most senior ones, adopt honesty as a way of life. It is ridiculous and outdated, I agree, but one must take account of reality. Pazair believes in his office and fulfils it with passion.'

The pretty brunette was nervous, and unsure what to do. 'I was wrong about him.'

'I don't like people who fail. When you work for me, you succeed.'

'If he has a weakness, I'll find it.'

'And what if he hasn't?'

'Then . . . he must be given one – without his knowledge.'

'That's an excellent idea. What do you suggest?'

'I'll have to think. I might—'

'It is all thought out already. I have a simple plan, based on the trade in very special items. Will you still help me?'

'I am at your disposal.'

Bel-Tran gave his instructions. Tapeni's failure had confirmed him in his hatred of women: how right the Greeks were to consider them inferior to men. Egypt granted them too much status. An incompetent like Tapeni would end up becoming an encumbrance. It would be as well to get rid of her as soon as possible, at the same time demonstrating to Pazair that his famous justice was powerless.

In the open-air workshop, five men were hard at work. From acacia-wood, sycamore and tamarisk, they were making throwing-sticks, some stronger than others, some more expensive.

Kem was questioning the owner, a squat, heavy-faced fifty-year-old.

'Who are your customers?'

'Bird-catchers and hunters. Does that interest you?'

'Very much.'

'Why?'

'Have you committed any crimes?'

A workman whispered a few words in the owner's ear.

'The commander of the guards in my workshop! Are you looking for someone?'

'Did you make this throwing-stick?'

The owner examined the weapon intended to kill Pazair. 'It's fine work, very good quality. With this, you can hit a target a long way away.'

'Answer my question.'

'No, it wasn't me.'

'Which workshops are capable of making it?'

'I don't know.'

'I find that surprising.'

'Sorry, I can't help you. Another time, perhaps.'

When Kem turned and left the workshop without another word, the owner was much relieved. The commander wasn't as determined as people claimed.

When he shut the workshop at nightfall, he changed his opinion.

The Nubian's huge hand came down on his shoulder. 'You lied to me.'

'No I didn't, I—'

'Don't lie again. Do you not know that I am more savage than my baboon?'

'My workshop's doing well, I have good workers . . . Why are you victimizing me?'

'Tell me about this throwing-stick.'

'All right, I made it.'

'And who bought it?'

'No one. It was stolen.'

'When?'

'The day before yesterday.'

'Why didn't you tell me the truth earlier?'

'When I saw it in your hand, I was afraid it might have been used in some rather dubious affair. Wouldn't you have kept quiet in my place?'

'You've no idea of the thief's identity?'

'None at all. A valuable stick like that . . . I'd very much like to have it back.'

'You'll have to make do with my lenience.'

The trail leading to the shadow-eater had been cut off.

Neferet took charge of difficult cases and carried out delicate operations. Despite her position and her heavy administrative burden, she never refused to help in emergencies.

She was surprised when Sababu came to see her at the hospital, because all Sababu suffered from was rheumatism. Neferet had cured Sababu of an inflamed shoulder which had threatened to cost her the use of her arm, and her patient was profoundly grateful.

'Has your rheumatism worsened?' asked Neferet.

'No, the treatment is still working well. I've come knocking on your door for another reason.'

The beautiful Sababu was still fairly young – she admitted to being thirty – and she ran the most famous ale-house in Memphis, staffed with delectable girls, and worked as a much-sought-after prostitute. Skilfully made up, perfumed to just the right side of excess, knowing how to make the most of her looks, she mocked at convention. But she greatly admired the tjaty and his wife: the truth of their marriage, a union which nothing could damage, gave her confidence in a kind of life she herself would never know. Moreover, she had never detected any hostility or contempt in Neferet, only the wish to heal.

Sababu put a porcelain vase on the table in front of Neferet. 'Break it,' she said.

'Really? A fine vase like this?'

'Please break it.'

Neferet smashed the vase on the stone-paved floor. In the middle of the fragments lay a stone phallus and a lapis-lazuli vulva, both covered in Babylonian magical inscriptions.

'I discovered this smuggling by chance,' explained Sababu, 'but I'd have heard about it sooner or later. These sculptures are designed to reawaken desire in tired people, and to make barren women fertile. It's illegal to bring them into Egypt without declaring them. In other vases like this, I found alum, which is said to increase pleasure and combat impotence. I detest such artificial aids – they make love unnatural. Honour Egypt by halting this loathsome trade.'

Despite her activities, Sababu had a certain grandeur.

'Do you know who the smugglers are?' asked Neferet.

'All I know is that the deliveries are made on the western quay at night.'

'I'll see that something is done. Now, tell me, how is your shoulder?'

'I haven't had any more pain.'

'If it comes back, don't hesitate to consult me.'

'What will you do about the smuggling?'

'I shall tell the tjaty about it.'

Waves had formed on the river; they broke on the stones of an abandoned quay, towards which a boat was being rowed. The captain was skilful, and steered the boat gently in to the quay. At once a dozen men ran up, in a hurry to unload the cargo.

Their task was done and they were receiving their pay, in the form of amulets, from a woman when Kem deployed his men and proceeded to make rapid and problem-free arrests. Only the woman struggled and tried to get away.

Kem took a torch from one of his men and held it near her face. 'Lady Tapeni!'

'Let me go.'

'I'm afraid I must lock you up in prison. You are, after all, involved in smuggling.'

'I've got powerful friends – they'll protect me.'

'Who are they?'

'If you don't let me go, you'll regret it.'

'Bring her,' ordered Kem.

Tapeni struggled fiercely, but in vain. 'I take my orders from Bel-Tran.'

As he had hard proof, Pazair made judging the case a priority. Before convening the court, he arranged a confrontation between Tapeni and Bel-Tran.

The pretty brunette was very agitated; as soon as Bel-Tran arrived, she flew at him and demanded, 'Make them set me free, Bel-Tran.'

'If this woman does not calm down,' he said to Pazair, 'I shall leave. Why have I been summoned here?'

'The lady Tapeni accuses you of having employed her in connection with illegal trading.'

'That's ridiculous.'

'What do you mean, ridiculous?' she exclaimed. 'I was to sell those things to important citizens, in order to compromise them.'

'Tjaty, I think the lady Tapeni has lost her reason.'

'Don't use that tone of voice,' she retorted, 'or I'll tell the tjaty everything.'

'As you wish,' said Bel-Tran.

'But that's insane! Do you realize—'

'Your ravings don't interest me.'

'So you're abandoning me, are you? Well, so much the worse for you.' Tapeni turned to the tjaty. 'Among those important people, you were the prime target. What a scandal there'd have been if people had learnt that you and your lovely wife were indulging in distasteful practices. A good way of sullying your reputation, wasn't it? It was Bel-Tran's idea, and he told me to do it.'

'This is mere spiteful rambling,' sneered Bel-Tran.

'It's the truth!'

'Have you even the smallest piece of proof?'

'My word will be enough.'

'No one will doubt that you yourself are the author of this scheme – you were caught red-handed, Lady Tapeni. Your hatred for the tjaty has led you too far. Thanks to the gods, I have suspected you for a long time, and I had the courage to act. I'm proud of having denounced you.'

'Denounced . . .'

'That is correct,' nodded the tjaty. 'Bel-Tran wrote a report warning of your illegal activities. It was sent yesterday to Commander Kem and registered by his scribes.'

'My cooperation with the law is self-evident,' said Bel-Tran. 'I hope the lady Tapeni will be severely punished. Attacking public morality is an abominable crime.'

28

It took Pazair several hours of walking in the countryside, accompanied by Brave and Way-Finder, to calm his anger. Bel-Tran's triumphant smile was an insult to justice, a wound so deep that even Neferet could not heal it.

There was one small consolation: his enemy had lost one of his allies by betraying her. Tapeni had been sentenced to a short period in prison, and stripped of her civic rights. The great beneficiary of this situation was Suti, who, since divorce documents had been drawn up, would not now have to work for his ex-wife. The downfall of the weaver, caught in the trap of her own greed, would give him back his freedom.

The donkey's gentle pace and the dog's happy confidence calmed Pazair's heart, and as he walked the serenity of the countryside and the nobility of the Nile dispelled his distress. At that moment, he would have liked to confront Bel-Tran, man to man, and wring his neck. But that was a childish whim, because Bel-Tran had so arranged mattters that if he were killed it would in no way prevent Ramses' downfall and Egypt's descent into a world where materialism ruled as the absolute master.

How defenceless Pazair felt in the face of such a monster! Usually tjaties, even if they were men of age and experience, did not master their work until two or three years had gone by. Now destiny demanded that young Pazair must save Egypt before the next flood – but without giving him any real weapons to use. Knowing the enemy's identity was not enough. Was it worth continuing to fight, when the battle was lost in advance?

Way-Finder's keen eye and Brave's friendly gaze were decisive encouragements. Divine forces were embodied in the donkey and the dog: bearers of the Invisible, they traced the paths of the heart, outside which no life had meaning. With them, he would defend the cause of Ma'at, the frail and luminous goddess of justice.

Kem was beside himself. 'With all due respect, Tjaty Pazair, I must tell you that your behaviour was absolutely stupid! Alone like that, in the middle of the countryside—'

'I had an escort.'

'Why in Pharaoh's name did you do something so risky?'

'I could no longer bear my office, the administration, the scribes . . . My task is to impose respect for the law, and yet I have to bow before Bel-Tran when he sneers at me, sure of his victory.'

'What has changed, compared to the day of your appointment? You knew all that already.'

Pazair sighed. 'You're right, of course.'

'Instead of feeling sorry for yourself, you ought to be dealing with an worrying affair which has caused turmoil in Abydos province. I'm told that two people have been seriously wounded, and there has been a violent altercation between the priests of the great temple and the emissaries of the state, and a refusal to undertake compulsory work duties – all serious offences. They'll reach your court eventually, but by then it may be too late. I suggest you strike while the iron is hot.'

Spring had brought warmth, at least in the daytime. Though

the nights were still cool and conducive to sleep, the midday sun was beginning to burn, while the harvest was just starting. The tjaty's garden was a glorious display: the flowers rivalled each other in beauty, composing a harmonious blend of red, yellow, blue, violet and orange.

When he ventured into this paradise, immediately after he awoke, Pazair headed towards the lake. As he had assumed, Neferet was having her first bathe. She swam naked, effortlessly, ceaselessly reborn in her own movements. He thought of the moment when he had gazed upon her like this, at that blessed hour when love had united them on this earth and for eternity.

'Isn't the water rather cold?'

'For you, yes – you'd catch a chill.'

'I certainly would not.'

When she emerged from the pool, he wrapped her in a linen sheet and kissed her ardently.

After a moment, she drew back a little and said, 'Bel-Tran won't allow new hospitals to be built in the provinces.'

'It doen't matter. Your file will reach me soon, and, as it's so well put together, I can approve it without fear of being accused of favouritism.'

'Yesterday, he left Memphis for Abydos.'

'Are you sure?'

'I was told by a doctor who met him on the quayside. My colleagues are beginning to realize the danger. They no longer sing Bel-Tran's praises, and some of them even think you ought to distance yourself from him.'

'More minor disturbances have broken out in Abydos. I'm going there this very day.'

Nowhere was more magical than Abydos, the vast Temple of Osiris, where the mysteries of the murdered and reborn god were celebrated by a few initiates, including Pharaoh. Like his father, Seti, Ramses had enlarged and improved the site, and he had granted the priests the use of a vast cultivable estate so that they should not suffer from material worries.

When they reached the landing-stage, it was not the High Priest of Abydos who came forward to greet the tjaty, but Kani, from the temple at Karnak. The two men embraced warmly.

'I dared not hope that you would come,' said Kani.

'Kem told me. Is it really that serious?'

'I'm afraid so, but a long investigation would have been necessary before calling on you. You shall lead it yourself. My colleague at Abydos is ill, and he asked for my help in resisting the unreasonable demands being made of him.'

'What demands?'

'The same as are being made of me and the other priests in charge of the sacred places: that we agree to put the craftsmen employed at the temple at the disposal of the state. Since last month, several provincial governors have improperly requisitioned temple craftsmen and have decreed compulsory work duties, while the large workshops only demand support workers from early autumn, after the start of the flood.'

The octopus was continuing to stretch out its tentacles and defy the tjaty. Fortunately, he had already set off back to Memphis, so Pazair might have a chance to lop off a tentacle or two.

'I was told people have been wounded,' cut in Kem.

'That's right: two peasants who refused to obey the guards' orders. Their family has worked for the temple for a thousand years, so they refuse to be transferred to another estate.'

'Who sent the guards?'

'I don't know. There are rumblings of rebellion, Pazair. The peasants are both free men, and they won't let themselves be moved about like pieces on a gaming-board.'

Fomenting unrest by breaking the laws of work: so that was Bel-Tran had now dreamt up. Choosing Abydos as the

195

first seat of rebellion was a clever idea: the region was considered sacred territory, so its economic and social upheavals would be seen as an example in other areas.

The tjaty would have liked to meditate in the awe-inspiring Temple of Osiris, to which his rank gave him access, but the situation was too urgent for that joy.

He hurried to the nearest village. As soon as they arrived, Kem, in his strong voice, called the villagers to assemble in the main square, near the bread oven. The message spread with surprising speed: the fact that the tjaty himself might address the most humble of citizens seemed like a miracle. People ran up from the fields, the granaries, the gardens, anxious not to miss the event.

Pazair began his speech by celebrating the power of Pharaoh: only he could give life, prosperity and health to his people. Then he reminded them that requisitioning workers was illegal, and would be severely punished, according to the ancient law, which was still in force. The guilty parties would lose their posts, receive two hundred strokes of the rod, would themselves carry out the work they had wanted to assign unjustly, and would then be imprisoned.

These words dispelled the villagers' anxiety and anger. A hundred mouths opened and spoke the name of the troublemaker. He was the stable-master Fekty, 'the Shaven One', owner of a big house beside the Nile and a farm where he bred horses, the liveliest of which were destined for the royal stables. He was authoritarian and brutal, but up to now had been content with his ostentatiously comfortable life, and had not bothered the temple workers.

Five men had just been taken to his property by force.

'I know him,' Kem told Pazair, as the two men, accompanied by Killer, neared Fekty's horse-farm. 'He's the officer who sentenced me for a theft I did not commit, and who cut off my nose.'

'And now you're commander of the security guards.'

'Don't worry, I shan't lose my temper.'

'If he's innocent, I can't authorize you to arrest him.'

'Let's hope he's guilty.'

'You represent force, Kem. Let it remain obedient to the law.'

'Shall we go into the house?'

But leaning against one of the columns of the wooden porch was a man armed with a spear. 'No one may pass.'

'Lower your weapon,' ordered Kem.

'Go away, black man, or I'll disembowel you.'

Killer grabbed the spear, wrenched it out of the man's hands and snapped it in two. The man yelled in panic, and rushed off into the estate. Kem, Killer and Pazair ran after him. Two magnificent horses were being put through their paces, but they were terrified when they saw Killer: they reared, threw their riders and bolted into the countryside.

Several guards armed with daggers and spears emerged from a flat-roofed building and barred the way to the intruders. Killer's red eyes began to grow menacing.

A bald man with a powerful chest pushed them aside and squared up to the trio. 'What is the meaning of this intrusion?'

'Are you Fekty?' asked Pazair.

'Yes, and this estate belongs to me. If you don't leave at once, and take your monster with you, you'll get a good thrashing.'

'Do you know the penalty for attacking the tjaty of Egypt?'

'The tjaty . . . Is that a joke?'

'Bring me a piece of limestone.'

Pazair imprinted his seal upon it, and Fekty sulkily ordered his men to disperse.

'The tjaty here,' said Fekty. 'That doesn't make sense. And that tall black man with you, who is that? But wait . . . I know him. It's him, it really is him!'

197

Fekty turned to run away, but was stopped in his tracks by Killer, who seized him and threw him to the ground.

'Aren't you in the army any more?' asked Kem.

'No. I prefer breeding and training horses. But there's no need to rake up that old story, is there?'

'You're the one who brought it up.'

'I acted in all conscience, you know. Besides, it hasn't stopped you making a career for yourself. You're one of the tjaty's bodyguards, aren't you?'

'I'm commander of Memphis's security guards.'

'You, Kem?'

The Nubian reached out and lifted the sweat-soaked Fekty off his feet. 'Where are you hiding the five artisans you brought here by force?'

'Me? That's slander!'

'Are your men spreading panic by calling themselves security guards?'

'Vicious gossip!'

'We shall make your men face the complainants in court.'

A horrible smile twisted the bald man's mouth out of shape. 'I won't allow it.'

'You are subject to our authority,' Pazair reminded him. 'I consider it is necessary to search your estate – after disarming your men, of course.'

Fekty's men were reluctant to lay down their weapons, but Killer soon encouraged them. Leaping from one to the next, striking a forearm, an elbow or a wrist, he picked up spears and daggers, while Kem made sure that not even the most resentful tried to fight back. The tjaty's presence calmed the men's anger, to the great displeasure of Fekty, who felt betrayed by his own men.

Killer led the tjaty to a grain-store, inside which the five workmen were locked away. They were very talkative when they were freed, and explained that they had been forced, under threats, to restore a wall of the house and repair furniture.

In the presence of the accused, the tjaty himself registered their depositions. Fekty was recognized as guilty of misappropriating public work and of illegal requisitioning.

Kem picked up a heavy stick. 'The tjaty has authorized me to carry out the first part of the sentence.'

'Don't do that!' cried Fekty. 'You'll kill me!'

'It's possible there might be an accident – sometimes I don't know my own strength.'

'What do you want to know?'

'Who put you up to this?'

'No one.'

'You're a very bad liar.' The stick rose.

'No! You're right: I had my orders.'

'From Bel-Tran?'

'What good does it do you to know that? He'll deny it.'

'If that's all you have to say, here are two hundred strokes of the rod in accordance with the law.'

Fekty grovelled at Kem's feet, watched with indifference by Killer. 'If I cooperate, will you take me to prison without beating me?'

'That depends on the tjaty.'

Pazair gave his permission.

'What happened here is nothing,' said Fekty. 'Take a look at the activities of the office that receives foreign workers.'

29

Memphis was dozing under the hot spring sun. In the offices of the secretariat responsible for receiving foreign workers, it was time for the afternoon nap. A dozen or so Greeks, Phoenicians and Syrians were waiting for the scribes to attend to their cases.

When Pazair entered the small room where the foreigners were waiting, they stood up, thinking that here at last was someone in authority; the tjaty did not disabuse them. Interrupting the din and the flood of protests, a young Phoenician appointed himself spokesman.

'We want work,' he said.

'What were you promised?' asked Pazair.

'That we would get it, because all our applications are in order.'

'What is your trade?'

'I'm a good carpenter and I know a workshop ready to take me on.'

'What is it offering you?'

'Beer, bread, dried fish or meat, and vegetables every day; oil, pomade and perfume every ten days; clothes and sandals as and when I need them. Eight days' work and then two days' rest, not counting festivals and legal holidays. No absence without good reason.'

'Those are the conditions that Egyptians accept. Are you satisfied with them?'

'They're much better than in my own country, but I and the others need this office's agreement. Why have we been stuck here for more than a week?'

Pazair questioned the others; they were all in the same position.

'Are you going to give us the authorization?' asked the Phoenician.

'This very day.'

A plump scribe burst into the gathering. 'What's going on here? Kindly sit down and be quiet. Otherwise, as head of this department I shall have you ejected.'

'Your manners are dreadful,' said Pazair.

'And just who may you be?'

'The tjaty of Egypt.'

There was a long silence. The foreigners were torn between hope and fear, while the scribe stared at the seal Pazair set on a scrap of papyrus.

'Forgive me, my lord' he stammered, 'but we were not notified of your visit.'

'Why have you not given these men the authorization they need? Their applications are in order.'

'Overwork, too few staff, the—'

'Nonsense. Before coming here, I examined the workings of your department, and you have all the resources and staff you need. You are well paid, and you pay only one-tenth in tax and receive gratuities you do not have to declare. You have an attractive house, a pleasant garden, a chariot and a boat, and you employ two servants. Am I wrong?'

'No, my lord . . .'

The other scribes had finished their midday meal and came hurrying back to their offices.

'Tell your people to issue the authorizations,' ordered Pazair, 'and come with me.'

The two men went out into the narrow streets of Memphis, where the scribe seemed ill at ease mingling with the common folk.

'Four hours' work in the morning,' said Pazair, 'and four in the afternoon after a long break for your meal. Is that how you are meant to work every day?'

'Indeed.'

'It seems you don't keep to it.'

'We do our best.'

'By doing too little work, and doing it badly, you wrong those who rely on your decisions.'

'That certainly isn't my intention, my lord, I assure you.'

'Nevertheless, the result is deplorable.'

'Oh, my lord, I think you're being rather too severe.'

'On the contrary, I am not being severe enough.'

'Assigning work to foreigners isn't an easy task. They sometimes have a sour disposition, don't speak our language properly, and are slow to adapt to our way of life.'

'I agree, but look around you: a lot of traders and craftsmen are foreigners, or the sons of foreigners, who came to settle here. So long as they respect our laws, they are welcome. I would like to consult your lists.'

The scribe looked most uncomfortable. 'It's a little delicate . . .'

'Why?'

'We are in the middle of reorganizing our files, and it won't be finished for several months. As soon as it's finished, I will notify you.'

'Not good enough. I am in a hurry.'

'But it really is impossible.'

'I shan't be put off by an administrative jumble. Let us go back into your office.' He saw with interest that the scribe's hands began to shake.

The information Pazair had obtained was good, but how could he exploit it? There could be no doubt that the department was involved in widespread illegal activity; but the nature of that activity still had to be determined so that the evil could be rooted out.

The head of the department had not lied: the archives were spread out all over the floors of the oblong rooms in which they were kept. Several scribes were stacking up wooden tablets and numbering papyri.

'When did you begin this task?' asked Pazair.

'Yesterday,' replied the head scribe.

'Who gave you the order?'

The man hesitated, but the tjaty's expression convinced him it would be unwise to lie. 'The Double White House, my lord. According to long-established custom, it wishes to know the names of the immigrants and the nature of their work, in order to set the level of their taxes.'

'Well, then, let us look.'

'My lord, it's impossible, really impossible.'

'That way of thinking reminds me of my early days as a judge in Memphis. You may withdraw. Two volunteers will assist me.'

'My role is to help you, and—'

'Go home. We shall meet again tomorrow.'

Pazair's tone brooked no argument. Two young scribes, employed in the department for a few months, were happy to help the tjaty, who took off his robe and sandals and got down on his knees to sort the documents.

The task seemed insurmountable, but Pazair hoped that chance would grant him a clue, however small, which would set him on the right track.

'It's strange,' remarked the younger scribe. 'Under the old department head, Sechem, we wouldn't have had to do things in such a rush.'

'When was he replaced?' asked Pazair.

'At the beginning of the month.'

'Where does he live?'

'In the garden district, beside the great spring.'

Pazair left the offices.

Kem, who had been standing guard on the threshold, told him, 'Nothing to report. Killer is patrolling around the building.'

'Please apprehend a witness and bring him here.'

Sechem, 'the Faithful One', was an old man, gentle and timid. The summons had frightened him, and his appearance before the tjaty plunged him into visible anguish. Pazair found it difficult to imagine him as a criminal, but he had learnt to distrust appearances.

'Why did you leave your post?' he asked.

'I had orders from above, my lord. I was transferred to a less senior role, controlling the movement of boats.'

'What had you done wrong?'

'As far as I know, nothing,' said Sechem. 'I'd worked in this department for twenty years, and never missed a single day, but I made the mistake of opposing instructions I believed to be wrong.'

'Please be specific.'

'I criticized the delay over issuing authorizations, and still more the absence of checks as regards hired workers.'

'Were you worried that your pay might be reduced?'

'No, my lord! When a foreigner hires out his services to the owner of an estate or an overseer of craftsmen, he commands a good wage, and quite quickly acquires land and a house that he can leave to his descendants. I do not understand why, for the last three months, most applicants been sent to a warfleet boatyard under the auspices of the Double White House.'

'Show me the lists.'

'Certainly, my lord – all I have to do is consult the archives.'

'I fear you may have an unpleasant surprise.'

When he saw the state of his former office, Sechem was close to despair. 'This reorganization is pointless.'

'How were the lists of hired persons registered?'

'On sycamore tablets.'

'Will you be able to find them in this mess?'

'I hope so, my lord.'

But fresh disappointment awaited them: after searching fruitlessly until after dark, Sechem gave his verdict. 'They've disappeared. But the drafts should still exist. Even incomplete, they'll be useful.'

The two young scribes removed the relevant limestone fragments from the rubbish heap where they had been thrown. By the light of the torches, Sechem picked out his precious drafts.

The war-fleet boatyard was like a bustling bee-hive. The overseers were snapping out orders to carpenters, who were working on long acacia-wood planks. Specialists were assembling a ship's hull, others were putting a ship's rail in place. With practised skill, they were creating a ship by placing piece upon piece, fastening them together with tenon-and-mortise joints. In another part of the boatyard, workers were caulking boats, while their colleagues were making oars and tillers.

'No entry,' a supervisor told Pazair, who was accompanied by Kem and Killer.

'Not even for the tjaty?'

'You are . . . ?'

'Call your superior.'

The man needed no further asking.

A tall, confident man with an assured voice soon arrived at a run. He recognized Kem and Killer, and bowed before the tjaty.

'How may I be of service to you, Tjaty?' he asked.

'I should like to meet the foreigners listed here.' Pazair handed the overseer a papyrus.

The man looked at it, then shook his head. 'I don't know any of them.'

'Think carefully.'

'No, I assure you—'

'I have official documents proving that, over the last three months, you have taken on about fifty foreigners. Where are they?'

The man's reaction was instant. He ran off so quickly towards the street that Killer seemed caught unawares; but the baboon leapt over a low wall and jumped on to the back of the fugitive, forcing his face into the ground.

Kem pulled him up by the hair. 'We're listening, my fine fellow.'

The farm, which lay to the north of Memphis, was enormous. The tjaty and a detachment of Kem's men entered the estate in the middle of the afternoon and hailed a goose-herd.

'Where are the foreigners?' asked Pazair.

The number of guards so alarmed the peasant that he couldn't speak. He pointed at a nearby stable.

When the tjaty went toward it, several men armed with sickles and staves barred his way.

'Do not use violence,' Pazair warned them, 'and give us free access to that building.'

A hot-head brandished his sickle. A dagger thrown by Kem sank into his forearm, and all resistance ceased.

In the stable, they found about fifty foreigners, all in chains, occupied in milking cows and sorting grain. The tjaty ordered that they were to be freed and their guards imprisoned.

Bel-Tran laughed about the incident. 'Slaves? Yes, as there are in Greece, and as there soon will be all over the world. Slavery is the future of mankind, my dear Pazair. It provides docile, cheap workers, and with it we shall develop a programme of extremely profitable projects.'

'Must I remind you that slavery is against the law of Ma'at and forbidden in Egypt?'

'If you're hoping to incriminate me, you may as well give up. You won't find any link between me, the boatyard, the farm and the department for foreign workers. Between ourselves, I will confess that I was trying an experiment – you have interrupted it inopportunely, but it was already bearing fruit. Your laws are outdated. When will you understand that the Egypt of Ramses is dead?'

'Why do you hate people so much?'

'Only two races exist: those who dominate and those who are dominated. I belong to the first; the second must obey me. That is the only law in force.'

'Only in your mind, Bel-Tran.'

'Many of our leading citizens agree with me, because they hope to become dominant. Even if their hopes are disappointed, they will have been useful to me.'

'So long as I am tjaty, no one will be a slave on Egyptian soil.'

'This rear-guard action ought to sadden me, but your point-less gestures are rather entertaining. Stop wearing yourself out, Pazair. You know as well as I do that your efforts are ridiculous.'

'I shall fight you to my last breath.'

30

Suti stroked his acacia-wood bow lovingly, and checked the integrity of the wood, the tension of the string and the flexibility of the frame.

'Haven't you anything better to do?' asked Panther affectionately.

'If you want to be a queen, I must have a weapon I can trust.'

'You have an army, so use it.'

'Do you think it can beat the Egyptian troops?'

'First, let's deal with the desert guards and impose our law in the sands. Libyans and Nubians are collaborating under your command – that's a miracle in itself. Tell them to fight, and they'll obey you without question. You are the master of gold, Suti. Conquer the land whose lords we shall be.'

'You really are mad.'

'You want revenge, my love, revenge on your friend Pazair and on your cursed Egypt. With gold and warriors, you will get it.' And she showered him with fiery, passionate kisses.

Convinced that an exciting adventure lay ahead, Suti ran about his camp. The fierce Libyan raiders were equipped with tents and blankets to make life almost pleasant in the middle of the desert. The Nubians, excellent hunters, tracked game.

But the high feeling of the first days was fading away. The

208

Libyans were at last realizing that Adafi really was dead, and that Suti had killed him. They had given their word before the gods, and so had to keep it, but silent opposition began to spread.

At its head was Jossete, a short, stocky, black-haired man; quick and agile, he was an expert with the knife. He had been Adafi's right-hand man, and was growing more and more resentful of Suti's seizure of power.

Suti inspected each encampment and congratulated his men; they were looking after their weapons, training and taking care to keep themselves clean.

Accompanied by five soldiers, Jossete interrupted Suti, who was talking to a group of Libyans on their return from an exercise.

'Where are you taking us?' he asked.

'That is not your concern,' said Suti.

'I don't like that answer.'

'I didn't like your question.'

Jossete's thick eyebrows knitted in a scowl. 'People don't talk to me like that.'

'A good soldier's most important qualities are obedience and respect.'

'Provided he has a good leader.'

'Are you saying I'm not?'

'How dare you compare yourself to Adafi?'

'I didn't lose, he did – even though he cheated.'

'Are you accusing him of dishonesty?'

'You buried the archer yourself.'

With a lightning-swift lunge, Jossete tried to plunge his dagger into Suti's belly, but the Egyptian parried the attack with an elbow in the Libyan's chest, and knocked him over. Before Jossete could get up, Suti stamped his head down into the sand and held it there with his heel.

'Either you obey me, or you suffocate.'

Suti's expression dissuaded the Libyans from helping their

comrade. Jossete let go of his knife and punched the ground, in a sign of submission.

'Very well. You may breathe.'

Suti raised his heel. Jossete spat out sand and rolled on to his side.

'Listen to me closely, little traitor,' said Suti. 'The gods enabled me to kill a cheat and to take command of a good army, and I took the chance they gave me. You will keep quiet, and you will fight for me. Otherwise, you can get out.'

Jossete returned to the ranks, his eyes cast down.

Suti's army headed north, along the Nile Valley, keeping well away from inhabited areas and taking the most difficult and least frequented route. With an innate feel for command, the young soldier knew how to share out hard toil and inspire trust in his men; no one challenged his authority.

He and Panther rode on horseback at the head of their troops. She relished every second of this impossible conquest, as if she had become the owner of the inhospitable land around them. Constantly alert, Suti listened to the desert.

'We've outwitted the All-Seeing Ones,' she declared.

'The golden goddess is wrong: they've been on our trail for two days.'

'How do you know?'

'Are you casting doubt on my instinct?'

'Why don't they attack?'

'Because there are too many of us. They'll have to group several patrols together.'

'Let's strike first.'

'No, we'll wait.'

'You don't want to kill Egyptians, do you? That's it, your big idea! To get yourself filled full of arrows by your countrymen.'

'If we can't get rid of them, how can I offer you a kingdom?'

*

Accompanied by their ferocious dogs, the All-Seeing Ones constantly criss-crossed the expanses of desert, capturing any sand-travellers who resorted to pillage, protecting the caravans and ensuring the miners' safety. Not a single nomad's movements went unnoticed, not a single predator enjoyed his crime for long. For decades, the desert patrols had nipped in the bud the smallest attempt to disturb the established order.

When a lone scout had reported an armed band coming from the south, none of the officers had believed him. It had taken a report – an alarming one – from a full patrol to spur them into action, necessitating the coordination of patrols spread out across a vast area.

Once all their patrols had joined up, the All-Seeing Ones were unsure what to do next. Who were these strange soldiers, who was commanding them, and what did they want? The unexpected alliance of Nubians and Libyans meant that a hard fight lay ahead, but the desert guards were keen to wipe out the intruders without calling on the army for help, so as to boost their reputation and earn a valuable reward.

The enemy had made a serious mistake by camping behind the line of hills from where the All-Seeing Ones would launch their assault; they would attack at nightfall, when the lookouts' attention was waning. First, they would encircle them; next, they would send over a murderous volley of arrows; lastly, they would finish off any remaining resistance by hand-to-hand fighting. The operation would be quick and brutal: any prisoners taken would be made to talk.

When the desert blushed red as the sun set, the wind began to blow, whipping up the sand; the All-Seeing Ones tried in vain to spot the enemy's lookouts. Wary of a trap, they advanced with extreme caution. When they reached the summit of the hills, they had still not seen a single adversary.

From their favourable position on the high ground, they surveyed the camp: to their astonishment, it was empty. Abandoned chariots, horses wandering loose, folded tents – all bore witness to the strange army's disarray. Obviously, knowing they had been spotted, the ill-assorted band had chosen to disperse.

It would be an easy victory indeed, and it would be followed by a determined pursuit and the arrest of every single intruder. The desert guards never allowed themselves to loot or pillage. They would draw up a detailed list of everything they seized, and the state would then award them part of it.

Warily, they entered the camp in small groups, covering each other. Some of the boldest men reached the chariots, took off the protective covers and found gold ingots. Immediately they called to their colleagues, who gathered around the treasure. Fascinated, most of them dropped their weapons and stood lost in contemplation of the precious metal.

Suddenly, in a dozen different places, the desert rose up.

Suti and his men had hidden by burying themselves in the sand. Staking their success on the attraction exerted by an empty camp and the cargo of gold, they knew that their ordeal would be short. They charged the All-Seeing Ones from the rear; surrounded, the guards realized that resistance was futile.

Suti climbed up on a chariot and addressed the defeated men.

'If you are reasonable, you'll have nothing to fear. Not only will your lives be spared, but you will get rich, like the Libyans and Nubians are under my command. My name is Suti, and before commanding this army I served as a chariot officer in the Egyptian army. I am the man who rid that army of a stain on its honour by ridding it of the traitor and murderer General Asher. It was I who carried out the sentence laid down by the law of the desert. Today, I am the master of gold.'

Several of the All-Seeing Ones recognized Suti. His reputation had travelled beyond the walls of Memphis, and some already considered him a legendary hero.

'Weren't you imprisoned in the fortress of Tjaru?' asked an officer.

'The garrison tried to kill me by offering me up to the Nubians as a sacrificial victim; but the golden goddess was watching over me.'

Panther came forward, lit by the last rays of the sunset, which set her golden crown, collar and bracelets aflame. Victors and vanquished alike were subjugated by the appearance of the famous goddess, who had at last returned from the mysterious, savage South to bring the joys of love to Egypt.

They submitted, prostrating themselves in the sand.

The celebration was well under way. Men were juggling with gold, drinking, mapping out a splendid future, singing of the beauty of the golden goddess.

'Are you happy?' Panther asked Suti.

'Things could be worse.'

'I was wondering how you'd manage not to kill any Egyptians . . . You're becoming a good general, thanks to me.'

'This coalition is very fragile.'

'It's strong enough for us.'

'What do you want to conquer?'

'Whatever presents itself. Standing still is unbearable – we must move forward, create our own horizon.'

Dagger raised, Jossete emerged from the darkness and charged at Suti. Swift as a cat, Suti leapt aside, dodging the fierce blow. Once her initial fear had passed, Panther was amused by the attack. The difference between the two men's size and strength was such that her lover would have no difficulty breaking the nasty little Libyan.

Suti struck empty air. Encouraged again, Jossete aimed at his heart. Quick reflexes saved the Egyptian, but he lost his balance getting free, and fell backwards.

Panther disarmed the attacker with a kick to his wrist. Murderous rage increased Jossete's strength tenfold. He flung her aside, seized a block of stone and brought it down on Suti's skull. Suti was not quick enough: he twisted so that the stone missed his head, but it landed on his arm and he gave a shout of pain.

Jossete howled with joy. Lifting the bloody stone high over his head, he stood in front of the wounded man. 'Die, you Egyptian dog!'

Eyes staring, mouth open, the Libyan dropped his improvised weapon and collapsed beside Suti, dead before he touched the ground. Panther had aimed well, plunging her dagger into the back of Jossete's neck.

'Why did you defend yourself so badly?' she asked.

'I can't see in the darkness any more . . . I'm blind.'

Panther helped him to his feet.

He grimaced. 'My arm . . . It's broken.'

Panther took him to the old Nubian warrior.

'Lay him on his back,' he ordered two soldiers, 'and place a roll of fabric between his shoulder-blades. You, on the left; you, on the right.'

The two soldiers pulled the wounded man's arms. The old man found the fracture in the forearm and put the bones back in place, ignoring Suti's cries of pain. Two splints padded with linen would aid his recovery.

'It's nothing serious,' pronounced the old man. 'He can march and he can command.'

Despite the pain, Suti got up. 'Take me to my tent,' he whispered in Panther's ear.

He walked slowly, so as not to stumble. She guided him to his tent and helped him to sit down.

'No one must know I'm blind.'

'Go to sleep. I'll keep watch.'

At dawn, the pain awoke Suti. The landscape he gazed upon seemed so wondrous that he soon forgot his pain.

'I can see, Panther, I can see!'

'The light . . . The light has cured you.'

'I know what it was: an attack of night blindness. It will happen again, at random. The only person who can cure me is Neferet.'

'We're a long way from Memphis,' Panther pointed out.

'Come with me.'

Jumping on to his horse, he led her off on a ride. They passed between the dunes, galloped along the bed of a dried-up river and climbed a stony hillside.

From the top, they saw a magnificent view.

'Look, Panther, look at the white city on the horizon. That's Kebet, and that's where we're going.'

31

The intense heat of early summer had plunged the vast burial-ground of Saqqara into a stupor; work on excavating tombs had slowed down, if not stopped. The priests whose task was to maintain the *ka*, the immortal energy, moved about increasingly slowly. Only Djui the embalmer had no chance of sleep: he had been brought three corpses, which must be prepared as quickly as possible for the journey to the otherworld. Although he was pale with fatigue, and still unshaven, he set to work at once. He extracted the entrails and embalmed the bodies more or less elaborately, according to the price paid.

In his few spare minutes, he took flowers to shrines whose owners offered him a small fee for doing so, a useful addition to his salary. One morning, as he was doing so, he met the tjaty and his wife on the path leading to Branir's tomb. Djui bowed deeply to them.

Time had not lessened the pain or healed the wound. Without Branir, Pazair and Neferet felt like orphans; their murdered master could never be replaced. He had been the embodiment of a perfect wisdom, the radiant wisdom of Egypt, which Bel-Tran and his henchmen were trying to destroy.

In venerating Branir's memory, Pazair and Neferet linked themselves to the long line of founding ancestors, who had valued peaceful truth and serene justice on which they had built a land of water and sunshine. Branir had not been annihilated; his invisible presence guided them, his spirit was creating a path they could not yet make out. Only the communion of hearts, beyond the borders of death, could help them follow that path.

The tjaty met the king in secret, in the Temple of Ptah. Officially, Ramses was residing in the beautiful city of Pi-Ramses, at the heart of the Delta, to benefit from the pleasant climate there.

'Our enemies must think me desperate and defeated,' said the king.

'We have less than three months left, Majesty.'

'Have you made any progress?'

'Nothing very satisfactory. I've won some small victories, but they aren't enough to trouble Bel-Tran.'

'What about his accomplices?'

'There are still a lot of them,' said Pazair, 'though I have managed to eliminate a few.'

'As have I. At Pi-Ramses, I have purged the troops in charge of watching the borders with Asia. Some senior officers were taking illicit payments from the Double White House, through several different organizations. Bel-Tran has a twisted mind. To detect the effects of his actions, we must search for the complicated twists and turns of his plotting. Let us continue to erode the ground beneath him.'

Pazair sighed. 'I seem to find new rottenness almost every day.'

'Have you found the Testament of the Gods?'

'No, Majesty, and I still have no leads.'

'And Branir's murderer?'

'Nothing concrete.'

'We must strike hard,' said Ramses, 'and discover the exact limits of Bel-Tran's domain. As time is so short, we shall proceed to a census.'

'But, Majesty, will that not take a long time?'

'Ask Bagey for help, and enlist all the state secretariats – the provincial governors must devote themselves to this task as a priority. In less than a fortnight, we shall have the first results. I want to know the real state of the country and the extent of this conspiracy.'

Bagey was weary and bowed with age, and his legs were swollen, but he nevertheless greeted Pazair amiably. His wife, though, was not best pleased by the visit: she hated seeing her husband being bothered like this and dragged out of his retirement.

Pazair noted that the little town house was getting into a sad state: in some places, the plaster was falling off the walls. He did not say a word, for fear of annoying the old man. He would send a team of workmen to repair and repaint all the houses in the street – including Bagey's, naturally. He would pay for the repairs himself.

'A census?' Bagey was astonished. 'That's an onerous undertaking.'

'The last one was five years ago. I feel it would be useful to have current information.'

'You are right.'

'I'd like to do it quickly.'

'That isn't impossible, provided you have the full support of the king's messengers.'

The messengers were an elite body who distributed instructions from the central government; the speed at which reforms could be implemented depended largely on their efficiency.

'I'll take you to the census secretariat,' said Bagey. 'You'd have understood eventually how it works, but going there now will save you a few days.'

'Please take my travelling-chair.'

'If you insist.'

*

Every single royal messenger was present. When the tjaty opened the session of his council by hanging a figurine of Ma'at on his gold chain, everyone bowed before the goddess of justice.

Pazair was dressed in the traditional garb of a tjaty: a long, weighted apron cut from thick, stiff material; his body entirely covered with the exception of his shoulders. He sat down on a straight-backed chair.

'I have summoned you, on Pharaoh's orders, to entrust you with an exceptionally important mission: a census as swift as the flight of a bird. I wish to know the names of the owners of fields and cultivable lands, the area they hold, the number of head of livestock and their owners, the nature and quantity of produce and resources, the number of inhabitants. I don't need to remind you that wilful falsehood or lies of omission are serious offences, carrying severe penalties.'

A messenger asked permission to speak. 'The census is usually carried out over several months. Why must this one be done so quickly?'

'I must take decisions concerning trade and resources, and I need to know if the state of the country has changed greatly in the last five years. Afterwards, we shall refine the results.'

'It won't be easy to meet your demands,' said the head of the messengers, 'but we'll manage it if we gather each day's information very quickly. Can you tell us more about your reasons for the census? Is it a matter of preparing a new tax system?'

'No census has ever been taken with that motive. As always, the goal will be full employment and a just sharing out of tasks. You have my word, by the Rule.'

'You shall have the first information within a week.'

At Karnak, the tamarisks were flowering between the sphinxes that denied outsiders access to the temple. The early summer was spreading its sweet scents, the stones of the temple were bedecked in warm colours, and the bronze of the great gates gleamed.

At the Temple of Mut, Neferet was presiding over the annual assembly of the principal towns' head doctors, who had been initiated into the secrets of their craft at the temple. They raised problems of public health and shared major discoveries which would benefit remedy-makers, animal-doctors, tooth-doctors, eye-doctors, 'shepherds of the anus',* 'they who know the humours and the hidden organs', and other specialists. For the most part elderly, they admired their superior's clear face, swanlike neck, slender waist and delicate wrists and ankles. On her head she wore a diadem of lotus-flowers surrounded by small beads. At her throat hung the turquoise amulet Branir had given her, to protect her from harmful influences.

Kani, the High Priest of Karnak, opened the session. His skin was still brown and deeply lined from his years as a gardener, and bore traces of abscesses on his neck from the days when he had had to carry heavy yokes. And he still made no attempt to charm people.

He said, 'Thanks to the gods, this country's doctors are led by an exceptional woman, whose concern is to improve care and not to increase her own prestige. After an unhappy period, we have returned to the righteous tradition taught by Imhotep. Let us never again deviate from it, and Egypt will know health of both body and soul.'

Neferet disliked making speeches and did not now inflict one on her colleagues; instead she invited them so speak. Their statements were brief and worthwhile. They reported improved methods of operating, notably in the fields of child-bearing and eye diseases, and the creation of new remedies based on exotic plants. Several stressed the need to maintain the high level of training for doctors, even if their studies

*Gastro-enterologists.

were long and several years of practical experience were required before they were considered fully trained.

Neferet agreed with all these points. But, despite the congenial atmosphere, Kani sensed that she was tense, almost anxious.

'A census is being carried out,' she told her audience, 'and, thanks to the royal messengers' diligence, some results are already known. One of them concerns us directly: the population is growing much too fast in some provinces. If that growth continues unchecked, the people will be reduced to terrible poverty.'*

'What do you wish us to do?'

'Village doctors must advise on methods of preventing pregnancy.'

'Your predecessor ended that policy, because the state had to give out the preventive remedies free of charge.'

'That was both stupid and dangerous. Let us return to giving out remedies based on acacia – the acid in the spines is highly effective.'

'That is true, my lady, but to preserve it it must be ground with dates and honey – and honey is expensive.'

'Over-large families will ruin the villages; we doctors must convince parents of this reality. As for the honey, I shall ask the tjaty to set aside enough of the harvest for our use.'

At dusk, Neferet set off along the path leading to the Temple of Ptah. Set apart from the great east–west axis, the spine of the immense Karnak complex, the little temple nestled in the heart of an island of trees.

Priests greeted her, and then Neferet went alone into the shrine, where a statue of the lion-goddess Sekhmet stood. Sekhmet was the patron of doctors and the incarnation of the

*In the era of Ramses II, Egypt's population, according to estimates which are difficult to verify, was about 4 million. Modern Egypt will soon have over 60 million inhabitants.

mysterious force that both caused illnesses and produced their remedies. Without her aid, no doctor could heal.

The goddess, who had a woman's body and a fierce lioness's face, was surrounded by darkness. The last ray of the setting sun entered through a slit in the ceiling, lighting up the terrifying deity's face.

The miracle happened again, as it had done on their first encounter: the lioness smiled. Her face softened, and she lowered her gaze to look at her servant. Neferet had come to ask her for her wisdom, and she communed with the spirit of the living stone. Through the goddess's immutable presence, the knowledge of energy was transmitted, an energy of which the human being was only a fleeting form.

The young woman spent the night in prayer; from being a pupil of Sekhmet, she became her sister and confidante. When the clear light of morning rendered the statue fearsome again, Neferet was no longer afraid of it.

A strong rumour had spread across Memphis: the tjaty's audience would be a very special one. Not only had the Nine Friends of Pharaoh been summoned, but also many courtiers were hurrying into the pillared hall so as not to miss the audience. Some speculated that Pazair would announce his resignation, that he had been crushed by the weight of his responsibilities; others said something stunning had happened, with unforeseen consequences.

Contrary to his usual custom, Pazair had not organized a restricted council, but had opened the double doors of the audience chamber. On this beautiful morning, he was confronting the entire court.

'On Pharaoh's orders, I have carried out a census. Thanks to exceptionally good work by the king's messengers, the first stage has already been completed.'

'He's trying to curry favour with a notoriously difficult body of men,' whispered an old courtier.

'And not forgetting to take the credit for their work himself,' added his neighbour.

'I must inform you of the results,' continued Pazair.

An unpleasant shiver ran through the assembled throng. The gravity of his voice made everyone fear that something terrible had happened.

'The population is growing too fast in three Northern and two Southern provinces. This necessitates action by the Health secretariat, which will stop the rise as quickly as possible by educating families.'

No one made an unfavourable comment.

'The possessions of the temples, if they are still intact, are gravely threatened, as are those of the villages. Without direct intervention on my part, the whole landscape of Egypt's trade and resources will soon be thrown into disarray, and you will no longer recognize the land of your ancestors.'

The courtiers began to whisper and exchange looks: they found the declaration exaggerated and unfounded.

'Of course,' Pazair went on, 'this is not merely an opinion but is based on verified facts whose seriousness cannot escape you.'

'I would ask you to set out those facts clearly,' said the Overseer of Fields.

'According to the reports gathered by the royal messengers, about half of all lands have passed into the direct or indirect control of the Double White House. A number of provincial temples are unaware that they will, before long, be deprived of their harvests. Many small and medium-sized farmers have unknowingly got into debt, and will either become tenants or be expelled. The balance between private and state lands is on the point of breaking down. It is the same for livestock and crafts.'

All eyes converged on Bel-Tran, who was sitting near the tjaty, to the right. Surprise and anger mingled in his eyes. Lips pursed, nostrils pinched, neck stiff, he raged silently.

'The policy carried out before my appointment,' said Pazair, 'was heading in a direction of which I disapprove. The census has revealed its excesses, which I intend to curb without delay, through decrees signed by Pharaoh. By respecting her ancestral values Egypt will preserve her greatness and the goodness of her people; so I shall ask the head of the Double White House to follow my instructions faithfully and to cancel injustices.'

Publicly disowned, but charged with a new mission, would Bel-Tran withdraw or submit? Heavy, massive, he advanced and stood before the tjaty.

'You have my loyalty, Tjaty,' he said. 'Command, and I shall obey.'

A murmur of satisfaction showed the court's assent. The crisis had been averted: Bel-Tran had realized the error of his ways, and the tjaty was not condemning him. Pazair's moderation was widely approved: despite his youth, he had subtlety and knew how to be diplomatic, without departing from his irreproachable line of conduct.

'Lastly,' said the tjaty, 'I shall not introduce compulsory registration of births, deaths, marriages and divorces. Such a measure would restrict freedom, by putting in writing events which concern only the interested parties and those close to them, not the state. We must not strangle our society by binding it in archaic and over-rigid modes of government. When Pharaoh is crowned, we do not mention his age, but celebrate his office. Let us preserve that state of mind, which is more concerned with non-temporal truth than with perishable details, and Egypt will remain in harmony, in the heavens' image.'

32

Silkis was afraid, unable to abate her husband's anger. He was suffering from a severe attack of cramps, and had no feeling in his fingers or toes. In his rage, he broke precious vases, tore up new papyri and insulted the gods. Not even his young wife's charms soothed him.

Silkis withdrew into her apartments, where she swallowed a brew of date-juice, leaves of the castor-oil plant and sycamore-milk, designed to ease the fire that burnt in her intestines. One doctor had warned her about the bad state of the veins in her thighs, another had expressed anxiety about the heat she constantly felt in her anus; she had sent them away, before accepting treatment from a specialist who had given her an enema of woman's milk.

Her belly continued to hurt, as if she were paying for her crimes. She longed to confide her nightmares to the dream-interpreter and to ask Neferet to treat her, but the first had left Memphis and the second had become her enemy.

Bel-Tran burst into her bedchamber. 'So you're ill yet again, are you?'

'It isn't my fault. You know a plague's torturing me.'

'I pay for the best doctors to treat you.'

'The only one who can cure me is Neferet.'

'Nonsense!' snapped Bel-Tran. 'She doesn't know any more than the others.'

'You're wrong; she does.'

'Have I made a single mistake since I began rising to power? I've made you one of the richest women in the land, and soon you'll be the richest of all. And I shall hold supreme power, through my puppets.'

'But Pazair frightens you.'

'No, he irritates me, by behaving like the tjaty he thinks he is.'

'His actions have brought him a good deal of sympathy. Some people who used to support you have changed their minds.'

'Fools! They'll regret it. Anyone who hasn't obeyed me to the letter will be reduced to the rank of slave.'

Silkis lay down, exhausted. 'Couldn't you be content with the wealth you already have – and look after me?'

'In ten weeks' time, we shall be the masters of the land – and you want to give up because of your health? You really are mad, my poor Silkis.'

She stood up, and gripped the belt of his kilt. 'Tell me the truth. Have I really still got a place in your heart and your head?'

'What do you mean?'

'I'm young and pretty, but my nerves are fragile and my belly is not always welcoming. Have you chosen someone else to be your future queen?'

He slapped her, forcing her to let go. 'I made you, Silkis, and I shall continue to do so. As long as you carry out my orders, you have nothing to fear.'

She did not cry, and forgot to simper. Her child-woman's face became as cold as Greek marble. 'And suppose I leave you?'

Bel-Tran smiled. 'You love me too much, my darling, and you love your comfort too much. I know your vices. We're inseparable – we've denied the gods together, lied together,

226

overturned the law and the Rule together. There could be no better guarantee of unfailing loyalty.'

'Delicious,' agreed Pazair, emerging from the water.

Neferet was checking the copper band that ran round the inside of the pool and kept it permanently clean. The sun turned her naked skin golden as drops of water trickled down it.

Pazair dived, swam underwater, and took her gently by the waist before surfacing and kissing her on the throat.

'They'll be waiting for me at the hospital,' she said.

'They can wait a little longer.'

'And shouldn't you go to the palace?'

'I don't know any more.'

Her resistance was feigned; languidly, she gave way. Pazair held her close and took her to the stone rim of the pool. Still embracing each other, they lay down on the hot paving stones and gave free rein to their desire.

A raucous voice shattered the peace.

'Way-Finder,' said Neferet.

'That braying means a friend's arrived.'

A few minutes later, Kem came and greeted the tjaty and his wife. Brave, asleep at the foot of a sycamore, opened one eye and went back to sleep, his head resting on his crossed paws.

'Your performance at the council is being praised highly,' he told Pazair. 'The criticism at court has been silenced, and there's no longer any scepticism. You're regarded as a true first minister again.'

'But what about Bel-Tran?' asked Neferet anxiously.

'He's getting more and more worried. Some leading citizens are refusing his invitations to dinner, and others are closing their doors to him. It is whispered that, if he puts another foot wrong, you'll replace him without warning. You've struck him a mortal blow.'

'I only wish I had,' said Pazair.

'Little by little, you're cutting away his power.'

'That isn't much consolation.'

'Even if he has got a decisive weapon, will he actually be able to use it?'

'Let's not think of that. We must go on as before.'

The Nubian folded his arms. 'To hear you, anyone would think that righteousness is the kingdom's only chance of survival.'

'Don't you believe that?'

'It cost me my nose, and it'll cost you your life.'

Pazair smiled. 'Let's try to prove that prophecy wrong.'

'How much time have we left?'

'I owe you the truth: ten weeks.'

'What about the shadow-eater?' asked Neferet.

'I dare not believe he's given up,' replied Kem, 'but he lost his battles with Killer, so he may have begun to have doubts. If he has, perhaps he's intending to give up the fight.'

'Are you becoming an optimist?

'Don't worry: I shan't lower my guard.'

Smiling, Neferet looked closely at the Nubian. 'This isn't merely a courtesy visit, is it?'

'You know me too well.'

'There's a sparkle in your eyes. Is there a glimmer of hope?'

'We've picked up Mentmose's trail.'

'In Memphis?'

Kem shook his head. 'According to my informant, who saw him leave Bel-Tran's house, he took the road to the North.'

'You could have stopped him,' said Pazair.

'That would have been a mistake – it's better to find out where he's going.'

'So long as we don't lose him.'

'He didn't take a boat, probably so that he could pass unnoticed – he knows my men are looking for him. By taking dirt roads, he'll avoid our checkpoints.'

'Is someone following him?' asked Pazair.

'Yes, my best trackers. As soon as he reaches his goal, I'll be informed.'

'Let me know at once, and I'll go with you.'

'That wouldn't be wise.'

'You'll need a judge to question him, and who better than the tjaty himself?'

Pazair was convinced he would get a decisive result, so Neferet had failed to persuade him to give up a wild escapade which was likely to be dangerous, despite the presence of Kem and Killer.

Surely Mentmose must know more about Branir's murder? The tjaty would not pass up the slightest chance of learning the truth. Mentmose would talk.

While Pazair was waiting for Kem's signal, Neferet and her concerned colleagues were implementing, throughout the country, the programme of enabling families to limit the number of their children. In accordance with the tjaty's decree, the necessary remedies were again to be distributed free of charge. Village doctors, whose office would regain its old importance, would form a permanent information service. From now on, the Health secretariat would oversee controls on birthrates.

Unlike her predecessor, Neferet had not moved into the government buildings set aside for her and her close colleagues. She preferred to remain in her old office at the central hospital in Memphis, so as to stay in contact with the sick and with those who prepared the remedies. She listened, advised and reassured. Each day, she tried to push back the limits of suffering, and each day she suffered defeats from which she drew hope for future victories. She also concerned herself with editing medical writings,* which had been handed down since the time of the pyramids and ceaselessly improved upon; a specialist college of scribes described successful experiments and noted down the treatments.

After carrying out an eye operation, designed to prevent the build-up of pressure in the eye, Neferet was washing her hands when a young doctor told her of an emergency. She was tired, and asked him to deal with it, but he said the patient insisted on seeing Neferet and only Neferet.

The woman was seated, her head covered by a veil.

'What is wrong with you?' asked Neferet.

The patient did not reply.

'I must examine you.'

Silkis lifted her veil. 'Treat me, Neferet, please. If you don't, I shall die.'

'There are excellent doctors here. Consult them.'

'But you're the only one who can cure me – no one else can.'

'You're the wife of a vile and destructive man, a perjurer and a liar. Staying at his side proves your complicity in his crimes. That is what is eating away at your soul and your body.'

'I haven't committed any crimes. I have to obey Bel-Tran – he made me, he—'

'Are you nothing more than an object?'

'You don't understand.'

'No, I don't, and I won't treat you.'

'I'm your friend, Neferet, your loyal and sincere friend. You have my whole-hearted admiration, so won't you trust me?'

*A few have survived: they deal with gynaecology, the respiratory passages, stomach disorders, the urinary tracts, ophthalmology, cranial surgery and veterinary medicine. Unfortunately, only a tiny part of the art of Egyptian medicine has come down to us.

'If you leave Bel-Tran, I'll believe you. Otherwise you must stop lying to me and to yourself.'

Silkis said plaintively, 'If you treat me, Bel-Tran will reward you, I swear it! It's the only way to save Pazair.'

'Are you sure of that?'

Silkis relaxed. 'At last you're facing facts.'

'I face them all the time.'

'Bel-Tran is preparing another future, a wonderfully attractive one. It will be like me – beautiful and seductive.'

'You'll be cruelly disappointed.'

Silkis's smile froze. 'Why do you say that?'

'Because you are basing that future on ambition, greed and hatred. It will offer you nothing else unless you give up your madness.'

'So you don't trust me.'

'You are an accomplice to murder, and sooner or later you will appear before the tjaty's court of justice.'

The child-woman went into a fury. 'That was your last chance, Neferet! By linking your destiny to Pazair's, by refusing to treat me, you have condemned yourself to ignominy. The next time we see each other, you will be my slave.'

33

In the words of a popular song, 'Merchants sail up and down the river, busy as flies, transport goods from one city to another, and supply him who has nothing.'

Pazair stood apart from the other passengers on the boat. They were Syrians, Greeks, Cypriots and Phoenicians, all debating, comparing their prices and dividing up their future clientele. No one would have recognized the tjaty of Egypt in this young, plainly dressed man, whose only baggage was the worn-out mat he slept on. On the cabin roof, which was piled high with bundles, Killer kept watch. His calmness meant that the shadow-eater was nowhere near. Kem stayed up at the prow, his head encased in a hood to hide his identity; some of his men, disguised as Greeks and Syrians, mingled with the other passengers. Fortunately, the merchants were too busy adding up their profits to be interested in anyone else.

The boat moved fast, before a brisk wind. The captain and his crew would be paid a good bonus if they reached their destination earlier than expected: the foreign traders were men in a hurry.

An argument broke out between some Syrians and Greeks. The former offered the latter necklaces of semi-precious stones in exchange for vases from Rhodes, but the Greeks scorned the offer, regarding it as inadequate. Their attitude surprised Pazair, for the exchange seemed fair.

232

The incident calmed the men's trade-fever, and each withdrew into his own thoughts as they moved down the Nile. After taking 'the Great River', which crossed the Delta, the trading-ship left the cape to the east, and took the 'Waters of Ra', a waterway separate from the main course, and headed towards the crossroads of routes serving Canaan and Phoenicia.

The Greeks disembarked during a brief stop in open country. Kem followed them, as did Pazair and Killer. The dilapidated landing-stage looked abandoned; all around were papyrus forests and marshes. Ducks flapped out of the way.

'This is where Mentmose joined a group of Greek traders,' explained Kem. 'They took a dirt track leading south-east. If we follow them, we'll catch up with him.'

The merchants were talking among themselves warily: they were unhappy about the trio's presence.

One of them, who had a slight limp, came over to them. 'What do you want?' he asked.

'Loans,' replied Pazair.

'In this benighted place?'

'At Memphis, no one will give us anything any more.'

'Has your business failed?'

'There are certain things we can't do, because we have too many ideas and not enough money. If we can accompany you, perhaps we'll find some rather more understanding people.'

The Greek seemed satisfied. 'You haven't chosen too badly. But tell me: your baboon, there, is it for sale?'

'Not at the moment,' replied Kem.

'There are a lot of keen collectors.'

'He's a good animal, quiet and docile.'

'He'll do as a guarantee for you – you'll get a good price for him.'

'Will it be a long journey?' asked Pazair.

'Two hours' walk – we've been waiting for the donkeys.'

As soon as the donkeys arrived, the caravan set off, at the

donkeys' regular pace. Although they were heavily laden, they neither stumbled not looked unhappy, being used to hard work. The men slaked their thirst several times, and Pazair moistened the donkeys' mouths.

After crossing an abandoned field, they found journey's end: a small town with low houses, protected by a curtain-wall.

'I can't see a temple,' said Pazair in great surprise. 'No great gateways, no monumental gates, no banners fluttering in the wind.'

'There's no need for sacred things here,' said a Greek in amusement. 'The only god this city knows is profit. We all serve him faithfully, and we're doing very well out of him.'

A crowd of donkeys and merchants was entering the main gateway, which was watched by two good-humoured guards. People bumped into each other over, hailed each other, trod on each other's toes, and almost drowned in the continuous tide that invaded the narrow streets. The Canaanites had pointed beards and luxuriant side-whiskers, and wore their thick hair tied on the top of the head with a band. They went barefoot, but proudly wore striped mantles, which they bought from the Phoenicians, past masters of the art of calculating in one's head. Canaanites, Libyans and Syrians bore down on the Greeks' shops, which were bursting with imported products, notably slender, shapely vases and toilet items. Even Hittites were buying honey and wine, as vital to their table as their rituals. Kem's men melted into the crowds to await his signal.

Watching all this activity, Pazair soon noticed something strange: the buyers did not offer anything in exchange for the goods they acquired. At the end of heated negotiations, all they did was shake hands with the seller.

With Kem and Killer at his heels, Pazair went over to a small, talkative Greek with a beard, who was displaying beautiful silver cups.

'I'd like that one,' he said.

'You have good taste. I'm really surprised.'

'Why?'

'That's my favourite. Letting it go would make me sadder than I can say; but, alas, that is the hard law of trade. Touch it, young man, stroke it. Believe me, it's worth it – there's isn't a craftsman alive who could make another like it.'

'How much is it?'

'Feast upon its beauty, imagine it in your home, think of the envious, admiring looks on your friends' faces. First, you will refuse to tell them the name of the trader with whom you made this incredible deal, then you'll confess: who but Pericles sells such works of art?'

'It must be very expensive,' said Pazair.

'What does the price matter, when art reaches such perfection? Make an offer. Pericles is listening.'

'A spotted cow?'

The Greek's expression became one of profound astonishment. 'I don't like that sort of joke.'

'Is it too little?'

'Your humour's getting feeble, and I've no time to waste.' Annoyed, he moved on to another customer.

Pazair was disappointed. He thought he had proposed an exchange in his own disfavour.

The tjaty went to another Greek's stall and the transaction, with a few variations, was repeated. At the crucial moment, Pazair held out his hand. The trader gripped it loosely, then, astounded, withdrew his hand.

'But . . . your hand's empty!'

'What should it contain?'

'Do you think my vases are free? Money, of course.'

'I haven't got any.'

'Then go to an exchange-house and borrow some.'

'Where will I find one?'

'On the main street – there are more than a dozen.'

Bemused, Pazair followed the merchant's instructions.

The street came out on a square bordered by strange shops. Pazair looked at them; they were indeed 'exchange-houses', a term not used in Egypt. He went to the nearest one and joined the queue.

At the entrance were two armed men examined the tjaty from head to foot, and checking that he was not hiding a dagger.

Inside were several very busy people. One of them was placing small, round pieces of metal on a scale, weighing them, then arranging them in different pigeonholes.

'Deposit or withdrawal?' a scribe asked Pazair.

'Deposit.'

'List your possessions.'

'I . . .'

'Hurry up, other customers are waiting.'

'Because of the enormous amount I've brought with me, I should like to discuss its value with the exchange-house's most senior official.'

'He's busy.'

'When may I see him?'

'One moment.'

The scribe returned a few minutes later, and said the meeting was fixed for sunset.

So money, 'the great twisted one', had been introduced into this closed city. Money, in the form of coins in circulation, had been invented by the Greeks decades ago, but had been kept out of Egypt because it would put an end to the economy of barter and lead to the irremediable decay of society.* 'The twisted one' proclaimed the pre-eminence of having lots of

*We note the existence of money in the XXXth dynasty; the monetary system was, however, not yet in force. It did not make its appearance in Egypt until under the Ptolemies, who were Greek.

money, increased humans' natural greed and made them apply monetary values detached from reality. Tjaties fixed the price of products and foods according to a reference which was not circulated and did not materialize in little circles of silver or copper – they were a veritable prison for individuals.

The director of the exchange-house was a round man with a square face, aged about fifty. Originally from Mycenae, he had recreated the atmosphere of his native house: little terracotta statuettes, marble effigies of Greek heroes, the principal passages from the Odyssey on papyrus, long-necked vases decorated with the exploits of Heracles.

'I am told that you are planning to grant us a large deposit,' he said.

'That is correct,' said Pazair.

'Of what kind?'

'I have many possessions.'

'Livestock?'

'Yes.'

'Grain?'

'Yes.'

'Boats?'

'Yes.'

'And other things as well?'

'Many other things.'

The director looked impressed.

'Have you enough coins here?' asked Pazair.

'I think so, but . . .'

'What is it?'

'Your appearance . . . gives no indication of such wealth.'

'When travelling, I prefer not to wear expensive clothes.'

'I understand, but I would like . . .'

'Proof of my wealth?'

The director nodded.

'Give me a clay tablet.'

'I would prefer to register your declaration on papyrus.'

'I have something more reliable to offer you. Give me that tablet.'

Taken aback, the director did so.

Pazair printed his seal deeply in the clay. 'Is this guarantee enough for you?'

The Greek gazed at the tjaty's seal, his eyes bulging. 'What . . . what do you want?'

'A fugitive from justice has visited you.'

'Me? That's impossible!'

'His name is Mentmose, and he used to command Memphis's security guards before he broke the law and was exiled. His presence on Egyptian soil is a major offence, which you ought to have reported.'

'I assure you that—'

'Don't lie,' advised the tjaty. 'I know that Mentmose came here on the orders of the head of the Double White House.'

The director's defences crumbled. 'How could I refuse to see him? He claimed to be from the authorities.'

'What did he want you to do?'

'To extend our exchange activities to the whole of the Delta.'

'Where is he hiding?'

'Not here – he left for the port of Raqote.'

'Have you forgotten that the circulation of money is forbidden and that those guilty of that crime are subject to heavy penalties?'

'My affairs are perfectly legal.'

'Have you received a decree signed by me?'

'Mentmose assured me that exchange-house activities were regarded as an accepted fact, and that they would become widespread in the near future.'

'You have been unwise. In Egypt, law is more than just a word.'

'You won't resist us for long. Progress is founded on exchange-houses, and—'

'It's a kind of progress we do not want.'

'I'm not the only one who says that. All my colleagues—'

'Let us go and meet them. Show me round this town.'

34

Full of hope, the director of the exchange-house presented the tjaty, accompanied by Killer, to his colleagues. They were charged with smuggling in money, controlling their customers' money, fixing the levels of loans and carrying out exchange transactions so as to make as much profit as possible from them. To a man, the directors insisted that their dealings brought great advantages. If a strong state could manipulate the system as it wished, why should it not utilize for its own benefit the possessions its subjects would be obliged to entrust to the exchange-houses?

While the tjaty was listening to the lecture, Kem's men, at a signal from their commander, dispensed with their Greek and Libyan accoutrements, and closed the gates of the city, despite the protests of an anxious crowd. Three men tried to climb a wall and get away, but their plumpness was their undoing: unable to reach the top of the wall, they were arrested and taken to Kem.

The most agitated of them said vehemently, 'Let us go at once.'

'You're guilty of illegally receiving coinage,' said Kem.

'You have no right to judge us.'

'I must take you before a court.'

When the three were in the presence of the tjaty, who listed his title and his offices, their scorn disappeared, and they began to wail.

'Forgive us. It was a mistake on our part, a regrettable mistake. We're honest traders, and we—'

'What are your names and professions?' asked Pazair.

The three men were Egyptians from the Delta, makers of furniture. Part of their production was not declared to the authorities, but was sent to the Greek city.

'It seems that you are piling up illegal profits and so harming your countrymen. Do you contest those facts?'

There were no protests.

'Don't deal harshly with us. We deluded ourselves.'

'I shall be content to apply our laws.'

Pazair set up his court in the main square. The jury was made up of Kem and five Egyptian peasants whom he had brought in from the nearest farm.

The many accused, most of whom were Greeks, did not contest the charges or the proposed sentence. The jury unanimously adopted the punishment that the tjaty wished for: immediate expulsion of the guilty parties and permanent banishment from Egyptian soil. The coins seized would be melted down, and the metal obtained would be given to the temples, where it would be transformed into ritual objects. As for the city, it would still be allowed to house foreign traders, so long as they observed the laws of Egypt.

The leader of the exchange-house directors thanked the tjaty.

'I was afraid the punishment would be more severe,' he confessed. 'They say the prison camp at Khargeh is hell on earth.'

'I survived it.'

'You?' said the man incredulously.

'Mentmose hoped that my bones would whiten in the sand there.'

'In your place, I wouldn't underestimate him – he's cunning and dangerous.'

'I am aware of that.'

'Do you realize that, by putting an end to the development of the monetary system, you will draw down on yourself the hatred of a formidable enemy? You are destroying one of Bel-Tran's main sources of wealth.'

'I am glad to hear it.'

'How long do you hope to remain tjaty?'

'As long as Pharaoh wishes me to.'

Pazair, Kem and Killer took passage on a fast boat bound for the coastal city of Raqote. The tjaty loved the lush greenness of the Delta landscape, where countless canals and streams intersected. The further north one went, the more the waters extended their kingdom. The Nile grew wider, preparing for its wedding with a dreamy, affectionate sea, which would intoxicate the last lands, with their indeterminate shapes. A world died in a bluish infinity and was reborn in the form of waves.

A significant part of Raqote's livelihood was fishing. Many Delta fisheries had set up their main premises in the areas around the little port, where different races mingled. In the open air, at the market or in warehouses, skilled workers washed the fish, gutted them and flattened them out; then they hung them on strips of wood to dry in the sun, or buried them in hot sand or in a cleansing mud. Next, they were salted; the finest pieces were kept in oil, the eggs of grey mullet put on one side for preparing a special delicacy. Rich people enjoyed fresh fish, grilled and covered in a sauce containing cumin, oregano, coriander and pepper; the ordinary people ate dried fish, a daily food as basic as bread. A grey mullet was equivalent in value to a jar of beer, and a basket of Nile perch to a fine amulet.

Pazair was astonished by the quietness in the town: not a song, not a gathering, no passionate bargaining, no caravans of donkeys coming and going. On the wharf, men were sleeping, stretched out on fishing-nets; hardly any boats were moored alongside.

A large, low house with a flat roof contained the secretariats that dealt with the registration of catches and their despatch.

Pazair and Kem went in.

The place was empty. No documents, as if the archives had never existed; not even a scribe's brush or rough notes. Not a clue to indicate that scribes had worked here.

'Mentmose can't be far away,' suggested Kem, gesturing at the baboon, which was getting restive. 'Killer knows he's here somewhere.'

The baboon prowled round the building and set off towards the port; Kem and Pazair followed. When they reached the docks Killer went to one of the few moored boats, a shabby, badly maintained one. At Kem's hail, the crew, five evil-smelling men armed with fish-gutting knives, emerged from their torpor.

'Go away,' said one. 'You're not from these parts.'

'Are you the last inhabitants of Raqote?'

'Go away.'

'I am Kem, commander of Memphis's security guards. Answer me, or you'll be in trouble.'

'Black men belong in the South, not here. Go back where you came from.'

'Will you obey the orders of the tjaty, who's here with me?'

The fisherman burst out laughing. 'The tjaty's lounging in his office in Memphis! In Raqote, we're the law.'

'I want to know what has happened here,' said Pazair sternly.

The man turned to his friends. 'Did you hear that? He thinks he's the great judge. Perhaps he thinks he can frighten us with his monkey.'

Killer had many good qualities and one failing: sensitivity.

Being a security guard, he hated hearing people mock the state's power. His sudden bound caught his opponent by surprise, and the baboon disarmed him by biting his wrist. The second man was stunned, before he could move, by a punch on the back of the neck. As for the third, Killer charged at his legs and knocked him over. Kem took care of the last two, who were no match at all for him.

He dragged upright the only fisherman who could still talk, and demanded, 'Why is the town deserted?'

'The tjaty's orders.'

'Passed on by whom?'

'His personal messenger, Mentmose.'

'Have you met him?'

'Everybody here knows him. He's had problems, it seems, but they've been sorted out. Since he's been working with the law again, he's got on very well with the port authorities. There are whispers that he pays them Greek money, metal coins, and that he'll make his friends rich, so they follow his instructions to the letter.'

'What were his instructions?' asked Kem.

'To throw the reserves of smoked fish into the river and then to leave Raqote at once because there was a dangerous disease in the town. The scribes left first, then the ordinary townsfolk, and the workmen followed them.'

'But you didn't?'

'I and my comrades didn't know where to go.'

Killer leapt up and down.

'You're in Mentmose's pay, aren't you?'

'No, we—'

Killer gripped the fisherman's throat tightly; there was fierce anger in his red eyes.

'Yes, yes, we're waiting for him!' gasped the fisherman.

'Where is he hiding?'

'In the marsh, to the west.'

'What is he doing?'

'He's destroying the tablets and papyri we took out of the secretariats.'

'When did he leave?'

'A little after sunrise. When he comes back, we're to take him to the great canal, and we'll go to Memphis with him. He promised each of us a house and a field.'

'And what if he breaks his promise?'

The fisherman raised horrified eyes to Kem's face. 'He couldn't – not a promise like that.'

'Mentmose's word is worth nothing – he's a born liar. For instance, he's never worked for Tjaty Pazair, no matter what he told you. Now, get into this boat and take us to him. If you help us, we'll be lenient with you.'

The boat travelled through expanses which were half water, half grass, where Kem and Pazair would never have been able to find the way. Disturbed, black ibis soared up into the sky, where little round clouds were pushed along by the north wind. All along the hull slithered snakes, as greenish as the opaque water.

In this inhospitable labyrinth, the fisherman made surprisingly good progress.

'I'm taking a shortcut,' he explained. 'Mentmose is some way ahead of us, but we'll catch up with him before he rejoins the main canal where the transport boats ply.'

Kem lent a hand at the oars, Pazair scanned the horizon, and Killer dozed. The time passed too quickly. The tjaty wondered if their guide was tricking them, but Killer's calmness reassured him.

When eventually Killer stood up on his hind legs, the three men began to think that their pursuit had been successful. A few moments later, within sight of the great canal, they spotted another boat. There was only one person aboard, a man with a bald, pink pate which shone in the sunlight.

'Mentmose!' shouted Kem. 'Stop, Mentmose!'

Mentmose speeded up, but the distance between the boats grew inexorably smaller.

Realizing that he could not escape, Mentmose turned to face his pursuers. A javelin, thrown hard and accurately, hit the fisherman in the chest, and the unfortunate man fell overboard and sank into the marsh.

'Get behind me,' Kem ordered the tjaty.

Killer dived into the water.

Mentmose aimed a second javelin at Kem, who ducked at the last moment and dodged it. Pazair, rowing awkwardly, got the boat stuck in a bed of water lilies, prised her free and set off again.

A third javelin in his hand, Mentmose hesitated. Which should he kill first, Pazair or Kem?

Surging up out of the water, Killer gripped the prow of Mentmose's boat and shook it, trying to capsize it, but Mentmose first smashed down on to his paw the stone weight that served as an anchor, and then tried to pierce the paw and nail it to the wood with his javelin. Badly wounded, Killer let go of the prow, just as Kem leapt across from his own boat.

Although he was fat and unused to exercise, Mentmose defended himself with unexpected vigour; his javelin-point grazed Kem's cheek. Unbalanced, Kem fell to the bottom of the boat, while with his forearm he parried a fierce blow; the javelin stuck between two planks. Pazair came alongside Mentmose, who pushed away the tjaty's boat; Kem gripped his adversary's foot, and Mentmose fell into the marsh.

'Stop trying to resist,' ordered Pazair. 'You are our prisoner.'

Mentmose had kept hold of his weapon, and he aimed it at the tjaty. Suddenly, he shrieked in pain, put his hand to his neck, swayed, and sank down into the murky water. Peering over the side of the boat, Pazair saw a catfish sneak off into the reeds that bordered the canal. He recognized it as of a kind rather rare in the Nile: it sometimes drowned people by rendering them unconscious.*

Kem, half mad with worry, spotted Killer struggling against the current. He threw himself into the water and helped him climb back into the boat. With great dignity, the baboon showed him his wound, as if apologizing for failing to arrest the suspect.

'It's a pity,' said Kem. 'But at least Mentmose will never speak again.'

Depressed and shocked, the tjaty was silent as they set off back to Memphis. He had reduced the size of Bel-Tran's secret empire a little more, but at the cost of the fisherman's life, and all lives were precious, even that of Mentmose's accomplice.

Kem examined Killer's wound, which fortunately turned out to be minor. Neferet would oversee his complete recovery.

As he worked, Kem sensed that Pazair was unhappy. He said, 'Mentmose is no loss. He was repulsive, like rotten, worm-eaten fruit.'

'Why do Bel-Tran's people commit so many atrocities? His ambition causes nothing but ill fortune and unhappiness.'

'You're our rampart against the demons. Don't give up.'

'I was expecting to see that justice was respected, not to investigate Branir's murder and live through so many crises. The office of tjaty is "more bitter than bile": that's what the king told me at my enthronement.'

Killer laid his wounded paw on the tjaty's shoulder; he did not remove it until they arrived at Memphis.

With Kem's help, Pazair wrote a long report on recent events. Hardly had they finished when, as they were relaxing in Pazair's garden, a scribe brought him a sealed papyrus.

Malapterurus electricus is a sort of electric catfish; when shocked, its victim receives a discharge of around 200 volts.

Addressed to the tjaty, it came from Raqote and was marked 'Urgent' and 'Confidential'.

Pazair broke the seal, and perused the astonishing message. He read out to Kem:

I, Mentmose, former commander of Memphis's security guards, who was unjustly condemned, denounce Tjaty Pazair as incompetent, criminal and irresponsible. In front of many witnesses, he threw the reserves of dried fish into the sea, and thus deprived the people of the Delta of their basic food for several weeks. I address this complaint to the tjaty himself; in accordance with the law, he will be forced to convene his own trial.

'So,' said Kem, 'that's why Mentmose destroyed all the fisheries' scrolls at Raqote: so that they couldn't contradict him.'

'He was right about one thing,' said Pazair. 'The accusation may be a shameless lie, but I shall be obliged to prove my innocence through a trial. There will have to be a reconstruction, witnesses will have to be called, and Mentmose's foul dealings proved. And all during that time, Bel-Tran will be able to do as he pleases.'

Kem scratched his wooden nose. 'Sending you that letter wouldn't be enough on its own. Mentmose would also have had to lodge an official complaint through Bel-Tran or a senior official, so that you'd be forced to take account of his accusation.'

'Of course.'

'So all there is at the moment is this papyrus.'

'That's right, but it's enough to initiate the court case.'

'If it didn't exist, this matter wouldn't exist, either, would it?'

'I cannot possibly destroy it.'

'But I can.' Kem snatched the papyrus from Pazair and ripped it into a thousand pieces, which were scattered by the wind.

35

Suti and Panther gazed at the beautiful city of Kebet, capital of the fifth province of Upper Egypt, whose white houses gleamed in the sunshine. It stood on the right bank of the Nile, about two days' journey to the north-west of Karnak. From here, trade caravans left for the Red Sea ports and teams of miners departed for the sites in the eastern desert. It was here that Suti had enlisted as a miner, in order to track down General Asher.

Suti's motley army approached the fort guarding the road to the city's main entrance. It was forbidden to move around the area without authorization, and travellers had to be accompanied by guards who checked their identity and ensured their safety.

The officers at the guard-post could not believe their eyes. Where had this ill-assorted band sprung from? And could it really be made up of Libyans, Nubians and All-Seeing Ones? Anyone would have sworn they were fraternizing, whereas the All-Seeing Ones ought to have been surrounding their securely bound prisoners.

Alone, Suti went towards the guards' commander, who was armed with a sword.

With his long hair, bronzed skin, bare chest decorated with a broad collar of gold, and bracelets emphasizing the strength of his arms, he had the proud bearing of a true general bringing back his men from a victorious campaign.

'My name is Suti, and I am an Egyptian like you. Why should we kill each other?'

'Where have you come from?' asked the commander.

'You can see it: from the desert, which we have conquered.'

'But that's illegal.'

'My law, and that of my men, is the law of the desert: if you defy it, you'll die pointlessly. We're going to take control of this town. Join us – you'll do well out of it.'

The guard hesitated. 'Are those really All-Seeing Ones under your command?'

'They're reasonable people. I offer them more than they could ever hope for elsewhere.' Suti threw a gold ingot at the guard's feet. 'That is a modest gift, to help prevent carnage.'

The man picked up the treasure, his eyes bulging.

'My reserves of gold are inexhaustible,' said Suti. 'Go and alert the military governor of the town. I shall wait for him here.'

Like most Egyptian cities, Kebet did not shelter behind walls, so while the guard was delivering the message Suti ordered his soldiers to surround the town, so as to control the ways in and out.

Panther took her lover tenderly by the left arm, like a faithful wife. Covered in golden jewellery, she truly resembled a goddess, born from the marriage of the sky and the desert.

'Aren't you going to fight, my love?' she asked.

'A bloodless victory would be preferable, wouldn't it?'

'I'm not Egyptian. I'd rather see your countrymen being felled by mine. Libyans aren't afraid to fight.'

'This is not the right moment to provoke me.'

'It's always the right moment.' She kissed him with a conqueror's ardour, excited at the idea of becoming queen of Kebet.

The town's military governor soon arrived. He surveyed Suti with an expert eye: he had had a long career in the army, during which he had fought no less an enemy than the Hittites. Now he was preparing for a comfortable retirement in a village near Karnak; he suffered from painful joints, and so confined himself to routine work, well away from the exercise yards. At Kebet, there was no risk of heavy fighting: because of its strategic position it was protected by a detachment of guards, which discouraged smugglers and thieves. The city was prepared to repel raids by looters, but not to drive away formidable soldiers like these.

Behind Suti were well-equipped chariots; to his right, Nubian archers; to his left, Libyan javelin-throwers; in the distance, standing on rocky outcrops, the All-Seeing Ones. And that superb woman, with the fair hair, the coppery skin and the gold jewellery! Although he did not believe in the legends, the governor thought she really might come from the otherworld, perhaps from the mysterious isles that lay at the ends of the earth.

'What are your demands?' he asked Suti.

'That you hand Kebet over to me, so that I can set up my own administration.'

'That's impossible.'

'I am Egyptian,' said Suti, 'and I served in my country's army. Now I have not only my own army but vast wealth, which I have decided to use to benefit the town of the miners and gold-seekers.'

'Was it really you who accused Asher of treachery and murder?'

'It was.'

'You were right,' said the governor. 'He was a corrupt man, without a shred of honour. May the gods ensure that he never reappears.'

'You need not fear that: the desert has swallowed him up.'

'Justice has been done.'

'I'd like to prevent fighting between brothers.'

'I must ensure that public order is respected.'

'I have no intention of disturbing it.'

'Your army doesn't seem exactly peaceable.'

'Unless there's provocation, it will be.'

'What are your conditions?'

'The mayor of Kebet is a tired old man, with no energy left. Let him yield his place to me.'

'The transfer of power would not be valid without the agreement of the provincial governor and the tjaty.'

'We'll begin by driving out this senile old man,' decreed Panther, 'and then destiny shall decide.'

'Take me to him,' ordered Suti.

The mayor of Kebet was eating juicy olives, while listening to a young and extremely talented harp-player; a lover of music, he spent more and more of his time in leisure pursuits. The administration of Kebet presented few difficulties: strong contingents of desert guards ensured security, the people were well fed, specialists dealt with matters concerning metals and precious minerals, and the temple was testimony to the town's prosperity.

The military governor's visit was an unwelcome interruption, but the mayor agreed to see him.

'This is Suti,' said the soldier.

'Suti? General Asher's accuser?'

'The very same.'

'I am happy to welcome you to Kebet. Would you like some cool beer?'

'Very much,' said Suti.

The harp-player withdrew, and cup-bearers brought cups and the delicious brew.

'We are on the verge of disaster,' declared the military governor.

The mayor started. 'What are you saying?'

'Suti's army has encircled the town. If we fight, many people will be killed or injured.'

'An army? With real soldiers?'

The soldier nodded. 'Nubians, who are excellent archers, Libyans, who excel with the javelin, and . . . All-Seeing-Ones.'

'That's insane! I demand that these traitors be arrested and beaten.'

'It won't be easy to persuade them,' objected Suti.

'Not easy? Just where do you think you are?'

'In my own town.'

'Have you gone mad?'

'His army looks formidable,' said the soldier.

'Call for reinforcements!'

'I shall attack before they can get here,' said Suti.

'Arrest this man, Governor,' cried the mayor.

'That would be a mistake,' warned Suti. 'The golden goddess would put the town to fire and the sword.'

'The golden goddess?' asked the mayor.

'She has come back from the distant South, with the key to inexhaustible riches. Welcome her, and you'll find happiness and prosperity. Reject her, and destruction will be visited on your city.'

'Are you so sure you'll win?'

'I have nothing to lose; you have.'

'Aren't you afraid of death?'

'It's been my companion for a long time. The Syrian bear, Asher the traitor and the Nubian bandits all failed to kill me. But try, if you like.'

The mayor thought fast. A good mayor had to be a good negotiator: he had to resolve a thousand conflicts by using the weapon of diplomacy.

He said, 'It seems I must take you seriously, Suti.'

'That would be best.'

'What do you propose?'

'That you give up your office and that I become master of this town.'

'That's unrealistic.'

'I know the soul of this city. It will accept us as rulers, the golden goddess and myself.'

'Your seizure of power will be only an illusion. As soon as the news gets out, the army will dislodge you.'

'It will be a fine battle.'

'Disband your troops.'

'I'm going to rejoin the golden goddess,' declared Suti. 'I'll give you an hour to think about it. Either you accept my proposal or we attack.'

Arm in arm, Suti and Panther gazed at Kebet. They thought of the explorers who had set out along dangerous ways, in quest of treasure they had dreamt of a thousand times. How many had been guided by the gazelle of Isis to the right deposit? How many had come back alive, to marvel at the vast easterly curve of the Nile, around the city of the gold-seekers?

The Nubians were chanting, the Libyans were eating, the All-Seeing Ones were checking the chariots. No one spoke, for they were all awaiting the inevitable clash that would soak the roads and the fields with blood. But some were tired of wandering, some aspired to undreamt-of riches, some wanted to fight in order to prove their bravery. All were under the spell of Panther's beauty and Suti's determination.

'Will the city surrender?' she asked.

'It makes little difference to me.'

'You'll never kill your Egyptian brothers.'

'You shall have your town. In Egypt we worship women who can embody goddesses.'

'You won't escape me by dying in battle.'

'You're Libyan, but you love my land. Its magic has conquered you.'

'If it absorbs you, I'll follow you. My sorcery will be the stronger.'

The military governor arrived before the deadline. 'The mayor accepts your terms,' he said.'

Panther smiled; Suti remained impassive.

'On one condition: that you promise not to sack or pillage the town.'

'We've come to give,' said Suti, 'not to take.'

At the head of their army, the couple entered the town.

The news had already spread, and the inhabitants had gathered on the main road and at the crossroads. Suti told the Nubians to take off the sheets of linen covering the chariots.

The gold shone. Never had the Kebetites seen so much.

Little girls threw flowers to the Nubians, little boys ran alongside the soldiers. In less than an hour, the whole town was celebrating the return of the golden goddess, and singing the legend of the hero Suti, defeater of the demons of the night and discoverer of a giant goldmine.

'You look anxious,' Panther said to Suti.

'This may be a trap.'

The procession went to the mayor's house, an attractive house in the centre of the city, surrounded by a garden. Suti looked hard at the roofs: bow in hand, he was ready to launch an arrow at any hidden archer.

But nothing happened. An enthusiastic crowd surged in from the outskirts of town, convinced that a miracle had just happened. The golden goddess's return would make Kebet the wealthiest city in all Egypt.

On the threshold of the house, the serving-women had spread marigolds, forming an orange carpet. Lotus-flowers in their hands, they welcomed the goddess and General Suti. Delighted, Panther gratified them with a smile and set off royally along a path bordered with tamarisks.

'This house is absolutely charming. Look at its white front, the tall, slender pillars, the lintels decorated with palm-fronds . . . I shall feel at home here. And look over there – that's a

255

stable. We shall go riding, before bathing and drinking sweet wine.'

The inside of the house also charmed her. The mayor had good taste: on the walls were paintings of wild ducks in flight and the luxuriant life of a lake. A wild cat was shown climbing along a papyrus stalk to reach a nest full of birds' eggs, a real feast in prospect.

Panther entered the bedchamber, took off her gold collar and lay down on the ebony-wood bed.

'You are a conqueror, Suti. Love me.'

The new master of Kebet could not resist that appeal.

That evening, a great feast was given for the citizens. Even the humblest folk ate roast meat and drank fine wines. Hundreds of lamps lit the streets, where people danced till dawn. The leading citizens promised to obey Suti and Panther and lauded the beauty of the golden goddess, who received their homage graciously.

'Why is the former mayor not here?' Suti asked the military governor.

'He has left the city.'

'Without my permission?'

'Enjoy your reign – it will be a short one. The mayor will alert the army, and the tjaty will re-establish order in the town.'

'Tjaty Pazair?'

'His reputation grows all the time. He is a just man, but stern.'

'The confrontation will be most interesting.'

'If you're wise you'll surrender.'

Suti smiled. 'I'm a madman, Governor, a madman with unpredictable reactions. My law is the law of the desert, which laughs at rules.'

'At least spare the civilians.'

'Death spares no one. Get drunk: tomorrow, we shall drink

blood and tears.' Suti put his hands over his eyes. 'Go and find the golden goddess. I wish to speak to her.'

Panther was enjoying the song of a harp-player, who invited the diners to enjoy the present moment while tasting in it the flavour of eternity. An army of admirers were devouring her with their eyes. When the governor gave her Suti's message, she hurried back. She found Suti staring gazing fixedly into the distance.

'I'm blind again,' he whispered. 'Take my arm and lead me to the bedchamber. No one must know what's happened.'

A number of revellers hailed the couple, whose disappearance marked the end of the celebration.

When they reached their bedchamber, Suti lay down on his back.

'Neferet will cure you,' said Panther. 'I shall go and fetch her myself.'

'There won't be time.'

'Why not?'

'Because Tjaty Pazair will send the army to kill us.'

36

Neferet bowed before Tuya, Ramses' mother, and said, 'I am at your service, Majesty.'

'It is I who should bow to Egypt's principal doctor. Your work over these past few months has been remarkable.'

Tuya was a haughty woman, with a thin, straight nose, stern eyes, high cheekbones and an almost square chin. She enjoyed unchallenged moral authority. The head of a large household, with a palace in every large town, she advised rathered than ordered, and made sure people respected the values that had made the Egyptian monarchy secure. The Mother of Pharaoh belonged to a line of eminent women. It was queens of her stamp who had expelled the Hyksos invaders and founded the Theban empire, whose legacy had been inherited by the Ramses dynasty.

However, Tuya was deeply worried: for several months, she had been excluded from her son's confidences. Without actually disowning her, Ramses had distanced himself from her, as if he bore so weighty a secret that he could not confide even in his mother.

'How is your health, Majesty?' asked Neferet.

'Thanks to your treatment, I am marvellously well, although my eyes burn a little.'

'Why did you not consult me sooner?'

'My daily duties . . . But yourself? Are you properly attentive to your own health?'

'I have no time to think about it.'

'Well, Neferet, you must. If you were to fall ill, many patients would sink into despair.'

'Let me examine you, Majesty.'

The reason for the burning was easy to establish: the Mother of Pharaoh was suffering from an irritation of the eye-membrane. Neferet prescribed a remedy made from bat droppings, which would soothe the inflammation without causing any new problems.*

'You will be cured within a week, Majesty. But please do not forget your usual eye-drops. Your eyes have greatly improved, but the treatment must be continued.'

'I thoroughly dislike having to concern myself with my own health – I would disobey any other doctor. Only Egypt deserves our attention. How is your husband bearing the weight of his office?'

'It is as heavy as a block of granite and as bitter as bile. But he will not give in.'

'I knew that the moment I first met him. At court, he is admired, feared and envied: that is the proof of his skill. His appointment caused great surprise and there has been no shortage of critics, but through what he has done he has silenced his detractors, to the point where Tjaty Bagey has been forgotten. That is no mean achievement.'

'Pazair cares little for the opinions of others.'

'That is all to the good. So long as he remains impervious to blame and praise alike, he will be a good tjaty. The king values his integrity and even grants him his trust. In other words, Pazair knows Ramses' most secret preoccupations,

*Bat droppings, which are rich in vitamin A, are also an excellent antibiotic; in other words, the modern treatment corresponds to that of the ancient Egyptians.

the ones I do not know. And you know them too, Neferet, because you and your husband form a single being. That is the truth, is it not?'

'It is the truth.'

'Is the kingdom in danger?'

'Yes, Majesty, great danger.'

'I have known that since Ramses ceased to confide in me – no doubt he feared I might do something too high-handed, and perhaps he was right. However, now it is Pazair who is directing the battle.'

'Our enemies are formidable.'

'That is why it is time I intervened. The tjaty will not dare ask for my direct support, but I must help him. Whom does he fear?'

'Bel-Tran.'

'I detest upstarts,' declared Tuya. 'But fortunately their greed eventually destroys them. I assume he has the support of his wife?'

'Indeed, Majesty. She is his accomplice.'

'You may leave that goose to me. Her way of bobbing her neck when she greets me exasperates me.'

'Please do not underestimate her – she is dangerous.'

'Thanks to you, my sight is still excellent. I shall deal with that little snake.'

'Majesty, I must tell you that Pazair is in great distress at the thought of presiding over the ceremony when foreign tributes are presented. He is hoping that the king will return from Pi-Ramses in time to take that role himself.'

'Tell him there is no hope of it. Pharaoh's mood is increasingly sombre. He no longer leaves his palace, grants no audiences, and leaves the tjaty to take care of all day-to-day matters.'

'Is he ill?'

'His teeth are probably troubling him.'

'Do you wish me to examine him?'

'He has just dismissed his personal tooth-doctor as incompetent. After the ceremony, you shall accompany me to Pi-Ramses.'

A flotilla from the North brought the foreign envoys. No other boat was permitted on the river while the flotilla docked and moored, which process was overseen by the river guards. On the quay, the head of the Foreign Affairs secretariat welcomed Egypt's guests, who were ushered into comfortable travelling-chairs, followed by their retinues. The imposing procession set off for the palace.

Pharaoh's vassals and trading-partners had come, as they did every year, to pay him homage by bringing tributes. This year Memphis had been granted two days' holiday and would celebrate the peace that had been securely established through Ramses' wisdom and resolve.

Seated on a low-backed throne, dressed in the great robe of his office, weighted and stiff, a sceptre in his right hand, the figurine of Ma'at at his throat, Pazair was extremely nervous. Behind him, on his right, was the Mother of Pharaoh; in the first row were the Friends of Pharaoh, including Bel-Tran, who looked exultant. Silkis was wearing a new gown, which made some less wealthy courtiers' wives turn pale with envy. Bagey had agreed to assist his successor by advising him on protocol, and his presence reassured Pazair. The copper heart Bagey wore on his chest would symbolize, in the ambassadors' eyes, the trust that Ramses still had in him, and would prove that the change of tjaty did not mean a break in Egypt's foreign policy.

Pazair was authorized to direct the ceremony in the king's absence; last year, Bagey had performed this duty. The young tjaty would have preferred to remain in the background, but he knew how important the ceremony was: the visitors must leave satisfied, so that relations with their countries remained good. In exchange for the gifts, they hoped for consideration

261

and understanding of their trading situation. The tjaty must tread a path between excessive strength and culpable weakness. One serious mistake by him, and the balance would be destroyed.

This was probably the last time the ancient ritual would take place. Bel-Tran would dispense with it, because it showed no tangible profit. He would ignore the fact that it was on a foundation of reciprocity, discretion and mutual respect that the sages of the time of the pyramids had built a happy civilization.

Bel-Tran's insolent satisfaction troubled Pazair. The closure of the Greek exchange-houses had dealt him a serious blow, but he seemed hardly to care. Had it come too late to slow his onward march? With less than two months before the festival of regeneration and the king's forced abdication, Bel-Tran might be content to wait, without stirring up any more trouble.

Waiting . . . A tremendous ordeal for an ambitious man whose normal state was feverish activity. Many complaints had reached the tjaty, begging him to replace Bel-Tran with someone calmer and less tyrannical. He tortured his subordinates by refusing to grant them any rest. Under the pretext of urgent work, he overwhelmed them with made-up cases in order to keep a firm hand on them and prevent them from thinking. There had been occasional protests: Bel-Tran's methods were brutal, and he showed no consideration to employees who did not want to be reduced solely to their skills at work. He cared nothing for that: the amount of work a man did was all that counted with him. Anyone who opposed him was dispensed with.

Some of his allies had, with the greatest discretion, opened their hearts to the tjaty. They were tired of Bel-Tran's incessant talk, when he lost himself in interminable speeches in which he promised the moon; they were tiring of his duplicity and his sometimes crude lies. His determination to be regent, no matter what the circumstances, revealed the extent of his rapacity. A few provincial leaders, who at first had been won over, were now displaying polite indifference.

Pazair was making progress. Little by little, he was revealing the man's true character: inconstant and untrustworthy. The danger he represented had not lessened, but his persuasive abilities were fading day by day.

So why did Bel-Tran look so happy?

A priest announced the visitors, and silence fell over the tjaty's audience chamber.

The envoys came from Damascus, Byblos, Palmyra, Aleppo, Ugarit, Qadesh, the Hittite lands, Syria, Phoenicia, Canaan, Minoa, Cyprus, Arabia, Africa and Asia, from ports, trading cities and capitals. Not one came empty-handed.

The delegate from the mysterious land of Punt, an African paradise, was a small man with very dark skin and curly hair. He offered the skins of wild animals, incense, ostrich eggs and feathers. The Nubian envoy was greatly liked by those watching, for his refinement: a kilt cut from a leopard-skin, covered by a pleated skirt, a coloured feather in his hair, silver earrings and wide bracelets. His servants laid jars of oil, shields, gold and incense at the foot of the throne, while cheetahs on leashes and a giraffe filed past.

Minoan fashion provoked amusement: black hair with locks of unequal length, beardless, straight-nosed faces, low-cut kilts trimmed with braid and decorated with diamond-shapes and rectangles, sandals with turned-up toes. The envoy laid down daggers, swords, animal-headed vases, ewers and cups. He was followed by the envoy from Byblos, a loyal ally of Egypt, who brought ox-hides, rope and rolls of papyrus.

Each envoy bowed before the tjaty and spoke time-honoured words: 'Receive my country's tribute, brought in homage to His Majesty, Pharaoh of Upper and Lower Egypt, in order to seal peace.'

The representative from Asia, where the Egyptian army had fought hard battles in a past that Ramses believed had gone by, arrived accompanied by his wife. He wore a kilt decorated with tassels and a red and blue tunic with long sleeves tied with thongs; she wore a tiered skirt and a striped cape. Their tribute, to the court's astonishment, was the smallest. Usually Asia closed the ceremony by laying before Pharaoh or the tjaty copper ingots, lapis-lazuli, turquoises, lengths of rare wood, jars of ointment, harnesses for horses, bows, quivers full of arrows, and daggers, not to mention bears, lions and bulls for the royal menagerie. This time, all the envoy offered were a few cups, some jars of oil and jewellery of no great value.

When he greeted the tjaty, he showed no emotion. Nevertheless, the message was clear: Asia was addressing grave reproaches to Egypt. If the reasons for the discord were not brought to light and the causes dispelled with all possible speed, the spectre of war would reappear.

While Memphis was feasting, from the docks to the craftsmen's districts, Pazair received the Asian envoy privately. No scribe or other official was present: before declarations were registered and took on a formal nature, attempts must be made to re-establish harmony.

The envoy had lively eyes and an incisive way with words. 'Why did Ramses not preside over the ceremony himself?'

'He is at Pi-Ramses, as he was last year, to oversee the building of a new temple.'

'Has Tjaty Bagey been disowned?'

'By no means – as you saw.'

'His presence and the copper heart he still wears. Yes, I noted those signs that he is still respected. But you are very young, Tjaty Pazair. Why has Ramses entrusted you with this office, one which everyone knows is overwhelming?'

'Bagey felt too tired to continue. He asked permission to retire, and the king granted his request.'

'That does not answer my question.'

'Who can know the secrets of a pharaoh's thoughts?'

'His tjaty,' said the envoy.

'I am not certain that I do.'

'So you are merely a puppet.'

'That is for you to judge.'

'My opinion is based on facts: you were a minor provincial judge and Ramses has made you first minister of Egypt. I have known the king for ten years; he is never wrong about the worth of those around him. You must be an exceptional person, Tjaty Pazair.'

'It is my turn to question you, if you will allow me to.'

'That is your duty.'

'What did the slightness of your tribute signify?'

'Did it seem insufficient?'

'You know what you have done: that it verges on an insult.'

'"Verges on", indeed. It shows my restraint and a last wish for conciliation, following an insult we have suffered.'

'I don't understand.'

'People boast of your love for the truth. Is it only a fable?'

'On the name of Pharaoh, I swear I do not know your grievances.'

The Asian ambassador was shaken; his tone became less acid. 'That is very strange. Have you lost control of your secretariats, and in particular of the Double White House?'

'I disliked certain practices dating from before my appointment, and I proceeded to reform them. Have you been the victim of an offensive act about which I have not been informed?'

'That word is far too weak! It would be more correct to speak of a crime so serious that it could lead to a break in relations between our countries – even to war.'

Pazair tried to mask his anxiety, but his voice was unsteady. 'Will you enlighten me?'

'I have difficulty believing that you are not responsible.'

'As tjaty, I accept the responsibility; but, at the risk of appearing ridiculous, I confirm that I know nothing about it. How can I make amends for this offence if I do not know what it is?'

'Egyptians often mock our taste for cunning and conspiracies. I fear that you may yourself have fallen victim to them. Your youth does not win only friends, it seems.'

'Pray explain.'

'Either you are the most accomplished of actors or you will not be tjaty for much longer. Have you heard tell of our trade exchanges?'

Pazair did not flinch, despite the biting sarcasm. Even if the envoy thought him both incompetent and ignorant, he must learn the truth.

'When we send you our goods,' continued the envoy, 'the Double White House sends us their equivalent in gold. That is the custom, and has been ever since peace was established.'

'Has the delivery not been made?'

'The ingots arrived, but the gold was of very bad quality, poorly purified and brittle, only good enough to please a few backward nomads. By sending us unusable gold, Egypt made a mockery of us. The integrity of Ramses himself is implicated: we consider that he has broken his word.'

So that was why Bel-Tran had looked so pleased with himself. Destroying Ramses' prestige in Asia would enable him to pose as a saviour, determined to correct the king's misdeeds.

'There has been a mistake,' said Pazair, 'not an attempt to offend you.'

'The Double White House does not act alone, so far as I know! It obeyed orders from above.'

'Consider that you have been the victim of flawed procedures and a lack of coordination between the secretariats I head, but do not see hostility in it. I myself shall inform the king of my own incompetence.'

The envoy regarded him thoughtfully. 'You have been betrayed, have you not?'

'It is up to me to be aware of that and to take the necessary measures. Otherwise, you will soon be dealing with a new tjaty.'

'I would regret that.'

'Will you accept my most sincere apologies?'

'I believe you, but Asia demands reparation, in accordance with custom. Send double the agreed quantity of gold, as soon as possible. If you do not, I fear war is inevitable.'

Pazair and Neferet were preparing to leave for Pi-Ramses when a royal messenger asked to see the tjaty as a matter of urgency.

'Something serious has happened, Tjaty,' he said. 'The mayor of Kebet has been driven from his city by an armed band of Libyans and Nubians.'

'Was anyone injured?'

'No. They seized the town without waging battle. Some of the All-Seeing Ones have joined the rebels, and the military governor dared not resist.'

'Who is in command of the rebels?'

'A man named Suti, aided by a golden goddess who has subjugated the population.'

Immense joy flooded Pazair: Suti was alive – very much alive! It was marvellous news, even if his much-hoped-for reappearance had occurred in rather chaotic circumstances.

'The soldiers stationed in Thebes are ready for action; their commander merely awaits your orders. As soon as you have signed the necessary documents, I shall ensure that they get to him. According to him, order will soon be re-established. Even if the rebels are properly armed, there are too few of them to resist a full-scale attack.'

'As soon as I return from Pi-Ramses, I shall deal with the matter myself. In the meantime, our soldiers are to surround the city and pitch camp in defensive positions. They are to allow through food caravans and merchants, so that the town will not go short of anything. Inform Suti that I shall come to Kebet as soon as possible and that I shall negotiate with him.'

37

From the terrace of the sumptuous house that had been set aside for them, Pazair and Neferet gazed out over Ramses' favourite city, Pi-Ramses, whose name meant 'Domain of Ramses' or 'Temple of Ramses'. It stood not far from Avaris – hated capital of the Hyksos invaders, who had been driven out at the start of the New Kingdom – and at the king's instigation had become the largest city in the Delta, with some hundred thousand inhabitants. It had many temples, dedicated to Amon, Ra, Ptah, the formidable Set, lord of storms, Sekhmet and Astarte, a goddess who had been brought to Egypt by the Hyksos. The army had three barracks; and to the south lay the port, with its many store-houses and workshops. At the centre stood the royal palace, which was surrounded by the houses of the nobles and senior officials, and a large ornamental lake.

In the hot season, Pi-Ramses enjoyed an agreeable climate, for the city lay between two branches of the Nile, 'the Waters of Ra' and 'the Waters of Avaris'; many canals crossed it, and ponds full of fish provided fishermen with an opportunity to indulge in their favourite pursuit.

The site had not been chosen by chance. Pi-Ramses was ideally placed for observing the Delta and Asia, and a perfect departure-point for Pharaoh's soldiers in the event of disturbances in the protectorates. The sons of the nobility vied with one another in their eagerness to serve in the chariot corps or to ride magnificent horses, swift and highly strung. The city's carpenters, boat-builders and metalworkers, who had been provided with excellent equipment, were often visited by the king, who took a keen interest in their work.

'What joy to dwell in Pi-Ramses,' declared a popular song. 'No more beautiful city exists. There, the small is given as much consideration as the great, the acacia and the sycamore dispense their shade to walkers, the palaces dazzle with gold and turquoise, the wind is gentle, the birds play around the pools.'

During an all-too-short morning, the tjaty and his wife had sampled the tranquillity of the orchards and the olive groves, surrounded by vineyards producing a fine wine which was served at festivals and feasts. The grain-stores reached almost to the sky. The fronts of the opulent houses were glazed with blue tiles, which had earned Pi-Ramses its nickname of 'the Turquoise City'. On the threshold of the brick homes built between the great houses, children were eating apples and pomegranates, and playing with wooden dolls. They laughed at the pretentious scribes and cheered the chariot officers.

The dream was but a brief one. Although the fruit might taste like honey and the garden of his house be a paradise, the tjaty was preparing to confront Pharaoh. According to what the Mother of Pharaoh had said in confidence, the king no longer believed in his tjaty's success. His isolation was that of a condemned man, without hope.

Neferet was painting her face. Using small, bulbous-ended sticks, she drew lines round her eyes with kohl. The box in which face-paints were kept bore the significant name of 'That Which Opens the Sight'. Round her waist, Pazair slipped the belt of amethyst beads, including parts in worked gold, that Neferet loved so much.

'Will you come with me to the palace?' he asked.

'My presence there has been requested.'

'I'm afraid, Neferet, afraid of having disappointed the king.'

She leant back, laying her head on Pazair's shoulder. 'My hand will always be in your hand,' she whispered. 'My greatest happiness is to walk with you in a secluded garden, where the only sound is the wind's voice. Your hand will always be in mine, for my heart is drunk with joy when we are together. What more could anyone want, tjaty of Egypt?'

The palace guard was changed three times a month, on the first, eleventh and twenty-first days. Each time they came on duty, they received meat, wine and cakes, plus the normal wage, paid in grain. For the tjaty's arrival, the men formed a guard of honour; his visit would mean a fine bonus for them.

A steward welcomed Pazair and Neferet, and told them, 'Pharaoh awaits you in the garden.' He led them through the summer palace. The entrance hall, with its white walls and coloured flagstones, led to several audience chambers decorated with tiles glazed in yellow and brown, with dots of blue, red and black. In the throne room, cartouches containing the king's name formed friezes. The reception halls reserved for greeting foreign rulers shimmered with pictures: naked girls swimming, birds in flight and turquoise landscapes enchanted the eye.

The ancients had said that Egypt should resemble an immense garden in which the most diverse species lived in peace. Ramses endeavoured to realize that wish by planting many, many trees. When Pazair and Neferet saw him he was kneeling down, planting an apple tree. On his wrists he wore his favourite gold and lapis-lazuli bracelets, their upper part decorated with wild ducks.

Ten paces away stood Ramses' finest bodyguard: a half-tame lion which had accompanied the young king on the battlefields of Asia at the start of his reign. Named Invincible, it obeyed no one but its master; anyone who approached the king with hostile intentions would have been torn to pieces.

The tjaty stepped forward; Neferet waited inside a shelter near a pond where fish were frolicking.

'How fares the kingdom, Pazair?' The king turned his back on his tjaty.

'As badly as it could, Majesty.'

'Were there problems at the tribute ceremony?'

'The Asian envoy is extremely unhappy.'

'Asia is a permanent danger. Its peoples do not like peace – they take advantage of it to prepare for the next war. I have strengthened the western and eastern frontiers with chains of fortresses; the former will prevent the Libyans from invading us, and the latter the Asians. Archers and footsoldiers have received orders to watch day and night, and to communicate with each other by signals. Here, at Pi-Ramses, I receive daily reports on events in the Asian princedoms, and I also receive reports on the activities of my tjaty.'

The king stood up and turned to face Pazair. 'Some nobles are complaining; some provincial governors are protesting; the court feels slighted. "If the tjaty is wrong," says the Rule, "let him not hide his mistake in darkness. Rather, let him make it public and make it known that he will rectify it."'

'What fault am I guilty of, Majesty?'

'Did you not punish dignitaries and senior officials by having them beaten? Those who carried out the base tasks even sang: "Fine gifts for you who have never received the like".'

'I was not aware of that detail, but the law was applied, to the rich as to the poor. The higher the guilty party's rank, the more severe the punishment.'

'Do you deny nothing?'

'Nothing.'

Ramses embraced Pazair. 'Then I am happy. The exercise of power has not changed you.'

'I feared I had disappointed you.'

'The Greek traders sent me a complaint filling an interminable scroll. Did you stop their trade?'

'I put an end to the smuggling of coins and the setting up of exchange-houses on our territory.'

'The mark of Bel-Tran, of course.'

'The culprits have been expelled, and Bel-Tran's main source of wealth has thus been cut off. Some of his friends are disappointed, and have distanced themselves from him.'

'As soon as he takes power, he will introduce the circulation of money.'

'We still have a few weeks left, Majesty.'

'Without the Testament of the Gods, I shall be compelled to abdicate.'

'Will Bel-Tran be able to rule, weakened as he is?'

'He will destroy rather than give up. Men of his type are not rare, but up to now we have succeeded in keeping them away from the throne.'

'Let us still hope.'

'What does Asia accuse us of?' asked Ramses.

'Bel-Tran had poor-quality gold sent to them.'

'The worst insult imaginable! Did the envoy threaten you?'

'There is only one way to prevent war: by sending twice the agreed quantity.'

'Have we enough?'

'No, Majesty. Bel-Tran took care to empty our reserves.'

'Asia will consider that I have broken my word. One more reason to justify my abdication – and Bel-Tran will play at being the country's saviour.'

Pazair said hesitantly, 'We may have one last chance.'

'Do not keep me waiting.'

'Suti is in Kebet, accompanied by a golden goddess. I wonder, might he know the whereabouts of easily accessible treasure?'

'Go and ask him.'

'Majesty, the matter is not so simple.'

'Why not?'

'Because Suti is at the head of an armed band. He has driven out the mayor of Kebet and controls the city.'

'That is insurrection.'

'Our troops have surrounded Kebet, but I have forbidden them to attack. The invasion was peaceful – we have no deaths or injuries to mourn.'

'What are you going to dare ask of me, Pazair?'

'If I succeed in persuading Suti to help us, impunity for him.'

'He escaped from the fortress in Nubia, and he has committed an act of insubordination of exceptional gravity.'

'He was the victim of injustice and has always served Egypt with devotion. Does that not deserve leniency?'

'Put aside your friendship, Tjaty, and conform to the Rule. Let order be re-established.'

Pazair bowed.

Ramses, accompanied by the lion, went to the shelter where Neferet was waiting.

'Well, Neferet, are you ready to torture me?'

Neferet's examination lasted more than an hour. Ramses was suffering from inflammation of the joints, and to control the pain she prescribed daily decoctions of willow bark.* She also found that several fillings in his teeth were in urgent need of replacement. In the palace laboratory, she prepared a mixture of pistachio resin, Nubian earth, honey, crushed grindstone, green eye drops and fragments of copper, with which to fill the king's teeth, and she advised him to give up chewing papyrus-shoots, so as to avoid premature wearing-out of the teeth.

'Are you hopeful, Neferet?'

*From which our modern aspirin is derived.

'To be completely honest, I fear there may be an abscess at the base of an upper left rear tooth – you should receive much more regular checks. However, we shall avoid having to take out the tooth, if you treat your gums with frequent applications of mother-tincture of calendula.'

Neferet washed her hands; Ramses rinsed his mouth with natron.

He said, 'What concerns me is not my future but Egypt's. I know of your ability to detect the invisible: like my father, you sense the lines of power that hide behind appearance. I ask again: are you hopeful?'

'Must I answer you?'

'Does that mean you despair?'

'Branir's soul protects Egypt: his sufferings will not have been in vain. In the very depths of the darkness, a light will be born.'

The Nubians, stationed on the roofs of the houses in Kebet, were keeping watch on the surrounding areas. Every three hours, the old warrior reported to Suti.

This time, he was breathless with haste. 'Hundreds of soldiers – they came up the Nile.'

'Are we surrounded?'

'Yes, though at the moment they're keeping their distance and holding their positions. If they attack, we'll have no chance.'

'Tell your men to rest.'

'I don't trust the Libyans. All they think of is stealing and playing dice.'

'The All-Seeing Ones are watching them.'

'And when will they turn against you?'

'When my gold runs out – and it's inexhaustible.'

Sceptical, the old warrior returned to the terrace of the mayor's house, from where he gazed out at the Nile. Already he was tiring of the desert.

Kebet held its breath. Everyone knew the army would soon attack. If Suti's men surrendered, a bloodbath would be averted, but Panther was inflexible and persuaded her faithful to resist or face terrible punishments. The golden goddess had not come back from the distant South to surrender to the first soldiers she encountered. Soon her empire would extend to the sea, and anyone who obeyed her would know limitless joy.

How could they not believe in Suti's power? The light of another world shone within him; his bearing could only be that of a demi-god. A stranger to fear, he gave courage to men who had never had it. The All-Seeing Ones dreamt of a leader like him, who could command without raising his voice, who could draw the sturdiest bow and shatter the skulls of the cowardly. The legend of Suti was growing: he had penetrated the mountains' secret places and extracted the rarest metals from their bellies. Anyone who dared attack him would fall prey to flames which sprang from the bowels of the earth.

'You've cast a spell on this town and its people,' Suti said to Panther, who was lying beside the pool after bathing.

'This is only a start, my darling. Kebet will soon seem too small for us.'

'Your dream's going to turn into a nightmare. We shan't be able to hold out for long against the Egyptian army.'

Panther seized him round the neck and pulled him down beside her. 'Don't you believe in your golden goddess any more?'

'I must be mad. Why else would I listen to you?'

'Because I keep saving your life. Don't concern yourself with this nightmare, but be content with the dream – doesn't it have the colours of gold?'

Suti would have liked to resist her, but had to admit that he was soon overcome. The mere touch of her golden skin, with its exotic scent, awoke a desire as tempestuous as the Nile in flood. He at once took the initiative and intoxicated her with caresses. Consenting, Panther became gentleness itself, before throwing Suti on to his side and falling with him into the lake.

Their bodies were still united when the old warrior interrupted them.

'An Egyptian officer wishes to speak with you. He's at the main entrance, beside the Nile.'

'Is he alone?'

'Alone and unarmed.'

The town fell silent, when Suti met the officer of the Army of Amon, who was dressed in a coloured coat of mail.

'Are you Suti, who drove out the mayor of Kebet?' asked the officer.

'The mayor offered me his position.'

'And do you command the rebels?'

'I have the honour to be the leader of free men.'

'Your lookouts have seen that we came in force. However strong you are in battle, you will be wiped out.'

'In the chariot corps, my best instructor advised me to distrust vanity. What's more, I have never yet yielded to threats.'

'Do you refuse to surrender?'

'Can you doubt it?'

'Any attempt at escape is bound to fail.'

'Attack – we're ready.'

'That decision will be made not by me but by the tjaty. Until he arrives, you will receive provisions as normal.'

'When will he get here?'

'Take advantage of this respite. As soon as Tjaty Pazair disembarks, he will lead us to victory and re-establish order.'

277

38

Silkis could not wait for Bel-Tran to come home. She rushed round the house, called conflicting instructions to her servants, ran into the garden, slapped her daughter, who had stolen a pastry, and let her son chase a cat, which took refuge up a tree. Then she turned her attention to the midday meal, told the cook to prepare different dishes, and lectured her children.

As soon as Bel-Tran arrived she rushed to the door of the house. 'My darling, it's wonderful!'

Scarcely giving him time to get down from his travelling-chair, she pulled so hard on his linen wrap, which protected his sensitive shoulders from the sun, that she tore it.

'Be careful! That cost a fortune.'

'Come quickly. I've some incredible news for you. I've poured you some wine in your favourite cup.'

More child-woman than ever, Silkis simpered all the way through the brief walk to her bedchamber, and enlivened the way high-pitched laughter.

'This morning,' she said 'I received a message from the palace.' From a chest she took a message marked with the king's seal. 'An invitation from the Mother of Pharaoh – for me! What a triumph!'

'An invitation?'

'To her very own palace! All Memphis shall know of this.'

Puzzled, Bel-Tran read the papyrus. It was written in the Mother of Pharaoh's own hand. The fact that she had not used the services of her personal scribe indicated the very marked interest she had in meeting Silkis.

'Several great ladies of the court have been hoping for this honour for years – and I have been given it!'

'It's surprising, though.'

'Surprising? Not at all! It is thanks to you, darling. Tuya is an intelligent woman, and very close to her son. He must have made her understand that his reign is about to end, and she is preparing for the future. She will try to become friends with me, so that you will let her keep her prerogatives and privileges.'

'That assumes that Ramses has told her the truth,' said Bel-Tran.

'He may have confined himself to telling her about his abdication. Tiredness, ill health, his failure to introduce new ways to Egypt – whatever reason he gave, Tuya knows change is coming and she's worried about her future. What better way to ingratiate herself with you than by introducing me into her circle of confidantes? The old lady is very cunning, but she knows she's lost. If we're her enemies, she'll lose her palaces, her household and her wealth. At her age, that would be unbearable.'

'Making use of her prestige in the country would not be a bad idea. If she sanctions the new power, it will take root very quickly and there will be very little opposition. I dared not hope for such a gift from destiny.'

'How should I behave?' asked Silkis, very excited.

'With respect and goodwill. Grant all her requests, and make her understand that we accept her help and her submission.'

'And what if she asks about her son's fate?'

'Ramses will withdraw into a temple in Nubia, where he will grow old with the priests. As soon as our new order is in place and there can be no going back, we'll get rid of both mother and son. We cannot let the past encumber us.'

'You're wonderful, my darling.'

Kem was in a bad mood. If Pazair had little taste for worldly things and protocol, Kem positively detested them. Obliged to wear elaborate clothing worthy of his rank, he felt ridiculous. The barber had dressed his hair, put on his wig, and shaved and perfumed him, and a painter had coloured his wooden nose black. For more than an hour he had been waiting in the antechamber, and he resented this waste of time. But he could not refuse to answer a summons from the Mother of Pharaoh.

At last, a steward showed him into Tuya's office, an austere place decorated with maps of the country and stelae dedicated to the ancestors. Although she was much shorter than the Nubian, the Mother of Pharaoh impressed him more than a wild animal about to spring.

'I wanted to test your patience,' she said. 'A commander of soldiers must never lose his head.'

Kem did not know if he ought to remain standing, sit down, answer or keep silent.

'What do you think of Tjaty Pazair?' asked Tuya.

'He is a just man – the only just man I know. If you wish to hear criticisms of him, Majesty, ask someone else.' Kem immediately realized that his blunt answer had been inexcusably lacking in courtesy.

'You have more character than your miserable pre-decessor, but you practise the art of polite conversation rather less well,' said the queen drily.

'I spoke the truth, Majesty.'

'As a commander should.'

'I care nothing for my rank or my title. I accepted them only in order to help Pazair.'

'The tjaty is fortunate, and I like men who are fortunate. Therefore you shall help him.'

'How?'

'I want to know everything about the lady Silkis.'

As soon as the tjaty's boat was announced, the river guards cleared a path to the main quay of Memphis. The heavy transport ships manoeuvred with the grace of dragonflies, and found their places without colliding.

The shadow-eater had spent the night on the roof of a grain-store between the trade-control office and a papyrus storehouse. Having committed his crime, he would escape by that route. At the port offices all he had had to do was listen, and he had gained detailed information about Pazair's return from Pi-Ramses. The security measures put in place by Kem meant that improvization was out of the question.

The shadow-eater's plan rested on a plausible supposition: to avoid the crowds, Pazair would not take the main road from the port to the palace. Instead, surrounded by guards, he would take the road past the grain-store – it was narrow, but a chariot could just get through.

The very chariot in which he would ride had just halted, right below the shadow-eater.

This time the throwing-stick would not miss its target. The stick was a simple one, from a lot sold off cheaply in the market because they were second-hand. The seller had not noticed the assassin as he mingled with a group of noisy buyers. Like them, he had offered fresh onions in exchange.

Having committed the crime, he would re-establish contact with Bel-Tran. The latter's position was becoming more and more shaky, and many people predicted that he would soon fall from power. By killing Pazair, the shadow-eater would give him back the certainty of victory.

No doubt Bel-Tran would think of killing him, not of rewarding him, so he would take precautions. They would meet in a deserted place, and Bel-Tran would come alone. If they agreed on mutual silence, Bel-Tran would leave alive and triumphant; if not, the shadow-eater would close his employer's mouth for ever. His demands would not alarm Bel-Tran: more gold, immunity, an official position under another name, and a large house in the Delta. It would be as if the shadow-eater had never existed. And, one day, Bel-Tran would need his services again . . . A reign built on murder was being consolidated, thanks to him.

On the quay were Kem and Killer. The shadow-eater's last anxiety was dispelled: the wind was strong, and it was blowing in the right direction. The baboon would not catch his scent and would have no chance of blocking the throwing-stick, which would not fly in a curve but would fall from the sky as swiftly as a bolt of lightning. There was just one difficulty: the narrowness of the angle. But cold rage and the desire to succeed would make the assassin's aim perfectly true.

The tjaty's boat moored. Pazair and Neferet disembarked, and were immediately surrounded by Kem and his men. After greeting the couple by bowing his head, Killer went to the head of the procession.

He avoided the main road and set off along the narrow street. The wind unsettled the baboon, whose nostrils flared in vain.

In a few seconds, the tjaty would halt before his chariot. In the time it took him to step aboard, the throwing-stick would fracture his head.

Arm bent, the shadow-eater concentrated. Kem and Killer stood on either side of the chariot. The Nubian helped Neferet to climb in. Behind her was Pazair. The shadow-eater stood up, saw Pazair's profile and kept hold of his weapon to the last moment, though it was already leaving his hand.

A man stepped in front of Pazair, masking him.

Bel-Tran had just saved the man whose death he so desired.

'I must speak to you at once,' said Bel-Tran, his hurried

words and jerky movements made Killer even more unsettled.

'Is it so urgent?' asked Pazair, surprised.

'Your office tells me your meetings have been cancelled for several days.'

'I do not believe I am required to account to you for how I spend my time.'

'The situation is extremely serious: I appeal to you in the name of Ma'at.'

Bel-Tran did not speak those words lightly before several witnesses, including Kem. The declaration was so solemn that the tjaty must accede to the request, provided it was well founded.

'She will answer you by her Rule. Be at my office in two hours.'

The wind died, and Killer raised his eyes to the skyline. The shadow-eater flattened himself against the roof. Wriggling on his belly, he beat a retreat. When he heard the tjaty's chariot moving away, he bit his lips until they bled.

The tjaty congratulated young Bak, who had become his personal scribe. The youth, who was scrupulous and hard-working, permitted no ambiguity in the wording of official documents. Pazair had entrusted to him the task of examining decrees and communications, in order to forestall criticism from officials and the population.

'Your work gives complete satisfaction, Bak, but it would be advisable for you to move to another department.'

The youth blanched. 'What have I done wrong?'

'Nothing.'

'Be honest, I beg you.'

'I repeat, nothing.'

'In that case, why transfer me?' asked Bak.

'For your own good.'

'My own good? But I'm happy here. Have I annoyed somebody?'

'On the contrary, your tact is admired by all the scribes.'

'Tell me the truth.'

'Well, it would be wise to distance yourself from me.'

'I won't do it.'

'My future is very uncertain,' said Pazair, 'and so is that of anyone close to me.'

'It's that man Bel-Tran, isn't it? He's trying to bring about your downfall.'

'It's pointless for you to be dragged down with me. If you move to another department, you'll be safe.'

'Such cowardice would be disgusting. Whatever happens, I want to stay with you.'

'You're very young. Why risk your career?'

'I don't care about my career. You've given me your trust, and I owe you mine.'

'Are you fully aware of how unwise you're being?'

'If you were in my place, would you do otherwise?'

Pazair gave in. 'Check this text concerning a tree plantation in the northern part of Memphis. There must be no argument about the chosen locations.'

Wild with joy, Bak returned to work.

His expression darkened when he showed Bel-Tran into the tjaty's office.

Seated in the scribe's position on the floor, Pazair was writing a letter to the provincial governors regarding the next annual flood; they were to check that the earthen banks and retaining-pools were in good condition, so that the country would gain the full benefit of the fertilizing waters.

Bel-Tran, who was wearing a new robe with exaggerated pleats, remained standing.

'I am listening,' said the tjaty without looking up. 'Would you oblige me by not losing yourself in unnecessary talk?'

'Do you know the extent of your power?'

'I am more concerned with my duties.'

'You occupy a crucial post, Pazair. If grave misdeeds are

committed at the highest level of the state, it is up to you to see that justice is done.'

'I dislike insinuations.'

'Then I'll speak plainly. You are the only person who can judge the members of the royal family – even the king himself, if he betrays his country.'

'Do you dare to speak of treason?'

'Ramses is guilty.'

'Who accuses him?'

'I do, so that our moral values may be respected. By sending poor-quality gold to our Asian friends, Ramses endangered Egypt. He must face trial before your court.'

'It was you who sent that gold.'

'Pharaoh does not allow anyone else to handle Asian affairs, and no one will believe that one of his ministers acted against his wishes.'

'As you say, it is up to me to establish the truth. Ramses is not guilty, and I shall prove that.'

'I shall provide evidence against him. As tjaty, you will be obliged to take account of it and to begin the trial process.'

'The preparations will take a very long time.'

Bel-Tran lost his temper. 'Don't you understand that I'm offering you one last chance? By becoming the king's accuser, you will save yourself. The most influential people in the country are rallying to my cause. Ramses is a man alone, abandoned by everyone.'

'He will still have his tjaty.'

'Your successor will convict you of treason.'

'Let us place our trust in Ma'at.'

'You will have deserved your sad fate, Pazair.'

'Our deeds will be weighed on the scales of the afterlife, both mine and yours.'

Scowling, Bel-Tran swept out.

When he had gone, Bak came in handed Pazair a strange missive. 'I think it may be urgent.'

Pazair read the papyrus. 'You were right to show it to me before I left.'

The little Theban village ought to have been dozing in the hot sunshine, shaded by the palm-trees. But only the oxen and the donkeys were resting, for the whole population had gathered in the dusty square where the local court sat.

The headman was at last having his revenge on the old shepherd Pepy, a real savage, who lived apart from other people, preferring the company of ibis and crocodiles, and who hid in the papyrus thickets as soon as a taxation scribe appeared. Since he had not paid taxes for years, the headman had decided that his modest piece of land, a few acres beside the river, should become the property of the village.

Leaning on his gnarled staff, the old man had emerged from his lair to defend his cause. The village judge, a peasant who was a friend of the headman and a childhood enemy of Pepy, seemed little disposed to hear the shepherd's arguments, despite several protests.

'Here is the judgement: it is decided that—'

'The investigation was inadequate.'

'Who dares interrupt me?' demanded the judge.

Pazair strode forward. 'The tjaty of Egypt.'

Everyone recognized Pazair, because he had been born in this village and had begun his career as a judge here. Astonished and full of admiration, they bowed.

'According to the law, I shall head this court,' he decreed.

'It's a complicated matter,' grumbled the headman.

'I know that very well, thanks to the documents brought to me by the official in charge of messages.'

'The charges against Pepy—'

'His debts have been settled, therefore the matter is reduced to nothing. The shepherd shall keep the land that was bequeathed to him by his father's father.'

Everyone cheered the tjaty, and brought him beer and flowers.

At last he was alone with the hero of the day.

'I knew you'd come back,' said Pepy. 'You chose your moment well. You aren't a bad fellow at heart, despite your strange profession.'

'As you see, a judge can be just.'

'All the same, I go on distrusting them. Are you coming back to settle here?'

'Unfortunately not. I have to go to Kebet.'

'It's a tough job, being tjaty. Keep everyone happy – that's what people expect from you.'

'Sometimes I think I'll collapse under the weight of my burdens.'

'Be like the palm-tree. The more you pull it downwards, the more you try to bend it, the more it springs up and points towards the sky.'

39

Panther ate a slice of watermelon, bathed, dried herself in the sun, drank some cool beer and snuggled up to Suti, who was staring at the western bank of the Nile.

'What is it?' she asked.

'Why don't they attack?'

'Tjaty's orders, remember.'

'If Pazair comes, we—'

'He won't come – he's deserted you now that you're a rebel and an outlaw. When our nerves are at breaking-point, there will be an explosion of dissent, and soon the Libyans will clash with the Nubians, and the All-Seeing Ones will return to their duties. The army won't even have to fight.'

Suti stroked her hair. 'What do you suggest?'

'Let's break out. While our soldiers still obey us, let's take advantage of their longing for victory.'

'We'll be slaughtered.'

'How do you know? We are accustomed to miracles, you and I. If we win, Thebes will be in prospect. Kebet seems too small now, and this gloominess doesn't suit you.'

He took her by the hips and lifted her up. Her breasts level with her lover's eyes, her head thrown back, her golden hair drowned in sunshine, her arms outstretched, she sighed with contentment.

'Make me die of love,' she begged.

*

The Nile was beginning to look different. An experienced eye could see that the blue of the river was becoming less bright, as if the first silt, arriving from the far-off South, was beginning to darken it. It was nearly the end of the harvest; in the countryside, threshing was being done.

Guarded by Kem and Killer, Pazair had slept in his own village, beneath the stars. When he was a young judge, he had often enjoyed that pleasure, relishing the scents of the night and the colours of dawn.

'We're going to Kebet,' he told Kem. 'I shall persuade Suti to give up his insane plans.'

'How will you do that?'

'He'll listen to me.'

'You know very well he won't.'

'We're blood-brothers; we understand each other beyond words.'

'I shan't let you face him alone.'

'It's the only way.'

Pazair turned to leave, then stopped in his tracks. He must be dreaming: Neferet had emerged from the palm-grove and was coming towards him. She was ethereal, radiant, her brow decorated with a diadem of lotus-flowers, her turquoise amulet at her throat.

When he took her in his arms, he found that she was close to tears.

'I had a terrible dream,' she explained. 'You were dying, alone, beside the Nile, and calling to me. I have come to thwart fate.'

It would be a huge risk, but the shadow-eater had no choice. The tjaty would never be more vulnerable than at Kebet. In Memphis he was becoming untouchable. In addition to Kem's close protection, luck was helping him. Some might have claimed that the gods were watching over Pazair, but although the idea crossed his mind from time to time the shadow-eater refused to believe it. Success was a capricious thing; it would eventually change sides.

Indiscreet words had filtered through. In the market, there was talk of a band of rebels who had come out of the desert, seized Kebet and were threatening Thebes. Rapid action by the army had reassured the people, but they wondered what punishment the tjaty would inflict on the insurgents. The fact that the tjaty himself had taken charge of re-establishing order was approved of by everyone. Pazair did not behave like an ordinary official, shut away in his office: he was like a man on the ground, swift to act.

The shadow-eater felt a crawling sensation in his fingers. He remembered his first murder, in the service of the conspirators led by Bel-Tran. As he stepped on to the boat that would take him to Kebet, he felt certain that, this time, he would succeed.

'The tjaty!' roared a Nubian lookout.

The inhabitants of Kebet ran out into the streets. People spoke of an attack, a regiment of archers, several wheeled siege-towers, hundreds of chariots.

Suti addressed them from the terrace of the mayor's house, and re-established calm.

'It is indeed Tjaty Pazair,' he announced loudly. 'He is wearing his official robe and he is alone.'

'What about the army?' asked a frightened woman.

'There are no soldiers with him.'

'What are you planning to do?'

'Walk out of the main entrance and go to meet him.'

Panther tried to hold him back. 'It's a trick – you'll be killed by archers.'

'You don't know Pazair very well.'

'But supposing his troops betray him?'

'He'd die with me.'

'Don't listen to him. Don't yield ground in anything.'

'Go and reassure your people, Golden Goddess.'

From the prow of a warship, Neferet, Kem and Killer – who had all been obliged to remain aboard – watched Pazair. Neferet was in mortal fear, while Kem could not stop blaming himself.

'Pazair's being stubborn because he gave his word – I ought to have locked him up,' growled Kem.

'Suti won't hurt him.'

'We don't know how he's changed. The taste for power may have sent him mad. What kind of man will the tjaty find himself up against?'

'He'll be able to persuade him,' said Neferet.

'I can't stay here doing nothing. I'm going after him.'

'No, Kem. You must respect his promise.'

'If anything happens to him, I'll raze this town to the ground.'

The tjaty took the narrow, paved street leading from the landing-stage, which was dotted with small altars where priests laid offerings during processions. He halted a dozen paces from the main entrance to Kebet, on the Nile side. There he waited, arms hanging by his sides, very dignified in his stiff, heavy robe.

Suti appeared. Long-haired and bronzed, his powerful build more pronounced than before, he was wearing a gold collar; at the belt of his kilt hung a dagger with a gold hilt.

'Who's going to approach whom?' asked Suti.

'Do you still respect our hierarchy?'

Suti came forward. The two men were face to face.

'You abandoned me, Pazair.'

'Never – not for one single moment.'

'Do you expect me to believe that?'

'Have I ever lied to you? My position as tjaty forbade me to violate the law by overturning the judgement against you.

291

The Tjaru garrison didn't pursue you after your escape because I ordered them to remain in the fortress. After that I lost track of you, but I knew you'd come back. I swore I'd be present when you did, and here I am. I'd have preferred you to reappear more discreetly, but I'm content with this.'

'In your eyes, I'm a rebel.'

'I've had no complaints to that effect.'

'I invaded Kebet.'

'No one was killed or wounded, and there was no conflict of any sort.'

'But what about the mayor?'

'He went to the army, which is on manoeuvres near here. From my point of view, nothing irrevocable has been done.'

'You're forgetting that the law condemned me to become Tapeni's slave.'

'Not any more. She's been stripped of her rights as a citizen, as punishment for trying to form an alliance with Bel-Tran. She had no idea of how much he hates women.'

'Which means that . . .'

'That a final divorce will be pronounced if you wish. You could even demand a share of her possessions, but I'd advise against it because it would probably mean a long court case.'

'I don't want her possessions,' said Suti fiercely.

'Has your golden goddess given you so many that you don't need any more?'

'Panther saved my life in Nubia. But she can't come back to Egypt: the court sentenced her to perpetual exile.'

'Ah, but her punishment was linked to yours. Besides, her heroism in saving the life of an Egyptian soldier means I am authorized to review the judgment. Panther is free to move about in our land.'

'Are you telling the truth?'

'As tjaty, I can't do anything else. These decisions, taken in all equity, will be approved by a court.'

'I don't believe it.'

'You should,' said Pazair. 'It isn't only your blood-brother telling you, it's the tjaty of Egypt.'

'Aren't you putting your position at risk?'

'It won't make much difference: as soon as the annual flood begins, I'll be dismissed and imprisoned anyway – Bel-Tran and his allies seem unstoppable. Besides, there's a threat of war.'

'With the Asians?'

'Bel-Tran sent them poor-quality gold, but of course the blame falls on Pharaoh. To mend matters we'd have to offer them double, but Bel-Tran saw to it that our stocks of gold are low, and there isn't time to replenish them – whichever way I turn, the trap springs shut. But at least I can save you and Panther. Enjoy Egypt during these last weeks before Ramses' abdication, and then leave. The country will become a hell, subject to the law of Greek money, profit and the cruellest materialism.'

'I've got gold.'

'The gold that Asher stole and you retrieved?'

'It would be almost enough to pay Egypt's debts.'

Pazair felt hope begin to revive. 'If it were, we could avoid an invasion.'

'You ought to be more curious.'

'Do you mean you refuse?'

'You don't understand,' said Suti. 'I rediscovered the lost City of Gold in the desert. I've got more gold that I can count. To Kebet, I offer a chariot full of ingots; to Egypt, I offer gold in the amount of her debt.'

'But will Panther agree?'

'You'll need a great deal of diplomacy – this is your chance to prove your talent.'

The two friends fell into each other's arms.

During the festivals of Min, its patron god, Kebet threw itself into one of Egypt's most unbridled celebrations. As the power regulating the fecundity of the heavens and the earth, Min incited boys and girls to join in the mutual expression of their desire. When the peace agreement was proclaimed, joy exploded with an excitement worthy of these traditional celebrations.

The tjaty had decided that Kebet should benefit from Suti's gold, which was exempted from taxes. The Libyans were enlisted as footsoldiers in the army corps stationed at Thebes, and the Nubians as elite archers; and the All-Seeing Ones resumed their missions keeping watch over the caravans and miners; none of the groups was punished.

The soldiers of the regular army had no equals in banqueting and joking. In the hot summer night, laughter rang out endlessly, under the protection of the full moon. Suti and Panther received Pazair and Neferet in the mayor's house, which had been officially placed at the tjaty's disposal.

Although bedecked in dazzling gold jewellery, Panther wore a sulky expression. 'I won't leave Kebet. We conquered it – it belongs to us.'

'Stop dreaming,' advised Suti. 'We haven't got any troops any more.'

'No, but we've got enough gold to buy the whole of Egypt.'

'Why not begin by saving her?' suggested Pazair.

'What? Save my hereditary enemy?'

'It's in your interests, too, to prevent an Asian invasion. If it happened, I wouldn't give much for your treasure.'

Panther looked at Neferet, hoping for her approval, but Neferet said, 'I agree with the tjaty. What use will your fortune be if you can't spend it?'

Panther respected Neferet. Assailed by doubt, unsettled, she stood up and paced up and down the big guest hall.

'What are your requirements?' asked Pazair.

'If we're going to save Egypt,' declared Panther haughtily, 'we have the right to be very greedy. Since we are in the presence of the tjaty, we might as well be blunt: what is he prepared to grant us?'

'Nothing.'

She started. 'What do you mean, "nothing"?'

'Both of you will be cleared of all charges and declared innocent before the law, because you haven't committed a crime. The mayor will accept your apologies and the gold that will enrich his city, and Kebet will owe its prosperity and happiness to you. Isn't that worth something?'

Suti burst out laughing. 'My blood-brother's incredible! Justice speaks through his mouth, but he hasn't forgotten diplomacy. Have you by any chance become a real tjaty?'

'I'm doing my best to be one.'

'Ramses was a genius when he chose you. And I'm lucky to be your friend.'

Panther flamed with anger. 'What kingdom will you offer me, Suti?'

'Isn't my life enough for you, Golden Goddess?'

She charged at him and hammered her fists against his chest. 'I ought to have killed you!'

'Don't give up hope – you may yet.' He gained control of her and held her tightly to him. 'Did you really see yourself as a leading provincial citizen?'

Bursting out laughing in her turn, Panther pulled herself out of his arms and picked up a jar of wine. But when she offered it to Suti, instead of taking it he put his hand over his eyes.

'He's night-blind because of a scorpion's sting,' she cried, dropping the jar.

Neferet said soothingly, 'Don't worry. Night-blindness may be rare but I know I can and shall cure it. Wait here while I go to the hospital workshops.'

To Neferet's relief, the workshops had all the necessary ingredients she needed. On her return to the mayor's house she gave Suti a medicine composed of the humour extracted from pigs' eyes, galenite, yellow ochre and fermented honey, crushed and reduced into a compacted mass. Then she administered a decoction of beef liver, which he must take each day for three months in order to be completely cured.

Reassured, Panther soon went to sleep, and Neferet also dozed off. Suti and Pazair went out and walked through the town's quiet streets, followed at a discreet distance by Killer.

Suti gazed up at the stars, feasting his eyes on their light. 'It's miraculous,' he said. 'Neferet's brought me back to life.'

'Your good luck is still with you,' said Pazair.

'How do matters stand for the kingdom?'

'Even with your help, I'm not sure I can save it.'

'Why don't you simply arrest Bel-Tran and throw him into prison?'

'I've often meant to, but that wouldn't tear up the roots of the evil.'

'If the cause is lost, don't sacrifice yourself.'

'So long as there's even a shadow of hope, I shall carry out the duties entrusted to me.'

'Stubbornness is one of your many failings. Why keep hitting your head against a wall? For once, just listen to me. I've got a better idea.'

The two men passed a group of Libyans leaning against the door of a tavern. Drunk on beer, they were snoring.

Suti once again raised his eyes to the sky, only too happy to see the moon and the stars. At that moment Killer gave a warning howl, and Suti spotted an archer standing on a roof, on the point of firing.

Leaping sideways, he put himself in front of Pazair. The arrow took Suti in the chest, just above the heart, and he collapsed. The shadow-eater jumped into a chariot and fled.

40

The operation began at dawn and lasted three hours. Exhausted from lack of sleep, Neferet drew the energy she needed from the very depths of herself, to avoid making a mistake. She was assisted by two Kebet doctors who had experience of treating the All-Seeing Ones' wounds.

Before removing the arrow, Neferet rendered Suti unconscious. At brief intervals, she gave him ten doses of a powder composed of opium, mandragora root and siliceous stone; during the operation, an assistant would mix more of the powder with vinegar and make the patient breathe in the acid vapours that came off it, so that he would not wake. For additional safety, one of the surgeons anointed Suti's body with a balm against pain, whose main component was mandragora root, a powerful sleeping-potion.

Neferet checked that her stone scalpels were sharp enough, then enlarged the wound in order to withdraw the arrowhead. The depth of the wound worried her. Fortunately, the channels of the heart had not been ruptured, but Suti had lost a lot of blood and was still bleeding. Having stopped the bleeding with compresses of linen soaked in honey, with slow, precise movements she repaired the tears; then she bound together the edges of the main wound with fine thread obtained from cattle intestines. For a few moments she hesitated: would it be necessary to seal the wound with skin taken from another part of his body? Trusting in her instinct and in Suti's robust constitution, she decided against. The skin's initial reaction confirmed her in her opinion; so she strengthened the suture points with strips of sticky fabric, covered with fat and honey. Then she bandaged the wounded man's chest with very soft vegetable fibre.

So far the operation had succeeded; but would Suti reawaken?

Ken inspected the roof from which the shadow-eater had fired. He picked up the Nubian bow the assassin had used. Killer had charged off in pursuit of the murderer's chariot, but had not managed to catch up with it. The man had disappeared into the countryside.

In vain, Kem sought reliable witnesses. Some had indeed seen a chariot leaving the city in the middle of the night, but no one could give a detailed description of the driver. Kem felt like tearing off his wooden nose and stamping on it. Only Killer's hand gripping his wrist stopped him.

'Thank you for your help, Killer,' said Kem.

But the baboon did not let go.

'What do you want?'

Killer turned his head to the left.

'Very well, I'll follow you.'

Killer led Kem to the corner of a narrow street and showed him a boundary stone which had been scratched by the passage of a chariot.

'He went that way, you're right, but . . .'

The baboon led him a little further along the street, bent over a pothole in the road, then stepped back, signalling to Kem to look at it. Interested, the Nubian did so. At the bottom of the pothole lay an obsidian knife.

'He must have dropped it without realizing.' Kem fingered the knife. 'Security Guard Killer, I think you've just given us a vital clue.'

*

When Suti opened his eyes, he saw Neferet smiling down at him.

'You gave me a bad fright,' she confessed.

'An arrow's nothing compared to a bear's claws. You've saved me for the second time.'

'Two finger-breadths lower, and the arrow would have pierced your heart.'

'Will there be any lasting damage?'

'Perhaps a scar, but frequent changes of dressings should prevent that.'

'And how soon will I be back on my feet?'

'Very soon, because you have a strong constitution – in fact, you seem even stronger than when you had your first operation.'

'Death is amusing itself with me.'

Neferet's voice shook with emotion. 'You sacrificed yourself for Pazair . . . I don't know how to thank you.'

Gently, he took her hand. 'Panther steals all the love I have; otherwise, how could I not be madly in love with you? No one will ever separate you and Pazair – even destiny would wear itself out trying. It happened to choose me to shield him last night. I'm proud of that, Neferet, very proud.'

'May Pazair speak to you?'

'If the doctor permits it.'

The tjaty was as moved as his wife. 'You shouldn't have risked your life, Suti.'

'I thought a tjaty didn't tell tall stories.'

'Are you in pain?'

'Neferet is an extraordinary doctor – I feel almost nothing.'

'The shadow-eater interrupted our conversation.'

'I remember,' said Suti.

'Then what's the piece of advice you were about to give me?'

'What, in your opinion, is my dearest wish?'

'According to you, to lead a great life, to love, celebrate, and get drunk with each new sun.'

'And what's yours?'

'You know that: to retire to my village with Neferet, far from the troubles that face me.'

'The desert's changed me, Pazair; that is my future and my real kingdom. I've learnt to share its secrets, to feed on its mystery. When I'm far away from it, I feel heavy and old, but as soon as the soles of my feet touch the sand I'm young and immortal. There's no true law but the law of the desert. You're of the same nature, so join me and let's go away together, leave this world of corruption and lies.'

'A tjaty exists to fight such wickedness and enable righteousness to reign.'

'And are you succeeding?'

'Every day brings its share of victories and defeats, but Ma'at still governs Egypt. If Bel-Tran ascends the throne, though, justice will leave this earth.'

'Don't wait for that to happen.'

'Help me fight this war.'

As if in refusal, Suti turned away, on to his side. 'Leave me to rest. How can I fight if I don't get enough sleep?'

A boat belonging to the Mother of Pharaoh had brought Silkis from Memphis to Pi-Ramses. In her cabin, which was airy and shaded from the fierce sun, she had enjoyed the care of attentive servants. She had been massaged and perfumed, and offered fruit juices and cool cloths to place on her brow and the nape of her neck, so that her journey was a delight.

At the landing-stage, a travelling-chair equipped with two sunshades awaited her. The journey was only brief, for Silkis was taken to the lake at the queen's residence. Two shade-bearers went down with her to the lakeside, and helped her in a blue-painted boat. Smoothly the oarsmen rowed her to an island in the middle of the lake, where Tuya was seated under a wooden canopy, reading poems from the Old Kingdom which celebrated the sublime beauty of the landscape and the respect that men should feel for the gods.

Silkis began to panic. Her linen gown was ostentatiously luxurious, and she wore many of her finest jewels, but would she be able to confront the richest and most influential woman in Egypt?

'Come and sit beside me, Lady Silkis,' said the queen.

To Silkis's great astonishment, the Mother of Pharaoh looked more like a woman of the people than the mother of the great Ramses. Her hair hung free, and she was barefoot, dressed in a simple white robe with straps; she wore no necklaces, no bracelets, not a trace of face-paint. But her voice pierced the soul.

'You must be feeling the heat, my child,' Tuya went on.

Incapable of speech, Silkis sat down on the grass, not thinking of the inevitable green stains on the expensive linen.

'Be at your ease. Swim, if you wish.'

'I . . . I do not wish, thank you, Majesty.'

'Would you like some cool beer?'

Paralysed with nerves, Silkis accepted a long vessel with a fine metal tube though which one sucked up the beer. She drank several mouthfuls, her eyes lowered, unable to meet Tuya's.

'I love these summer months,' said the queen. 'Their light is dazzlingly honest. Does the intense heat upset you?'

'It . . . it dries out the skin.'

'But surely you have a fine array of creams and lotions?'

'Yes, of course.'

'Do you spend a great deal of time making yourself beautiful?'

'Several hours a day – my husband is very demanding.'

'His has been a remarkable career, I am told.'

Silkis raised her head a little: the Mother of Pharaoh had

not taken long to approach the expected subject. Her fear
lessened: after all, this impressive woman, with her thin,
straight nose, pronounced cheekbones and square chin, was
soon going to be her obedient slave. Hatred invaded her, like
the hatred that had driven her to undress before the head of
the honour-guard so that her husband could kill him. Silkis
liked submitting to Bel-Tran, but she wanted her entourage to
grovel at her feet. The thought of beginning by humiliating
the Mother of Pharaoh gave her a feeling of ecstasy.

She said, 'Indeed, Majesty, "remarkable" is exactly the
right word.'

'A little accounting-scribe becoming the greatest man in
the kingdom – only Egypt allows that kind of rise to power.
But it is important not to lose one's humility when one
becomes great.'

Silkis frowned. 'Bel-Tran is honest, hardworking, and all
he thinks of is the common good.'

'The quest for power engenders conflicts, which I see only
from a great distance.'

Silkis was jubilant: the fish was taking the hook! To give
herself courage, she drank a little more beer; it was so
delicious that she felt quite relaxed.

'At Memphis, Majesty, there are whispers that the king is
ill.'

'He is very tired, Lady Silkis – his burdens are crushing.'

'Must he not soon celebrate a festival of regeneration?'

'That is the sacred tradition.'

'And . . . what if the magic ritual were to fail?'

'The gods would thus signify that a new pharaoh is called
to reign.'

Silkis's face lit up in a cruel smile. 'Would the gods be the
only ones implicated?'

'You are enigmatic.'

'Does Bel-Tran not possess the stuff of a king?'

Pensively, Tuya watched a flock of mallard glide across

the blue waters of the lake. 'Who are we, to claim to lift the veil of the future?'

'Bel-Tran can, Majesty.'

'Admirable.'

'He and I were counting on your support. Everyone knows that your judgments are very sure.'

'That is the role of the Mother of Pharaoh: to see and to advise.'

Silkis had won; she felt as light as a bird, as quick as a jackal, as sharp as a dagger-blade. Egypt belonged to her.

'How did your husband build up his fortune?' asked Tuya.

'By developing his papyrus business. Of course, he juggled with the accounts, as he has done everywhere he has been. No accounting-scribe has ever been his equal.'

'Has he ever been dishonest?'

Silkis became talkative. 'Majesty, business is business, is it not? If one wishes to reach the first rank, one must from time to time forget morality. Ordinary people become mired in it, but Bel-Tran has freed himself of that hindrance. In government he has overturned old habits. No one has noticed his misappropriations; the state has done well out of them, but so has he! And now it is too late to accuse him.'

'Has he ensured that you have a personal fortune?'

'Of course.'

'How?'

Silkis was exultant. 'In the most audacious way imaginable.'

'Enlighten me.'

'You will find it hard to believe, Majesty. It concerns an illicit traffic in papyri of the *Book of Going Forth by Day*. As the supplier to a good part of the nobility, he has taken it upon himself to find scribes capable of drawing the scenes and writing the texts relating to the resurrection of the deceased in the otherworld.'

'What is the nature of the deception?'

'It is threefold, First, he delivers papyrus of lower quality than that promised; then he reduces the length of the texts without reducing the price, and while paying the scribe very little; and lastly he does exactly the same thing with the pictures. The dead people's families are always so grief-stricken that they do not think to check. And I also have an enormous number of Greek coins resting in my coffers, awaiting the free circulation of money . . . What a revolution, Majesty! You will no longer recognize this old Egypt, hidebound in pointless traditions and outdated customs.'

'Those are your husband's words, if I am not much mistaken.'

'And the only ones the country should hear.'

'Have you no thoughts of your own?'

The question disconcerted Silkis. 'What do you mean?'

'Murder, theft, falsehood – do they seem to you to provide a good basis for a reign?'

Silkis was too excited for caution. 'If they are necessary, why not? We have gone too far to draw back. I myself am an accomplice of my husband, and as culpable as he is. I only regret not having killed Branir and Tjaty Pazair, the main obstacles to—' A sudden attack of dizziness made her sway; she put her hand to her brow. 'What's happening to me? Why did I confess all that to you?'

'Because you have drunk beer mixed with mandragora. Its taste is bland but it loosens the tongue, and with its help weak minds are freed of their secrets.'

'What did I say? What did I reveal to you?'

'If the mandragora acted so quickly,' said the Mother of Pharaoh, 'it is because you are in the habit of using drugs.'

'My stomach hurts!' Silkis stood up. The island and the sky seemed to move before her eyes. She fell to her knees, and hid her face in her hands.

'The illegal traffic in the *Book of Going Forth by Day* is an abominable crime,' declared Tuya. 'You have profited from the pain of others, with incredible cruelty. I myself shall lodge a complaint before the tjaty's court.'

'It will come to nothing,' said Silkis, raising her head. 'And soon you will be my servant.'

'You will not succeed,' said Tuya, 'for you carry failure within you and will never succeed in becoming a great lady in the land. Your depravity is known to all. No one will accept you, even if you do wield a measure of power. You will soon see that the situation is untenable. More determined women than you have been forced to renounce their ambitions.'

'Bel-Tran will crush you underfoot.'

'I am an old lady and do not fear bandits like him. My ancestors fought against invaders as dangerous as he is, and defeated them. If he was hoping for your support, he will be disappointed: you will be of no use to him at all.'

'I *will* help him, and we *will* succeed.'

'You will be not be able to help him. You have limited intelligence, fragile nerves, and you have no individual personality, only a destructive fire nourished by hatred and hypocrisy. Not only will you harm him, but also, sooner or later, you will betray him.'

Silkis writhed about, beating her clenched fists on the ground.

At a sign from Tuya, the blue boat drew up to the island shore.

'Take this woman back to the port,' Tuya ordered the crew, 'and ensure that she leaves Pi-Ramses immediately.'

Silkis was overwhelmed by a desire for sleep. As soon as she was aboard the boat, she collapsed, her head filled with unbearable buzzing as if bees were devouring her brain.

The Mother of Pharaoh gazed serenely at the peaceful waters of the ornamental lake, above which the swallows danced.

41

Leaning on Pazair's shoulder, Suti took his first steps on the deck of the boat taking them back to Memphis. Neferet watched, and was satisfied with his recovery.

Panther also gazed at her hero, at the same time dreaming of an immense river which would belong to him and of which she would be queen. From North to South and South to North, they would sail on a huge boat laden with gold which they would present to the villages spread out along the banks. If they could not conquer an empire by force, why not try gifts? The day the mines of the Lost City were exhausted, the whole country would celebrate the names of Panther and Suti. Lying on the cabin roof, she surrendered her copper-skinned body to the summer sun's burning caresses.

Neferet changed Suti's bandages. 'The wound looks very good. How do you feel?'

'I'm not strong enough to fight yet, but I can stand upright.'

'Please rest now. If you don't, your flesh will take longer to knit together.'

Suty lay down on a mat, in the shade of a cloth stretched between four poles. Sleep would help restore his strength.

Neferet went to the prow of the boat and looked out over the Nile. Pazair joined her, and put his arm round her.

'Do you think the flood will come early?' he asked.

'The level of the water's rising, but the colour's changing only slowly. We may have the benefit of a few days' respite.'

'When the star Sopdet shines in the sky, Isis will weep, and the energy of resurrection will bring to life the river born in the otherworld. Death will be defeated, as it is every year. And yet the Egypt of our forefathers will die.'

'Every night I call upon Branir's soul. I'm sure it isn't far from us.'

'I've failed completely,' said Pazair dejectedly. 'I've neither identified the assassin nor found the Testament of the Gods.'

Kem came over to them. 'Forgive me for disturbing you, but I'd like to suggest a promotion to you.'

Pazair was surprised. 'You, Kem, taking an interest in promotion?'

'Security Guard Killer has earned it.'

'Of course,' said Pazair. 'I should have thought of it long ago. If it weren't for him, I'd have travelled to the Western shore.'

'Not only did he save your life, but he's given us a means of identifying the shadow-eater. Doesn't that merit promotion and an increase in wages?'

'What means?' asked Pazair.

'Let Killer see his investigation through to the end. I'll help him.'

'Whom do you suspect?

'I still have a few checks to make before I know the murderer's name, but he won't escape us.'

'How long will your investigation take?

'A day at best,' said Kem, 'a week at worst. Killer will identify him as soon as he faces him.'

'You must arrest him so that he can be put on trial.'

'He's committed several murders.'

'Unless you persuade Killer to keep him alive, I shall be obliged to withdraw Killer from the inquiry.'

'The shadow-eater tried to kill him by sending another baboon against him. How could he forget that? Withdrawing him would be unjust.'

'It's vital that we find out if the shadow-eater is responsible for Branir's death, and which master he serves.'

'You will – and that's all I can promise you. If Killer's provoked, I shan't be able to restrain him. If it comes to a choice between the life of a brave creature and that of a monster, I know which I'll choose.'

'Be very careful, both of you.'

When Bel-Tran crossed the threshold of his house, no one came to meet him. Annoyed, he called for his steward. Only a gardener responded.

'Where is the steward?' demanded Bel-Tran.

'He has left, my lord, with two serving-women and your children.'

'What? Are you drunk?'

'He did, my lord, I assure you.'

Furious, Bel-Tran charged into the house and bumped into Silkis's personal handmaid.

'Where are my children?'

'They have gone to your house in the Delta, my lord.'

'On whose orders?'

'Your wife's.'

'And where is she?'

'In her bedchamber, my lord, but . . .'

'Well?'

'She is very unahppy – she hasn't stopped crying since she got back from Pi-Ramses.'

Bel-Tran strode through the house and burst into his wife's private apartments. She was lying motionless in bed, curled up, sobbing.

He shook her but she did not react.

'Why have you sent the children to the country? Answer

me!' He twisted her wrists, forcing her to sit up. 'Answer me, I order you.'

'They're in danger.'

'Nonsense.'

'And so am I.'

'What's happened?'

Sobbing, Silkis told him of her meeting with the Mother of Pharaoh, ending, 'That woman's a monster – she broke me.'

Bel-Tran did not take his wife's account lightly. He even made her repeat the accusations Tuya had made.

'Calm yourself, my darling,' he said when she had finished.

'It was a trap – she lured me into a trap.'

'Don't be afraid. Soon she'll have no power left.'

'You don't understand. I no longer have any chance whatever of being admitted to court. Every move I make will be criticized, every opinion challenged. Whatever I do, I shall be reviled. I couldn't bear persecution like that.'

'You must be calm.'

'Calm? When Tuya's ruining my reputation?' Silkis flew into a rage, shouting incomprehensible phrases which mingled the dream-interpreter, the shadow-eater, her children, an inaccessible throne and unbearable stomach pains.

When Bel-Tran left her he was in pensive mood. Tuya was a clear-sighted woman: Silkis's instability meant that she would indeed be unable to fit into the Egyptian court.

Panther was dreaming. The voyage on the Nile with Pazair and Neferet, in complete safety, was proving an unexpected time of peace in her tumultuous life. Without admitting it to Suti, she was dreaming of a big house surrounded by a garden, though she was ashamed of giving up her thirst for conquest, even for a few hours. Neferet's presence calmed the fire that had been burning her ever since she had first had to fight to survive. Panther was discovering the virtues of tenderness, which she had always despised as though it were a shameful disease. Egypt, the land she hated so much, was becoming her haven of peace.

She went in search of Pazair, and found him in his cabin, sitting on the floor, writing a decree relating to the protection, in each province, of animals it was forbidden to kill and eat.

'I must talk to you,' she declared solemnly.

'I'm listening.'

'Let's go on deck – I like looking at the Nile.'

Leaning on the rail like two awe-struck travellers, the pair watched the river and the life on its banks. On dirt tracks atop low hills, donkeys laden with grain ambled along; around the good-hearted beasts scampered chattering children. In the villages, in the shade of palm-trees, peasants were finishing the threshing to the sound of flutes playing ancient melodies. Everyone was waiting for the flood.

Panther said, 'I'm going to give you my gold, tjaty.'

'Suti and you discovered an abandoned mine; it belongs to you.'

'Keep all this wealth for the gods – they'll make better use of it than mortals would. But let me live here and forget the past.'

'I owe you the truth: in just one month, this country's soul will change utterly. It will undergo such upheavals that you won't recognize it any more.'

'A month's peace? That's a lot.'

'My friends will be hunted down, arrested, perhaps executed,' said Pazair. 'If you help me, you can be sure you'll be denounced.'

'I shan't go back on my decision. Take the gold, and prevent war with Asia.'

She turned and went back to the cabin roof, worshipper of a sun whose violence she had tamed.

Suti took her place beside the tjaty. 'I can walk,' he said, 'and move my left arm. It hurts a bit, but it's healing well. Your wife's a sorceress.'

'So is Panther,' said Pazair.

'She certainly is! The proof is that I haven't yet managed to free myself from her.'

'She's giving your gold to Egypt, to prevent war with the Asians.'

'I've no choice but to agree.'

'She wants to be happy with you. I think Egypt has won her over.'

'What a horrible future! Must I wipe out a regiment of Libyans to give her back her ferocity? But let's not talk about her – you're the one I'm worried about.'

'You know the truth,' said Pazair.

'Only part of it. But I can see that you're being hamstrung by your main failing: respect for other people.'

'That is the law of Ma'at.'

'Rubbish! You're at war, Pazair, and you're taking too many blows without returning them. Thanks to Neferet, in another week I'll be fit for the fight again. Let me act as I see fit and disrupt the enemy's game.'

'Will you step outside the path of the law?'

'When war's declared, one must make one's own path. Otherwise one's likely to fall into an ambush. Bel-Tran's merely an enemy like any other.'

Pazair shook his head. 'No, he isn't. He has a certain weapon against which neither you nor I can do anything.'

'What weapon?'

'I am sworn to silence.'

'You haven't much time left.'

'At the start of the flood, Ramses will abdicate. He will be unable to experience his regeneration.'

'You're being absurd. Up to now, you were probably right to be suspicious of everyone. But now you must bring together the people you trust, and tell them what this weapon is and the real reason why Ramses can't do anything. Together we'll find a way of parrying it.'

'I must ask Pharaoh. Only he can give me permission to tell you. You disembark at Memphis, and I'll go on to Pi-Ramses.'

In the great burial-ground of Saqqara, Neferet went to the tomb of Branir and laid lotus-flowers, cornflowers and lilies on the offering-table of the little shrine that was open to the living. By doing so, she remained in communion with the soul of Branir, whose body of light, summoned to the resurrection of Osiris, lay in a sarcophagus at the heart of the earth-mother.

Through a slit in one wall of the tomb, she looked at the statue of her murdered master. He was shown as if walking, his eyes raised to the sky.

To her surprise, the darkness seemed less profound than usual; she sensed that Branir's gaze was fixed upon her with rare intensity. These were no longer the eyes of a dead man, but those of a living man who had come back from the otherworld to give her a message beyond human words and thoughts.

Overwhelmed, she drove all thoughts out of her mind, so that her heart might perceive the truth of the ineffable. And Branir spoke to her, as he had done when alive, in his solemn, steady voice. He spoke of the Light that nourished the righteous, and of the beauty of paradise, where thought wandered among the stars.

When he fell silent, she knew he had opened a path which the tjaty must take. Evil's victory was not inevitable.

On her way out of the burial-ground, Neferet met Djui the embalmer, who was going back his workshop.

He bowed and said, 'I have cared for Branir's tomb, as you wished.'

'Thank you, Djui.'

'You look upset.'

'It's nothing.'

'Would you like some water?'

'No, thank you, I must go to the hospital. Goodbye.'

On tired feet, the embalmer made his way back, beneath the implacable sun, to a building with tiny windows; against its walls stood several sarcophagi of varying quality. The workshop was in an isolated place; in the distance were pyramids and tombs. A rocky hill blocked the view of the palm-trees and fields that bordered the desert.

Djui pushed the door, which opened with a creak. Once inside, he put on a goatskin apron covered with brownish stains, and unemotionally regarded the corpse he had been brought. He had been paid for a second-rank embalming, which necessitated the use of oils and unguents. Wearily, he picked up an iron hook, with which he would extract the brain of the deceased through the nostrils.

An obsidian knife was flung down at his feet.

'You lost this at Kebet,' said a deep voice behind him.

Very slowly, Djui turned round.

On the threshold of the workshop stood Kem.

'You're mistaken, Commander,' protested Djui.

'This is the knife you use to cut into a corpse's flank.'

'I'm not the only embalmer—'

'You're the only one who's been travelling a lot over the last few months.'

'That isn't a crime.'

'Every time you leave your post you have to make it known, or your colleagues would complain. Now, your movements coincided with those of the tjaty, whom you have several times tried – but failed – to kill.'

'My trade's so difficult that I often need to take a rest.'

'In your trade, people live apart from society and hardly ever leave their workplace. You've no family in Thebes.'

'It's a beautiful region – and I've a right to move around, just like anyone else.'

'You know a lot about poisons, don't you?' said Kem.

313

'What makes you say that?'

'I consulted your work record. Before becoming an embalmer, you were an assistant in a hospital workshop. Your knowledge of that environment was of great use in your crimes.'

'It isn't forbidden to change one's job.'

'You're also an excellent shot with the throwing-stick – your first trade was as a bird-hunter.'

'Is that, by any chance, a crime?'

'All the evidence agrees: you are the shadow-eater hired to assassinate Tjaty Pazair.'

'That's slander!'

'There's one piece of irrefutable proof: this expensive knife. At its base, it bears a distinctive mark, that of the embalmers, and a number which corresponds to the Saqqara workshop. You shouldn't have tried to use it, Djui, but you wouldn't be separated from it. It's the love of your trade that betrayed you, the love of death.'

'No court will consider that knife sufficient proof.'

'You know very well that it will. And the final confirmation is hidden here, I am sure of it.'

'You want to search my workshop?'

'More than want: I'm going to.'

'I won't let you – I'm innocent.'

'Than what are you afraid of?'

'This is my own domain, and no one has the right to violate it.'

'As commander of the security guards, I have. Now, before showing me your cellar, put down that iron hook. I don't like seeing you with a weapon in your hand.'

The embalmer obeyed.

'Lead the way.'

Djui went down the staircase, with its worn, slippery steps. Two torches, permanently lit, illuminated a huge cellar where sarcophagi were piled up. At the back were some twenty vases destined to receive the liver, lungs, stomach and intestines of the deceased.

'Open them,' ordered Kem.

'That would be sacrilege.'

'I'll risk it.' The Nubian removed a lid with a baboon's head, a second with a dog's and a third with a falcon's. The vases contained only viscera.

In the fourth, whose lid was in the form of a man's head, was a gold ingot. Kem looked further and found two more.

'Are these the price of your murders?'

Arms folded over his chest, Djui seemed almost indifferent. 'How much do you want?' he asked.

'How much are you offering?'

'If you've come without your baboon and without the tjaty, you're here to sell your silence. Will half of my profits be enough?'

'You'll also have to satisfy my curiosity. Who paid you?'

'Bel-Tran and his accomplices. But you and the tjaty have destroyed the band, and now only he and his wife are left to taunt you.' Djui smiled. 'She's a fine filly, believe me. She's the one who gave me my instructions when I had to kill an inconvenient witness.'

'Did you kill Branir?'

'I keep a list of my successes, so that I'll remember them when I'm old. Branir wasn't one of my victims. I wouldn't have balked at killing him, I assure you, but I wasn't asked to do it.'

'Then who did?'

Djui said with a shrug, 'I've no idea, and I don't care. You've done the right thing, Kem – I expected no less from you. I knew that if you identified me you wouldn't tell the tjaty, you'd come and demand your share.'

'Will you leave Pazair in peace now?'

'He'll be my only failure – unless you lend me a hand.'

The Nubian felt the weight of the ingots. 'They're magnificent.'

'Life is short. You have to know how to make the best of it.'

'But you've made two mistakes, Djui.'

'Never mind that. Let's talk about the future.'

'The first is that you underestimated me.'

'You mean you want everything?'

'A whole mountain of gold wouldn't be enough.'

'Are you joking?'

'You second mistake was thinking Killer would forgive you for sending a rival against him, to try to tear him to pieces. Other people might feel sorry for you, but I'm only a black man with unsophisticated feelings and he's a baboon and is over-sensitive and prone to bear grudges. Killer's my friend, and he almost died because of you. When he cries vengeance, I have to listen to him. And he'll see to it that you eat no more shadows.'

Killer appeared at the foot of the stairs.

Kem had never seen him so enraged: his eyes were bright red, his pelt bristled, his teeth were bared, and he gave a blood-curdling growl. No doubt remained as to Djui's guilt.

The shadow-eater backed away. And Killer sprang.

42

'Lie down,' Neferet told Suti.

'The pain has gone.'

'I must still check the channels of the heart and the circulation of energy.'

Neferet took his pulse in several places, while consulting the little water-clock that she wore at her wrist; inside were gradations in the form of dots on twelve vertical lines. She calculated the internal rhythms, compared them with one another, and established that the voice of the heart was powerful and regular.

'If I hadn't operated on you myself,' she said, 'I'd have difficulty believing you'd been wounded recently. The scarring has taken place twice as quickly as normal.'

'Tomorrow I shall practise with my bow – if the kingdom's principal doctor will permit it.'

'Don't ask too much of your muscles. Be patient.'

'I can't. I'd feel as though I were wasting my life. Shouldn't life be like the flight of a bird of prey, strong and unpredictable?'

'Spending time with the sick has made me accept all ways of life. However, I am obliged to re-bandage you in a way that will hamper your activities.'

'When will Pazair be back?'

'Tomorrow, at the latest.'

'I hope he's been persuasive enough. We must shake off this passivity.'

'You're a poor judge of him: since your unfortunate departure for Nubia, he's fought Bel-Tran and his allies day and night.'

'But he hasn't beaten them.'

'He's weakened them.'

'But not killed them.'

'The tjaty is the foremost servant of the law, and he must ensure it is respected.'

'The only law Bel-Tran knows is his own, so Pazair is fighting on uneven ground. When we were young, he took stock of the situation and then I dealt with it. If my target is clearly defined, I don't miss it.'

'Your help will be very valuable.'

'So long as I know everything, the same way you do.'

'There, I've finished bandaging you.'

Pi-Ramses was less joyous than usual. Soldiers had replaced passers-by, chariots were moving about the streets, and the war-fleet filled the port. In the barracks, which were on full alert, the footsoldiers were undertaking combat exercises. The archers were constantly at practice, and senior officers were checking the horses' tack. There was a scent of war in the air.

The palace guard had been doubled. Pazair's visit aroused no enthusiasm, as if his presence set a seal upon a decision everyone feared.

This time, Pazair did not find Pharaoh gardening. He and his generals were studying a large map of Asia laid out on the floor of the council chamber. The soldiers bowed before the tjaty.

'May I consult you, Majesty?'

Ramses dismissed his generals. When they had gone, he said, 'We're ready to fight, Pazair: the Army of Set is already deployed along the border. Our spies confirm that the Asian princedoms are trying to unite in order to mobilize as many soldiers as possible – it will be a fierce battle. My generals advise me to attack, as a preventive measure, but I would prefer to wait. Anyone would swear that the future belonged to me!'

'We can prevent war, Majesty.'

'How? Has there been a miracle?'

'We can use gold from a long-forgotten mine.'

'Is this information reliable?'

'An expedition is already on its way, with a map drawn by Suti.'

'But will the gold be enough?'

'Enough to satisfy Asia, Majesty.'

'And what does Suti want in return?'

'The desert.'

'Are you serious?'

'He is.'

Ramses thought for a moment. 'Would the post of commander of the All-Seeing Ones suit him?'

'I think it possible that all he wants is solitude.'

'Has he any more miracles concealed under his robe?'

'Suti wants to know the truth, Majesty. He suggested that I bring together the few people who have proved their loyalty and tell them the true reasons for your abdication.'

'A secret council . . .'

'A last council of war.'

'What do you think of the idea?'

'I have failed, because I have not recovered the Testament of the Gods. If you grant me permission, I shall mobilize our last forces in order to weaken Bel-Tran as much as possible.'

Silkis was suffering her third attack of hysteria since dawn. Three doctors had attended her bedside in turn, but without much success. The last gave her a sleeping-draught, in the hope that a deep sleep would bring her back to her senses, but as

319

soon as she awoke, in the middle of the afternoon, she became delirious, disturbing the whole house with her cries and her convulsions. Only more of the sleeping-draught could calm her, although the consequences of overuse were serious: a lessening of the brain's faculties and damage to the intestines.

Bel-Tran made the decision that had been forced upon him. He summoned a scribe and dictated to him the list of possessions he was bequeathing to his children, reducing those left to his wife to the absolute minimum required by the law. Contrary to custom, he had drawn up a very detailed marriage contract, which permitted him to manage his wife's fortune should she show a clear inability to do it herself. He had had that inability verified by three doctors, all of whom he had richly rewarded. Armed with these documents, Bel-Tran would have sole parental authority over his children, whose upbringing would be taken out of Silkis's hands.

The Mother of Pharaoh had done him a service by revealing his wife's true nature: an unstable creature, sometimes childish, sometimes cruel, incapable of occupying an important office. After serving him as a beautiful puppet at receptions and banquets, she had become a handicap.

The best place for her to be treated was in a specialized establishment housing the mentally ill. As soon as she was well enough to travel, he would send her to Phoenicia.

All that remained was to draw up the deed of divorce, a vital document since Silkis was still living in the family home. Bel-Tran could not wait for her departure. Once free of her, he would be ready to tackle the last obstacle separating him from the realization of his dream. That was how one travelled the path to power, dispensing with one's useless travelling-companions.

All Egypt was invoking the flood. The earth was cracked open, as if dead; scorched, singed, dried out by a burning wind, it was dying of thirst, longing for the nourishing water that would soon climb the banks and push back the desert. A dull tiredness weighed down men and animals alike, dust covered the trees, the last small areas of greenery were shrivelling, exhausted. However, work did not stop. Teams came one after another, cleaning out the canals, repairing the wells and the irrigation systems, strengthening the earthen retaining-banks by scooping back up the soil that had fallen down and stopping up the cracks. The children were set to filling jars with dried fruit, people's main food during the period when the water covered the lands.

As he sailed back from Pi-Ramses, Pazair sensed the suffering and hope of his land. Soon Bel-Tran would attack the water itself, criticizing it for not being present all year. The regime he imposed would shatter the country's alliance with the gods and nature. By destroying the delicate balance that had been respected by nineteen dynasties of pharaohs, he would leave the field open to the forces of evil.

When his boat docked in Memphis, Kem and Killer were waiting on the quay.

'Djui was the shadow-eater,' said Kem.

'Did he kill Branir?'

'No, but he was Bel-Tran's paid assassin. He murdered the surviving members of the honour-guard and Bel-Tran's accomplices. And he's the one who tried to kill you.'

'Have you imprisoned him?'

'Killer did not grant him his forgiveness. I've dictated my testimony to a scribe. It contains charges against Bel-Tran, complete with names and dates. Now you are safe.'

Accompanied by Way-Finder, who carried a full water-skin, Suti came hurrying along the quay. 'Did Ramses agree?' he asked.

'Yes.'

'Convene your council at once. I'm ready to fight.'

'Before that, I'd like to try one last thing.'

321

'We haven't much time.'

'Messengers bearing my summons have already left. The council will be convened tomorrow.'

'This is your last chance,' warned Suti.

'Egypt's last chance.'

'What is this "last thing"?'

'I shan't take any risks, Suti.'

'Take me with you.'

'And Killer, too,' urged Kem.

'I can't,' replied the tjaty. 'I must be alone.'

Lisht, two days' journey to the south of the burial-ground at Saqqara, was still living in the age of the Middle Kingdom, a time of peace and prosperity. There stood temples and pyramids, dedicated to Amenemhat I and Sesostris I, powerful pharaohs of the dynasty who had made Egypt happy again after a troubled period. Since that far-off era, seven hundred years before the reign of Ramses II, the memory of the illustrious sovereigns had been respected. *Ka* priests celebrated the daily rites, so that the dead kings' souls might remain present on earth and inspire their successors' actions.

Not far from the fields, the pyramid of Sesostris I was being rebuilt, following the collapse of part of its covering of white limestone, which came from the quarry at Tura.

Bel-Tran's chariot, driven by a former army officer, took the road that bordered the desert. It halted at the start of the covered way that led up to the pyramid. Agitatedly, Bel-Tran leapt out of the vehicle and shouted for a priest. His angry voice sounded most incongruous in the silence that pervaded the site.

A shaven-headed priest emerged from a shrine.

'I am Bel-Tran. The tjaty summoned me here.'

'Follow me,' said the priest.

Bel-Tran was uneasy. He liked neither the pyramids nor the ancient shrines whose builders had raised colossal stone blocks, manipulating them with incredible skill. The temples were an obstacle to his plans; destroying them would be a priority of the new regime. As long as men, no matter how few, escaped the universal law of profit, they would hinder a country's development.

The priest led the way down a narrow causeway on whose walls relief carvings showed the king making offerings to the gods. The priest walked slowly, so Bel-Tran had to rein in his pace. He cursed the time he was losing and the summons to this forgotten place.

At the top of the causeway a temple had been built against the wall of the pyramid. The priest turned to the left, crossed a small pillared hall and halted before a flight of stairs.

'Go up,' he said. 'The tjaty awaits you at the top of the pyramid.'

'Why up there?'

'He is overseeing the work.'

'Is the climb dangerous?'

'The steps beneath the covering have been laid bare. If you climb carefully, you'll be safe.'

Bel-Tran did not admit to the priest that he got dizzy in high places; drawing back would have made him look ridiculous. Against his better judgement, he set off for the top of the pyramid, some sixty cubits above.

He climbed slowly, watched by stone-cutters busy restoring the covering. Eyes glued to the stones, his feet clumsy, he hauled himself to the summit, a platform deprived of its little pyramid. This had been removed and entrusted to the goldsmiths, so that they could cover it with fine gold.

Pazair held out his hand to Bel-Tran and helped him to stand up.

'The landscape is beautiful, isn't it?'

Bel-Tran swayed, closed his eyes, and managed to keep his balance.

'From the top of a pyramid,' the tjaty continued, 'Egypt is unveiled. Have you noticed the abrupt break between the

323

fields and the desert, between the black earth and the red earth, between Horus's domain and Set's? And yet they are indivisible and complementary. The cultivated land shows the eternal dance of the seasons, the desert the fire of that which never changes.'

'Why did you bring me here?'

'Do you know the name of this pyramid?'

'I couldn't care less.'

'It is called "the Watcher of the Two Lands", and in watching them it creates their unity. If the ancients devoted their energies to building monuments like this, if we build temples and houses of eternity, it is because no harmony is possible without them.'

'They're just pointless piles of stones,' sneered Bel-Tran.

'They're the foundation of our society. The world beyond inspires our government, the eternity of our deeds, for day-to-day mundanities are not enough to feed men.'

'That's outdated idealism.'

'Your policy will ruin Egypt, Bel-Tran, and will soil you.'

'I'll hire the finest washermen.'

'The soul cannot be washed so easily.'

'Are you a tjaty or a priest?'

'Both: the tjaty is a priest of Ma'at. Has the goddess of righteousness never won your heart?'

'All things considered, I hate women. If you've nothing else to say, I shall go down.'

'I thought you were my friend when we helped each other. In those days you were only a papyrus-maker and I was a minor judge lost in a great city. I did not even wonder about your sincerity. You seemed animated by a true faith in your work in the service of the country. When I think of that period, I still find it hard to believe that you were lying all the time.'

A strong wind began to blow. Thrown off balance, Bel-Tran grabbed hold of Pazair.

'But you were, weren't you?' Pazair went on. 'You were play-acting right from our first meeting.'

'I was hoping to persuade you and use you – and I confess I was disappointed when I failed. Your stubbornness and your narrow views have often exasperated me, but making use of you wasn't too difficult.'

'What does the past matter? Change your life, Bel-Tran. Use your skills in the service of Pharaoh and the people of Egypt, renounce your over-arching ambition, and you'll know the happiness of righteous people.'

'What ridiculous words ... You don't believe them yourself, I hope?

'Why lead a whole people to disaster?'

'Although you may be tjaty, you know nothing of the taste for power. I know it; this country is rightfully mine, for I am capable of imposing my rule on it.'

The rising wind obliged the two men to speak loudly and distinctly. In the distance, the palm-trees bent, their fronds intermingling, and moaned as though they would break. Whirlwinds of sand rose to attack the pyramid.

'Forget your own interest, Bel-Tran; it will lead you to nothingness.'

'Branir would not have been proud of you and your foolishness. By helping me, you have proved your incompetence; by torturing me like this, your stupidity.'

'Did you kill him?'

'I never dirty my hands, Pazair.'

'Never speak the name of Branir again.'

In Pazair's eyes, Bel-Tran saw his death. In terror, he took a step back and lost his balance.

Pazair caught him by the wrist; his heart pounding, Bel-Tran climbed down the pyramid, gripping every stone tightly.

The tjaty's gaze weighed down on him, as the storm-wind was unleashed.

43

Since the end of spring the Nile waters had been green; now a month later, they were turning brown, laden with mud and silt. In the fields, work stopped; with the end of threshing began a long holiday. Those who wanted to earn more would go to work on the large construction sites, when the annual flood facilitated the transport by boat of enormous stone blocks.

One worry haunted everyone: would the water rise high enough to quench the earth's thirst and make it fertile? To solicit the gods' favour, villagers and town-dwellers offered the river little terracotta or porcelain figurines representing a fat man with pendulous breasts, his head crowned with plants; he symbolized Hapy, the flood's dynamic energy, a formidable power which made the fields grow green.

In about twenty days' time, Hapy would swell to the point of invading the Two Lands and turning Egypt into a kind of immense lake, in which everyone moved between villages in boats. In about twenty days' time, Ramses would abdicate in favour of Bel-Tran.

The tjaty bent down to stroke his dog, who had been treated to a bone which he had chewed, buried and then unearthed from its hiding-place; Brave, too, too was feeling the effects of this period, heavy with fears and uncertainties. Pazair was concerned for the future of his faithful companions: who would take care of the dog and the donkey when he was arrested and deported? Way-Finder, accustomed to his peaceful retirement, would be sent back to the dusty tracks and made to carry heavy loads again. His two companions, friends for so long, would die of broken hearts.

Pazair held his wife close. 'You must leave, Neferet, leave Egypt before it's too late.'

'Are you suggesting that I desert you?'

'Bel-Tran's heart is a dried-out husk. Greed and ambition have replaced all feeling, and nothing can move him any more.'

'That cannot have surprised you.'

'I hoped the voice of the pyramids would reawaken his deadened conscience, but all I did was intensify his thirst for power. Save yourself; save Brave and Way-Finder.'

'As tjaty, would you permit Egypt's principal doctor to abandon her post when a grave sickness has stricken the kingdom? However the adventure may end, we shall experience it together, all of us. Ask Brave and Way-Finder: neither of them will leave you.'

Hand in hand, Pazair and Neferet looked round the garden, where Mischief was frolicking, forever in search of delicacies. So close to the cataclysm, they drank in the scented peace of this place, sheltered from the tumult; that morning, they had bathed in the ornamental lake, before taking a walk in the shade.

'The tjaty's guests have arrived,' said the head steward.

Kem and Killer greeted the guards at the gate, walked along the tamarisk-lined path, meditated before the shrine of the ancestors, washed their hands and feet on the threshold of the house, crossed the entrance hall and took their places in the four-pillared chamber where the tjaty and his wife were seated. Their arrival was soon followed by those of Tuya, Bagey, Kani and Suti.

'With the king's permission,' said Pazair, 'I can reveal to you that the Great Pyramid of Khufu, which Pharaoh alone is permitted to enter, was desecrated by Bel-Tran, his wife and three accomplices, Denes the ship-owner, Kadash the tooth-doctor and Sheshi the inventor, all three of whom are now dead, as you know. The conspirators violated the sarcophagus, and stole the gold mask, the great collar, the adze of sky-iron and the gold cubit. Some of those treasures have been recovered, but the most important one is still missing. It is the Testament of the Gods, contained in the copper case which the king must hold in his right hand during his festival of regeneration, before showing it to the people and the priests. This document, passed down from pharaoh to pharaoh, gives each reigning king his legitimacy. Who could ever have imagined that anyone would commit such a profane act and such a theft?

'My master, Branir, was murdered because he stood in the rebels' way; and Djui the embalmer became a shadow-eater in the pay of Bel-Tran. Kem and Killer have put an end to Djui's criminal activities, but we have still not identified Branir's murderer and we have been unable to recover the Testament of the Gods and return it to the king. On the first day of the New Year, Ramses will be forced to abdicate and offer the throne to Bel-Tran. Bel-Tran will close the temples, introduce the circulation of coins and adopt one law: the law of profit.'

A long and heavy silence followed the tjaty's explanation. The members of the secret council were devastated: as ancient predictions had feared, the heavens were falling upon their heads.*

Suti was the first to react. 'However precious this document may be, it won't be enough to make Bel-Tran a respected pharaoh, truly capable of ruling the country.'

---

*According to mythology, the sky rested on four great pillars, and, if the harmony with the gods was broken, might collapse upon the troublemakers, human beings.

'You're right,' said Pazair. 'That's why he has spent so much time corrupting the country's government and economy, and creating his network of useful alliances.'

'Haven't you tried to dismantle the network?'

'The monster's heads grow back as soon as they're cut off.'

'Your predictions are too gloomy,' said Bagey. 'Many officials will refuse to take orders from a man like Bel-Tran.'

'The Egyptian government has a strong sense of tradition,' objected Pazair, 'and it will obey the pharaoh.'

'Let's start organizing armed resistance,' proposed Suti. 'Between us, we control a lot of territory. The tjaty should coordinate the forces at his disposal.'

Kani asked to speak, and went straight to the heart of the matter. 'The temples will never accept the financial and other upheavals Bel-Tran intends to impose, because they would lead the whole country to misery and civil war. Pharaoh is the servant of the temple in spirit. If he betrayed that prime duty, he would be nothing but a political leader to whom we no longer owed obedience.'

'In that case,' agreed Bagey, 'the government would be freed from its promises. It swore an oath of loyalty to the mediator between heaven and earth, not to a despot.'

'The Health secretariat will stop functioning,' said Neferet. 'It's linked to the temples, so it will reject the new power.'

'With supporters like you,' said the Mother of Pharaoh, her voice full of emotion, 'all is not yet lost. You should know that the court is hostile to Bel-Tran and that it will never accept at its heart the lady Silkis, whose depravities are well known to everyone.'

'That's splendid, Majesty!' exclaimed Suti. 'Have you managed to sow discord between that pair of criminals?'

'I do not know, but that cruel, perverse child-woman has a

329

fragile mind. If I see clearly, Bel-Tran will soon desert her, or else she will betray him. When she came to Pi-Ramses, hoping to ensure my complicity, she seemed certain of success; when she left, her mind had been shipwrecked. One question, Tjaty Pazair: why are only some of the Friends of Pharaoh here?'

'Because neither Pharaoh nor I have identified all Bel-Tran's active or passive supporters. The king decided to conceal the truth, so as to continue the fight as long as possible without letting the enemy know what he was doing.'

'You have dealt Bel-Tran some severe blows.'

'But none has been decisive, unfortunately. Resistance itself won't be easy, because Bel-Tran has infiltrated the transport systems and the army.'

'The security guards will back you,' declared Kem, 'and Suti's prestige with the All-Seeing Ones is so great that he'll have no difficulty mobilizing them.'

'Doesn't Pharaoh control the troops stationed in Pi-Ramses?' asked Suti.

'That is why he is there,' said Pazair.

'The troops based in Thebes will listen to me,' said Kani.

'Appoint me general in Memphis,' said Suti. 'I know how to talk to soldiers.'

This proposition was unanimously approved by the secret council.

'There remains the matter of transport, which the Double White House controls,' Pazair reminded them. 'And I haven't mentioned the irrigation secretariats or the officials in charge of canals, whom Bel-Tran has been trying to bribe and corrupt for several months. As for the provincial governors, some have distanced themselves from him, but others still believe in his promises. I fear there may be civil war, which will result in many deaths.'

'What other solution is there?' asked Tuya. 'Either we all abdicate before Bel-Tran, and the Egypt of Ma'at is dead, or else we reject his tyranny and keep hope alive, even at the cost of our lives.'

After overcoming the opposition of his wife, who resented his taking on all this work, Bagey helped Pazair draw up decrees relating to the management of estates after the flood and the repair of damaged irrigation pools. He set up a programme of major civil and religious works, over a period of three years. These documents would demonstrate that the tjaty was planning to act in the long term and that no upheaval threatened Ramses' reign.

The festival of regeneration was going to be impressive. One after another, the provincial governors, accompanied by the statues of their local gods, were already arriving in Memphis. Housed in the palace, with the consideration due to their rank, they conversed with the tjaty, whose authority and courtesy pleased them. At Saqqara, in the Djoser enclosure, the priests were preparing the great courtyard where Ramses, wearing the Double Crown, would reunite the North and the South in his symbolic being. In this magical space, he would commune with each divine power, in order to regain his strength and be able to go on ruling.

Suti's reputation had spread quickly, and his appointment aroused great enthusiasm in the Memphis barracks. The new general immediately gathered his troops together, and told them that the war in Asia had been averted and that they would receive a special bonus. The young general's fame reached a peak at a banquet thrown for the troops. Who but Ramses could guarantee lasting peace, a prospect which delighted the soldiers?

The guards felt greater and greater admiration for Kem, whose unwavering devotion to the tjaty was known to all. He had no need to give a speech to maintain his men's loyalty.

In every temple in Egypt, on the advice of High Priest Kani, people were preparing for the worst. Nevertheless, the priests who specialized in tending the divine energy changed nothing in the established sequence of days and nights; the dawn, noon and sunset rites were celebrated regularly, as they had been since the earliest days of the pharaohs.

The Mother of Pharaoh granted numerous audiences and spoke with the most influential courtiers, senior government officials attached to the royal household, scribes in charge of educating the elite, and noble ladies responsible for court protocol. Bel-Tran was considered a troublemaker, and Silkis unbalanced: the fact that they wanted to belong to the monarchy's inner circle seemed insane, a matter for laughter.

Bel-Tran was not laughing. The vast offensive Pazair was leading had borne some fruit. In his own government, he was having difficulty making himself obeyed and had to lose his temper more and more often with negligent underlings.

An alarming rumour was spreading: immediately after Ramses' regeneration, the tjaty would appoint a new head of the Double White House, and Bel-Tran – who was too ambitious, too hasty, and would never be anything more than an upstart – would be sent back to his papyrus works in the Delta. Some people were hawking confidential information, suggesting that the Mother of Pharaoh had lodged a complaint with the tjaty about an illegal traffic in the *Book of Going Forth by Day*. Bel-Tran's rise to power had been fast: would his downfall be even faster?

To these difficulties was added the prolonged absence of Silkis, who seldom left her apartments. It was said that she was suffering from an incurable sickness which preventing her from appearing at the banquets she used to love so much.

Bel-Tran cursed, but continued preparing his vengeance. Whatever opposition might arise would be swept away. Becoming Pharaoh meant holding the sacred power before which the people bowed. Rebellion against the king was the ultimate crime, and therefore attracted the ultimate punishment, so once Bel-Tran was enthroned the faint-hearts would rally to him, and Pazair's support would melt away. Bel-Tran had been a traitor to his word and his oaths for so long that he now distrusted all promises. When force spoke, weakness and evasion answered.

Pazair had the power of a leader, but had lost his way by placing it in the service of an outdated law. A man of the past, attached to old-fashioned values, incapable of understanding the demands of the future, he must die. As the shadow-eater had failed to kill him, Bel-Tran would deal with him in his own way, by having him convicted of negligence and high treason – after all, the tjaty had opposed the necessary reforms and the transformation of the state. There was only a fortnight to wait: a fortnight until his triumph, a fortnight until the downfall of that inflexible, stubborn tjaty.

Bel-Tran, in whom tension was growing greater and greater, no longer went home. Silkis's rapid physical deterioration horrified him; the divorce papers were in order and he had no desire to see that faded woman again.

He remained in his office after the scribes had left, and thought about his plans and the many decisions he would have to take in a short time. He would strike swiftly and hard.

Four smokeless oil-lamps provided sufficient light to work by. Unable to sleep, Bel-Tran spent the night checking the elements of his plans for the economy. Although many of his networks had been dismantled, those which remained would be maintained by the money-exchangers and Greek traders, and would impose his views on the population. It would be easy, because his main weapon, whose nature Pazair would not know until the last moment, would be used with devastating effectiveness.

A sound made Bel-Tran start. At this late hour, the building was deserted.

He stood up and called, 'Who's there?'

The only answer was silence. Reassured, he remembered that the night patrol ensured the offices' safety. He sat back down on the floor and unrolled an accounting-papyrus, a plan of the new taxation system.

A powerful forearm hooked round his neck. Half-strangled, Bel-Tran flailed his arms, trying to break free.

'Keep quiet or I'll stick a dagger in your side.'

Bel-Tran knew that voice.

'What do you want?'

'To ask you a question. If you answer, your life will be spared.'

'Who are you?'

'Knowing that won't be any use to you.'

'I'll never give in to threats.'

'You aren't brave enough to hold out.'

'I know who you are – Suti!'

'General Suti.'

'You won't harm me.'

'Don't be too sure of that.'

'The tjaty will condemn you.'

'He doesn't know what I'm doing. Torturing someone like you doesn't worry me. If that's what the truth costs, I'm willing to pay.'

Bel-Tran realized that Suti was not joking. 'What is your question?'

'Where is the Testament of the Gods?'

'I don't know.'

'That's enough, Bel-Tran. The time for lies is over.'

'Let me go! I'll talk.'

The stranglehold loosened.

Bel-Tran rubbed his neck and looked at the dagger Suti was brandishing. 'Even if you stick that blade in my belly, you won't learn any more.'

'Let's try.'

The blade pricked Bel-Tran's flesh and, to Suti's astonishment, he smiled.

'Do you want to die?'

'Killing me would be stupid; I don't know where the Testament of the Gods is hidden.'

'You're lying again.'

'Use that dagger and you'll be committing a useless murder.'

In the face of such disturbing self-assurance, Suti hesitated. Bel-Tran ought to have been shaking with fear, almost fainting at the thought of failing so close to his goal because of this brutal intervention.'

'Get out of here, Suti,' said Bel-Tran. 'You're wasting your time.'

44

By the time Suti had finished telling Pazair about his attempt to make Bel-Tran talk he needed a cup of cool beer. He drained the cup, but he was still thirsty.

'It was incredible,' he said, 'unbelievable. But Bel-Tran wasn't lying, I'm sure of that. He really doesn't know where the Testament of the Gods is hidden.'

Neferet brought Suti some more beer. Mischief jumped on to his shoulder, dipped a finger in the cup, leapt up the trunk of the nearest sycamore tree and hid in the foliage.

'I'm afraid he may have deceived you. He's a formidable talker, a past master of the art of dissembling.'

'But this time he was telling the truth, even if it doesn't make sense. Believe me: I was ready to run him through, but that revelation took away my desire to do so. I'm lost. It is up to you to give us direction, Tjaty.'

The gatekeeper came up to them and told Neferet that a woman was at the entrance and insisted on speaking to her. Neferet said he might show her into the garden.

The woman turned out to be Silkis's personal maid, who prostrated herself before Neferet. 'My lady, my mistress is dying. She's asking for you.'

Silkis would never see her children again. When she had read the divorce document, which had been given to her by a scribe without Bel-Tran's knowledge, she had had an attack of hysteria which left her utterly without strength. All around her, everything was soiled; despite treatment by a doctor, her intestinal bleeding had not stopped.

Looking at herself in a mirror, Silkis had been appalled. Who was that witch with swollen eyes, misshapen face and spoilt teeth? Trampling on the mirror had not removed the horror: Silkis could feel the degradation of her body, rapid and unstoppable.

When her legs gave way beneath her, she could not get up. The huge house was almost deserted – only a gardener and a maid remained. They picked her up and laid her on her bed. She was delirious, howling, then fell into a lethargy, only to become delirious once again. Silkis was rotting away from inside.

In a moment of lucidity, she ordered her servant to fetch Neferet. And Neferet came.

Beautiful, radiant, peaceful, she looked down at Silkis. 'Do you want to be taken to the hospital?'

'It would be no use – I'm going to die. Dare tell me otherwise.'

'I should sound you.'

'You don't need to – your experience will tell you the truth. I'm horrible, aren't I?' Silkis tore at her face with her nails. 'I hate you, Neferet. I hate you because you have everything I've ever dreamt of and will never have.'

'Hasn't Bel-Tran given you all you could want?'

'He's left me because I'm ill and ugly – it's a properly drawn up divorce. I hate you and Pazair!'

'How are we responsible for your unhappiness?'

Silkis leant her head to one side; her hair was sticky with unhealthy sweat. 'I almost won, Neferet, I almost crushed you, you and your tjaty. I was the most hypocritical of women. I made you trust me, I won your friendship – with the sole intention of harming you and defeating you. You'd have been my slave, forced to obey me every moment of the day.'

'Where has your husband hidden the Testament of the Gods?' asked Neferet.

'I don't know.'

'Bel-Tran has perverted you.'

'Don't believe that! We've been in full agreement, ever since the start of the conspiracy – not once have I opposed his decisions. The murder of the honour-guard, the shadow-eater's crimes, the assassination of Pazair . . . I wanted them, approved of them, and congratulated myself on them. I was the one who passed on the orders, and I wrote the message luring Pazair to Branir's house. Pazair in the prison camp, accused of murdering his master – what a victory!'

'Why do you hate us so much?'

'To give Bel-Tran the highest position in the land, so that he'd raise me to his level. I was determined to lie, plot and deceive anyone, in order to achieve that. And now he's left me, because my body has betrayed me.'

'Did the needle that killed Branir belong to you?'

'I didn't kill him. Bel-Tran's wrong to leave me, but the real guilty party is you! If you'd treated me, I'd have kept my husband instead of rotting away here, alone and abandoned.'

'Who murdered Branir?'

An evil smile lit up the misshapen face. 'You and Pazair are on completely the wrong track, and when you understand, it will be too late – much too late. From the depths of hell where demons burn my soul, I shall witness your downfall, beautiful Neferet.' Silkis vomited.

Neferet called the maid. 'Wash her and purge this room with herbal fumes. I shall send you a doctor from the hospital.'

Silkis sat up, madness in her eyes. 'Come back, Bel-Tran, come back! We'll tread them all underfoot, we'll—' Her breath failed. Head flung back, arms flung outwards, she collapsed and lay still.

*

The coming of Akhet, the time of the flood, affirmed the reign of Isis, queen of the stars, the great sorceress whose generous, inexhaustible bosom gave rise to all forms of life. Women and little girls, evoking her benefits, prepared their most beautiful dresses for the great festival to be held on the first day of the flood. On the island of Philae, the goddess's sacred territory in the extreme South of Egypt, the priestesses were practising musical pieces to be played as the waters rose.

At Saqqara, the priests were ready. In each shrine in the courtyard where the regeneration would take place, a statue of a god had been placed. Pharaoh would climb a stairway and kiss the stone body, brought to life by a supernatural force; it would enter him and rejuvenate him. Fashioned by the divine powers, a masterpiece conceived by the Principle and made concrete by the temple, Pharaoh, the link between the visible and the Invisible, would be filled with the energy necessary to maintain the union of the Two Lands. In this way he would ensure the unity of his people and lead them towards bliss, in this life and in the world beyond.

When Ramses arrived in Memphis, three days before the festival of regeneration, the court was there in full to greet him. The Mother of Pharaoh wished him success in the ritual ordeal, the dignitaries assured him of their confidence. The king stated that the peace with Asia would be lasting and that he would continue, after the festival, to reign according to the eternal law of Ma'at.

As soon as the brief ceremony was over, Ramses shut himself away with his tjaty.

'Anything new?' he asked.

'Yes, Majesty, but it's rather worrying. Despite being handled somewhat roughly by Suti, Bel-Tran says he does not know where the Testament of the Gods is hidden.'

'A crude lie.'

'We must assume not.'

'What conclusions can be drawn from that?'

'That neither you nor anybody else will be able to present the Testament to the priests, the court and the people.'

Ramses was troubled. 'Could our enemies have destroyed it?'

'There is serious dissension among them. Bel-Tran has killed his accomplices and is divorcing his wife.'

'If he has not got the Testament, what is he planning to do?'

'I made a final attempt to appeal to the glimmer of light in his heart, but it was fruitless.'

'So he has not given up.'

'Silkis, in her delirium, claimed that we are wrong.'

'What did she mean?'

'I do not know, Majesty.'

'I shall abdicate before the start of the ritual, and will lay my sceptres and my crowns before the one gate in the sacred enclosure of Saqqara. Instead of my regeneration, the priests will celebrate the coronation of my enemy.'

'The officials who oversee the waters are quite clear: the flood will indeed begin the day after tomorrow.'

'The Nile will flood the land of the pharaohs for the last time, Pazair. When it returns next year, it will nourish a tyrant.'

'Resistance is being organized, Majesty. Bel-Tran's reign is likely to be an extremely difficult one.'

'The title of Pharaoh alone is enough to compel obedience. He will soon regain the ground he has lost.'

'Without the Testament?'

'He did lie to Suti. I am withdrawing into the Temple of Ptah. We shall meet again before the enclosure gate at Saqqara. You were a good tjaty, Pazair, and the country will not forget you.'

'I have failed, Majesty.'

'This evil was wholly unknown to us, so we did not have the means to fight it.'

*

The news spread from South to North: the flood would be perfect, neither too low nor too high. No province would go short of water, no village would suffer. Pharaoh still enjoyed the gods' favour, because it had been shown that he could still feed his people. Ramses' regeneration would make him the greatest of kings, before whom the entire earth would prostrate itself.

There was bustling activity around all the river-gauges; marks on the stone walls would enable the rate of the waters' rise and the energy of Hapy to be evaluated. The speed of the current and the Nile's brownish colour told people that the annual miracle was about to happen. Joy filled everyone's heart, and the celebration would commence within the hour.

The tjaty's secret council, meeting again, could not hide their near-despair. Tuya felt the weight of her years; Bagey was more and more stooped; Suti's many wounds were hurting; Kem hung his head, as if he were ashamed of his wooden nose; Kani's face had become more deeply lined than ever; Pazair's dignity was steeped in desperation. They had all done their utmost, in their own domains, but they had failed. What would remain of undertakings made here or there, when the new pharaoh dictated his law?

'Don't stay in Memphis,' advised Pazair. 'I shall stay, but I've hired a boat to take my household to the South. From Elephantine it will be easy to reach Nubia, and they can hide there.'

'I have no intention of abandoning my son,' declared Tuya.

'Silkis is dying, Majesty,' said Pazair worriedly. 'Bel-Tran will hold you responsible for her death and will show you no mercy.'

'My mind is made up, Tjaty. I am staying.'

'And so am I,' said Bagey. 'At my age, I am no longer afraid of anything.'

'I am sorry,' said Pazair, 'but I must disagree with you. You embody a tradition whose destruction Bel-Tran demands.'

'He will break his teeth on my old bones. My presence, beside Ramses and the Mother of Pharaoh, might even encourage him to moderation.'

'In the name of myself and all the other High Priests,' said Kani, 'I shall see Bel-Tran as soon as he is enthroned and will emphasize our attachment to the laws and virtues that made Egypt great. He shall know that the temples will not grant their support to a tyrant.'

'Your life will be in danger.'

'That is of no importance.'

'Pazair, I must stay to protect you,' said Suti.

'And so must I,' said Kem. 'I serve the tjaty and no one else.'

Moved to tears, Tjaty Pazair closed his last council with an appeal to Ma'at, whose Rule would survive after the extinction of humanity.

After telling Pazair about her last visit to Branir's tomb, Neferet left for the hospital, to operate on a patient with a broken skull and to give her colleagues final advice. She had confirmed that the communion with her master's soul had not been an illusion. Although she could not translate the message from the otherworld into human words, she was convinced Branir would not abandon them.

Alone before the shrine of the ancestors, Pazair let his thoughts wander in the past. Since he had held the office of tjaty, he had had hardly any time to meditate like this, detached from a reality which had slipped from his grasp. The mind, that mad monkey which must be kept chained up, had been pacified; his thoughts flew free, keen and clear-cut as an ibis's beak.

He went over the facts one by one, from the crucial moment when, refusing to sanction the transfer of the head guard of the Giza sphinx, he had unwittingly thwarted the conspirators' plan. His determined search for the truth had been strewn with traps and dangers, but he had not lost heart. Today, although he knew the identities of most of the conspirators, including Bel-Tran and Silkis, although he had solved parts of the puzzle and knew what the outcome of the plot would be, Pazair felt he had been fooled. Swept up in a whirl of activity, he had not stepped back far enough to see clearly.

Brave lifted his head and growled softly: someone was coming. In the garden, though the moon was still shining, birds were beginning to awake and sing gaily. Someone slipped along the edge of the lotus pond and made for the porch. Pazair held the dog back by the collar.

An emissary from Bel-Tran, charged with killing him? A second shadow-eater, whom Killer had not stopped? The tjaty prepared himself for death. He would be the first to fall beneath the blows delivered by the new master of Egypt, so eager to wipe out his opponents.

There was no sign of Way-Finder. Pazair was afraid the intruder might have slit the donkey's throat. He would beg him, no doubt fruitlessly, to spare Brave.

She appeared in the moonlight, a short sword in her hand, her bare breasts covered with strange signs, her brow decorated with black and white stripes.

'Panther!'

'I must kill Bel-Tran.'

'Is your face painted for war?'

'It was the custom in my tribe. He won't escape my magic.'

'I'm afraid he will,' said Pazair.

'Where is he hiding?'

'In his office at the Double White House, and he's well guarded. After Suti's visit, he's not taking any risks. Don't go there, Panther. You'll be arrested or killed.'

Her mouth took on a sullen pout. 'Then it's all over . . .'

'Persuade Suti to leave Memphis straight away – tonight. Hide in Nubia, work your goldmine, and be happy. Don't be destroyed with me.'

'I promised the demons of the night to kill that monster and I shall keep my promise.'

'Why take such a terrible risk?'

'Because Bel-Tran wants to harm Neferet, and I won't let anyone destroy her happiness.'

Panther ran off across the garden, and Pazair saw her scale the surrounding wall with the grace of a cat.

Brave went back to sleep, and Pazair returned to his thoughts. Odd details came back to him and, so as not to forget them, he noted them down on clay tablets.

As the work progressed, other aspects of his investigation, neglected until now, came to light. Pazair grouped the evidence, drew provisional conclusions and forged strange paths, which reason forbade him to take seriously.

When Neferet came back, at sunrise, Brave and Mischief greeted her joyfully.

Pazair took her in his arms. 'You're exhausted.'

'The operation was difficult, and then I had to put my affairs in order. My successor will have no difficulty continuing my work.'

'Rest now.'

'I'm not sleepy.'

Neferet looked at the scores of clay tablets piled beside him. 'Have you been working all night?'

'I've been stupid.'

'Why do you say such a thing?'

'And not only stupid but blind, because I refused to see the truth. That's an unforgivable sin for a tjaty, a sin which would have plunged Egypt into misfortune. But you were right, and something wonderful happened: the soul of Branir spoke to me.'

'Do you mean . . . ?'

'I know where the Testament of the Gods is.'

45

As the star Sopdet shone in the east, companion of the rising sun, the birth of the flood was proclaimed throughout the land. After several days' anxiety, the new year was surging up out of the restorative tide. The rejoicing would be especially great because the festival would also celebrate Ramses' regeneration.

Demons, miasmas and invisible dangers had been defeated. Thanks to the principal doctor's conjurations, the terrifying Sekhmet had not sent her hordes of diseases against Egypt. Everyone filled a blue porcelain vase with the water of the new year, which held within it the very first light; keeping it in one's home ensured prosperity.

At the palace, there was no deviation from custom. A silver vase containing the precious water was placed at the foot of the throne where Ramses had been sitting since first light.

The king wore no crown, collar or bracelets, merely a simple white kilt in the style of the Old Kingdom.

Pazair bowed before him. 'The year will be happy, Majesty. The flood is perfect.'

'But Egypt will soon know disaster . . .'

'I hope I have accomplished my mission.'

'I do not blame you for anything.'

'I beg you, Majesty, to put on the insignia of power.'

'A futile request, Tjaty. That power no longer exists.'

345

'It is intact and will remain so.'

'Are you making mock of me, at the very moment when Bel-Tran is about to appear in this throne-room and seize Egypt?'

'He will not come.'

'Have you lost your mind?'

'Bel-Tran is not the leader of the conspirators, Majesty. He led those who violated the Great Pyramid, but the real leader did not take part in the expedition. Kem suggested this idea to me while we were speculating about the number of plotters, but my ears remained closed. As we discovered the extent of their plan, Bel-Tran imposed himself as their spokesman, while his master remained hidden in the shadows. I believe I know not only that master's name but also the hiding-place of the Testament of the Gods.'

'Shall we find it in time?'

'I am sure that we shall.'

Ramses stood up, put on the great ceremonial gold collar and silver bracelets, set the Blue Crown upon his head, took up the sceptre of command in his right hand and sat down on the throne.

The head steward came in and asked permission to speak: Bagey was requesting an audience.

The king concealed his impatience. 'Would his presence hinder you, Tjaty?'

'No, Majesty.'

The former tjaty approached, his face grim, his gait stiff. The only jewellery he wore was the symbol of his former office, a copper heart attached to a chain about his neck.

'Our defeat is not yet certain,' said the king. 'Pazair thinks that—' He broke off in surprise: Bagey had not bowed before him.

'Majesty, this is the man of whom I spoke,' said Pazair.

The king was stunned. 'You, Bagey? My former tjaty?'

'Give me the sceptre of command,' said Bagey. 'You are no longer fit to rule.'

'What demon has taken hold of your mind? To think that you, of all people, could commit this treachery . . .'

Bagey smiled. 'Bel-Tran persuaded me that he is right. The world he wants, which he and I shall fashion together, suits me. My coronation will not surprise anyone, and will reassure the country. By the time the people notice the transformations Bel-Tran and I have made, it will be too late. Those who do not follow us will fall by the wayside, where their corpses will turn to dried-out husks.'

'You are no longer the man I knew, the honest, incorruptible judge preoccupied with truth.'

'The times are changing, and so are men.'

Pazair cut in, 'Before meeting Bel-Tran, you were content to serve Pharaoh and to apply the law, with an almost excessive severity. But Bel-Tran showed you a new and shimmering horizon, and he was able to buy your conscience because it was for sale.'

Bagey remained icily calm.

'You had to ensure your children's future,' continued Pazair. 'So, although you showed an ostentatious distaste for material possessions, you became the accomplice of a man whose main characteristic is greed. And you are greedy, too, because you covet supreme power.'

'We have talked enough,' said Bagey dryly, holding out his hand. 'The sceptre of command, Majesty, and the crown.'

'We must appear before the high priests and the court.'

'I am glad of it. You shall renounce the throne in my favour.'

Pazair seized Bagey's copper heart, and pulled it towards him so hard that its chain broke. He handed it to the king. 'Open this dead heart, Majesty.'

With his sceptre, Ramses smashed it.

Inside lay the Testament of the Gods.

Bagey stood rooted to the spot.

'Coward among cowards!' exclaimed the king.

347

Bagey drew back. His cold eyes contemplated Pazair.

'The truth did not appear to me until tonight,' confessed the tjaty in a calm voice. 'I trusted you completely, so to me it was inconceivable that you were in alliance with a creature like Bel-Tran, and still less that you were the rebels' secret leader. You wagered on my credulity and you almost won.

'And yet I ought to have suspected you a long time ago. Who but the tjaty could have ordered the transfer of the Sphinx's head guard, and then laid the responsibility at the door of General Asher, whose treason he knew? Who but the tjaty could pull the strings of government and build such a conspiracy? Who else could so easily have manipulated Mentmose, who was so preoccupied with keeping his job that he obeyed orders without understanding them? Who allowed Bel-Tran to climb the stairway to power without hindrance? If I had not become tjaty myself, I would never have realized the full scope of this office and the range of action it implies.'

'Did you yield to Bel-Tran's threats or to his blackmail?' asked Pharaoh.

Bagey said nothing, so Pazair answered for him.

'Bel-Tran outlined a brilliant future for him, in which he would at last occupy the highest position in Egypt, and Bagey knew how to make use of a crude but all-conquering man. He hid in the shadows, while Bel-Tran showed himself. All his life, Bagey has hidden behind rules and the dryness of the surveyor's maps, for his heart is inhabited only by cowardice. I realized that when, faced with difficult circumstances in which we had to confront enemies together, he preferred to make his escape rather than help me. Sensitivity and love of life are unknown to Bagey. His thoroughness was merely a mask for fanaticism.'

Ramses' eyes blazed with anger. 'And you dared wear the tjaty's heart round your neck, making people believe that you were Pharaoh's conscience!'

348

Before the king's wrath Bagey drew back a few paces, but he still glared at Pazair.

'Bagey and Bel-Tran,' Pazair went on, 'based their strategy on lies. Their accomplices did not know of Bagey's role – in fact, they even despised him – and that deceived me. When the old tooth-doctor Qadash became a hindrance, Bagey gave the order for him to be killed, and the same fate would have befallen the ship-owner Denes and the inventor Sheshi if Princess Hattusa had not taken her own vengeance.* As for my death, it was to make up for the disappointment of seeing the post of tjaty elude Bel-Tran. When I was unexpectedly appointed, he hoped to corrupt me, and when that failed he tried to discredit me. When that also failed, all he had left was murder.'

No emotion showed on Bagey's face; he seemed indifferent to the enumeration of his crimes.

'Thanks to Bagey, Bel-Tran was progressing safely. No one would ever have thought of looking for the Testament of the Gods in the copper heart, symbol of the tjaty's awareness of his duties, a symbol Pharaoh had permitted Bagey to continue wearing after he retired, in recognition of the services he had rendered. Bagey had foreseen that you would make that generous gesture, Majesty. Leaving nothing to chance, he used it as the best and most inaccessible of hiding-places. Lurking in the shadows, he would not be identified before he seized power. Until the very last moment, we would concentrate on Bel-Tran – and all the while Bagey was a member of my secret council and was informing his accomplice of my decisions.'

As if being close to the throne was becoming intolerable, Bagey moved further away.

'The only point on which I was right,' stated Pazair, 'is the link between Branir's murder and the conspiracy. But how

*See *Secrets of the Desert*.

could I have dreamt that you were mixed up in this appalling crime, either directly or indirectly? I was a feeble tjaty, with my legal procedures, my blindness and my trust in your integrity. There again, you calculated right – until the dawn of this wonderful day when Pharaoh Ramses will be regenerated. Branir had to be killed because, as High Priest of Karnak, he would have occupied a powerful position and would have provided me with means of investigation I did not then have. Now, who knew that Branir was to become High Priest? Only five people. Three of them were above suspicion: the king, Branir's predecessor at Karnak, and yourself. The other two, though, were excellent suspects: Nebamon, principal doctor of Egypt, who hoped to kill me and marry Neferet, and his accomplice Commander Mentmose, who did not hesitate to send me to the prison camp, even though he knew I was innocent. For a long time I believed that one or the other was guilty, before I became certain that they had not made any attempt on my master's life. The murder weapon, the mother-of-pearl needle, seemed to indicate a woman. I followed false trails, thinking of Denes's wife, of Tapeni, and of Silkis. That Branir made no attempt to defend himself when the needle was stabbed into his neck meant that the killer must belong to Branir's small inner circle, must be lacking in all sensitivity, must be capable of killing a sage and accepting that he would be damned, and must show perfect accuracy in the murder. Now, the investigation established that the three ladies were not guilty of this crime. Neither was Branir's predecessor, who has not left Karnak since his retirement, and therefore could not have been in Memphis on the day of the murder.'

'Aren't you forgetting the shadow-eater?' asked Bagey.

'Kem's interrogation of him dispelled all my doubts: he did not kill Branir. That leaves only you, Bagey.'

The accused made no denial.

'You were familiar with his home and his habits. On the

pretext of congratulating him on becoming High Priest, you visited him at a time when no one would see you. A man of the darkness, you know how to pass unnoticed. He turned his back on you and you stabbed him with a needle you had stolen from Silkis during one of your secret conversations at Bel-Tran's house. Never was a greater act of cowardice committed on this earth.

'After that, your successes came thick and fast: Branir was dead, Mentmose could not identify you, Neferet was under Nebamon's authority, Suti was reduced to impotence, Bel-Tran was soon to be tjaty, and Ramses would be constrained to abdicate in your favour. But you underestimated the power of Branir's soul and forgot the presence of the world beyond. Killing me was not enough: you also had to stop Neferet realizing the truth. You and Bel-Tran have nothing but contempt for women, but you were wrong to overlook her. Without her I would have failed, and you would have become the masters of Egypt.'

'Let me leave the country with my family,' said Bagey in a husky voice. 'My wife and children are innocent.'

'No. You shall be judged,' decreed Pharaoh.

'I served you faithfully for many years, and was never rewarded according to my true worth. Bel-Tran saw that. What was Branir, what is this miserable creature Pazair, beside me and my knowledge?'

'You were a false sage,' said Ramses, 'the worst of all criminals. The monster you nourished within yourself destroyed you.'

On this day of celebration, the Double White House was deserted. Worried that Suti might attack him again, Bel-Tran had not stood down the guards, and had even demanded that they increase their vigilance. The people's revelry amused him: they did not yet know that they were cheering a deposed monarch. When the truth became known, no one would be surprised that a discredited Ramses should stand down in favour of Bagey, who was respected by all. They would trust the former tjaty, who have never shown any sign of ambition.

Bel-Tran consulted his water-clock. By now, Ramses would have abdicated, and Bagey, installed on the throne with the sceptre of command in his hand, would have summoned a scribe to note down his first decree: that Pazair be dismissed and imprisoned for treason, and that Bel-Tran be appointed tjaty. In a few minutes, a delegation would come to fetch Bel-Tran and take him to the palace, where he would attend the new monarch's coronation.

Bagey would soon become drunk on a power he did not know how to wield. Bel-Tran would flatter him skilfully for as long as necessary, and would meanwhile do as he pleased. As soon as the state was in his hands, he would get rid of the old man – assuming sickness did not do the job for him.

From his window, Bel-Tran saw Kem coming towards the Double White House at the head of a squadron of guards. Why was the Nubian still in his post? Bagey must have forgotten to replace him. Bel-Tran would not make that kind of mistake: he would at once surround himself with subordinates devoted to his cause.

Kem's martial bearing was strange: he did not look like a defeated man being compelled to carry out an unpleasant order. However, Bagey had assured Bel-Tran there was no risk of failure: no one would ever find the Testament of the Gods.

The Double White House guards lowered their weapons and allowed Kem to pass. Bel-Tran panicked: something had gone wrong. He left his office and ran downstairs to where there was an emergency door, in case of fire. The bolt drew back with a grating noise, and Bel-Tran entered a passageway that led to a garden. Slipping between clumps of flowers, he slid along the surrounding wall.

As he was preparing to knock out the guard posted at the

gate opening on to the grounds of the Double White House, something landed on his shoulders and knocked him over. Bel-Tran's face was squashed into the soft earth, which had recently been watered. Killer's fist flattened him to the ground.

Watched by the High Priests of Iunu, Memphis and Karnak, Pharaoh united the North and South, and entered the court-yard of regeneration. Alone before the gods, he shared the secret of their incarnation, then came back into the world of men, and returned to his palace.

Ramses wore the Double Crown, and held in his right hand the leather case containing the Testament of the Gods. From the palace's 'Window of Appearance', the king showed his people the document that made him a rightful sovereign.

Ibis took to the skies from all four points of the compass to spread the news. From Minoa to Asia, from Phoenicia to Nubia, vassals, allies and enemies would all know that Ramses' reign was continuing.

On the fifteenth day of the flood, the celebrations were at their height.

From the terrace of his palace, Ramses and his tjaty looked out over the city, which was lit up by countless lamps. In the hot summer nights, Egypt thought only of pleasure and the joy of living.

'What a magnificent sight,' said Pharaoh.

'Indeed it is, Majesty. Looking at it, I cannot understand why evil took hold of Bagey.'

'Because evil had dwelt in him since birth. I made a mistake in appointing him tjaty, but the gods enabled me to correct it by choosing you. A man's deepest nature never changes. It is up to us, who are in charge of the people's destiny, and who have inherited a kind of wisdom, to learn how to discern it. Now, justice must be done; upon it, and upon it alone, rest a country's greatness and happiness.'

353

46

'May we distinguish truth from falsehood,' declared Pharaoh, 'and protect the weak to save them from the powerful.'

The tjaty's court was in session. The three accused, Bagey, Bel-Tran and Silkis, must answer for their crimes before Pazair and a jury made up of Kani, Kem, an overseer, a weaving-woman, and a priestess of Hathor.

The tjaty read out the charges, not omitting a single detail. Bagey showed no emotion and apparently took no interest in the accusations against him. Bel-Tran protested, gesticulated, insulted the judges and claimed that he had acted properly. Silkis had been given permission to remain at home because of her poor health. When Kem had handed her the document concerning her, she had taken refuge in silence.

After a brief deliberation, the jury reached its verdict, which Pazair approved.

'Bagey, Bel-Tran and Silkis, having been found guilty of conspiracy against the king's person, perjury, of crime and complicity in crime, treason and rebellion against Ma'at, are condemned to death, both on this earth and in the afterlife. Henceforth, Bagey shall be called "the Coward", Bel-Tran "the Greedy One", and Silkis "the Hypocrite"; they shall bear these names for all eternity. As they are enemies of the Light, their effigies and their names shall be drawn with fresh ink on pieces of papyrus, which will be attached to wax figures in their image, pierced with a spear, trampled underfoot, then thrown into the fire. In this way, all trace of the three criminals shall be erased, in this world and the next.'

When Kem brought the poison to Silkis, so that she could carry out the sentence herself, the maid informed him that she had died shortly after learning her own and her accomplices' names of infamy. The Hypocrite had expired in a last attack of hysteria; her corpse was burnt.

Bel-Tran had been locked away in the barracks under General Suti's command. He occupied a cell with whitewashed walls, where he paced up and down, his eyes fixed on the phial of poison that Kem had placed in the centre of the room. The Greedy One was so afraid that he could not accept the idea of taking his own life. When the door opened, he thought of charging at the arrival, knocking him down and running away.

But the apparition rooted him to the spot.

Panther, her body covered with war paint, was threatening him with a short sword; in her left hand, she held a leather bag. The young woman's gaze was terrifying. Bel-Tran backed away, until the wall prevented him from going any further.

'Sit,' ordered Panther.

Bel-Tran obeyed.

'Since you're so greedy, eat.'

'Is it poison?'

'No, it's your favourite food.'

Laying her sword-blade against Bel-Tran's neck, she forced him to part his lips and poured the contents of the bag into his mouth: Greek silver coins.

'Stuff yourself, Greedy One! Stuff yourself into nothingness!'

The summer sun was reflecting off the faces of the Great Pyramid of Khufu, covered once more with white limestone from Tura. The whole structure was transformed into a powerful petrified ray of light, so intense that no one could bear to look directly at it.

His legs swollen, his back bent, the Coward followed Ramses with difficulty; the tjaty brought up the rear. The trio crossed the threshold of the great monument and continued along an upward-sloping corridor. Gasping for breath, Branir's murderer moved more and more slowly; climbing the great gallery was torture. When would this climb end?

After bending almost double, he entered a vast chamber with bare walls, whose covering was in the form of nine gigantic granite flagstones. At the far end was an empty sarcophagus.

'This is the place you wished so much to conquer,' said Ramses. 'Your five accomplices, who defiled it, have been punished. You, coward among cowards, gaze upon the energy centre of the country, decipher the secret you wanted to steal.'

The Coward hesitated, suspecting a trap.

'Go,' ordered the king, 'explore the most inaccessible domain in Egypt.'

The Coward grew bolder. He slid along a wall like a thief, searched in vain for an inscription, a hiding-place for precious items, and arrived at the sarcophagus, over which he bent.

'But . . . it's empty.'

'Your accomplices looted it, didn't they? But look more closely.'

'Nothing. There is nothing there.'

'Since you are blind, go.'

'Go?'

'Leave the pyramid. Disappear.'

'You are permitting me to leave?'

Pharaoh remained silent. The Coward entered the low, narrow corridor, and ran down the great gallery.

Ramses turned to Pazair. 'I have not forgotten the sentence

of death, Tjaty. For cowards, the most violent poison is the noonday sun. It will strike him as he emerges from the pyramid, and it will utterly destroy him.'

'Are you not the only person permitted to enter this shrine, Majesty?'

'You have become my heart, Pazair. Come to the sarcophagus.'

The two men laid their hands upon Egypt's founding stone.

'I, Ramses, son of the Light, decree that no visible body shall again rest in this sarcophagus. From this void is born the creative energy without which a reign would be nothing but a paltry government of men. Look, tjaty of Egypt, look beyond life, and worship its presence. Do not forget it, when you hand down justice.'

When Pharaoh and his tjaty emerged from the Great Pyramid, they were bathed in the gentle rays of sunset; inside the stone giant, time had been abolished. The guards had long since carried away the charred body of the Coward, who had been struck dead on the threshold of the Temple of Purification.

Suti could not keep still: despite the importance of the ceremony, Panther was late. Although she had refused to tell him why her body was covered in warlike paint-markings, he was convinced that only she would have been cruel enough to suffocate the Greedy One with silver. Kem, content to verify that the condemned man was dead, did not open an investigation. The dead man's body would be burnt, like those of his accomplices.

The whole court had travelled to Karnak. No one wanted to miss the magnificent ceremony during which Ramses would reward the tjaty, whose praises were being sung throughout the Two Lands. In the front row, beside Kem in his ceremonial dress, were Way-Finder, Brave and Killer, who had been raised to the rank of captain. They all wore dignified expressions. Mischief, Neferet's little green monkey, had wisely perched on her mistress's shoulder.

As soon as the festivities were over, Suti would leave for the Great South, in order to restore the Lost City and enable gold and silver to be mined again. At the heart of the desert, he would feast upon sublime dawns.

At last Panther arrived, bedecked with collars and bracelets of lapis-lazuli, compelling admiration from even the most resolutely unimpressed. Her golden hair, the plumes of an indomitable wild creature, aroused a good deal of feminine jealousy. Panther threw hate-filled looks at a few beauties who were gazing too longingly at General Suti's fine figure.

Silence fell when Pharaoh, carrying a gold cubit, walked towards Pazair and Neferet, who were standing side by side in the middle of the sun-filled courtyard.

'You have saved Egypt from chaos, rebellion and ill fortune. Receive this symbol: may it be your goal and your destiny. Through it Ma'at is expressed, the intangible foundation upon which righteous deeds are built. May the goddess of truth never leave your heart.'

Pharaoh himself consecrated the new statue of Branir, which was placed in the secret part of the temple, with those of the other sages who had been admitted to the shrine. The statue showed him as an elderly scribe looking down at an unrolled papyrus, on which were written the ritual words: 'You who see me, greet my *ka*, recite the offertory words for me; pour a libation of water, and the same will be done for you.' Branir's eyes sparkled with life: quartz for the eyelids, rock crystal for the white of the eye, and obsidian for the pupil, produced a gaze filled with eternity.

When the summer night glittered above Karnak, Neferet and Pazair gazed upwards. At the zenith of the celestial vault, a new star had appeared; it crossed the sky and joined with the pole star. Henceforth the soul of Branir, now at peace, would dwell with the gods.

From the banks of the Nile rose up the song of the ancestors: 'May hearts be gentle, O inhabitants of the Two Lands. The time of happiness is come, for justice has resumed its rightful place. Truth drives out falsehood, the greedy are driven back, those who transgress the Rule fall to the ground. The gods are filled with delight, and we are living through wondrous days, in joy and light.'